ALSO BY JESSICA KNOLL

Luckiest Girl Alive

THE FAVOURITE SISTER

JESSICA KNOLL

MACMILLAN

First published in the United States 2018 by Simon & Schuster

First published in the UK 2018 by Macmillan
an imprint of Pan Macmillan
20 New Wharf Road, London N1 9RR
Associated companies throughout the world
www.panmacmillan.com

ISBN 978-1-5098-3996-4

1 3 5 7 9 8 6 4 2

A CIP catalogue record for this book is available from the British Library.

Printed and bound by CPI Group (UK) Ltd, Croydon, CR0 4YY

For the women who know that feeling

Sisterhood is powerful. It kills. Mostly sisters.

—Ti-Grace Atkinson

PROLOGUE

Kelly: The Interview

Present day

A man whose name I do not know slides his hand under the hem of my new blouse, connecting the cable to the lavalier mic clipped to my collar. He asks me to say something—sound check—and for a single, reckless beat, I consider the truth. *Brett is dead and I'm not innocent.*

"Testing. Testing. One. Two. Three." I'm not only dishonest. I'm unoriginal.

The sound guy listens to the playback. "Keep your hair off your left shoulder as much as you can," he tells me. I haven't had my ends trimmed in months, and not because my grief has bested my vanity. I'm hoping viewers are better able to see the resemblance to my sister. I have nice hair. Brett had beautiful hair.

"Thanks," I reply, wishing I could remember his name. Brett would have known it. She made a point of being on a first-name basis with the crew—from the gaffer to the ever-rotating harem of production assistants. My sister's specialty was making under-appreciated people feel appreciated. It's a testament to that quality that we are all gathered here today, some of us prepared to tell heroic lies about her.

Acoustics isolated, I take my seat before Camera A with the grim poise of a fallen soldier's widow. The small room is cozy as a Christmas card—fire going, overstuffed chairs. This is my first time in Jesse Barnes's apartment, and I was dismayed to discover that while richly appointed, it is not much bigger than my one-bedroom in Battery Park that atrophies my savings on the fifteenth of every month. Jesse Barnes has a hit reality show on a prestige cable channel and all she has to show for it is nine hundred square feet. New York does not have the real estate for any more success stories.

Jesse emerges from her bedroom and frowns at me. "Better," she says, meaning my outfit. I agonized over what to wear for this interview, scouring the flash-sale sites, until finally giving myself permission to shop the full-price racks at Ann Taylor. Not Loft. When you are going on TV to talk about your little sister, dead at twenty-seven, you spring for the core product.

I showed up for the interview fifteen minutes early (location one, Jesse's living room), feeling spruce in a starched white button-down and black pants that hook above my belly button. Jesse barely glanced at me and called over her stylist with an excoriating sigh, like she was expecting me to disappoint her. My grieving big sister costume has since been reimagined with the help of a pair of large ripped jeans and sneakers, though we kept the fitted button-down *for contrast,* rolling up the sleeves and knotting it at the waist. *This is an intimate fireside chat in my living room, not a network interview with Diane Sawyer on a soundstage,* Jesse told the stylist, speaking about me as though I were not standing right next to her. She noticed but did not comment on the price tag, still attached to the interior seam of the rejected pair of black pants by a small brass safety pin. Diane Sawyer actually wanted to interview me on a soundstage for half a million dollars, but I said no, for Jesse, and I'm a single mother wearing clothes I'll try to return tomorrow.

Jesse Barnes sits down across from me and does a very confusing thing. She smiles at me. All morning, she has oscillated between picking me apart and ignoring me, which is not an easy thing to do in such tight quarters. Jesse Barnes knows what really happened and that's why she's of two minds about me. She needs me, that's for sure, so you would think she would smile at me more. The problem is that I need her too.

"You feel okay about this?" she asks, sounding almost nervous. All around us, yellow sandbags moor light stands, their naked bulbs too bright to look at directly. *It's like we're preparing for a natural disaster*, I thought the first time I saw them, not too long ago.

"I do," I tell her with the confidence I've learned to fake as a mother. *What's my father's name?* I don't know. *What if a man comes to my school with a gun?* That will never happen.

"Let's make this quick for both of our sakes," Jesse says, raising her phone to her face to brush up on her interview questions, one combat boot bobbing. *Jesse dresses like a goth lesbian Audrey Hepburn*, Brett told me before I met her for the first time, and then she actually repeated the witticism to Jesse's face, as though to prove to me that unlike the other women, Jesse was her friend and not just her boss. Jesse and I were on our way to friendship before Brett died, our one inside joke igniting a blaze of insecurity in my sister that had remained mostly contained since she became famous. This fear that we might regress to our childhood roles—me the golden child, Brett the reprobate—was a fire that nothing could put out entirely. *At least you didn't have the shitty childhood*, she would say whenever something bad happened to me in adulthood, as though I had no right to complain about needing a root canal now because I was Mom's favorite growing up. What Brett never understood was that Mom preferred me because she could control me, and that made for a shitty childhood in its own right. I was the *yes* daughter, and for the record what that got me wasn't love. What that got me was a lowering limbo bar, until I couldn't bend any deeper. So I snapped.

"We're good, Jess," Lisa says. Lisa is our showrunner and the only person in this room who wasn't enamored with Brett while she was alive. Well, besides me. Don't get me wrong—I loved my sister, but I saw her too.

There are the last-minute preparations: a dab of Vaseline in the bow of my lips, a spritz of hairspray from the on-set hairdresser, smile check—no breakfast in our teeth. The set clears, leaving only the main players. It is not the most ideal of circumstances, but not even a year ago, I could only dream that Saluté would be promoting *The Kelly Courtney Interview Special* on the sides of MTA buses.

Jesse begins. "Kelly, I want to thank you so much for agreeing to share your story with the Saluté community." She is speaking in a gentle lilt, but her eyes are flat and hard. "Let me start by saying how profoundly sorry I am for your loss. I know I speak on behalf of the entire Saluté family when I say we are all grieving." She pauses long enough for me to thank her. "That grief, as I'm sure you know, is a tornado of emotions. Hurt, shock, confusion, *anger*." A bead of Jesse's spit lands just below my eye. I wipe it away and realize it looks like I am wiping away a tear when Jesse clucks. "How are you holding up?"

"I'm hanging in there." I picture my fingers monkey-gripping the edge of a rooftop, cartoon clouds separating me from the gawkers on the street below: *Am I really going to do it?* Something Stephanie must have thought. How many times?

"I noticed you're wearing your sister's ring," Jesse says. "Can you share the significance of that with the people at home?"

My right hand flies to my left, shielding the gold signet as though Jesse has threatened to take it from me. "The women had these rings made after the first season of the show," I explain, my thumb brushing the letterpressed metal. Like everything of Brett's but her shoes, the ring is too big on me. On cold days I have to wear it on my thumb. "They're inscribed *SS*, for Standing Sisters."

"What does Standing Sisters signify?"

That the lethal casting process you subjected them to every year didn't bring them to their knees. Production was notorious for toying with the women between seasons. They brought in new women, younger women, smarter women, richer women, put them on tape, and sent them to the network to consider. Potential "new hires," all under the guise of keeping the cast fresh. But they also made sure the old women heard about it, that they knew *no one* was irreplaceable. If they wanted to come back, they had better dance for their dinner. And the old women would do anything to come back. No one ever left the show of her own accord, despite what previously axed *Diggers* have claimed in the press. You were fired or you died, and honestly, dying might be better. Once you were fired, it was over anyway.

It was a point of pride for Jen Greenberg, Stephanie Simmons, and my sister that they were original *Goal Diggers* who withstood every between-season casting gauntlet. They had these rings made to congratulate themselves and, let's be real, to assert their authority over the newbies like me.

"The rings are our promises to each other that as women, we will raise each other up," I revise.

"As women, we *must* make this commitment to one another," Jesse says with the vigor of someone who believes herself, "especially when the world is designed to keep us down. And I have to give it to you, Kelly, because after what happened to Brett, I think most of us would understand if you wanted to back off, sell your share in the company, and hand over the reins. Instead, you've taken complete creative control and doubled your revenue, all while raising the most thoughtful, caring, and enterprising teenager I've ever met. You're not just standing. You're thriving."

The mention of my daughter gets my heart going at a primal pace. *Keep her out of this,* I think, unfairly, since I'm the one who brought her into *this* in the first place.

"Kelly," Jesse continues, "the network faced a great deal of flak when we announced that we were not only moving forward with airing season four as planned, but that we would be sharing the footage of that day uncensored. But as a show dedicated to the empowerment and advancement of women, we felt it was our responsibility to lay bare the truth of domestic violence. I know, as your friend, you agreed with Saluté. Would you talk to me a little bit about that?"

Even though I know we are not and never will be "friends," the word sends a warm spike through my middle. To be a part of Jesse's orbit is a fantastic thing. I'm sorry this is the way it had to happen—of course I am, I'm not a monster—but I shouldn't have to feel guilty about it either. Everything Jesse just said about me is true. I have revitalized the company. I have doubled our revenue. I have raised an exceptional daughter. I deserve to be here, maybe even more than Brett ever did.

"I think of it like this, Jesse," I answer. "That if what had happened to my sister had happened to me, I wouldn't want the truth *censored*"—this verbal mirroring is met with an almost imperceptible nod of approval from Jesse—"just because it makes people uncomfortable. We should be made uncomfortable by domestic violence. We should be traumatized by it. It's the only way we are ever going to be motivated to do anything about it." The tenor of my voice has intensified, and Jesse reaches out and catches my hand in hers. The gesture produces a clapping sound, as though we have high-fived.

"Why don't we start from the beginning?" she suggests, her pulse electric beneath my fingertips. *She's not nervous,* I realize. *She's excited.*

My mother always told me to make my own money so that a man could never tell me what to do. (Like my father ever told *her* what to do.) But here I am, doing that, or trying to at least, just to take orders from a woman who would not hesitate to hit me harder than any man ever could if I do not do as she says. I do not have independence. I do not have desirable options. What am I to do but to start from our version of the beginning?

PART I

Pre-Production • May 2017

CHAPTER 1

Brett

Would-be yoga instructor number four has punk blond hair and a bodybuilder's tan. Her name is Maureen and she's an ex-housewife who has spent the last seven years working on a documentary about the exodus of the Anlo-Ewe tribe from Notsé to the southeastern corner of the Republic of Ghana. If it were up to me, I'd say look no further.

"Thank you for coming all the way up here to see us," Kelly says with a pleasant smile she doesn't intend Maureen to ever see again. I know she decided against her the moment she took off her coat to reveal her pink sports bra and mommy gut. Kelly never got mommy gut after she had a baby, and so she believes mommy gut is not a result of biology but a choice. Wrong choice.

I've stayed mostly silent during the interview—this is Kelly's thing—though not in writing—but Maureen turns to me, wringing her hands, shyly.

"At the risk of sounding like a total brownnoser," she says, "I can't leave here without saying how lucky this generation of young girls is to have someone like you on their TV screens. Maybe I would have come into my own sooner if I had someone like you to show me how great life can be when you embrace your authentic self. Would have saved my kids a lot of fucking grief." She slaps a hand over her mouth. "Shit." Her eyes go wide. "Shit!" Wider still. "Why can't I stop? I'm so sorry."

I glance at my twelve-year-old niece sitting in the corner, texting deafly. She wasn't supposed to be here today, but the babysitter's dog ate a grape. Toxic, apparently. I turn back to Maureen. "How. Dare. You."

The silence stretches, uncomfortably. Only when it becomes unbearable do I flash her a grin and repeat, "How *fucking* dare you."

"Oh, you're kidding!" Maureen doubles over with relief, resting her hands on her knees. She releases a breath between her teeth; half whistle, half laugh.

"*Easy,*" my sister mutters, reminding me of our mother in two terrifying consonants. Our mother could silence a car alarm going off all night with the slow turn of her head.

"Your daughter is stunning, by the way," Maureen addresses Kelly, changing tack in an attempt to placate my stern-lipped sister, but it is the exact worst thing she could have said about her daughter. *Stunning. Striking. Exotic. That face. That hair.* All of it makes the green tendon in Kelly's neck throb. *My daughter is not some rarefied tropical fruit,* she sometimes snaps at well-meaning strangers. *She is a twelve-year-old* girl. *Just call her pretty.*

Maureen sees the expression on Kelly's face and laughs, nervously, turning to appeal to me one last time. "You should know that there's already a wait list for your book at my local library. Only two people ahead of me, but still. You haven't even *published* it yet."

I offer her the plate of Grindstone artisanal doughnuts. *What's wrong with Dunkin'?* I wanted to know. But Kelly had read about designer doughnuts on *Grub Street* and insisted we stop in Sag Harbor on the way. "You get the bacon maple for that." I wink at Maureen and she blushes like a much younger woman who married a man despite all those fantasies, starring her best friend.

"Do you get that a lot?" the *New York* magazine reporter asks when Maureen is gone. Erin, I think she said her name was. "Women who credit their coming out to you?"

"All the time."

"Why do you think that is?"

I lace my fingers behind my head and kick up my feet. *Cocky*, straight women often call me with a giggle. "Gay looks good on me, I guess."

Kelly makes that face our mother warned would stick. I wish she were alive so that I could tell her she was right about something, at least.

"It's working for you," Erin agrees, blushing. "Whew!" She fans her cheeks. "Where's the bathroom in here?"

"Down the hallway on the left," Kelly tells her.

"No, Brett," Kelly says, quietly, as soon as the bathroom door shuts. She means Maureen. No, Brett, we aren't hiring her. No, Brett, it's not your call. I reach for Erin's recorder and switch it off so Kelly isn't caught fat/age/tan shaming on tape.

"Hey," I hold up my phone to take an Instagram story of our surroundings, "the yoga studio is your baby." I type NEW SPOKE SPACE COMING JUNE '17. Click, done. Search for the location. Montauk End of the World doesn't come up for a while. Service is wonky out here, which reminds me . . . "By the way," I say to Kelly, "it's *out* here."

Kelly stares at me, blankly.

"You said thank you for coming all the way *up* here to see us. Montauk isn't up. It's east. You want people to think you're an old pro at the Hamptons scene . . ." I pull my sweatshirt over my head and pet the static out of my famous hair.

This is, in fact, Kelly's first time *out* here. A ticket to a comedy show, I realized, after mentioning it to the commercial designer I've hired to transform the abandoned hardware store on Montauk's Main Street into a pop-up yoga studio. A pop-up yoga studio on Montauk's Main Street. If you're worried I've become more basic than the insult "basic," you should be.

"Never been to Montauk before?" the designer had repeated back to us in slow disbelief, as if my sister had never seen avocado toast on a menu, or heard Justin Bieber's music. He spread a palm over his throat, choking on Kelly's quaintness.

And so earlier, as Kelly and I were setting up the space for the yoga instructor auditions, Kelly told me not to mention anything about it being her first time in Montauk to the *New York* magazine reporter who was on her way *out here* to document the first hiring call for the yoga studio.

I tried to parse her reasoning before asking about it. Kelly gets cranky when you ask her to explain things she thinks should be obvious, another fetching facet of her personality she got from our mother. "Why not?" I'd finally been forced to ask. I couldn't for the life of me figure out why it would be a bad thing for people to know this was Kelly's first time in Montauk. I've barely been to Montauk, and, if anything, it better serves our "brand"—yup, still the grossest word in the English language—that Kelly has never spent a summer mainlining rosé in a slutty one-piece at Gurney's. We are the *people's* fitness studio.

"Because I don't want anything that makes us look inexperienced in the press," she said, flicking open a yoga mat. "I'm worried how it looks to our investors, like we're little girls playing with Monopoly money."

Well, I thought but didn't have the energy to say, *they aren't our investors. They're my investors. So don't lose any sleep over it.* But I let it slide. I have enough headaches in my life right now. No need to get hung up on the delusional statements of a stay-at-home mom who still hasn't accepted the fact that her tubby little sister is the overachiever now.

And overachiever I am. Since filming wrapped last season, I've raised $23.4 million to expand the location of my spin studio, WeSPOKE. Coming fall 2017, SPOKE will open on the Upper West Side and Soho, and, if this yoga thing does well for us, we have our eye on a space just down the block from our original SPOKE location in the Flatiron, the premier zip code for boutique studio fitness in Manhattan. Not bad for a twenty-seven-year-old community-college dropout who, up until three years ago, was living in her sister's basement in New Jersey.

I should be proud, and I am, but . . . I don't know. I can't help but feel conflicted about the expansion. I loved our scrappy little studio when it was a self-governing affair: There was no board to answer to, no human resources department, no numbingly dull talk of *the market*. Our seed capital came from an entrepreneurial contest I won when I was twenty-three. I never needed angel investors or bootstrappers, I never had to answer to anyone but myself. The grant money gave me the freedom to focus on the mission of SPOKE, which is and always will be to protect and educate the female Imazighen population of Morocco's High Atlas Mountains.

Imazighen women and girls—some as young as eight—walk, on average, four miles a day under a gruesome 14 UV Index sun just to bring home a single jerrican of water. It's a woman's duty to provide clean water for her family, and the task often prevents them from attending school and entering the workforce later in life. Then there is the issue of their safety. One in five Imazighen women have been sexually assaulted on their way to the well, sometimes by groups of men who hide in the bushes and wait for the youngest walkers. When I heard this, I had to act, and I knew other women would be compelled to as well if I made it easy for them. For every fifth ride at SPOKE, we provide a bike to an Imazighen family in need. The bikes reduce the time of the water-gathering task (from hours to minutes) so that young girls are home in time for school and their moms can go to work. The bikes mobilize girls who haven't even gotten their periods yet to outpace a gang of rapists.

That was my pitch, and not a single investor bought it. They were all men, and they all thought New York City women were too self-absorbed to care. But these days, it's cool to care. It's mandatory to support the sisterhood. Women are spokes in the same wheel, trying their best to move each other forward. That's SPOKE's mission statement. Kelly came up with it. Beautiful, huh? Myself, I preferred *Get off your privileged ass and think of someone else for a change*, but Kelly made the point that we'd probably catch more flies with honey.

Of course, when we didn't, Kelly lost interest. She laughed at me when I showed her the article I'd clipped from the *Out* magazine

I found in the doctor's waiting room, detailing the entrepreneurial contest for budding LGBTQ business owners. *That's a long shot,* she said, but I've always had a strong arm.

I'd peeled apart a folding chair and said, "The Hamptons are absolutely lovely and they should stay that way, but they won't, not with pop-up yoga studios opening where the hardware store is supposed to be."

Kelly had sighed. "There's a client base out here, though."

I'd set the box of Grindstone doughnuts on the seat of the chair. I'd already eaten two—classic Boston crème and blueberry basil with lemon ricotta frosting. The sugar remained a burning ring in my throat, demanding more. *Better than an orgasm,* people say about good food, but that isn't quite right. Food is what happens before the orgasm, the building of something great, the wonderfully excruciating plea to *keep going, keep going.* Too many women deny themselves this pleasure, and I decided long ago I would not be one of them. Almost one third of young women would trade a year of their lives to have the perfect body. This is not because women are shallow, or because they have their priorities out of whack. It is because society makes life miserable for women who are not thin. I am part of a small but growing minority determined to change that. SPOKE is the first exercise studio that mentions nothing about transforming your body, because study after study proves that your physical body has so little to do with health. Healthy people are people who feel connected to their communities, who are loved and supported by those around them, and who have a sense of purpose in their lives. Healthy women do not waste their precious energy separating egg whites from egg yolks.

"How about this," I said to Kelly. "I won't mention anything about this being your first time in Montauk if you consider the free memberships for the locals."

"No, Brett," Kelly said, her favorite refrain. "Someone in this family needs to graduate from college."

"Half a degree from Dartmouth is like a full degree from CUNY," I pointed out.

"I'll get a scholarship," Layla had said, dutifully. Little perfect angel that she is, she had found a broom and was sweeping the area around the yoga mat, because it was dirty and the instructors were going to be auditioning barefooted. When Layla was born, the doctor told me she had 25 percent of my genes, but I think those cells have copied and split a few times since then. It was Layla's idea to curate an Instagram account and online shop that hawks the wares of Imazighen women. The feed is filled with gorgeous rag rugs, pottery, and cold-pressed olive oil, and 100 percent of the proceeds go back to the women of the High Atlas Mountains. Just like her auntie, Layla thinks with her heart, not her wallet. We have Kelly for that.

"It's not that easy to get a scholarship, Layla," Kelly said. "Especially to a top school."

"Uhhhhh," I said, making prolonged eye contact with Layla, whose smile was a dare: *Say it.* "I think she'll be fine."

"Don't do that, Brett," Kelly muttered, plopping into a chair while her daughter continued to sweep the floors.

I walked over to her and rested my hands on the back of her chair, bringing my face close enough for her to smell the lavender rose poppy seed *we could have just gone to Dunkin'* doughnut on my breath. "Pretending to be colorblind is just as offensive as the n-word, you know."

Kelly covered my whole face with her palm and shoved me away. "*Stop.*" It came out an exhausted plea. Kelly is a mother, and heretofore exhausted in a way that I as a child-free individual running a multimillion-dollar corporation cannot begin to even contemplate.

Kelly had Layla when she was nineteen years old, in a confounding act of defiance against our recently deceased mother. Growing up, my mother's shadow darted after Kelly as she moved between AP classes, piano lessons, Habitat for Humanity, SAT tutors, college essay editors, college interview coaches, Dartmouth, premed summer sessions, and finally, a fellowship with the International School of Global Health in North Africa that Kelly returned from motherless, pregnant, and more chill than I'd ever seen her. Our mom was far from the traditional definition of a tiger mom. Her fixed state was mopey, immobilized, one stain on her blouse away from crying. Kelly was the court jester, but instead of juggling and telling jokes, she got straight As and played Bach with soft fingers. When our mother died (took *three* strokes), Kelly was released from duty. Why she decided to celebrate her freedom by holding out her wrists for another set of handcuffs still escapes me, but then we wouldn't have Layla, who, listen, I know on a subliminal level has to love my sister more than she loves me. But it doesn't feel that way. Not to me and not to Kelly either. And it's a reversal of fortunes for both of us.

Because when I was in high school, I was the least loved. I was smoking pot when I should have been in Spanish class, piercing my nose instead of my ear cartilage, eating white cheddar Cheez-Its for breakfast, and looking more and more like my mother every day, an *egregious* crime, in her eyes. I never understood it. Kelly may have gotten the thin genes but my mother and I got *face.* A boy in high school once said that if you put my head on Kelly's body we could be a supermodel. And this is the problem with the way girls are raised, because both of us were flattered. One of us even gave him a blow job.

—

Erin returns from the bathroom, shaking her wet hands. "No paper towels in there," she says. I stick my hands in my sweatshirt and reach out to dry hers. For a moment, our fingers intertwine through the terry cloth material, and we feel that our hands are the same size. I love introducing other women to the eroticism of equality.

"Thanks." Erin is *flushed.* She takes a seat next to me, pressing play on her recorder with a cutely scolding glance in my direction. I lift a hand with a shrug—*No idea how that happened*—and a prism of light distracts her.

"Ah," she says. "There's the famous ring."

I hold out my hand so we can both admire the gold signet I wear on my pinkie. "It's a little cocktail-hour-at-the-club for me," I say, "but I got absolutely no say in the design."

When the show was renewed for the third season, Jen, Steph, and

I realized we were the only original cast members still standing, and Steph proposed having rings made to commemorate this momentous achievement. She sent me a link to the website of a designer Gwyneth Paltrow featured on *Goop,* $108 for an inch of plated gold, plus the cost to have them engraved *SS,* for Standing Sisters. This was before the $23.4 million, the book deal, and the speaking fees that still haven't made me rich, because it is very hard to be rich in New York City. *Does Claire's still exist?* I texted back. *On me,* was Steph's response. A lot of things were *on Steph,* and despite what she tells you, she likes it that way. Sometimes, I catch Kelly staring at the ring. She'll look away when she realizes she's been seen, sheepish, like a guy busted staring at your tits when you bend over to pick up something that's fallen on the ground.

Erin's attention travels up my bare arm. "Is that new?"

I flex my bicep for her. I am not the type of woman who gets a tattoo on the nape of her neck or the underside of her wrist. "A woman needs a man—"

"Like a fish needs a bicycle," Erin finishes. *Another Straight Girl Flirts with Me (And I Love It)* should be the name of my fucking memoir.

"That's so clever," Erin gushes. "Especially with the reference to the bicycle."

"Oh, Brett is *extremely* clever." Kelly gets me in a headlock and gives me a noogie, her preferred method of attack whenever she feels like anyone is stroking my ego too hard. She likes to try to break off my Cher hair at the root. I sink my teeth into her arm hard enough to taste her Bliss body lotion, the only body lotion Kelly can afford at Bluemercury, and she releases me with a sharp cry.

Erin reaches out and irons my hair back into place.

"Can you please tell everyone it's real?" I ask her.

"Hair is real." Erin pretends to jot it down in a pretend notebook. "It's interesting," she says, "but I'm noticing a pattern here that the show parallels. You as the little sister to the group."

"Mmmm," I say, unconvinced. "I think Jen Greenberg would rather hump a hot dog than share a bloodline with me."

Erin controls her laugh, but her eyes are twinkling with shared detestation for Jen. "I'm sure that's not true."

There is no love lost between Jen Greenberg and me. We were acquainted through the wellness industry years ago, something approaching friends that first season. Viewers watched as I grew close to her famous humanist mother, Yvette, who loves Jen because she has to and me because she does, and everyone thinks this is why we can't speak the other's name without a lip curl of contempt. The reality is that there is a gap between Jen's onscreen persona (Vegan. Groovy.) and real-life one (Vegan. Mega bitch.), and I have no patience for that particular brand of inauthenticity.

And guess what? It's okay that we do not get along. It is a dangerous thing to conflate feminism with liking all women. It limits women to being one thing, *likable*, when feminism is about allowing women to be all shades of all things, even if that thing is a snake oil saleswoman.

Erin continues, "I guess I just mean everyone has their role, right? You're the baby. The scrappy up-and-comer. Stephanie is the grand dame. The one with it all—money, success, love. Jen is obviously feminist royalty and Lauren's the straw that stirs the drink. Hayley was, I don't know . . . I guess she was the normal one?"

And that's why you're speaking about her in the past tense. Hayley's obituary came in the form of an *Us Weekly* announcement detailing her desire to concentrate on new and exciting business opportunities. As if the whole point of the show isn't to document that very thing. I liked Hayley and I think she had another season in her, but she got greedy, asking for all that money when she was bringing nothing to the table.

Cast members drop every year and I see no reason to go into crisis mode worrying that I might be next. We all have a story that will come to an end at some point or another, no use making myself crazy trying to manipulate the inevitable, as is the way of some of the cast. Still, I'd rather deal with that than with my sister, buzzing in my ear the last few weeks. *Would the producers consider her to replace Hayley? Would I talk to Lisa again? Would I talk to Jesse this time?*

I submit. "I guess I'm kind of the underdog."

One side of Erin's mouth tugs down, wryly. "*Well.* If the underdog has three million followers on Instagram while the rest of the cast has yet to break a mil. But in terms of your socioeconomic standing, yes, though I'm so interested to see how this season plays out now that you're catching up to everyone else financially. It seems like you're really firing on all cylinders, you know? You're in a serious relationship with a drop-dead gorgeous human rights lawyer—"

"Who volunteers with sexual assault survivors and speaks five languages," I pad.

Erin laughs. "Who volunteers with sexual assault survivors and speaks five languages. Then you've got the book deal. The two new studios. You're trying your hand at yoga. All of this, it's *going* to cause a power shift in the group. I mean," she smirks—not at me; at *her*, "it already has, hasn't it?"

Kelly watches me, curious how this is going to go. This is the first time anyone in the press has asked me about *her*. Stephanie. My former best friend.

I gather my wits and say, "I'm not one for beating around the bush."

Erin leans forward with a collaborating smile, as though to assure me we can shape this any way I want if I'm willing to spill the tea. "I heard you and Stephanie had a fight and are no longer talking."

I speak around her, to Kelly, "It was on *TMZ*, right? So it has to be true."

Erin shrugs, unfazed. "*TMZ* was the first to break the news about Michael Jackson's death and the Kim Kardashian robbery."

"I love *TMZ*." Kelly grins at me, thrilled to see me in the hot seat. Kelly knows all about my falling-out with Stephanie. But unlike *TMZ*, and unlike what I'm about to tell Erin, she knows the truth, and I can count on her to keep it a secret. Sisters are reliably good for two things: hating and loving.

"We haven't spoken in six months," I admit.

Erin purses her lips, saddened by this news. But the sadness is only an angle to solicit more information. "I loved your friendship with Stephanie. It felt important to see a relationship like that between two women. Important and remarkable, especially for the reality TV landscape that feeds off women in conflict. And you didn't—" She cuts herself off, searching for a better phrasing. "I don't want to sound blamey. I guess I'm trying to understand how two women whose bond seemed unbreakable don't reconnect given the serious revelations made by one in her memoir." She waits for me to respond. I wait for a question to actually be asked. "Unless . . ." Erin squints as if to filter out everyone and everything but me. "Unless you already knew about the sexual abuse?"

I am prepared for this. "Stephanie is a really private person."

"So . . . you did know?"

"Just because we're going through a rough patch right now doesn't mean I'd betray her confidences. Violence against women, and particularly women of color, is a cause I feel very strongly about. I would never want to speak for Stephanie about her own experience."

Erin frowns and nods: *Fair enough*. "Clearly, you still care about her. Does this mean we'll get to see a reconciliation next season?"

I gaze at the old cash register in the corner. There's still a dish of Bazooka Bubble Gum on the counter. I'd like to keep that, if possible. Some original touches as penance for the fresh hell of athleisure that's about to rain down on this unsuspecting corner of an innocent fishing village. "It's really up to her. She's the one who is upset with me. Maybe it's for all the reasons you said. I know she's having her big moment with her memoir right now, a moment I want to make clear is well-deserved, but maybe she liked me better when I was the *underdog*."

Erin props her elbow on the folding table, resting her chin on her fist, giving me her best *I'm listening* eyes. "Or do you think it's because you wouldn't pass on an advance copy of her book to Rihanna?"

I do a double take. Not even *TMZ* knew about the Rihanna part. Yet.

"Full disclosure." Erin raises her hand like she's about to take an oath. "I called Stephanie for a quote earlier this week."

It's a good thing I'm sitting down because I'm pretty sure my kneecaps have liquefied. She called Stephanie? Does she *know*?

"I had pitched this as a piece about our new yoga suite," Kelly inserts with an amicable smile. And it's true, she did. I didn't see the need to have a member of the press present for today, but Kelly wants it printed in *New York* magazine that she is chief of SPOKE's first foray into exploiting an ancient and sacred practice for its low overhead.

In addition to being SPOKE's bookkeeper and also a .000000001 percent investor (she generously threw in 2K of the money Mom left us in her will), it was Kelly's idea to expand into yoga. The pop-up studio is a trial run. If it does well for us, I promised Kelly that FLOW would be her domain. But for that to happen, Kelly needs to hire some instructors. Before Maureen there was Amal, who blew something called a Handstand Scorpion and spoke too high, like a little girl. How could anyone relax into something called King Pigeon with that voice? Before that was Justin, who was otherwise perfect if not for his declaration that he would require a 20 percent raise to leave his post at Pure Yoga. Next! Kirsten's capital offense was her uninspiring sequencing.

I paw through the stack of resumés. "Kirsten. I want to give her a call back. She was good. I liked her."

Kelly squares the pile of resumés I just cluttered. "Not Maureen?"

I tug my sweatshirt on. The sleeves are still wet from Erin's hands. "Bitch should have preordered my book."

"Jesus," Kelly gasps, horrified. "Please tell me that's off the record, Erica."

Erica. Not Erin. Panic pole-axes me. Have I been calling an important reporter by the wrong name all morning? I retrace our conversation and take a metaphorical exhale, realizing I'm in the clear. Names are *my thing*. I'm slipping. I've allowed this Stephanie pettiness to distract me. Thank God for Kelly, who handles the details so that I can focus on the big picture. I remind myself this is why I need her around. Because lately, I've been thinking that maybe I don't.

Kelly reaches for the passenger-side sun visor and flips it open, hauling her twenty-pound makeup kit into her lap. She brought the whole thing with her, like some kind of traveling theater dancer.

"I'll be really quiet," Layla says from the back seat.

"Layls, honey, it's not appropriate," Kelly says, glazing her lips with a gloss so thick and pink it could be the coating on the strawberry doughnut no one wanted. Her nice clear skin doesn't need the airbrush foundation she thinks it does and she's put a meticulous, embarrassing wave in her hair. I don't know much about fashion or designer doughnuts—neither does Kelly, but she's trying and only occasionally hitting the mark—but I know that no woman in New York is spending hours trying to make her hair look messy anymore. At least her outfit looks good. She showed up at my apartment last week with ten abominably short dresses. I was tempted to let her meet Jesse looking like she was attending a divorce party at a lounge in Hoboken, but then I remembered how every August, Mom would take only Kelly shopping for new school clothes. Her rationale was that most little sisters wear their older sister's clothes, and why should she have to pay for two wardrobes just because I couldn't *get ahold of myself*? As though my skinny self was on the lam and I was expected to chase after her, a normative body bounty hunter, spinning a lasso above my head. Every August at the Gap cash register, Kelly would pretend to change her mind about a pair of jeans, or a flannel button-down, and run back into the dressing room to find the item of clothing she wanted to replace it with. What she would really do is grab something in my size so that I had at least one new item of clothing with which to start the school year. One time, I came downstairs in a gray waffle sweatshirt, a premier selection from the Gap's 1997 fall sportswear collection, and just as Mom started to say something, Kelly cried, "I got a B-minus on my Spanish quiz!" It was the Courtney family equivalent of taking a bullet. That's a fucking sister. And so, I asked my girlfriend if she would lend Kelly that Stevie Nicks–looking dress she bought on the top floor of Barneys that Zara is also selling for a tenth of the price. Arch and my sister wear the same size. Arch and my sister have gotten ahold of themselves.

"It's not like you planned it like this," I say. "The babysitter fell through."

"For fuck's sake, Brett!" Kelly turns away from the mirror, only her bottom lip pink. Sure, it's okay for *her* to curse in front of Layla. "Be on my side for once. Be on my side for *this*." Kelly is a nervous wreck for this meeting because she actually thinks she has a chance, though Jesse Barnes, creator and executive producer of the number two reality program in the highly prized eighteen- to forty-nine-year-old demographic on Tuesday nights, would never seriously consider casting her in Hayley's vacant spot. But as soon as *New York* mag suggested photos of the pop-up yoga studio on site, Kelly started: *What if we swung by Jesse's after for lunch?* Jesse spends almost every weekend of the year in her Montauk house, even during the off-season, and Kelly has now gotten it into her head that her way on to the show is through Jesse, even though I told her that Jesse is too senior to get involved at the casting level. Lisa, our showrunner, is the one Jesse trusts to make those decisions. But Kelly tried Lisa last year and both of us got a caning for it. *DEAR FUCKING BRETT,* Lisa wrote me after the coffee meeting I arranged between the two, *THANKS FOR OMITTING THE FACT THAT YOUR SISTER HAS FUCKING UDDERS AND WASTING MY FUCKING TIME.*

I didn't tell Lisa that Kelly was a single mother to a preteen girl because she never would have taken the meeting otherwise, and I needed Kelly to hear for herself that she's not right for a show about young women who have eschewed marriage (generally) and babies (specifically) in favor of building their empires. But Kelly doesn't understand that unlike mommy gut, motherhood is a choice. And in the eyes of Jesse Barnes, it's the wrong one.

—

For half the year, Jesse Barnes lives in a two-bedroom, one-bath 1960s beach bungalow that hugs the edge of a mythical clay cliff in Montauk. Of course she has the means to knock it down and build some glass-walled spaceship like most people would do. Most people aren't Jesse Barnes. A woman living alone in a big ole house almost always invites the question of how she's going to fill it. Partner, kids, multiple rescue dogs, each with its own Instagram account. But a five-million-dollar shack in the most expensive beach destination in the country answers that question with gorgeous restraint. A woman in a home only big enough for herself is the ultimate fuck you to patriarchal society. It says *I am enough for me.*

We're greeted at the door by Hank, still in his orange wellies from his sail earlier that morning. Jesse met Hank years ago on a Montauk fishing dock and started buying swordfish and sea bass from him directly. From time to time, she pays him to fix up things around the house.

"Hi, girls," Hank says. I let that slide because Hank is in his seventies. But *Diggers* have rules. The establishing tenet: We're women. Not girls. I am a twenty-seven-year-old pioneer in the wellness space who reincorporated her company as a B-corp without needing to hire a lawyer. Would you refer to my male equivalent as a boy? Try saying it out loud. It sounds non-native. "She's in the back." He beckons us with three craggled fingers.

Through the double sliding glass doors I see that Jesse is reading *The New Yorker*—ha!—on a lounge chair by the tarp-covered pool, a Southwestern striped wool silk blanket draped over her legs. Kelly is doing her best not to stare, but Kelly is incapable of affecting disinterest in the face of something fantastically interesting. Jesse Barnes, whether you consider her the first feminist voice of reality TV (the *New York Times*) or a feminist fraud (*The New Yorker*), is nothing if not fantastically interesting.

"Hi!" Kelly says, much too ardently, before Hank can even introduce us. Jesse stiffens, but she smiles, graciously.

"Kelly!" Jesse says, standing to give her a hug. Kelly has met Jesse before, in headquarters and at the reunions, but it was only for the briefest of moments. Up close, without camera makeup and beauty lighting, she finally gets to see what I see: that the heartthrob of the butch community has pretty pink cheeks and a pink chin, hair just a little too dark for her complexion.

"Wow," Jesse holds Kelly at an arm's length, appraisingly, "look how gorgeous you are!" If Kelly were my size, no one would call her gorgeous. Her face is inoffensive and unremarkable.

"Can you believe she has a twelve-year-old?" I go in for a hug with Jesse, Kelly's glare torching my back. I know she thinks I'm trying to sabotage her by bringing up the fact that she's a mother. But it's not that. It's that I'm not going to pretend like my niece doesn't exist so Kelly can break one thousand followers on Twitter, which is what we would have to do in order for Kelly to be cast in Hayley's spot.

The show is founded on the radical notion that women are people first, and once women have kids, they cede everything to the black hole of motherhood. I want to make it clear that this is Jesse's worldview, but I don't think she's wrong either. We have choices as women, and there is no right one to make—especially because no matter what you decide, the world will tell you you're doing it wrong. But when you make the choice to become a mother, it becomes the choice that defines you, fair or not. Case in point: the *New York Times* obit for Yvonne Brill, eighty-eight-year-old rocket scientist. *She made a mean beef stroganoff, followed her husband from job to job and took eight years off from work to raise three children. "The world's best mom," her son Matthew said.* This is what the editors chose to lead with, about a woman whose inventions made satellites possible.

And motherhood is a limitation that women themselves have internalized. Go on, right now, and look up the Instagram and Twitter profiles of all the men you know. How many of them list father or husband to @theirwife'sname in their bios? Not many, I'd guess, because men are raised to view themselves as multifaceted beings, with complexities and contradictions and prismatic identities. And when they only have a certain number of characters in which to describe themselves, when they reduce themselves to just one or two things, it is more likely their profession, and maybe their allegiance to a certain sports team, than their family.

So there are mothers and unmothers, and while neither choice is the easy one to make, motherhood is at least the comfortable one. The one society has come to expect from us. Same goes for marriage, same goes for changing your last name to match your husband's, for him being the financial provider, moving for his job and learning to make a mean beef stroganoff. There is a rash of reality TV shows that either depict this conventional way of life (*Real Housewives*) or the aspiration to this way of life (*The Bachelor*). Mothers and wives and domestic goddesses and aspiring mothers, wives, and domestic goddesses get to see their likeness represented when they turn on the TV at all hours of the day.

But there was nothing for the unmothers, and the unwives, and the women who can't even scramble an egg. And there are a lot of us, more than ever before. A few years ago, when she was just thirty-nine and a network executive at Saluté, Jesse Barnes read Yvonne Brill's obit, and then she read the Pew statistics that showed that for the first time ever, women were outpacing men in college placement and in managerial positions. More women than ever before were out-earning their husbands, starting their own businesses, and choosing to delay marriage and children, or to withhold from both customs altogether. *Where are the reality TV avatars for these women?* Jesse wondered, and when she couldn't find them, she created them.

And because she was committed to assembling an ethnically, sexually, and physically diverse cast, I found a place where I fit, after not fitting in for the entirety of my life. *Goal Diggers* is the little corner of the reality TV landscape where women like me belong, and it's unfair—and typical—that a woman like Kelly, with her big boobs and her tiny waist, her socially sanctioned and exercised uterus, would stomp in and try to claim a piece of this scant land for herself.

"Unbelievable," Kelly declares. Jesse has led us to the edge of the property, where the Atlantic recycles itself brutally against the base of the cliff. These are not the turquoise waters of Carnival Cruise Line commercials or the gentle brown waves I learned to bodysurf at the Jersey Shore. This is the tank that housed Moby Dick. These are steel-colored waves that will make a missing person out of you. Of all the slippery bitches I know—and I know a few—the ocean takes it by a landslide.

"This house was originally built two hundred feet from the bluff," Jesse says, sending an apologetic wink my way. I've heard this story many times over.

I raise a hand in permission. "No. Tell her."

Jesse explains how the land has eroded—one hundred and seventy-five feet in the forty-one years since the house was constructed. She's had to apply for an emergency approval from the East Hampton Planning Department to have the house relocated closer to the road.

"Wouldn't it be easier to tear it down and build a new one?" Kelly asks, and I squeeze my eyes shut, mortified.

"This house was built on the site of a former World War II bunker and constructed from the structure's original cement." Jesse gives Kelly a tolerant smile and starts back toward the picnic table without having to explain further.

Hank has left silk wool and alpaca blankets folded in our seats, blue striped for me, gray for Kelly. We drape them over our shoulders and nod our heads when Hank offers us red wine. Jesse is watching Kelly, and when my sister realizes it, she frames her chin with her hands and gives a big, fifth-grade-picture-day smile. Sometimes Kelly is funny.

Jesse laughs. "I guess I'm just trying to find the resemblance."

"We sneeze in threes," I say, tartly. Maybe if my hair were its natural color and my thighs didn't touch, Jesse would see the resemblance. Stephanie pays a bitchy therapist a lot of money to exorcise her demons and she once tried to play armchair with me, proposing that in high school, I gained weight and covered my arms in tattoos as a defense mechanism against comparisons to Kelly. Kelly was the pretty one, the smart one, the one who was going places. Sabotaging my looks, failing in school, disappointing my mother for sport, it was all less of an emotional risk than trying to measure up to Kelly's legacy and failing.

And by the way, Stephanie added, *the average woman in America wears a size eighteen. So you're not fat.* If everyone could stop assuming that I care about being skinny that would be *so* great. *You're showing young girls that you don't have to be thin to be beautiful*, many a freshly body positive women's mag editor has started off an interview with me, causing my pelvic floor to seize up in a fit of fury. *No*, I correct them, *I'm showing young girls that you don't have to be beautiful to matter*. The thinking that women of all shapes and sizes can be beautiful is still hugely problematic, because it is predicated on the idea that the most important thing a woman has to offer the world is her appearance. Men are raised to worry about their legacies, not their upper arm and thigh fat, stretch marks, crows-feet, saggy elbows, ugly armpits, thin eyelashes, and normal-smelling genitals. This is how society keeps us out of the C-suite—it booby-traps the way to the top with self-loathing, then reroutes us on a never-ending path of self-improvement.

"Did you find a space?" Jesse asks us.

"We found a space," I say.

"*Oh!*" Jesse turns to me. "Where?"

"You know where Puff 'n' Putt is?" Kelly interjects, annoyingly.

"The mini golf place?" Jesse asks.

Kelly nods. "We are *right* across the street. That hardware store shut down. It's such a great location."

"And we hardly have to do anything to it," I rub my fingers together, signifying *money*, "which is good because I'm going to be eating a lot of ramen during this expansion." Kelly pierces my thigh with a fake fingernail under the table. I wrap a fist around her finger and twist, doing my best, one-handed, to inflict an injury with a very racist name that wasn't yet considered offensive when we were kids in the nineties. It was in the nineties that Kelly and I should have outgrown the roughhousing, only it intensified with age, and now it's like we're adult thumb-suckers or something else worthy of a spot on TLC's *My Strange Addiction*. The longest break we've ever taken from our weekly wrestling matches was ten years ago, when Layla was two, and only because we realized we were scaring the shit out of her. She would come running in when she heard the rumbling start, sobbing and shrieking, "No hurt! No hurt!"

We never talked about stopping. We just did, for a while. Then one day, while Layla was napping, Kelly opened the refrigerator to find that I drank the last can of her Diet Coke. She dragged me off the couch by my ponytail and we went at it silently until it was time for Kelly to wake up Layla. And that's been our routine ever since—quiet, private violence. We know it's perverse. We know we should stop. But it's an outlet for words that would hurt more to say.

Kelly bumps the table trying to wrestle her finger free from my death grip, and Jesse trains an eye on both of us, curiously. We sit up straight and give her our best *You imagined it* smile.

"We're doing okay for ourselves," Kelly says, rubbing *her* fingers together coyly. "Most Series A capital efforts raise between two and fourteen million dollars. We did almost triple that."

"I'm not surprised," Jesse says. "SPOKE is such a great concept."

"Yeah, but that has less to do with it than you'd think," Kelly says. "The key to breaking that fourteen-million-dollar glass ceiling is a unicorn valuation of the company, and, because it's a private company, making sure that the valuation is disseminated publicly to create a bidder's urgency in the private equity firm world."

Jesse blinks like she's been spun around on the dance floor one too many times. "Jesus," she says to me, "she's like John Nash with a great rack."

I feel a ridiculous spear of jealousy. Jesse has been known to make somewhat lecherous comments to young, pretty women, but I prefer to be the target of them, thank you very much. "Kelly has whatever the opposite of mom brain is," I say, pettily. Kelly makes *Shut up!* eyes at me for bringing up Layla again. I make them right back at her.

Kelly would prefer everyone think we're on the up-and-up now that our funding has been so widely reported in the press. She thinks this makes her a more desirable candidate, even though being broke is what got me my job on the show in the first place. The producers didn't initially conceive of a *Digger* in financial straits, but finding an enigmatic gay millennial proved a harder task than they realized, and Jesse was not about to cast the show without at least one of her people represented.

Once I was in the mix, the producers realized that I added some much-needed texture to the group. I'm the Greek Chorus, the one the audience is rolling their eyes with when Lauren sets off the airport metal detector because she forgot to remove both—count them, *both*—her Cartier Love bracelets.

Erin or Erica or whatever the fuck her name is was right that the power dynamics are about to shift this season, and I'm nervous about how that's going to play out in terms of audience reception. I've always been the little guy, the relatable one, the favorite, and I want to make it clear that as I move up in the world, my triumph comes not from being able to afford rent on an apartment with a dishwasher, but in being able to give back to the women who need it most.

Jesse arches an eyebrow, sexily. She's a forever bachelorette, a serial model dater who throws pizza parties on this very cliff with the likes of Sheryl Sandberg and Alec Baldwin. Viewers are always calling in to her aftershow, wanting to know when the two of us are just going to admit we're having an affair. I have something to admit, but it's not that. "In any case," she says, "with a *unicorn valuation,*" she directs her smile at Kelly, "I don't think you'll be dining daily on ramen much longer."

I point to the sky. "From your lips. But that money doesn't go to us yet. It's all for the new studios and our e-bikes."

"Brett is being modest," Kelly insists, tucking her hair behind her ear to pass off my girlfriend's diamond huggie as her own. Neither of us draw a salary from SPOKE yet, but I make my living through speaking engagements and brand extensions like the book. The show pays less than five thousand a year and for good reason—producers wanted to attract young women who were already established, not those looking for a lily pad.

"The money will come if you keep doing what you're good at," Jesse says. She raises her glass. "Cheers. To the new yoga studio and the book deal and the Series A money *and* the new girlfriend. Jesus, *chica*. You've got a few things going on, huh?"

I do a little dance in my seat and Jesse laughs. "When do I get to meet her?"

"I'll set something on the calendar soon," I promise.

"Does big sister approve of bae?" Jesse asks Kelly.

Kelly tilts her head, confused.

"'Bae,' Kel." I laugh at her. "It means, like, significant other." To Jesse, I explain, "She doesn't get out much."

"I know what 'bae' means." Kelly tosses her hair. She got highlights for this meeting. They made her too blond.

"You *lie*!"

Kelly turns to Jesse with an expression that makes my heart thump like a sneaker in the dryer. Shit. I shouldn't have antagonized her like that in front of Jesse. "You want to know what I think of *bae*?" Kelly asks, pausing long enough to make me squirm. "We adore her," she finally says, much too glowingly.

"So your daughter has met her," Jesse infers.

Kelly looks mortified to have reminded Jesse she is a mom for the third time in ten minutes. "Yes. Um. My daughter. Layla."

"Pretty name," Jesse says, hollowly. She turns to me. "Brett, I'm assuming none of the other women have met her?"

"No. No one. Yet."

"Not even Stephanie?"

"We met after Stephanie and I . . . you know . . ." I trail off and Jesse smiles at me like she does know but she still wants to hear me say it. "Come on," I groan. "You know what happened."

"Could I hear it from you and not *TMZ*?" She bats her eyelashes.

I sigh, using my hand to deepen the part in my hair. Massaging the truth for Jesse is dangerous, but Stephanie has left me no other choice. "She started to get funny after I got my book deal. Like . . . I could tell she wasn't happy for me. There was no congratulations. It was just right off the bat, how much was my advance and this immediate assumption that I would ghost it. And when I started talking about moving out, it was like she wanted to scare me into staying." I have lived with Stephanie (and Vince, the Husband) on and off for the last few years. The first time, we were filming season two, which made for a darling storyline. Then I met my ex-girlfriend and moved in with her. When the ex and I broke up last year, Sarah got the apartment until the lease ran out and in the meantime, I returned to chez Simmons. My stay was notably less darling the second time around.

"Steph just got very scoldy," I continue, scrunching up my face remembering what it was like as things started to sour for us. "She kept reminding me that book advances are paid in installments and five hundred K actually isn't as much money as I think it is because it's doled out over the course of a few years and taxes and blah blah. I read the payment schedule in my contract. I got it. I wasn't trying to buy a brownstone on the Upper East Side. I'm twenty-seven years old. I'm just looking to get my own *place*. It was very much the big guy wagging his finger at the little guy to keep me in my place."

"And this was all before her memoir came out?" Jesse clarifies, resting her pink cheek in her small palm.

I nod. "And I thought what you're probably thinking. She's stressed. She's only ever written fiction and now here she is, making these major and incredibly painful revelations about her life. I was willing to let it pass. But then . . ." I sigh. Up until now, nothing has been a lie. There is no turning back after this. "She wanted me to pass an advance copy of the new book to Rihanna. She wanted her to share it on her social, and she also thought Rihanna should play her if the book came out and was a big hit and they wanted to make it into a movie."

"It would be a great part for Rihanna," Jesse says.

"If Rihanna were five years older and straightened her hair to within an inch of its life and dressed like a local newswoman, then yes, maybe."

"Come on now," Jesse teases, thinking I'm just jealous.

"I can admit when someone has hit a home run. Stephanie is so brave for coming forward about what she went through when she was younger. She's helping so many women find their voices. But that doesn't give her a free pass to place unfair demands on our friendship. Rihanna attended one class and I didn't feel comfortable emailing her out of the blue to push my castmate's book on her. That's a grimy move. I thought that as my friend, Stephanie would understand that. But that's not how she saw it. She thinks my ego is out of control and that I'm holding out on her. That after everything she's done for me, I owe her. Meanwhile, she was the one who insisted I move in with her. *Both times*. I'm obviously grateful"—I cradle my heart to prove how much her hospitality meant to me—"but I never asked. It's like she only helped me so she gets to say I owe her."

"It wouldn't have been appropriate," Kelly adds, coming to my defense with cool common sense. "We support Stephanie, but we are trying to cultivate a relationship between Rihanna's team and SPOKE, and we don't want to look like we're taking advantage of her generosity. Class bookings went up two hundred percent the day after those pictures of her surfaced on *People* and any asks we make of her must be strategic."

"And can I just add," I say, raising a hand like all other points are moot due to this one, "that the book has come out and been a smash hit and Stephanie's got the Oscar-Nominated Female Director attached to direct. She's *fine*."

"Have you reached out to congratulate her?" Jesse asks.

"Has she reached out to congratulate me on the expansion?"

"Good woman," Jesse says. "Don't do anything yet. Let's get the first confrontation on camera."

Hank appears, balancing a blond plank holding appetizers on the palm of his hand. He sets it in the center of the table and remains stooped to say into Kelly's ear, privately but not quietly, "Your daughter is asking if you have a charger in your purse."

Jesse pauses, a coin of sausage halfway to her mouth. "Your daughter?"

"Uh, yeah," Kelly says, fumbling through the impossible-to-pronounce purse my girlfriend also lent her for this occasion. "My childcare fell through, unfortunately. I have her waiting in the car—she's fine."

"Are you not married?" Jesse asks, and Kelly *uh-uhs* like she just wants to move off the subject as quickly as possible.

And that's when I notice it—the designing glint in Jesse's eyes. I realize, feeling a little faint, Kelly didn't just lose a point for having a kid out of wedlock. She gained one. I turn to my sister, looking at her through Jesse's lens: single mom, hustling to support her daughter and make a name for herself. Articulate, camera-friendly. And that's not even the best of it. The best of it is sitting in our junky car with a dead phone. Twenty feet—or however close the driveway is from the picnic table—is all that separates Kelly from getting the job. Because when Jesse sees that Layla is black, she will be smitten. That is a horrible thing to think, let alone be true. But for Jesse Barnes, nothing is more compelling than the tension between the conventional and the unconventional. Kelly, who looks like a woman who should have a big rock on her finger and a minivan full of budding athletes but instead chose to bring a mixed-race child into this world—independently—exemplifies that tension in a fresh and exciting way. I see that now. I just don't know how I didn't see that before.

"Alone?" Jesse frowns. "Why doesn't she join us?"

I need to speak up. Say anything to keep Layla from Jesse. I don't want my pure-hearted niece anywhere near this flaming Dumpster. Like parents who did drugs when they were younger but punish their kids when they find pot in their backpacks now, the show is only okay when I do it. "She's got her phone." I roll my eyes, good-naturedly, as if that's all anyone needs to survive these days.

"Her dead phone," Jesse reminds me. She looks at her watch. "It's lunchtime. Is she hungry?"

"There are doughnuts in the car," I say, too quickly.

Kelly turns to me, a curious expression on her face. Just minutes ago I was rubbing Layla's existence in Jesse's face, and now I want her to remain unseen and unheard. I know she's wondering—why?

"Doughnuts are not lunch," Jesse says.

"I can make her a grilled cheese," Hank offers.

"She does love grilled cheese, doesn't she, Brett?" Kelly smiles at me in a way I will slash her for later. She's picked up on my anxiety—there must be a good reason I am fighting so hard to keep Layla from

Jesse, a reason that may work in her favor. My sister's main fault is that she knows me too well, I realize, as she gets up and heads for the car to release Layla on Jesse.

"Sorry about this," I say to Jesse.

"Don't be," she says, "your sister is adorable. How old is she?"

I think on my feet. "She'll be thirty-two in October."

Jesse laughs at me. "That's like six months from now."

I hear Kelly and Layla approaching behind me, but I don't turn. I stay and watch the delight bloom in Jesse's face as her latest millennial disrupter actualizes.

"This is Layla," Kelly says. "She's very excited to meet you. She's a big fan."

"I admire all you do for women," Layla tells Jesse, taking Jesse's hand with the strong grip I taught her.

Jesse howls with laughter, making a performance out of clutching her hand after Layla lets go, as though Layla shook so hard she did damage to the bones.

Kelly is brightening, slowly, like one of those sunrise simulators designed to gently wake you in the morning. She throws up her hands, like this is what she has to deal with. Utter perfection for a child. "Layla is twelve going on twenty-five. Do you know she started an online shop to sell goods made by Imazighen women and children? She refuses to take a cut, but she figured out a way to earn money through sponsored posts."

"You're raising the next generation of *Goal Diggers*!" Jesse cries.

I can't even speak.

Kelly sets her hand on her daughter's head of curls, in case Jesse hasn't noticed how beautiful they are. As though she is a Realtor, showing her around an exclusive new listing—you think the kitchen is something, wait until you see the master bathroom. "She's pretty special."

"And with such great style. Look at you and your *Mansur Gavriel*." Jesse's pronunciation is viciously French.

"Brett got this for me," Layla says. She looks like a little off-duty model with the scuffed bag slouching next to her narrow hips.

And it's true I did. And it's also true Kelly tried to make her return it. It was a standoff that lasted nearly a week, with neither Layla nor I speaking much to Kelly, until finally, she spun on me when I asked her curiously why she was only wearing one earring that day. *Because I'm fucking tired and sick of being ganged up on by the two of you. She can fucking keep the poorest-made fucking five-hundred-dollar bag I've ever seen in my life. It has fucking scratches everywhere!*

It's supposed to scratch and wear and look used and cool, but I thought better of telling her that in the moment. The only way to let Kelly calm down is to let her spin out.

"It's going to look great on TV," Jesse says.

My niece and my sister also lose the ability to speak as they turn over Jesse's statement, to be sure they understand. "Wait?" Layla grins. She has a Lauren Hutton gap in her front teeth, just enough to give her angelic face some character. "You mean, like, *I'd* be on the show?"

"Would you like that?" Jesse asks.

Layla blinks at Jesse for a few seconds. Then she hoots so loudly a dog barks somewhere down the street.

Kelly shushes her, laughing. "But really, just like that?"

"It would be Layla *and* Kelly?" I say, stupid and shell-shocked.

"This is the perfect example of how to get more women into positions of leadership," Jesse says, in that rallying voice I usually find so inspiring. "I was just reading how family-controlled businesses have the largest number of female decision-makers. The three of you represent a new path to advancement that I think would be very beneficial for our viewers to see." Jesse seems to consider something. "We do have to take child labor laws into account, which requires permission from not only you, Kelly, but from her father. Will that be a problem?"

"My father is Nigerian and he lives in Morocco," Layla says, with an accusatory glance Kelly's way.

Jesse's face clouds. "So does that mean it would be a problem?"

Kelly rubs Layla's back, consolingly. "That's all we know about him, unfortunately. I never got his full name and by the time I realized I was pregnant, I was already back in the States with no way of getting in touch with him."

"Well," Jesse says to Layla, "I'm sorry, Layla. But it certainly makes things less complicated on our end."

"Shouldn't we talk to Lisa about this?" I try, pathetically. One last bid to stop this train before it leaves the station.

Jesse flicks away Lisa's authority with the back of her hand. "The show has gotten too narrow in its definition of a *Goal Digger*. We're a shoal of fish, not a school." She clasps her hands between her knees and addresses Layla like she's five, not twelve. "Do you know the difference between a shoal of fish and a school?"

"Um . . ." Layla thinks. "A school of fish swims in the same direction?" How the fuck does she know that? I don't even know that, at least not that succinctly.

"That's right!" Jesse exclaims. "A school of fish swims in the same direction, but a shoal of fish is a group of fish that stays together for social reasons. The group should make sense, socially, but it doesn't make for great TV when everyone is swimming in the same direction. So." She sets her hands on her thighs, like the start of a race. "Let's at least visit the process. Get both of you on tape. Submit it to the network, introduce you to Lisa, she's our showrunner, if you don't know . . ."

It feels like the iris of a camera is shrinking, narrowing, slowly isolating the terror on my face. I've always been afraid that Kelly was too smart and too primed for greatness to play second fiddle to me. It was only a matter of time before she became listless and bored, before Layla wasn't enough, before she would make a play for the top spot. It's starting. Her comeback. This will get ugly.

CHAPTER 2

Stephanie

T*he general who wins the battle makes many calculations.* I myself am down to two, side by side in my rift-sawn white oak custom closet: the Saint Laurent boots or the platform sneakers that everyone is wearing these days. I am not much for the sprezzatura pox that's claimed most of the women in New York. When I moved here, twelve years ago, women wore ballet flats on the subway, work heels hooked over the lip of their monogrammed Goyard totes. Sneakers were exclusively aerobic in purpose, never for cocktail dresses and Chanel, New York Fashion Week, and martinis at Bemelmans. Sometimes, even on Madison—even in the *eighties*—I feel like the last of my kind. Nobody gets dressed anymore.

I consider the boots, worried they say I'm doing *too* well, which I am. When your memoir about your abusive teenaged boyfriend has been top three on the bestseller list for the last four months with no sign of slowing down, an Oprah's Book Club pick, and an Oscar-nominated director's next passion project, there is never more of a right time to bow your head. People prefer acutely successful women to have *no idea how we got here*, to call ourselves lucky, blessed, *grateful*. I hook a finger through the sneaker's ornamental laces, considering their message on a spin. The sneakers literally level me. And people respond to approachable women, don't they? It's part of what the audience loved about Brett, part of what I loved about her, at least in the beginning. I pluck the other sneaker from its custom perch. Show, don't tell. The bedrock of what I do.

The Rangers' game goes mute as I descend the stairs to our living room. We have stairs in our prewar brownstone on the Upper East Side. This is not just architectural fact, it's consolatory, something Brett pointed out to lift my spirits two years ago, when my third book came out and bombed. *You have stairs in your apartment,* Brett said. *Fuck it. Not everything you do can be a win.* I thrill every time I upset these stairs. Vince is always threatening to fix them—rather, use my money to pay someone to fix them—but I savor their squeaks and grunts, audible reminders of my earning power. It is one of the few times I allow myself to dissociate, to think about how I will never be at the mercy of Lynn from Creative and Marketing Staffing Pros again, *creak,* because I started writing the blog on my lunch break, and, *creak,* through the 3:00 P.M. slump too, and it became popular enough to net me a mid-six-figures book deal. I will never have to deposit seven dollars into my bank account, *creak,* just to be able to make the minimum withdrawal of twenty, *creak.* Because I have sold over three million copies of my first two books and am on track to surpass that with my memoir, which the Sunday *Review* embraced, breathlessly. (*Finally.*) Then there is the million Warner Bros. paid for my life rights, and the half I'm getting to adapt my memoir for film. *Creak. Creak.* The last two stairs sound absurdist, like a witch opening a door to a haunted house that you will tour, scream-laughing. Vince is watching me from his favorite navy club chair. Navy is the only color I've allowed on this floor.

Vince looks confused when he sees me. "You're not going?"

It's the sneakers. My mother wore heels in her bathrobe and that's what I was taught. "I'm going," I say, sinking into his lap. "Do I look like a slob?"

"Oof!" He grimaces, squirming a bit. "Wait. Wait." He shifts me around on top of him. "That's better." He breathes a sigh of relief.

"Thanks," I crack, digging my knuckle into his bicep, still far from solid though I'm paying Hugh Jackman's trainer three times a week.

"Hey-ayy!" He clutches his shoulder, his lips an astonished *o*. How could *anyone* want to hurt Vince?

"You never answered me."

"What?"

"Do I look like a slob?"

Vince pushes his hair out of his eyes. Between him and Brett, sometimes I just want to superglue their hands to their sides. "But a sexy slob."

"Really?" I frown at my feet. "I just wanted to be comfortable."

"You look cool, babe," Vince says to the TV screen, lifting his glass of wine from the marble-topped side table. I can smell the vintage.

"Is that the 2005?" I ask, an edge creeping into my voice. I don't know much about wine, but I know I had to put a hold on Vince's credit card last year after a Christie's online auction for Fine and Rare Vintages ended in obscenity.

Vince quickly sets the glass back on the table and his hand gets lost in his hair again. "Nah. 2011 or something lame like that." He squeezes my side, and in a suggestive voice says, "You could stay, though." His hand moves lower. Squeezes there too. "And we could open that one."

I swat him away with a giggle. "I can't. I need to see them."

Vince holds up his hands. *He tried*. "I'll be waiting up." He purses his stained lips.

It's a chaste kiss—it always is, these days—but when I lean in, I get a whiff of his old Rutgers tee and can't help but feel pleased. BO is the scent of devotion in our marriage. Vince is not getting up to anything smelling like that. He means it when he says he will be waiting up. My husband is never more faithful than when he has to crane his neck to look up at me.

Jen and Lauren are already seated by the time I arrive at L'Artusi, which is an unremarkable observation unless you are dining in New

York City, where no restaurant will seat you until your entire party is present. A rule designed to keep your own illusions about yourself in check, I imagine. You've seen the original *Hamilton*—with Leslie Odom Jr.!—and you're wearing the Gucci loafers that are on back-order until next fall? Please let us know when your entire party has arrived.

Celebrity doesn't help. I've seen Larry David pacing the corridor of Fred's and Julianne Moore told it will be an hour-and-fifteen-minute wait at the original Meatball Shop, before the Upper East Side expansion robbed it of its kitsch mystique. So it's genuinely remarkable that when I arrive Jen and Lauren are seated, and it's genuinely a shame that it has nothing to do with the show, and everything to do with Jen Greenberg's mother. Yvette Greenberg isn't a celebrity, she's a *cause*.

I am self-conscious about the sneakers as I tail the hostess through the restaurant. I'm used to turning heads at this point, but before, I was half-defensive about it, feeling like people were gawking for the wrong reasons. No woman in New York would admit to reading my books before this year. Opening Didion or Wallace on the subway is as much a part of the dernier cri as the bedhead hair and the jeans that asexualize your butt. What *are* those about, anyway?

Up the stairs we go, to a table in the corner, where Lauren Bunn and Jen Greenberg are sitting shoulder to shoulder, facing me as though schoolgirls on a school bus. I am breathless to discover that they've left me the outside seat. It's customary for celebrities to sit with their backs to a restaurant, so that no one can snap a picture while they're sipping wine with one eye closed and sell it to *In Touch* to be strung up with the headline *Rehab for Reality Star!* When the *Diggers* dine out together, it's always a passive-aggressive tango for the outside chair, and it almost always ends up sagging beneath the weight of Brett's big butt. To have it reserved for me will go down as a flash point in our history. That isn't a chair; it's a throne.

Lauren rises when she sees me. "Rock star!" she cries, the way townsfolk would charge *witch* in seventeenth-century Salem. *Witch! Witch!* She flings her arms around my neck and I note the empty martini glass over her shoulder. Jen holds up two fingers. It's her second. We need to move fast.

She pulls away and holds me by the shoulders. "*You* are a rock star!" Her $250 micro-bladed eyebrows come together as she studies me up close. "You even look different." She pats me down, her hands finishing on my rear end, which she pumps and jiggles, her platonic expression that of a doctor performing a routine checkup. "You feel different."

"All right, all right." I laugh, removing her hands. *Blond and oversexualized* is Lauren's beat. She's like the poor man's Samantha Jones—too drunk to enjoy all the sex she has. "And what's different is these." I kick up the septuagenarian sole of my sneaker.

Lauren expands a hand over her breast and becomes momentarily Southern. "As I live and breathe."

Jen does not get up and fawn all over me, but she does provide me an excuse for my tardiness. "Traffic?" she asks, as I take my seat and spread a dinner linen over my lap.

"FDR was a mess," I tell her, even though it wasn't. Late is just another outside chair. Late is a muscle, flexing.

The waiter appears, one arm folded behind his back.

"The Monfalletto Barolo," Lauren says, before he can greet us.

"Excellent choice," he says, giving Lauren a little bow. She appraises his backside as he walks away.

"He's not even cute," Jen complains. Her brown eyes don't narrow, they just *are* narrow. *Jen looks like the angry stepsister of a Disney princess,* a TV critic once described her perfectly on Twitter.

"I don't like the cute ones." Lauren closes her lips around the toothpick in her drink, removing an olive with her front teeth. "You don't have to worry about *me* around your husband, Steph."

"Nice," Jen quips.

Lauren's mouth pops open. "I said Vince is *too* good-looking for me. It's a compliment!" She reassures me, the tiniest bit of fear in her eyes. "It's a *compliment*."

I don't smile but I do make a joke. "Where's the option on

SADIE for women who like uggos?" Lauren is the creator but *no longer* the CEO of a dating website that is, depending on whom you're speaking to, a bold challenge to the status quo or a rich girl's vanity project. If you are told the latter, you're speaking to Brett.

A clever phrase materializes. "Hots and nots," I suggest, feeling funny when Lauren's boisterous laugh stops the conversation at the table next to us. Funny was always Brett's thing. Now, all it takes is the palest attempt at humor, a small miracle given the fact that I was at the end of the couch at the last reunion.

The waiter returns, holding three gorgeous air-blown wineglasses. I do not stop him before he can place one in front of me, and Lauren notices, elated. "She's drinking!" she exclaims to Jen, with the momentous pride of a lesser woman who has just called up her family members to share that *the baby is walking*, something every baby ever has done since the dawn of time. I don't drink much or like children. I have my reasons for both.

"Unlike you," Jen says crisply to Lauren, "she has something to celebrate."

That was not said with love, but Lauren giggles anyway.

The server appears again, splashing Lauren's glass with a taste of the wine. He places the cork next to her fork for her consideration, a little blood-bottomed thumb.

"Excellent," Lauren concludes, tossing the whole thing back without really seeming to taste it.

"That's about all I can handle," I tell the server with self-effacing cheer midway through his pour. He rights the bottle and wipes its neck with a white dinner napkin.

"To season four," Lauren says, raising a glass. "And to the Oscar-Nominated Female fucking Director."

"Keep your voice down, crazy woman," I say, clinking Jen's glass lightly and waiting for someone to wag their finger at me, only no one does. Rule number two of *Goal Diggers of New York City*, no one is ever nuts, batshit, insane, sensitive, or emotional. No one overreacts. "Crazy" and its derivatives are words that have been used to shame women into compliance for centuries. The outside chair and a Chinese ducket on the word "crazy." Toto, I'm not at the end of the reunion couch anymore, which is where they stick you right before they fire you.

I make eye contact with Jen first, then Lauren. "I just need to say something."

"Speech." Lauren thumps a fist on the table. "Speech."

"No, seriously," I say, not laughing, and the smile vanishes from Lauren's face in a swift show of obedience. I rest my hands flat on the table, taking a moment to gather my thoughts. "I need to say that I'm indelibly touched by your support. Especially because I know the three of us have never been particularly close." My expression is full of remorse. *I let Brett turn me against you, and I see the error of my allegiance now—forgive me.* "The last few months have been equal parts exhausting and exhilarating. I never thought I would open up about my past in this way, and I continue to be surprised not only by the people who have shown up for me, but by those who have not."

I pause, and that's when I notice that Jen's nails are painted. Jen's nails are painted and she has traded her heavy-framed Moscot Mensch glasses for contacts and very possibly, Jen has gotten a boob job. The sexier styling seems an obvious message to the person who broke her heart last season: *This is what you're missing.* We have no idea who he is, if he even *is* a he. Jen refused to get into details at the reunion, telling us only that there had been someone "special" in the picture but insisting that it had ended, amicably, with agonized tears in her small eyes. In the three years I've known her, Jen has been notoriously tight-lipped about her love life, which infuriates Brett, perennial oversharer. But I always thought it wasn't so much Jen holding back as Jen not having much to tell. I have wondered, more than a few times, if Jen might have been a virgin before this "special" person came along. There is something about her that is inherently untouchable but prepared to be, in case anyone comes along who is up to the task. The gruffness is an obvious defense mechanism, allowing her to reject you first.

Of course, the viewers would be surprised to hear me describe our resident earth goddess as gruff. Jen presents much differently on camera, speaking in spiritual platitudes and extolling the virtues of veganism and plant-based alchemy, a lifestyle that has turned into her livelihood. Packets of super-herbs and adaptogens sell for seventeen dollars in her downtown juice bars that are frequent props in the Instagram stories of Gwyneth Paltrow and Busy Philipps. Last year, she opened a vegan restaurant on the corner of Broome and Orchard that has so many beautiful people willing to wait an hour for her air-baked sweet potato fries that plans are in the works to open locations on the Upper West Side and in Venice, for a cookbook and a national delivery service. No matter, her mother wishes she were more like Brett.

Lauren *tsks*. "I cannot believe Brett still hasn't reached out to you."

Jen shoots me a look.

"What?" Lauren asks, noticing. Jen gets very busy, straightening her silverware and ignoring the question. "*What?*" Lauren repeats.

"I have not heard from Brett," I say. "But I spoke to Lisa recently." I exhale, like what I'm about to say won't be easy for her to hear. "She told me they're going in a different direction with the new *Digger*."

"Okay . . . and?" Lauren looks as if there is a weight attached to her jaw, pulling everything in her expression down, down.

"They're bringing in Brett's sister and her niece to replace Hayley."

Lauren looks like she might short-circuit. "Brett's sister *and* Brett's niece?"

I nod.

"But . . ." Lauren brings her fingers to her temples with a soft moan, as though processing this new information is a painful endeavor. "How old is the niece?"

"Twelve," Jen says, stonily.

Lauren looks like she's about to cry. She sits there, her face growing hot, her breathing short and frantic, waiting desperately for one of us to say something that's going to make her feel better. "I don't understand," she says, finally. "She's going to be a cast member?"

"She's like a friend of the cast. It's the sister who is the cast member."

"And she has a twelve-year-old?" Lauren crows. "How *old* is she?"

"Our age," I say.

"Thirty-one," Jen clarifies, ruthlessly. I haven't been thirty-one for a few years now.

"Is she married?" Lauren asks, eyes shut, like she can't bear to look until she knows it's safe.

"No," I say. "Not married." Lauren opens her eyes with a sad, resigned sigh. The news is not great, but it is tolerable. Lauren would probably like to be married with a baby and two ugly nannies, but our master and commander doesn't want kids; henceforth, none of us are allowed to want them either. A few years ago I started to notice that mothers and not-mothers are equally fixated on childless women in their thirties, and in particular childless, *married* women in their thirties. How fun for me. It is a little like living in a swing state and being registered as an Independent. Both parties campaign fastidiously to get me on their side. The mothers make me promises like, *I'm not that maternal either, but you love them when they are your own.* The not-mothers rage against therapists and doctors who try to pathologize your reluctance for children. Neither party thinks they have anything in common with the other, which makes it all the more hilarious how much they do. It's human nature to want your decisions validated. You feel better about yourself and your life when others make the same choices as you do. Luckily for me, I have no problem validating this particular decision of Jesse's. Pathologize my contempt for kids all you want, I'll never have them.

"But she doesn't even live in the city," I continue. "I heard they're setting her up in Brett's apartment and Brett's going to move in with the new girlfriend."

"Like it's a storyline?"

"No, like . . . they're going to make it look like the sister has always lived here. No one's seen the apartment Brett is in right now so there won't be any confusion."

"Who *is* she?" Lauren demands. "Do you know her?"

"I've only met her here and there. But she basically handles all the day-to-day at SPOKE so that Brett can do the hard work of co-hosting the fourth hour of the *Today* show when Hoda goes on vacation."

There is a moment of bitter silence. None of us are over the fact that we weren't asked to do it.

"Fine," Lauren concedes. "I get the sister. I guess. But why are they making the niece a part of the show?"

"Well, now you're asking the right question," I tell her. A bread basket is delivered to the table and out of habit, everyone reaches for a piece. Rule number three of *Goal Diggers*, we eat carbs. We are emancipated from diets, and we exercise for health, not weight loss. Even if you starve yourself between takes like Lauren or suffer from orthorexia like Jen, you play your gourmandism for the cameras (or always, if you're Brett and you found a way to commoditize your thunder thighs). Jesse thinks we have seen too many white, straight women hawking flat tummy tea on Instagram. Women who refuse to eat processed food are passé.

"The niece is black," I say.

Lauren's jaw goes slack. "Is the sister black?"

My mouth full, I shake my head *no*.

"Then what? The niece is adopted?"

I shake my head again, unable to elucidate while chewing. I'm the only one who actually took a piece of bread in the end. Jen and Lauren remembered the cameras weren't around and returned their empty hands to their laps to be sniffed later.

"Stop making me dig, for Chrissakes!"

I swallow my food and tell her what I know. The data I've gathered from the field producer whose Net-a-Porter habit I shamelessly indulge every Christmas: that come season four, I will no longer be the onliest POC on the show. I felt both completely helpless and like

I had to do something after I found out. Something that would make me better, stronger, irreplaceable. But beyond the plans I'd already put into place, there was nothing I could think to do, and so I called Sally Hershberger and arranged a last-minute blowout, even though my hair is always perfect and I didn't have anywhere to go. Some of us eat our feelings; others turn a hot air stream and a round brush on them. I sat in the leather swivel chair with the junior stylist, the only one available at the last minute, and searched Layla Courtney on Instagram.

I have, of course, met Layla Courtney on a few occasions. A quiet, tall girl with wet hair in a high bun who unimpressed me greatly. What did Lisa see in her? What did *Jesse*? There were no Layla Courtneys on Instagram, and so I tried the mother. I turned up a scroll of Kelly Courtney variations, but only one with SPOKE in the handle and a light-skinned black girl in the profile picture. I felt like I was breathing fire ants as I thumbed her feed. Kelly and Layla at the Jersey Shore, Kelly and Layla at sixth-grade graduation last year, Kelly's big "announcement" with all of ninety-six likes that you should follow Layla over @souk_SPOKE, where she would be hawking the gimcrack rugs and pottery and clothing handcrafted by Imazighen women, who now have the opportunity to learn a skill and earn a living thanks to SPOKE. A quick Google of the word "souk" told me that it is Berber for market. A terrible name for an Instagram handle, nothing catchy about it, but still I felt light-headed when I clicked on Kelly's tag and saw that Layla's account already had 11K followers, and that nearly every picture of Layla, modeling the goods with her baby afro, was riddled with comments like *gorgeous girl, natural beauty, @ICManagement she on your radar???* I glanced at myself in the mirror, never one more honest than a hairdresser's. My hair was smooth and straight, a little bit of movement at the ends, the way I've worn it for twenty years. Even with the straightening treatments, no one ever called me gorgeous when I was the same age as this mouseburger, and I was.

So why am I up in arms? How could I possibly feel threatened by a twelve-year-old black girl with natural curls? Diversity is one of the pillars of our show. But Jesse, the empress regnant of reality television, never would have opened that door if there wasn't any green behind it. Advertisers desperately want to capture young viewers, and diversity (Or are we calling it inclusivity now? Better question: Which expression is more lucrative?) is of paramount importance to millennials. To us, I guess I could say. I did make the millennial cutoff by the skin of my teeth, and that was also part of the reason I didn't think I was coming back after the last reunion. No one survives the show past thirty-four.

I've managed to delay the inevitable for another year, and now I can't help but feel my replacement is being groomed. Because Jesse didn't open the door for underrepresented women in the media as much as she did crack it. Just enough to allow Brett and me through for a short window of time. On a show with four to five players, any more than one gay woman and it becomes a lesbian show, any more than one *woman of color* and it becomes an ethnic show, and then advertisers start to worry about alienating the audience. That's not diversity; it's tokenism, and that's why it felt like a kick in the stomach when I found out that not only was my choice out of the running for Hayley's spot (we all hustle hard to replace outgoing *Diggers* with our friends), but that the new *Digger* satisfied a requirement that up until now only I could fulfill. Think of each of us as a pendant on a charm bracelet. I am the lock and Brett is the heart and Jen is the ballet slipper and Lauren is the ladybug. What we needed was a transgendered woman, not another lock.

"Aren't you pissed?" Lauren hisses, reaching for her wine and realizing it's empty. She pretends like she was really going for the bread, tearing off a small piece and docking it on her plate. "I would be so pissed if I were you."

I experience a flicker of appreciation for the woman I'd written off as a boy-crazy boozehound. I've never spoken to any of the *Diggers* about feeling like a box Jesse had to check to escape an evisceration from *Jezebel*, because Brett, the one who *should* get it, is utterly beguiled by Jesse, and Lauren and Jen could never even begin to empathize. Jen came to the attention of the producers by way of her mother and Lauren shouldn't be on the show at all. She's one of those Hitchcock blondes, from a family with its own crest. But she has mastered hi-lo style and drinks too much and talks about sex too loudly and you'd be hard pressed to find a single woman in the city who doesn't have her dating app hanging in the gallery of her mobile screen. Her name is Lauren Bunn and viewers call her Lauren Fun, and that has kept her safe, as has her willingness to go in for the kill when Lisa blows the whistle. She's the show's lovable hatchet man; indispensable, really.

But then Lauren clucks, "Your friend must be so disappointed," and I realize she meant I'm probably pissed that my hire was passed over, and that a small part of her is pleased by that.

There are precisely two seasons in a *Goal Digger*'s life: shooting season and killing season. Not even a week after we wrap, months before we film the reunion, it's customary for producers to approach each *Digger* and ask if we have any friends we would like to nominate for the next season of the show. We have no idea who is coming back and who is on the chopping block, though the position on the couch at the reunion some weeks later is normally a clue. The closer you are seated to Jesse, the better your odds. At this most recent reunion, filmed a month before my memoir came out and put me back in the game, I was on the end of the couch for the first time ever. The last book in my fiction series had flopped and I was growing long in the tooth. I nearly accepted my fate. The only *Digger* who has ever been where I was at and asked to return is Lauren, and I'm not willing to have my vagina steamed on camera or pose naked in a valiant effort to save the minks, high jinks Lauren has gotten up to in a single episode.

But. There is another option besides humiliating yourself for laughs. The producers are always looking to shake up the troupe, which is why the casting process starts anew the moment the mic packs come off. It's an unwritten rule that if you bring a woman to prod's attention and they like her and they cast her, you can buy yourself a stay of execution. The producers are not going to introduce a new *Digger* unless she has some sort of connection to the group. This isn't *Big Brother*, throw a bunch of strangers together and hope for pregnancy scares and cold-cocks. The show runs best when the group has history, allegiances, *grudges*. The moment filming ends, a *Digger* is campaigning for her hire for the next season, nary a modicum of concern that it may be at a current castmate's expense. If you're lucky enough to see your person cast, you enjoy one more benefit, which is that she provides you with her eternal loyalty. You never betray the *Digger* who brought you in.

Lauren was Jen's hire, in season two, and so for as long as she and Jen are on the show together, she will have to like who Jen likes and feud with who she doesn't. She's tiring of it, and I know she was pushing for her fellow Yalie, inventress of period-proof underwear, to replace Hayley so that she could boss someone around for a change. Better luck next season, Lauren.

The server reappears to ask us if we are ready to order.

Lauren and I sit in supportive silence as Jen explains to him that she's a friend of the chef's and she's called ahead about some dairy-free butternut squash soup.

"God, no." Lauren laughs, when the server asks us if we also have any dietary restrictions. "Let's do the fluke, the hamachi, the mushrooms, and the bucatini."

"Two orders of mushrooms," I say.

The server smiles, pleased with us and with himself. "My all-time favorite dish on the menu."

"She's married," Lauren growls, saucily.

"And you?" the server asks her.

Lauren waves her naked finger at him.

"Jesus God," Jen mutters. However long it's been since Jen has had sex, it's in dog years.

The waiter picks up the bottle to refill my glass and realizes it's empty. "Did we want to stick to this bottle?" Lauren circles her finger in the air, pantomiming a mini tornado: *another round*. Jen pokes me under the table. *Now,* before she gets too drunk to remember.

I reach for another piece of bread. "So, Laur, I'm not trying to blow your fuse here but there's more."

"Don't tell me," she says, pushing her plate away. "Brett is skinnier than me now."

Jen endorses the bon mot with a guffaw. She's always bristled at being grouped into the "wellness industry" with a woman who considers baked goods one of the major food groups. Likewise, Brett has taken Jen to task for her narrow and elitist definition of health, which contains but a single word—"thin." There is nothing healthy about a woman weighing the same as she did in the fifth grade, about a woman who rarely eats solid foods and who is so malnourished she cannot grow her hair past her ears. These are Brett's words, not mine, though I do wonder what she would say if she could see Jen now, with her shiny new lob and lusher-looking figure. *There is nothing healthy about a woman who changes her appearance to please a man,* probably.

"It's about the trip," I say to Lauren.

The Trip. Every season, the producers carve out a benchmark week to bring all the women together, no matter where we are in our cycle of loving and loathing each other. First season was quiet and cost effective: Jen's Hamptons house, to celebrate the opening of her pop-up juice truck in the parking lot of Ditch Plains. Second season, we were a bona fide sleeper hit thanks to the network's incessant Sunday afternoon marathons, and we could afford to go bigger: Paris, for the launch of the third book in my fiction series. (The Parisians have never called my books smut.) Last season, it was Los Angeles for the GLAAD awards. The show was up for Outstanding Reality Program—which we all understood to be Brett's nomination—and there was also a nomination in the Outstanding Talk Show category, for the episode of *60 Minutes* featuring Brett and all she was doing to help pave the way for other young, gay entrepreneurs.

As it's gone, the *Digger* who is at the heart of the trip is the *Digger* who gets the most flattering pass by the editor's hand and the most screen time for her product. And as it's gone, every woman gets her turn. Lauren isn't an original like Jen, Brett, and me, she doesn't wear the signet ring inscribed *SS*, but she's been with us since season two. This season we all assumed it would be her turn.

With as much compassion as I can muster, I say, "Lisa told me they want to calendar Morocco for some time in June."

"Morocco?" Lauren whispers in quiet defeat.

"Apparently SPOKE is releasing a line of electric bikes," Jen says. Her elfin face pinches in disgust. "Because what women like Brett need is a piece of exercise equipment to *reduce* the amount of movement in their day."

In all fairness, the e-bikes aren't for *women like Brett*. They're for women who have too much movement in their day to attend school and to earn a living. I hate that even a silent part of me is still sticking up for Brett, after what happened between us. "The good news is that they haven't booked the travel yet," I say, putting the devastating memory out of my mind. "If we make our concerns known, we can sway them. But we have to move fast and we have to show a united front. Lisa said Jesse feels very strongly that in the first season since the election we present women as magnanimously as possible."

"I see," Lauren sniffs, "and reversing sexist dating roles isn't magnanimous?"

"Not as magnanimous as keeping twelve-year-old African girls from getting raped," Jen replies.

"Who are these twelve-year-old African girls Brett is keeping from getting raped?" Lauren wants to know. "Honestly, does she have any hard data to prove this? Have we even talked to a single one of them? How do we even know it's true?"

I nod, animatedly. I want her riled up before I get to the point.

"So the show is now *The Brett Show*," Lauren says, her aggrieved voice crowd-surfing the din of the restaurant. "Or the SPOKE show or whatever it is. It's her whole fucking family and her business and she gets the trip two years in a row."

"It pays to play on the same team as your boss," Jen says, which was a claim I used to defend Brett against before I realized that Brett has absolutely benefited from being the same kind of different as Jesse. In our ecosystem, Brett is undoubtedly the most privileged of the bunch, and her advantages extend beyond the good edit. Jesse has made it abundantly clear that the show functions as a by-product of our already existing success. It is wonderful if it can enhance what we have already built for ourselves, but it is not there to lay the groundwork. In other words, we attract the show; the show does not attract us. For that reason, *Diggers* take home the same paltry salary of five thousand dollars a year for roughly one hundred twenty days of labor—and that's before taxes. We are not meant to need the money, and most of us don't, but ever since Jesse banished me to the end of the couch, I can no longer stomach the hypocrisy of my boss lambasting the wage gap in the *New York Times* while paying her own less than minimum wage. Jesse moves up the corporate ladder at the network as the show grows in popularity, getting richer off our backs while we are expected to just be grateful for the continued exposure. Hayley finally had enough of it, especially once one of the production coordinators suggested that Brett took Jesse's advice, asked for more money, and got it. I admired Hayley for going to bat for herself, but I also knew it was a suicide mission. Jesse would only see the attempt at a salary negotiation as ungrateful, and it would only end in her dismissal, which, of course, it did. Unless you are Brett Courtney, the show does not reward difficult women.

Brett is the teacher's pet, and funnily enough, one of her top complaints about Jen was that she received preferential treatment because of her mother. Introducing two people who are so much alike that they ultimately repel one another. Both are exhaustively preachy when it comes to their brand of health. Both are smug know-it-alls, believing their approach is the right one and if you don't do it their way then you are a moron who will probably get cancer soon. Something else they have in common, something I didn't discover until recently, is that they are both totally different people off camera than they are when we are rolling, though this could be said of all of us. It's not easy to maintain the dividing line between who we are on the show and who we actually are, to do the dirty, daily work of pulling up the weeds and clipping the undergrowth. But not all of us go around insisting *Who I am in real life is who I am on camera*, which Brett has said so often it should be her next hideous tattoo. The truth is that who Brett is on camera is who she has *become* in real life. TV-Brett metastasized.

Brett-Brett is in there, somewhere—I've had a brush with her—but she is like the last, smallest Russian nesting doll of the set.

Lauren groans. "What are we going to do about her?"

I glance at Jen again. She nods: *Go for it.* "I sent Lisa my schedule for the next few months," I say. "I have my book tour and Vince's birthday and a few other things on the calendar, and I just made it clear I would invite you two, and perhaps whoever the new cast member is—not if it's Kelly, obviously—but that was it."

"You think we shouldn't film with *the darling one,*" Lauren deduces with a snort. "That'll go over well."

"I just think we do our own thing and we let her do hers," I say, trying to keep it light. This isn't a blood pact. We don't need to draw knives and weapons. The most effective way to destroy someone on the show is to disengage, to deprive her of the drama, of the meaningful connections, of the great and powerful storyline. In our world, your sharpest weapon is a polite smile.

I can tell Lauren is still not sold.

I'm contemplative for a moment. "I've debated whether or not to tell you this," I say, and I have. I was hoping my case was solid without this.

Lauren says, at two martinis and two glasses of wine volume, "Just fucking tell me."

I avoid her eyes. I am sure she will be able to tell I am lying if I don't. "That thing in Page Six? The one about the—"

"I know which one you're referring to," Lauren says, and I look up to see that she's reddened. There have been several items in the *Post* about Lauren's drinking, but only one that cost her so much.

"Brett called that in," I practically whisper.

Lauren blinks, stunned.

"I only found out after the reunion," I rush to say. "I didn't know what to do. Brett and I were still friends and I felt a sense of loyalty—"

Lauren holds up her hand. "Why are you telling me this now?"

I check in with Jen. Are we that obvious? "This affects your business, Laur. This affects your *money.*"

"Why are you telling me this now?" Lauren repeats, her voice softer this time.

Jen and I check in with each other across the table, telepathically negotiating who should be the one to answer her. Jen didn't think it was necessary to tell Lauren that Brett was the one who sent the editors the video of a drunken Lauren fellating a baguette at Balthazar. I know Brett has a line into the editor of Page Six and I know *I* didn't do it, and Jen and Lauren are in lockstep. Who else could it have been? Lauren had been next to hysterical at the reunion, demanding to know who shared the video that resulted in a lifetime ban from her *favorite brunch place* and her father bringing in a seasoned CEO, effectively rendering Lauren's role at the company impotent.

Jen thinks telling Lauren not to film with Brett is enough to get Lauren not to film with Brett. She brought Lauren into the group and that buys unconditional servitude. But Lauren likes Brett, even though she is not supposed to, and I can't pretend that I don't understand. For a time, I didn't just like Brett, I loved her.

I decide to be the one to say it.

"What if you didn't drink this season?" I suggest to Lauren. "Make your sobriety a storyline. I think Jen and I, we could really support that. In a way Brett would never." This is me, sweetening the pot for Lauren, because I need her to commit to the mutiny. I need Brett gone. We all do.

"Rehab my image," Lauren says, her tone petulant.

"That's right!" I say, brightly, as though I am a game show host and she is a player who has guessed the answer to a deciding trivia question correctly.

Lauren folds her arms across her chest, huffily. "Our viewers are so proletarian. This is how people *drink* in New York. It's normal. I'm normal." Her eyes flit to my unfinished glass of Barolo. She wouldn't dare say it—*You're the one who's not normal.* At this age, in this world, she's not just deflecting. The fact that I drink in thimble portions makes her far more average than me.

Lauren sighs, fluffing her hair at the roots in a way she thinks gives her Brigitte Bardot volume when really, it just makes her look like she rubbed a balloon against her head. "Fine. I'll *say* I'm not drinking. Say it. I'm still going to, though."

"We figured." Jen shrugs.

"Fuck you, Greenberg," Lauren says with a smile. She raises her glass, seeming to come around more positively to the idea. "To not drinking this season."

I raise my own, laughing at the intended irony of the toast, relieved that everyone is so wholeheartedly on board. "To not drinking this season."

What kind of narcissist signs up for a reality show? is a question lobbed at me on Twitter often. There are not enough characters to capture the magic of Jesse Barnes when she turns it on. And she did turn it on for me in the beginning. Dinners at Le Bernardin where she quoted from my novels. A twenty-five-thousand-dollar donation made in my name to my favorite charity that provides writing mentorship to underprivileged girls. *SNL* after-parties, box seats at the Yankees game for Vince, front-row tickets to a Madonna concert, and backstage passes where I got to *meet* Madonna. And all the while, Jesse was in my ear, promising me this was not my mother's reality TV show. This was a show about women getting along, about women supporting one another, about women succeeding, about women who didn't need men. I was absolutely fooled.

Jesse might have meant some of it. I think she believed, on some level, that she would be at the forefront of a new kind of reality TV, living as we were in a time of performed girl power. Beyoncé had recently dropped a golden microphone on stage at the VMAs, backlit by the word *Feminist*. It was no longer mainstream suicide to care about the equality of the sexes. And then season one aired and the ratings were so dismal that they briefly canceled us.

Season two felt different from the start. We got a new showrunner, Lisa, who found Machiavellian ways to pit us against one another. We fought. We aligned. We were a massive hit. There have been many times I have wanted to walk away, but I didn't, and not because I am a narcissist.

It is because Diggers don't survive the push off the couch. Jesse sees to it. The invitations to events that claim to support women stop coming, A-listers you were paired with on Jesse's aftershow stop following you on Twitter, your businesses shutter, and the only magazine that wants to put you on the cover is *The Learning Annex*. It's happening to Hayley right now. I made the mistake of texting to ask if I would see her at Jesse's annual Halloween party, the one everyone who is anyone attends, and instead of saying yes, she hit me with a series of excuses so fraught my ulcers oozed. *I'm having a problem receiving messages lately. Mercury is in retrograde. At least my assistant tells me so. I haven't actually checked my email myself in a while. It's probably in my inbox. Where is it just in case? When? Want to grab a drink together before?* Ugh, I was nauseous for her. I knew *that feeling*. It's like heartbreak, but not, the way cramps hurt differently than a stomach bug, though the pain is similarly located. There is no word for it, but there should be. It is the sting, it is the sickness—because it is also contagious—of your fellow woman turning on you.

I know my storyline must come to an end at some point, that I cannot reserve a prime spot on the reunion couch forever. But I will not—I cannot—allow a parasite like Brett Courtney to edge me out.

CHAPTER 3

Brett

My father thinks it's a phase. My *lesbianism*.

He met one of my girlfriends once. Thanksgiving, two years ago, in San Diego, where he moved after Mom died. He's remarried now, to a vegetarian named Susan. Susan and my father treated my ex like a best gal pal from college who didn't have anywhere to go for the holiday because her parents were going through an ugly divorce. They stuck all of us—Layla, Kelly, Sarah, and me—in the second bedroom, mother and daughter in the bed, lezzies on the air mattress. There is a third bedroom in the San Diego house, but it's Dad's "office" and he had emails to send "very early in the morning."

It's not hard for me to imagine Mom's reaction. She was dead when I came out of the closet at twenty-two, but had she been alive, I doubt she would have so much as frowned, abiding as she did by the parenting rule that the best way to discipline your children when they "act out" is to ignore them. Between my maroon hair and my green hair and my purple hair, my tattoos and piercings, and a brief Wiccan stint after renting and keeping Blockbuster's copy of *The Craft*, I got ignored a lot growing up. But you better believe she would have been marching in the pussy parade as my star started to rise, as she saw that my gayness was intrinsic to my celebrity. And she would have adored

Arch. A lawyer for the A-C-L-*U*? She could have been a purple Communist with a sexual attraction to mangoes, and Mom would have set out the fancy Clinique lotion every time I brought her home.

Mom didn't go to college and while she occasionally flitted around in various retail capacities whenever we needed a little extra cash or she needed something to do, she never had a career. She came of age in a time when it was just as socially acceptable for a woman to get married at twenty-one and have her first child by twenty-three as it was to go to college and earn a paycheck. I don't think she had the confidence to continue her education, the path that was really in her blood. And so she was always a little bit defensive about being a young mother, getting it into her head that if she could raise a Mensa candidate it would somehow elevate her status in the eyes of second-wave feminists.

She chased accolades for Kelly before she could even walk, submitting her photo to Gerber baby contests and entering her into child beauty pageants. By the time I was born, four years later, she had so much time and money and *hope* vested in Kelly that it came down to another decision: Split the effort and risk turning out two mildly accomplished daughters, or go full throttle on the one who was already showing so much promise. Kelly was an honorable mention in the 1986 Gerber contest, so go full throttle on her she did.

My phone trembles in my hand as the R pulls into the Twenty-eighth Street station and catches a few bars of service. I look down. *Kelly*. Asking me how far away I am. The production meeting started eighteen minutes ago, but our booking system went down twenty minutes into the Rise and Resist class and I was on the phone with tech support for an hour and a half. I didn't even get a chance to shower and I'm still in my smelly spandex. *Ten minutes,* I tell her. *Is there food there?*

It's harder for me to imagine how Mom would have reacted to Kelly's about-face. And Layla. What kind of grandmother would she have been to Layla? My gut tells me not the kind who baked cookies and read bedtime stories, at least during those early years. Now that

Layla's older and has expressed an interest in SPOKE, she would have warmed. But I don't know if she would ever forgive Kelly for making her feel like she bet on the wrong horse.

Kelly was a sophomore at Dartmouth, studying abroad in Morocco, when Mom had her second stroke. I was fifteen, downstairs in the finished basement pretending to be researching a class project, actually in a sex chat room. Kelly was the one who turned me on to them. She once forgot to sign out of her account and when I opened up the browser, I discovered her screen name, *PrttynPink85*, and that her ambitions did not end outside of the classroom! I was floored, mostly because despite the fact that there were never any rules in place in our household, Kelly didn't date. It was assumed Kelly was more interested in microbial genetics or whatever the fuck they studied in AP chemistry than she was boys. My sister went to prom with her best friend, Mags, and came home early with a greasy-assed McDonald's bag. Looking back, I can see that Kelly was just taking her cues. Our mother made it very clear that high school was for getting into a top college, not for football games and fun. And so my sister went off to her Ivy a sexually frustrated virgin with a banging bod and an encyclopedia of knowledge thanks to her digital dalliances. None of us should have been surprised when she went on a fuck-crawl of Marrakesh two years later.

My mother's second stroke was minor, same as the first. She insisted Kelly stay abroad. Two days later she got up to use the bathroom and a pulmonary embolism took her down as she was washing her hands. She would have been relieved that it happened after she had gotten her pants back on—Mom was obediently ashamed of her ass. In a way I'm grateful that she was, because my inclination was always to do and be the opposite of whatever she expected of me. Body confidence is hard. Teenage rebellion comes with reserves.

My father and I called Kelly with the terrible news, and then we called her again . . . and again . . . and again. She had become increasingly difficult to get ahold of in the weeks leading up to Mom's death, even though my parents set her up with the priciest international plan AT&T had to offer. We left messages, telling her we needed to speak to her urgently. She must have heard the news in our voices, because she never called back. *She never called back.*

We got ahold of her professor, who told us that Kelly hadn't been to class in two days. For most students, this was unremarkable, but for Kelly—BRING IN THE NATIONAL GUARD. Through her roommate, we were able to track her whereabouts to the flat of the DJ at the American watering hole, who went by the name Fad. Only Fad. My father and I had to put the funeral on hold and *fly* to Marrakesh to drag my goodie-two-shoes sister out of the arms of a thirty-two-year-old man who wore tiny yellow sunglasses and double puka shell necklaces. Fad wasn't actually Moroccan, he'd emigrated from Nigeria as a kid, and that's about as much as Kelly knows about his background. I have determined that in another life, a life where he didn't dress like an aging MTV veejay on spring break, Fad-no-last-name-Fad must have invented the polio vaccine and maybe also cold-pressed coffee. Because how else do you end up with a Layla?

I should thank Fad not just for my niece but for dickmatizing my sister the way he did. Because if he hadn't, I never would have had a reason to travel to Morocco, and the idea for SPOKE never would have been born. And so it seems a bit of a moot point, what my mother would think of our lives now. Because nothing would have turned out this way if she hadn't died and Kelly hadn't fallen out of first place.

The train shudders into the Twenty-third Street station. I check my phone. I'm already late—what's five more to dash over to Third Ave and grab a bagel? The chance that there is any sort of substantial spread at the prod meeting is low. We're a month out from filming—those bitches are in conservation mode.

Only half the seats in the conference room are occupied, and yet the team has made a complete ring around the table by skipping chairs. Kelly has two empties to her right and three to her left. She's fighting to look like she doesn't care that no one wants to sit next to the weird new girl, but I can smell how much it actually bothers her. Seriously, when my sister is stressed, she emits the odor of sauerkraut.

Lisa, our showrunner, is at her rightful place at the head of the table. When she sees me, she drops her phone and cuts off a speaking field producer. They say that in meetings, women are interrupted at five times the rate that men are. I wonder how that number increases with Lisa Griffin in the room. "There's Miss *My Time Is More Important Than Your Time*. Twenty million in her bank account and she can't afford a fucking Rolex."

It's 23.4 million and it's in an LLC holding, but I don't correct Lisa. Lisa could eat me for breakfast—that is, if she ate breakfast. Two years ago she started drinking Jen's protein shakes and dancing with two-pound weights at Tracy Anderson. Now she wears mostly leather jeans and is smaller and meaner than ever. She resents my friendship with Jesse, and I'm sure she feels like I went around her to get Kelly on the show. If she only knew. "I am so, *so* sorry," I say, lifting my cross-body bag over my head and crabwalking between the wall and the table to take a seat next to Kelly. "We had a major technical glitch at the studio this morning."

"Thanks for being the one to deal with that," Kelly says, like I've done *her* such a favor, tending to an issue within my own company. Something about her appearance makes me do a double take, and it's not that she's trying too hard in strappy ankle heels and an off-the-shoulder top while Lauren and Jen are across from her looking every bit like they woke up like this in weird jeans, drinking matching coconut La Croixs. Monsters. Who likes the coconut? I can't decide if I'm embarrassed or vindicated by Kelly's sexy third-date getup. (*You're out of your league. I* told *you.*) If we should talk about hiring a stylist or if I should keep the float all to myself.

I'll sort it out later, because more pressing is the realization that Stephanie is running even later than I am. I shouldn't—*I shouldn't*—but I bristle. Stephanie was notorious for holding up filming in the early seasons, whether it was because she didn't like her hair or that the shoot started at ten and she just didn't feel like getting there at ten. She shaped up last season, after acquiring the nickname "Sleptanie" from viewers who complained on Twitter and Instagram that she had gotten boring, that she felt too *produced*. Sleptanie employs a glam squad—hair, makeup, personal stylist—and together they actually generate a *lookbook* for her each season. It's all in keeping with Sleptanie's very manufactured image of a modern woman killing it on all fronts: life, love, and real estate. Meanwhile, *Stephanie* is contemptuous of the readers who enjoy her fluffy series, her marriage is riddled with infidelity, she's been on and off antidepressants since she was a teenager, and her mother paid the down payment on the brownstone as a wedding gift. The audience wasn't connecting with her because there's not a hair out of place. You need a little bit of imperfection to make people feel like there's a human being underneath it all, but she could never quite bring herself to expose her real warts. She even had her agent negotiate *in her contract* that production could not shoot the outside of her house—for "security" purposes. Really, she's embarrassed she lives next to a dry cleaner's. But that brownstone would have cost millions more if it wasn't, millions more on top of that if it was even one more avenue west of First. Like I said, it's hard to be rich in New York, even for Stephanie Simmons.

The fact that she's back to her old ways means she's feeling pretty confident about her contract. Did she get a two-season renewal? No one gets a two-season renewal, but you don't show up late unless you can get away with being late, which is why I'm so mortified that I got held up this morning. I never want to look like I'm taking advantage of Jesse's obvious favoritism. Yes, I know it's there, but I will cut you if you suggest it's because we're both gay. How about Jesse and I are the only ones who can truly call ourselves self-made women? Jen may not come from the piles of money that Lauren and Steph do, but she was raised in Soho and has gotten by fine on her mother's name.

Oh, and in case Stephanie sold you the rags-to-riches story about scraping by on minimum wage when she first moved to New York—because she loves that one—here's the truth that she conveniently omits. Her mom was paying the rent on her one-bedroom on Seventy-sixth and Third and slipping her an allowance of two hundred and fifty a week. Stephanie may have run out of spending money from time to time, she may not have been able to go out to dinner as often as she would have liked or shopped on a whim, but she was far from fucking Fievel.

I take a seat and set my bag on the table, rummaging around for the everything bagel with vegetable cream cheese and tomato, my long-standing order at Pick A Bagel.

"Nice Chloé," Lauren says, slyly. She turns to Jen with a triumphant smirk, as if I have proven something on her behalf.

Arch had been on me to "invest" in a "power bag," and when I wouldn't do it myself, she took matters into her own hands. What the fuck kind of messed-up financial advice do we instill in women that even my Harvard-educated girlfriend has internalized it? Invest means put your money into something that has a return. Unless the cost of this bag included some kind of pension plan, I'm pretty sure Arch didn't invest in anything. She just bought something. "Thanks," I say. "It was a gift from my girlfriend."

"Nice girlfriend then." Lauren gives me a naughty little wink.

"Sorry I'm late," I say again, but specifically to Lauren and Jen this time. Clearly, they're pissed. Though the Green Menace is usually pissed about something. "The entire booking system crashed just as I was heading out the door."

"I know how *that* goes," Lauren says, wearily, not to be generous but to reinforce the fiction that she is on the ground at SADIE too. Lauren had a great idea—a dating website where the woman is the one to establish contact—but she never would have gotten it off the ground if her father hadn't provided her with a jumbo nest egg and a well-stocked corporate advisory board. Lauren has never been anything more than the face of SADIE. It's a great face, but lately, it's doing more harm than good.

I tip my head at Jen, who is going after my hairstyle now, I guess. "Liking the long hair, Greenberg." It's been three months since I've encountered the Green Menace in the wild, which isn't unusual at all, and not because we "hate" each other. If anything, production prefers we keep our distance during the off-season. They want us fresh when we see each other; they don't want alliances shifting when the cameras aren't around to capture it. It helps streamline the narrative if we can pick up right where we left off in the previous season.

"And *moi*?" Lauren asks, pumping an upturned palm by her head, which is zipped up prettily with a crown braid. Did you know that every fourteen seconds a woman in New York City succumbs to a crown braid? It's a *braidemic*. "I got carded at Gemma last night."

"Adorable," I tell her. "You look my age." Lauren barks, *Ha!* Jen texts someone.

I generally like Lauren. She's Lauren Fun! What's not to like? We've always treated each other like friends of a mutual friend who get along exceptionally well whenever occasion brings us together, who have each other's numbers but only so we can text logistics. *What time is (enter mutual friend's name) birthday dinner tonight again?* I think it's ridiculous that she's been sentenced to indentured servitude just because Jen brought her on the show—they know each other from summers in *Ohm-nah-gansett*. Jerk me. But the truth is I'm not interested in taking on Lauren as a real friend. I get all itchy around people who aren't honest with themselves, and Lauren crashes into that category headfirst double fisting tequila on the rocks and shouting *Let's do it again!* You could argue Steph suffers from the same affliction, but Steph *is* honest with herself. It's everyone else she's lying to, which is not necessarily a criticism. I just think she could be more strategic about which lies she tells.

Jen turns her infamous squint on our showrunner. "Lisa, I have to be on the east side at one for another meeting."

Jen has this expression about her, *Ugh, people, do I really have to talk to them?* There is something about her that is fundamentally unfuckable. I *guess* she's pretty—we're on TV, the network's not evolved enough to cast uggos yet—but it's an anemic kind of pretty. She's a whey-faced canvas upon which she's applied the "vegan boho" palette. Lots of tea-stained lace schmattas are involved. Maybe that's where this unsexiness comes from, the fact that she has no idea who she is or what she stands for. Everything is an imitation, flower child cosplay, with the end goal being money and success, rather than fulfillment and pleasure.

Even this bougier Jen before me feels like a well-thought-out move on the chessboard. Word is that Jen has glossed up her appearance to reignite her relationship with the person who put her heart through the Vitamix just before the last reunion. The third button of her linen shirt *is* undone. Saucy minx. But there is no way to know for sure, primarily because Jen refuses to talk about her personal life. This sends me into orbit. We are on a reality TV show! We signed up to share all aspects of our lives, even the humiliating heartbreak. I had to endure Sarah dumping me twice—once in real life and once again when it aired, but Jen has managed to wiggle off the hook. She wants the promotion and adoration of being on TV without having to make any of the sacrifices.

"Now that we are *all here*," Lisa tucks her chin and stares me down from the other end of the table, "let's get started."

Kelly picks up her production packet, her spine rod straight.

Now that we're all here? I glance at the door. "Steph lost in one of her two hundred rooms?"

The field producers laugh.

"Steph's not coming," Jen seems very pleased to tell me. Since when does Jen refer to Stephanie as *Steph*?

"She's not *coming*?" I survey the room, looking for anyone who is as gobsmacked as I am. We have never had a *Digger* skip the all-cast prod meeting before.

"She's in Chicago with Marc," Lauren volunteers, watching closely for my reaction, knowing I am well within my rights to bug out that Stephanie is in Chicago with our director of photography, *alone*. They don't film you early and alone unless they think your storyline is pertinent to the season. No one wanted to film me, early and alone, presiding over the yoga auditions.

I refuse to show that I care, but damnit, I care. "Why wouldn't we do it when she's back then?" I ask Lisa.

"Because," Lisa says, "you're all busy bitches and four out of five of you ain't bad." She picks up the production packet and flips the page. "Headline events . . ."

Everyone turns their attention to the packet before them. I try to focus too, but all I see are numbers and words instead of dates and locations. I detect movement and glance up in time to see Lauren lean into Jen's side and whisper something, holding a knuckle to her lips to contain a giggle. Jen manages to crack a smile without short-circuiting.

It's hard to believe that the very first episode of *Goal Diggers* kicked off with Jen and me shopping for recycled dresses at Reformation, hours before the party for the grand opening of her second Green Theory location. We were something resembling friends back then, butting heads once we realized that our definitions of health inherently threatened the other's business model, with hers being "skinny" and mine being "eat the doughnut." Truly, that is the crux of our issues—that and Jen's unmitigated disgust with my body—though Jen likes to make it out as though I "stole her mother." It's not my fault Yvette is disappointed in Jen for choosing a path in life that makes women smaller.

"We had talked about doing a ride to raise money for Lacey Rzeszowski's campaign," Kelly is suddenly saying, and I come to with her looking at me, encouragingly. We've been discussing ways for our businesses to acknowledge the results of the election.

I clear my throat. "Lacey . . . ?"

"Rzeszowski," Kelly prods. "We talked about this, remember? She's one of two hundred women who are running for political office for the first time this year? Making a bid for a seat in the New Jersey Assembly?"

I am drawing a blank. The Green Menace seizes the opportunity.

"One thing I'm in the process of doing is designing a limited line of juices called Clintonics," Jen says, her eyes ever narrow.

Lisa taps her pen against her forehead for a few moments, trying to work out what Jen has just said. "Oh my God," she says when it clicks. "*Clintonics.* Fucking hysterical." Yeah, so hysterical she doesn't even laugh.

Lauren nods. *Yeah! Yeah! Yeah!* Her energy is manic, depending on what she's on that day. "And they're supposed to be good for your voice, right, J?"

"They're concentrated with what we call 'the warming spices' in Ayurvedic culture," Jen says in a tone that tells me to prepare for terminal boredom. "Cinnamon, cardamom, and clove are traditionally used together to provide a diverse supply of antioxidants that help boost immunity, but tulsi is the new super spice that the homeopathic community has discovered supports lung and throat health. To help our voices as women carry."

There are mumbles around the room about how smart this is, how *timely*. I'm just thinking that of course that guy broke up with her. Jen's farts must smell like death.

"We could sell them at the front of SPOKE," Kelly suggests, tentatively, because she knows we have a strict policy about pushing food or drink on our customer. I feel strongly that SPOKE shouldn't influence women's dietary choices. They get enough of that everywhere else they go.

"You need a permit to sell outside of the restaurant and it's a pain in the ass to get," Jen says. "Plus, your girl doesn't really do the juice thing."

"I love them." Kelly shrugs, and I put my finger on it. Kelly's lost *weight.* It's only a few pounds, and I didn't notice in those duster cardigans she usually wears, but in that tight getup from Forever 21, her chest looks like a grill pan.

Jen raises her eyebrows, amused by this, and I can't say I blame her. If Jen's sister were here, sucking up to *me,* I'd be pretty fucking amused myself.

"Think on it," Lisa says, licking her finger and turning the page. "Let's talk Morocco."

Now it's my turn to sit up straighter. *Let's!* "I had a conversation with one of my investors last night. About funding the trip. Whatever we need. Travel, lodging, transportation. We're totally covered."

"Is big *daddy* single?" Lauren bats her eyelashes.

"Back off," Lisa says. "It's Greenberg who's in dire need of rebound D."

Jen turns a livid red.

"Wow, Laur." I fold my arms across my chest, glowering at her. "That's really sexist that you would just assume my investor is a man." An awkward hush falls over the room, and I let everyone stew in it a good long while. "Just kidding." I stretch my arms over my head with a leisurely yawn. "He's totally an old white dude from Texas."

Everyone but Jen laughs.

"Can we focus, please?" Lisa squeaks. Lisa is pushing fifty but has the voice of an eleven-year-old choirboy and this manages to make her all the more terrifying. There is something deeply disturbing about being told that you're about to become so irrelevant even your own grandchildren won't remember your name by a woman who sounds like Pinocchio, which is something Lisa said to Hayley when we went to Anguilla to shoot her new control-top swimsuit line. You haven't lived until Lisa has eviscerated you in an exotic location.

Lisa slaps the page of her production packet. "*Morocco,*" she says, impatiently. "We are thinking last week of June. We start filming June first so that's enough time for everyone to get their feet wet, work through their shit"—she points her pen at *me*—"and come together for a big, bleeding-heart getaway. My rough understanding is that we start the trip in Marrakesh, and then head out to one of these villages in the mountains."

Kelly raises her hand, as though she is in school. Lisa calls on her, playing along. "Yes, Miss Courtney?"

"Layla has become pen pals with a girl in the village of Aguergour. She's one of our top sellers on the shop. I thought it would be a nice moment for the two of them to meet in person."

There is silence all around, mine sharpest. This is the first I've heard of Layla's *pen pal*. Kelly learns fast. She always has.

Jen, of all people, is the one to say, "That sounds like a really powerful moment." But then she keeps talking. "The thing is, I don't think I can go in good faith. The CDC recommends a hepatitis A vaccination for Morocco, the makers of which are on PETA's list of companies that test on animals. They use baby bunny rabbits." Her chin quivers.

Lisa holds her hand up to silence me, though I haven't spoken. "Is that right?"

Jen dips her finger into a tub of lip balm free of parabens, sulfates, and phthalates and dots it on. That was a quick recovery—from almost crying over the baby bunny rabbits to an act of personal grooming. "But just because I can't make it doesn't mean it's not a great idea." She smiles at me, like she had to grease her lips just to get them to do that.

Now Lauren raises her hand. "I hate to pile on," she says. "But we're in app development for the new version of SADIE that's tailored for the LGBTQ community. My CEO is worried about me going to a country that prosecutes gays and lesbians for their sexuality."

Lisa works her pen between her thumb and index finger, index and middle, holding Lauren accountable in a thousand-yard stare. "Weren't you in Dubai over the holidays?"

Lauren dips her finger into Jen's tub of lip balm. "For one night." She rubs her lips together. "You can't fly direct to the Maldives."

I snort. "And where do the Maldives stand on gay and lesbian rights?"

Lauren gapes, opening and closing her shiny mouth a few times before a few sober brain cells bump into each other. "I read that your investor had his daughter's wedding at Trump Bedminster!" she cries, completely out of context. A field producer covers her mouth with the production packet in horror and I'm tempted to do the same. What she just said is true, but Lauren has never come for me before. A two-fingered chill walks my spine. What is *happening* here?

"*People! People!*" Lisa chirps in a way that makes Kelly bow her head and plug a finger in her ear. "Enough. Everyone is to mark June twenty-third to July second on their calendars. We will find a location that works for the group."

"Lisa," I sputter, "I *have* to go to Morocco this summer."

Lisa curls her lip, disgusted by my desperation. "We'll *figure it out,* Brett." She waits for Jen and Lauren to turn their attention back to the production packet. *What the fuck?* she mouths, jerking her head in their direction. I exaggerate my shrug to show I'm just as baffled as she is. Lisa rolls her eyes and mouths *Fuck my life,* both because she is almost fifty and doesn't realize that no one is saying that anymore and because what's my problem is Jesse's problem is Lisa's problem. That's always the way it's been. So why does this time feel different?

CHAPTER 4

Stephanie

"When I was sixteen, I entered an essay-writing contest at a major women's magazine and won. In the contest's half-century history, I was the youngest woman ever to take home the honor. *You have a voice beyond your years,* the editor in chief told me in a handwritten note, *and because of that we are willing to bend the rules for you.* I had lied about my age on the application form. Contestants had to be eighteen to enter. To this day I keep that note in my top desk drawer, reading it whenever my confidence wavers. It's a reminder that I once believed in myself so much that I, Stephanie Simmons, broke a rule.

"There were prizes. Publication, of course. Five thousand dollars, though that was incidental. I would have left all of it on the table for the trip into the city to meet with a literary agent. Mary Shelley began writing *Frankenstein* before she turned twenty. S. E. Hinton published *The Outsiders* when she was just sixteen. I had the first two chapters of my novel already drafted and an outline of the rest, and I planned on not just meeting with Ellen Leibowitz of the Ellen Leibowitz Agency to find out how the publishing world worked, but on pitching her and leaving with representation.

"'We'll make a day out of it!' my mother exclaimed after reading the letter from the editor in chief. Breakfast at the Plaza. Shopping at

Bloomingdale's. She would get a manicure while I was no doubt signing with the Ellen Leibowitz Literary Agency on Lexington Avenue ('Lexington Avenue is a very upscale street,' my mother said with authority when she looked up the address on the Internet.) We'd end the day with a celebratory drink at The Ritz Carlton in Battery Park, watching an orange sun glaze the Hudson. I would order an iced tea and my mother a glass of champagne, and when the bartender wasn't looking, we'd swap. 'Oh, Stephanie,' my mother said, pinning the letter to the refrigerator with a magnet from Baltusrol Golf Club (I was a single-digit handicap by the time I entered high school). 'Aren't you so proud of yourself?' Her blue eyes brimmed with tears, the effect infuriating and depleting all at once. *Let me have this*, I remember thinking, incapable of parsing what I wanted more: to break something or to sleep.

"I understand my anger and my exhaustion now. As a child, my mother was constantly asking me to perform for her, to reassure her that I was doing well, that I was thriving, that I was happy. That she was a good mother and that she had made the right choice in adopting me, defying all those who counseled against it. She was single, they told her. She was fifty. She was *white*. Did she have any idea how much work it took to raise a child in a *two*-parent family? Sure, she could afford help, but wasn't it a little bit cruel, wasn't it a little bit *selfish*, to bring up a black girl in a town as homogeneous as Summit, New Jersey, just because she missed her window to have a baby of her own? My mother was married briefly in her thirties, the ink barely dry on her divorce papers before her own mother was diagnosed with an aggressive and intractable form of breast cancer. She put her life on hold—thirteen years of it—to take care of her mother, and her death left a void for a new dependent. She was volunteering at a women's shelter when a counselor mentioned a friend's troubled teenage daughter had gotten pregnant, and that the family was looking to put the baby up for adoption. 'I didn't care if you were black, white, green, or polka-dotted', my mother told me the only time I asked her why I didn't look like her. 'I wanted you.' It was the closest we ever got to acknowledging my race.

"'You'll need an outfit for the interview,' my mother said, even though I didn't. When I went back to clean out the house after her death five years ago, I donated so many unworn pieces to that same women's shelter that a volunteer asked me if I had a clothing store that had gone out of business. But my mother insisted that I take my winnings and go to the Short Hills Mall two weeks before the meeting. 'So there's time to get to the tailor if we need to.' My mother loved the tailor. At five-foot-one and ninety-seven pounds, she needed his step stool more than I ever did. I had twenty five pounds and half a head on her by the time I could drive. People didn't know what to make of the two of us. This frail, glamorous white woman approaching her seventies and the young black girl dressed in her likeness. Was I her elderly aide? Her expensively turned-out housecleaner? I grew up stared at. Sometimes I wonder if it's the reason I feel comfortable buying tampons with a camera crew in tow."

The joke elicits a few laughs from the audience gathered to hear me read from my memoir at the Harold Washington Library Center in Chicago. *No,* I realize, my eyes settling on a woman in the third row. Not a laugh. A yawn.

"I asked my best friends to accompany me to Nordstrom," I continue, speaking over the voice inside my head that insists I am boring everyone. *Get to the good part already.* "As always, Ashley, Jenna, and Caitlin went best of three on a game of rock, paper, scissors to decide who got to drive my car to the mall that day. I hated my blue bimmer. I felt screamingly self-conscious behind the wheel, ever since the night a middle-aged white man saw me searching for my keys in the parking lot of Kings and called out, 'Hey! You! What are you doing to that car?' He probably had a daughter my age, but to him, I wasn't anybody's daughter, a promising young woman with the fifth-highest GPA in her class, a nationally ranked field hockey player, or a talent on the page. I was an anonymous, suspicious, and potentially threatening *you.* The word still makes me shrivel in shame. I tried to imagine any of my friends being addressed as such and could not. I saw the way grown-ups looked at them—with fondness, with amusement. *Oh, let them eat candy for breakfast now. Let them break curfew. Real life will come for them soon enough.* Some people got mulligans in life, but I learned early on I was not to be one of them.

"In the contemporary designers department of Nordstrom, my friends flung pantsuits and skirt suits and twinsets over the top of the dressing room door. 'Come out! Come out!' they chanted like little kids for their dinners, rotating their thumbs down or up, depending. 'I miss my tan,' Caitlin sighed wistfully when I emerged in a white turtleneck and short schoolgirl kilt that Jenna liked so much she went in search of her size and tried it on too. If there is such a thing as teacher's pet among a group of friends, then that was what I was. I was never going to call the shots, take the quarterback with the biceps to prom, or inspire copycats to steal my hairstyle. I was not a threat to my friends and that's why I never had to worry about falling out of favor with them. For a while I found the upside to this. No one ever ganged up on me, no one ever got three tickets to Pearl Jam and said to me, 'Sorry, you'll have to sit this one out,' which is something Ashley did to Jenna once because she had instant-messaged a guy Ashley liked. If the girls could only invite one friend to their beach house, it was always me. Number two wasn't such a bad place to sit, I reasoned. And this is the insidiousness of the world in which we live. It doesn't just discourage little black girls from being great. It makes them grateful they are not great.

"'What shoes, though?' Ashley asked after the unanimous vote in favor of a Theory pantsuit in navy. 'Nude pumps?' Caitlin suggested. 'Brown boots,' Jenna said with a sly grin. 'We wear the same size, right?' She did a spin in the new plaid miniskirt she was about to buy.

"We called for the salesperson, hoping she might bring us some footwear options, but she was nowhere to be found. I had been relieved that she had been rude not just to me but to all of us, which allowed me to pretend that it wasn't so much about the color of my skin as it was about my age. No doubt she dismissed us out of hand—just a bunch of bored teenagers here to not buy anything and leave the dressing room in shambles, which my friends routinely did when we shopped together. They made fun of me for neatly clipping trousers to their hangers and folding sweaters into tidy squares. 'Such a neat freak,' they said, and I let them think that was what it was about.

"The shoe department was on the other side of the escalators, but still close enough that I felt comfortable leaving my purse in the dressing room. There, standing before the full-length mirror in a pair of brown boots that really were the best choice for the Theory pantsuit, I saw the security guards before they tapped me on the shoulder from behind.

"They escorted me to a leather sofa outside the restrooms. A small crowd gathered, the way it did when the in-house pianist played a selection from *Phantom of the Opera,* watching as I was pressured to sign a statement admitting to an attempt to leave the store wearing the Theory pantsuit without paying for it. Jenna had walked out of the dressing room in a skirt she hadn't yet paid for, but two adult men hadn't been called in to isolate and intimidate her. 'She wasn't trying to steal it!' my friends cried in exasperation. 'Her purse is in the dressing room!' When the security guards threatened to call their parents, they became incensed. 'I'll call my parents and her mom, right now!' Ashley shouted with a defiance that crushed me. I had that nerve—would I ever feel safe enough to use it?

"Within half an hour, my mother arrived and cleared everything up, which is shorthand for me, apologizing to the saleswoman and the security guards for the misunderstanding and her, purchasing the pantsuit. (Jenna left the kilt in the dressing room in an act of revolt—'No way is that bitch making a commission off me,' she got to say with her nose in the air.) Two weeks later, sitting in the meeting with Ellen Leibowitz, that pantsuit felt like wearing a porcupine's coat inside out. The humiliating memory pricked me and pricked me, rendering me a stuttering, blushing child in front of an accomplished woman I had been dreaming about impressing for weeks. *'Oh, no,'* my mother exhaled when we met on Lexington Avenue afterward. She could see in my face that I had blown it. And instead of going downtown to celebrate, we just went home. I remember feeling relieved that it was rush hour, that the train was so crowded that we had to split up to find seats, that for the forty-one minutes it took to get from Penn Station to Summit I got to hold myself by the elbows and cry without having to consider my mother's feelings.

"In the weeks that followed, I didn't sleep. I slumbered. Like a character in a Disney story under a wart-nosed witch's spell. Even at sixteen I knew my propensity for sleep was not just a byproduct of a still-growing body and brain. I hungered for it like a meal, was addicted to it like sugar—a little bit was sometimes worse than none at all, because it only made me want more, more, *more*. Worse: sometimes, I heard things. Words and names, so clearly enunciated that the first few times it happened I looked over my shoulder, thinking someone had stepped into the room to speak to me. I'd seen the episode of *Sally Jessy Raphael* where she'd interviewed teenagers with schizophrenia, the kind that makes you hear voices. Not everyone who hears voices has schizophrenia, I later learned. But at the time, I was terrified something was wrong with me and terrified to be found out. I thought if I could just get some information about my family history, I could control whatever was happening to me. I thought I could get out ahead of it.

"I didn't tell anyone when I started the search for my biological mother. I didn't want to call any more attention to the fact that my make was different, or have to explain any of it to my adoptive mother, who would only hear that she wasn't enough of a mother for me. Lots of adoptees report wanting to meet their birth parents because they can never shake the feeling of rootlessness, or they want to make sense of their origin story, or they're simply curious about where they came from. My motivation was strictly clinical. I wanted to look my birth mother in the eye and ask her if she was sick and if I was going to get sick too, and if so, how could I get better before anyone noticed?

"My adoption was a closed adoption, which might have meant something in the 1980s. In the early aughts, around the time I started my search, the Internet may not have been what it is today, but you could pay to run a background check if you had a name. And I had a name. When I was seven, I'd come home from a movie with my mom to find a message from the housekeeper: Sheila Lott, 12:47 P.M. I would never have remembered this if not for my mother's pallor when she suggested I go read in my room for a bit. She'd spent all afternoon on the phone, her shrill terror occasionally snaking its way up our double staircase and interrupting my umpteenth reading of *Beezus and Ramona*. I had to memorize a new home phone number after that and all I knew was that Sheila Lott was to blame.

"There were ninety-seven Sheila Lotts on Foundit.com, thirty nine once I eliminated any over the age of forty, and seventeen once I narrowed down the ones who lived on the East Coast. At $24.95 a pop to 'get the report on,' I would have had to explain the charge of $424.15 on my credit card if I hadn't found her on my fourth try.

"I knew it was my mother the moment the image loaded. We had the same grouping of freckles under our eyes, the same sweeping, smooth foreheads. Had she been smiling in the mug shot, I was sure she'd get those brackets around her mouth, the ones that made my cheekbones appear both soft and sharply pronounced. A boy at my school once told me that when I smiled, I was prettier than most white girls he knew.

"My real mother was thirty-two, my adoptive mother's junior by thirty-five years, which made her fifteen when she had me. She had been arrested twice on drug charges. There was an address in Doylestown, Pennsylvania. Two weeks later, I told my mom I was helping set up for the Spring Saturday dance at school and crossed state lines in my blue bimmer. I didn't find my mom that day—it would take three more tries until I did that—but I did find A.J."

I could go on. I could turn the pages, recount the times A.J. elbowed me in the throat, sat on my chest, or covered my mouth and squeezed my nose until I was flapping like a fish on land. He never hit me. Never left a mark. He preferred me blue in the face, wheezing like a longtime smoker, burning for one good breath. I close my copy of *Seen*. It burns enough, remembering that day in Nordstrom. "Thank you."

The Cindy Pritzker Auditorium is silent a moment. Women look left and right, some with their hands poised to clap, as though they are unsure if I am finished or not. They left their jobs early and shelled out twenty-nine dollars a ticket to hear me describe what it feels like to be starved of oxygen for eighty-three seconds by the first man who ever told me he loved me. I have to say thank you again before I receive their applause.

I am still not used to it. How *different* the applause for my memoir is than it was for my fiction. At my early readings of the She's with Him series the reception was frisky, lanced with plenty of *Woo-woos!* and *Whoops!*, which always rankled. Yes, I wrote about sex, but I also wrote about identity, race, power, and the inescapable cycle of abuse. But that wasn't enough to quiet people down, to be heard, to be respected. You want a full-page review in the *New York Times*? You want serious clappers at your readings? Open a vein.

"Babe," Vince says, arms and mouth open wide, in this *Are you kidding me with what an absolute inspiration you are?* kind of way. He could just lean across the table and give me a kiss, but he comes around to my left so that Marc has to adjust the magnification of the Canon 5D. The producers left film of me, marching in protest of George Zimmerman's acquittal, on the cutting room floor in season one. 'Too polarizing,' I heard Jesse had said. Three years later, when enough white people agree that Black Lives Matter, Jesse sends a crew to document the scores of black women who gather to hear me say that sexual violence against us has gone unchecked for too long. To her, we're bulletproof coffee or millennial-pink blazers. Just another coastal-elite trend that she will tire of soon enough.

I kiss my husband on the mouth for the first time in a few weeks. Gwen, my editor, looks away when it lasts too long. One of the most frequent questions I've been asked since the memoir came out is how Vince feels about it, if he's disturbed at all by the revelation that the fictional couple in my trilogy is loosely based on my first relationship.

My husband and I don't keep secrets in our marriage. He already knew. That's what Gwen had me practice saying. And then she had Vince practice too: *My wife and I don't keep secrets in our marriage . . .*

Vince doesn't usually accompany me on the book tour—and for reasons I won't get into today, I prefer it that way—but he can always be counted on to show up when the cameras are around, because it's success through osmosis. All the glory and none of the work. Gwen has been referring to him as the Human Step and repeat since we've been on the road and she's exactly right. Get your book signed by Stephanie and your selfie taken with Vince, just to the right of her table. Even the serious clappers can't resist an Instagram photo-op with my husband, who at thirty-two should really be losing his hair by now.

The line disappears out the door, "All the way to the lobby," Gwen whispers to me, and there are two security guards on crowd control. No one is allowed in this room without buying a book. I have my Caran d'Ache ballpoint pen punched and ready to sign when Gwen waves over the first audience member. She can't be twenty-five and she wears a bright yellow cardigan, pulling across the chest to reveal a pink bra that matches the neon smear on her lips. Dark acne scars mottle her jawline and is she . . . ? Yes. She's already crying. My stomach gets that sensation, like it is a deep and maybe endless tunnel, like sadness will have a place to travel through me my whole life.

"Oh, sweetheart," I say, and I stand and wrap my arms around her. I learned early in the book tour: no silk blouses. The women destroy them.

"I want to leave," she sobs into my shoulder.

Ugh. So she's one of those. One who is still holding on, hoping it will get better. I could knit the world's least cozy quilt out of the things they've confessed on my shoulder: I'm so stupid. No one knows. My mom said it's nothing compared to what my dad did to her. I should be grateful. He has a job. I'm being dramatic. I have nowhere to go. I have no one. It's not that bad. It's not that bad. Black women are three times more likely to die at the hands of an abuser than white women. It's unconscionable that our government hasn't stepped up to do more for us. One of the things I'm planning on speaking about with the Female Director when I meet her in a few months is the possibility of an initiative specifically devoted to helping black women extricate themselves from their violent partners. I was thinking we could roll it out in tandem with the movie's release.

I pull away and pat her on the shoulder. "We're going to get you help, okay?" I beckon Gwen, who is armed with the numbers for Chicago's women's shelters and some of the national hotlines. She will call none of them. Or maybe she will, and he'll kill her anyway. As Gwen passes her the cards, I scrawl *Be strong* in the book she was forced to buy to enter this room.

A small woman steps forward next. It's nearly June but she's drowning in a heavy winter sweater, which either means she runs cold or she's covered in bruises. Her face is unsmiling as she passes me my book, telling me her name is Justine.

"I knew your mother," she waits to say until after I've signed.

Instantly the line ceases to exist. There is no one else in the room but this woman who knew my real mother. I was prepared for this at the signings in New York and New Jersey and Philadelphia, for long-lost relatives angry I've aired our family's dirty laundry, for the truthers with documents and police reports that fact-checkers missed. But here, in Chicago, in front of the cameras, I am completely defenseless and at the mercy of this frail, cold, and possibly battered old woman. Justine looks to be in her seventies, meaning she can't have been a peer of my mother's. If my mother were alive today she'd be approaching fifty. It takes a sizable amount of courage just to ask, "How did you know her?"

Justine nods, a single slow dip of her chin, as though she's gotten my attention now. "I grew up with *her* mother." Her pointer finger does a little leap, skipping a generation, the gold bracelets on her wrists caroling together. "Your grandmother. Your grandmother was a good woman." She makes a noise to back this up. "She tried everything to help Sheila. Rehab. Doctors. A program in California one time too. And Sheila, she wasn't a bad person. But she had her troubles with alcohol and with men. Your grandma did too. With men, that is. So many of us did back then." Justine's chin is held at a high, strong angle, but a tear slips down her face.

I pluck a tissue from the box on my table. I also learned on the last book tour: Keep tissues at the ready. "What happened to her?"

Justine blows her nose quietly, folding the tissue in half and taking her time slipping it into her purse. When she looks at me again, her eyes are dry. "She died. Twelve years ago this summer. She would have been so sorry this had happened to you. It was in your blood, for this to happen to you. But she would have been *proud*"—her voice wavers briefly on the word—"that you found a way to break the cycle. Promise me you'll stay away from it. Alcohol and bad men." Justine draws herself together with a deep breath, casting a steely glance first at Vince, then at me. "I only wish you had the courage to pay your respects at St. Mark's. We would have embraced you."

There is a resistance in my chest when I try to breathe, like I'm wearing one of those lead bibs in the dentist's office. In the book, I write that I stood across the street from the church during my mother's funeral service, watching the puny gathering process in and process out. Thinking about going inside was as close as I got. There just weren't enough people. I would have been noticed. I would have had to explain who I was.

But that's not what has left me short of breath. It was the very particular mention of St. Mark's that did that. And now I just want her to go away. I need her to go away. I say, with a note of finality in my voice, "Thank you for coming tonight, Justine."

"Well, okay now," she says, with a smile that says she gets it.

I wanted to be seen so badly I made it the title of my memoir. Whatever comes next, I asked for it. I had it coming.

CHAPTER 5

Brett

"Garbage?" Arch holds up a copy of *Business Plan Writing for Dummies* that's seen some things.

I reach for the tome and clutch it to my chest. "Never," I say, stroking its yellow-and-black cover with inflated sentimentality. "I can never throw this out."

"Holding on to it until you finally read it?" Kelly quips, tying off a garbage bag in my kitchen.

"Hey," I say, placing the book tenderly in the *keep* pile, "I don't have to move, you know."

"Then who are you planning to film with?" Kelly purses her lips at me, sassily, before heading toward the garbage room down the hall.

"Who are *you* planning on filming with?" I call after her, lamely. The door rebounds off the dead bolt, seeming a little bit stunned.

Arch looks up at me from the floor, where she's seated cross-legged, surrounded by old mail, DVDs, power cords, and Happy Belated Birthday cards from my dad and Susan. Her dark hair hangs over her shoulder in a long braid, and she worms it around her finger with a small, private smile. Arch is an only child and thereby endlessly amused by the ways in which Kelly is able to so easily irritate me.

"Well, that you can trash." I toe an old copy of *She's with Him: A Novel* by Stephanie Simmons. *People* promises on the cover: *The sexiest beach read you can pack in your beach bag right now.* Stephanie hated that her books were reduced to summer reads. They were *smarter* than that, exploring the nuances between working-class and white-collar blackness, and how they manifested in a romantic relationship. The *New York Times* did not agree. They passed on reviewing all three in the series, which chronicled the passionate-bordering-on-abusive relationship between a seventeen-year-old prep school girl and a seventeen-year-old rising football star from the wrong side of the tracks. Think *Fifty Shades of Grey* with black characters and writing that won't impair your IQ.

"Can I read it?" Layla asks, emerging from the bedroom wearing a pair of my earrings.

"When you're thirty-five," I tell her.

Arch flips open the book. "But she signed it," she says. Her lips trace the inscription, silently. She is still a moment, then looks up at me strangely.

"What does it say?" I ask, crouching down next to her to read it. *To the love of my life. Sorry, Vince!* She dated it *3.21.15*. "Whoa," I say, wholly unprepared for the burning tightness in my throat, that feeling like you're gurgling your heart. I can't believe that just two years separates that inscription and the news Lisa delivered yesterday.

"You're going to hate this," Lisa had said over the phone, a smile in her voice.

Stephanie, back from her book tour, had a private prod meeting with Lisa. Morocco isn't going to work for her either. The World Health Organization has issued a Zika warning for North Africa and, well, she'll let all of us do with that what we will.

I had to squeeze the phone tighter to keep it from sliding out of my damp hand. "She's *pregnant*?" For as long as I've known Stephanie, she has been adamant: Kids are for women with no other path to glory.

"She and Vince are talking about it."

"Oh, come the fuck on!"

"We will still film you going to Morocco," Lisa said, suddenly on speaker. I could hear her fingers playing the keyboard. I could feel her retreating, as though my spray of emotions had repelled her to the other side of the battlefield.

"It's not the same if I go alone," I said, trying to keep my voice level. Lisa has a freeze response to emotion. "You know that." If I go alone, the trip and all the Imazighen women who deserve visibility will be reduced to one, maybe two, segments within a single episode. They will be treated as filler, between a scene of Stephanie and Vince pretending like they still have sex and Lauren ordering a third glass of wine at lunch.

"Look." Lisa sighed. "They all think you got your turn last year with the L.A. trip. It's someone else's opportunity."

"The L.A. trip?" I repeated, incredulous. "That trip was for the group. It was for the show. It had nothing to do with SPOKE."

"I know."

"When we went to Paris, it was for Stephanie's book. When we went to the Hamptons, it was for Jen's juice stand. When we went to Anguilla, it was for Hayley's—"

"Hang on a sec?"

I was taken off speaker, and a muffled conversation between Lisa and nobody had ensued.

"Brett, I have to take this. It's the network."

"Sure." I know a *get me the fuck off this call* maneuver when I'm the target of one.

"It will work out," Lisa said. But then she stopped typing. "Or maybe you should talk to Stephanie. She's convinced them not to film with you."

I could feel my pulse in the button of my jeans. There is only one reason Stephanie would do such a thing, and it's not something our viewers would easily forgive.

I didn't try to talk to her. I couldn't. But there was someone else who would listen to me, who could possibly help, and so I called her and asked if we could meet anywhere, anytime, but soon.

"She was kidding," I say to Arch, who is still staring up at me, suspiciously, her red fingernail underlining Stephanie's inscription. *To the love of my life.*

"Then why are you blushing?" Arch asks, a salient point.

I take the book from her hands and carry it the few steps into the kitchen, chucking it into the recycle bin. I notice the garbage bag where we're dumping the contents of old condiments, horseradish and mustard, sriracha and grape jam, just as Kelly returns from the trash room. I see an opportunity to distract Arch from thinking whatever it is she is thinking that is making her look at me like that, and smash the open bag in Kelly's face.

"Brett!" she shrieks, doubling over with a hysterical retch. Layla shares my wounding laugh. Kelly is so *precious* sometimes. Kelly recovers and snatches a handful of my hair, dragging me left-ear-side down to the floor.

"Uncle!" I cry, the pain in my scalp ice-cold. "Uncle!" But when Kelly lets go—idiot, she knows we don't fight fair—I kick her in the shin so hard Arch moans in secondhand agony. Kelly crumples to the floor with a guttural sound, but it is just a fake out so she can spring on top of me, sending me onto my back, pinning my torso between her knees.

"I'm sorry!" I scream more than I laugh. Kelly is red-faced and breathing hard. "Oh, God, no! I'm so sorry!" Kelly leans over me, lips pursed, a line of spit stretching, lengthening, dangling inches from my face. "Layla!" I twist my head left and right. "Help me!"

"Stop it!" Layla cries. "Stop, Mom! Stop!" She looks around for something to throw at Kelly, landing on a rolled-together pair of socks in the laundry bin. *Bop!* They bounce off the back of Kelly's head, and it's as though a switch has been flipped. Kelly swings upright, the trail of spit attaching to her chin.

"I don't *like* when you guys do that," Layla says, sounding near tears. Arch scrambles to her feet, standing behind Layla and slicing a hand under her chin, making furious eyes at both of us—*cut it out.*

"Oh, we were just fooling around," Kelly assures Layla, wincing as she stands. She flicks her eyes at me—my turn to corroborate.

"We're not actually hurt, Layls!" I say, though the tender tempo of my scalp and the way Kelly is putting her weight on her left leg suggest otherwise. I glance at the clock on the microwave. "Eek! I have to meet Miss Greenberg soon. Layls, want to help me pick out my outfit? She's making us go somewhere fancy." I offer her my hand. She leaves me hanging for a few moments, mad at me for scaring her. "Please?" I stick out my lower lip. With a sigh, Layla threads her long fingers through mine and we head into my room. Kelly's room, now.

Yvette Greenberg is seated between an old-school finance guy and a Texan blonde in the golden tomb of Bemelmans, wearing wide, lightweight black pants, a white suiting vest, and red glasses, which she removes when she sees me to declare how *happy* I look. She licks her thumb to remove the lipstick mark on my left cheek, and for a moment, my mom isn't dead.

The bartender removes the silver triple-dish server from the bar top. "We'll replenish this and transfer to your table, Miss Greenberg."

Yvette mouths, *Thank you, Tommy.*

"I can't believe I got you all the way up here," Yvette says, sitting across from me and fluttering a few elegant fingers at the pianist over my shoulder. He purrs her name into the mic and she drapes her arm over the back of her chair with a laugh when light applause follows. The moment feels like it's mine too. It is the better accomplishment to be Yvette Linden Greenberg but a close second is to be in her company.

Yvette cups a hand around the side of her mouth. "And to think these fuckers wouldn't serve me in the eighties."

"Stop."

"That's why I'm a regular here now. You don't flee the places that discriminate against you, darling one. You occupy them." She leans back, melding into her seat, an unabashed spill of linen and resistance. "President Mandela told me that."

"You sure it wasn't Lennon?"

Yvette laughs, delighted that I'm impressed. And that's reason one of twenty-seven hundred that I love her. She doesn't play humble, the way most women have been brainwashed to do. I once told her in an email that I was lucky to have her in my life and she flipped the fuck out at me and lost all ability to punctuate. *YOU ARE NOT LUCKY BRETT!!!! YOU ARE TALENTED AND BRILLIANT AND STRONG AND I SEEK OUT TALENTED BRILLIANT STRONG WOMEN AND THATS WHY IM IN YOUR LIFE.* I was so moved I printed it out and tacked it behind my computer at SPOKE HQ.

The waiter appears, hand on his gut, asking what he can get for me. I point to Yvette's glass, and Yvette holds up two fingers. "Tanqueray and tonic."

The pianist starts in on Paul McCartney and Yvette leans forward on her elbows. "How have you *been*?" She reaches for my hand, the lines around her gray eyes long and thin, winging out like whiskers. It makes her look like she is always smiling, despite the more indelicate grooves between her brows, the heavy slabs of skin lumbering her eyes. The effect is that of someone who has seen a lot but remains cautiously optimistic about the state of humanity. Yvette rose to fame when she posed as a stewardess in the seventies, chronicling the abject sexism and misogyny that came with the line of work for *Esquire*. She also happens to have cheekbones for days, and was deemed *the foxy femi-nazi* by the *New York Post*. She's inaccurately held up as a symbol of the women's movement when Yvette is a crusader for intersectional activism, fighting oppression in *all* its forms: racial, sexual, religious, gendered, and on and on. She protested apartheid in South Africa and hosted the first women-only Seder in New York City. She coproduced an Oscar-winning documentary about the constitutional violations of the death penalty and founded a nonprofit for at-risk LGBTQ youth. She advised the 2005 MTA strike and she once seriously looked into adopting me. If aliens invade our planet one day, I would hold up Yvette as an example of why they should spare the human race.

My smile is lovestruck. "I have some news."

Yvette sucks in a giddy breath. "*Tell* me."

I pause for effect. "We're moving in together."

"Oh!" Yvette cries. "Oh, I knew it. I knew it as soon as I met her. She's special, Brett. And you're special." She puts her hand to her plump cheekbone, as though an exciting thought just occurred to her. "Do you think you'll get married?"

"Yvette. Pump the brakes, please."

"Why? You *should* get married. Everyone thinks I'm anti-marriage because I never did it, but I just never found the right person. Or maybe," she strokes the underside of her chin, coquettishly, "I just found too many right people."

I laugh. Yvette's roster reads like the guest list for Studio 54 in its heyday. "You've had a lot of fun."

"I'm still having a lot of fun. Maybe the most fun I've ever had." The song ends and Yvette booms, "Play 'Satisfaction'! I need some Mick in my life!" I nearly miss her wink.

"Shut the fuck up."

"I would never lie to you, my darling one."

"No," I say, "I believe you. I just need you to shut up before I spontaneously combust with jealousy."

"In any case," Yvette says, "it's probably better you hold off. If you get engaged Jesse would only try to commodify it for the show. She'd probably talk you into some god-awful spinoff." She puffs, full of disdain.

"That's something to consider," I murmur, noncommittally.

Our drinks arrive, frothy on top with extra lime juice, just the way Yvette makes them at home. We meet our glasses in the center of the table. "To the best medicine there is." Yvette does not mean gin. Sometimes I wonder if Jen's frigidity is a rebellion against her mother's resounding sex positivity.

Yvette tips her drink to her lips and laughs. "My daughter would die of embarrassment if I ever said such a thing in front of her. Speaking of. I heard you saw her recently." Her eyebrows slump together. They really only express in two directions: together or apart, concerned or conserving energy. Nothing surprises her enough to raise them anymore, though I could tell her some things.

"She looks really healthy," I tell Yvette, earnestly. It's a complicated dance, to be friends with the mother of a woman neither of us likes very much. My party line is this: I respect Jen but not necessarily the message her business sends to women, a hugely more forgiving position than Yvette has taken. If anything, my friendship with Yvette is predicated on her disappointment in her daughter's chosen profession and the positive spin I put on it. I remind her how impressive it is that Jen helms a multimillion-dollar company, that the investors have not felt the need to bring in a seasoned single Y chromosome to oil the machine. "That's a big deal, Yvette. Something to be really proud of," I'm always telling her, and sometimes I wonder if Yvette is even putting on her contempt a little bit. To force me to find things I admire about Jen.

"She's doing really well," Yvette says. "Professionally, that is. I just worry about her. I know she wants to find someone, to get married, and to have children. It feels like the show has steered her away from all of that."

The pianist holds the final key of "Tupelo Honey" and Yvette claps bossily, so that others put down their drinks and follow her lead. My heart races the applause as I ready myself to say what I came here to say. "Yvette, this is awkward. But I think Jen is trying to sabotage me."

Yvette appears truly stricken on my behalf. "*Sabotage* you?"

My eyes get a little teary because for a moment, I consider telling her everything. The truth. If anyone could understand it, it might be her.

Yvette's gentle gray eyes get even gentler. "Darling girl! What is it?"

I immediately change my mind. I cannot take the risk that Yvette may never look at me like this again, may never call me *darling girl*. "It has to do with the show."

Yvette makes a tickled noise that means *What now*. Yvette was once signed on as a recurring character, but she politely recused herself when Lisa became the showrunner in season two, the season our principles went down and our ratings went up. She's concerned we are contributing to a culture that paints female friendships as catty, conniving, and deceitful, rather than bucking that stereotype, as was the show's original intention. I hear that but unfortunately, no one is interested in watching a bunch of women get along. Jesse says it's our burden as the first feminist reality show to make the show palatable to the unwashed masses. She says it's no different than what I've done with SPOKE: helping third-world women by charging first-world women twenty-seven dollars to listen to Lady Gaga and pedal nowhere. Maybe one day we will live in a world that will binge on five independently successful women doing nothing but building each other up. Until then, we have to occasionally knock each other down.

"You know I told you that this year it was my turn to plan the trip," I say, "and that I wanted to take everyone to Morocco and introduce them to the women who are getting so much out of the bikes."

"It's wonderful," Yvette rests a cocktail straw next to the base of her glass, "when the show gets to be what it is."

"Except it's not happening anymore."

"I don't understand," Yvette says, lifting one hand in her confusion. "Why not?"

I give her the streamlined version: I had a falling-out with Stephanie, and the others seem to have chosen sides—her side—and now we may not be going to Morocco after all. I feel completely cheated out of a trip and unsupported by the other women when all I've ever done is support them, and worse, like I've misled my investors. I sold them on SPOKE getting a lot of airtime this season and now I'm worried they're going to feel duped.

"Here's what I think," Yvette says when I've finished my ramble. "First, breathe. *Breathe.* Take a deep breath and remember that whether or not the show gives Morocco the full treatment, it has no bearing on all the good you will do there."

Yvette pauses, and I realize she actually wants me to breathe. I take a deep inhale and look at her expectantly. She doesn't say anything so I take another.

"That being said," Yvette continues, appeased, "I don't believe in just sitting aside and letting others trample all over you. Stephanie has done a brave thing in telling her story, and I appreciate all she is doing to help women who have experienced similar traumas, but that does not make her beyond reproach. She is a very commanding personality and I don't think she always uses that power for good. Nearly all women can stand adversity, but if you want to test someone's character, give her power. Lincoln said that."

"You knew Lincoln too?"

"I'm that old, yes. And he was a great man." She draws her hands a foot apart, scrutinizes the distance, and adds another inch. "The greatest."

"Yvette!" I laugh.

"Good. See? You're laughing. Not dying." Her head traces the pattern of the music as she thinks for a moment. "I think you and my daughter need a face-to-face. No Lauren. No Stephanie. No Jesse and please God, no Lisa." Yvette grimaces. "I know you and Jen haven't always gotten along but Jen knows what it's like to have a lot to lose. I think you could appeal to her."

That was an odd thing to say—*Jen knows what it's like to have a lot to lose*—but I don't dig. I've already asked too much of her. "I feel like she'll never agree to meet me," I say.

Yvette *hmmms*, holding up her finger when she's got something. "How about this? We'll be at the house next week. Why don't you come out for the night? It will be peaceful. Private. You haven't even seen the remodel yet."

Jen and Yvette's 1880s whaler's cottage underwent an extensive face-lift this spring. I hear the East Hampton town council is none too pleased about it, which must mean it's spectacular.

"Huh." I consider. "I guess I could fold some work into it. You know we're doing this temporary yoga studio in Montauk and they're building out the old hardware store."

"Make it about work, don't make it about work, just come, Brett. You don't need an excuse to stay with me. You're family."

Yvette swipes her knuckle against my cheek, affectionately. Would she still love me like a daughter if she knew the truth? I lower my chin and take a lengthy pull from my cocktail straw. She would. I'm sure of it. It's not that bad, what happened.

Or is that just the Tanqueray, telling stories?

CHAPTER 6

Stephanie

I can hear the empty bottle of Sancerre in Lauren's laugh from the hallway. I rap my knuckles on Jen's door, inciting a fit of barking and a searing rebuke from Jen.

"Almond, *no*!" Jen is saying as she opens the door, wearing one of those x-small enormous linen sack dresses that are the true test of thinness these days—can you wear a tarp the size of lower Manhattan and not look obese? Congratulations, you are thin. She's restraining some sort of German shepherd–lab mix by the collar and her brown hair is longer than it was when I saw her last—extensions?

Cashew and Pecan, Jen's Frenchie and dachshund, swirl my ankles as I make my way into her McCondo, the thermostat set so low you would think the furniture was perishable. It continues to surprise me that hippie Jen, who was born and raised in a grungy loft in Soho, lives in one of these glass and steel luxury high-rises that geyser Bowery. With its white lacquer cabinetry, on-site housecleaning service, and hookups for smart technology, the place has all the charm of an airport hotel, making its fanciful décor all the odder. There are colorful kilims on the synthetic wood floors and a gallery of woven baskets on a wall without crown molding. If you're going to live in a space that didn't exist before the Obama administration, go to Mitchell Gold + Bob Williams and buy silver Greek key pillows and an acrylic coffee table and really *embrace* it. Instead, it's like she's taken a Renaissance painting from the Met and hung it in a gallery at the MoMA. She doesn't even really seem to like her dogs. Brett once said she adopts them for Instagram likes, which was very funny, sadly. I hate how infrequently I laugh now that Brett is no longer around.

Lauren is barefoot in the kitchen, pouring a glass of wine, which turns out to be for me. A year ago, I would have had a sip, then slunk off to the bathroom to dump it in the sink so that none of the women could give me any grief. A year ago, I was on sixty milligrams of Cymbalta.

"Welcome back from your book tour!" she greets me. "We have so much to tell you. Oh!" she says, looking down at my shoes. "I'm wearing the same Chanel espadrilles! Well. I was. *Somebody*"—she sticks her tongue out at Jen and I notice instantly that it's white—"told me to leave them at the door."

"Oh," I say, looking to Jen. "I can do that if you want." It's a weak offer. I really don't feel like unlacing the ankle straps.

"When you can stop yourself at two glasses of wine and I don't have to worry about you stepping on my dogs, you can leave your shoes on too," Jen ripostes, setting me at ease instantly. Still maintaining a healthy sense of deference, even after seeing Brett at the all-cast prod meeting. Around these parts, alliances have the life span of mayflies.

"I've had *one* glass of wine!" Lauren protests, reaching into her bra and extracting a small plastic baggie, the kind that contains an extra button for a new coat. She peels the seal apart and slips a finger inside, which explains the white tongue. "Coke math."

I take my wine and slide into a cantilevered chair with brown leather thatching before Lauren can ask me if I want any and, when I demur like I always do, pout and say I'm *no fun*. I was nervous to come here—it's like *Animal House* behind the scenes, and the other women have always ragged on me for my half-finished wine spritzers. I'm uptight, a control freak. I need to let loose, learn *to hang*, whatever that means. What they don't understand is that addiction runs in my blood, and that I pay a steep price for partying. They get hangovers; I get suicidal.

"Is this a celebration?" I ask, bringing my glass of wine to my lips cautiously. How much of it I'll drink depends on the answer.

"*I* think so," Lauren says, joining me in the sitting area, mere steps from the kitchen. On *House Hunters*, everyone is hot for open concept. In New York, there is no other choice.

Lauren tucks into the fold of the green velvet couch, one elbow propped on the back to keep her glass of wine level with her lips at all times. She's wearing red striped track pants and a white cashmere wife beater, a diamond "L" in one ear the length of a crayon. She looks absurd, and yet she is routinely lauded for her *bold* sense of style while the Internet makes fun of my anchorwoman clothes. *Why does Stephanie Simmons always dress like Kate Middleton visiting a children's cancer hospital?* the *New York* magazine recapper memorably asked. I have spoken to my stylist about edging up my look this season, and I suppose it's a positive sign Lauren and I are wearing the same pair of shoes.

Jen sets a cheeseboard on the coffee table, though calling it a cheeseboard is an offense to Brie. "Mushroom and olive pâté," Jen says, gesturing to a mealy brown lump surrounded by birdseed shards that I suppose are standing in for Carr's. A few years ago, Jen kept a food diary for Vogue.com, chronicling a day in the life of her wackadoodle diet. It was all bee pollen shakes and plant dust lattes until 3:00 P.M., at which point she indulged in a handful of activated walnuts. The thing went mega-viral, and among the five hundred and seventy-nine comments the piece elicited is the first-ever sighting of Jen's nickname, "the Green Menace." Though it was Brett who made it stick.

"And we *are* celebrating, by the way," Jen says, taking a seat without taking any food. "Because that little piggy will not be going to Morocco." She smirks and twists the cap on her Brill juice. Jen names her juices and powders and potions for characteristics the customer is looking to enhance. A former Saluté assistant once told me—under promise of Prada—that she glimpsed a search on

Urban Dictionary for the word "brill" on Jesse's computer screen. Brill: British slang for brilliant, American equivalent of "cool." In my opinion, Jesse has no business sporting a faux-hawk or those ghastly Stella McCartney creepers when she has to consult Urban Dictionary just to keep up with what the kids are talking about. You have no business treating the cast who made your show a hit like members of Menudo, putting us out to pasture at the ripe old age of thirty-four. That is decidedly un-*brill*.

Jen tips her head back and brings the juice to her lips. The sleeves of her dress gape open, like a wizard's cape, a long oval through which one of her breasts is clearly visible. The bohemian of the Bowery has very definitely gotten a boob job. The thought comes before I can reason with it: *I can't wait to tell Brett about this*. We used to drop nuggets of gossip about the other women at the other's feet, like cats with rodent corpses. I feel a pang of sadness for what was, but it perishes almost immediately. "Tell me everything," I nearly pant.

"Let's start with the sister." Lauren widens her eyes, blinks, and widens them once more.

"Have you met her before?" Jen wants to know.

"A few times," I say, and decide to be generous. "But I don't remember her being that bad." One of the great things about where I currently sit is that I can be generous and still experience the cathartic release of disparaging my opponents, because everyone down below is willing to do it for me.

"Okay," Lauren says, with a small, seated jump. "You know those Stuart Weitzman nudist shoes that everyone was wearing two years ago?"

"Except me," Jen says with a self-congratulatory laugh. "I'm too much of a hippie to be able to walk in those things."

Not too much of a hippie for implants.

"Well, the sister couldn't walk in them either. It looked like the first time she was wearing heels. And I'm pretty sure they were the Steve Madden knockoffs," Lauren says with a shudder. "In *patent* leather."

"Don't forget the off-the-shoulder top," Jen says.

Lauren turns to me. "She's first in line at Starbucks on pumpkin spice latte day, okay?"

I nod: *Say no more*. "And what, was the Big Chill wearing a seven-hundred-dollar tracksuit?" I ask. Not long after "the Green Menace" entered the *Digger* lexicon, a Jen supporter on Twitter (who we all agree was Jen in handle disguise) clapped back with a nickname of Miltonian perfection for Brett: "the Big Chill," referring to both her avaricious figure and her seemingly endless capacity for chill. Brett loves to brag that she's too lazy for fashion. That she has loftier things on her mind than *fashion*. That she is too broke for *fashion*. Such statements may have been true at one time. But I was twenty-three with a forehead free of injectibles once too, and you don't see me going around and shoving that expired bio into people's faces.

"*Brett*." Jen says her name with a scoff. "Brett was forty minutes late—"

"Oh, come on," Lauren chides. "Like *twenty*."

"It was ten-oh-*six* when she walked in!" Jen guffaws.

"She's such a hypocrite," I say, remembering how Brett could never let it go that I was late *twice* during season one, and only because the snotty makeup artist didn't stock a foundation darker than *Honey* in his dopp kit and I had to redo my face myself. Everyone thinks I'm so high maintenance because I've hired my own glam squad, but I'd like to see how they'd respond to production teaming them with a car mechanic for hair and makeup. That's how ill equipped their guy was to deal with a brown woman's face.

"In all fairness, she did have some kind of issue with her booking system," Lauren says. Pecan jumps onto the couch next to her and Lauren leans down to pet her, but before she can, Jen punts her off the couch with the heel of her hand.

"No jumping. On the. *Minotti couch*!" Jen booms. Suddenly there is a spray bottle in her hand, and she's vaporizing the dog into the kitchen. Lauren raises her eyebrows at me in silent consternation while Jen fights to affix a baby gate between the wall and the island, imprisoning a yapping Pecan. Cashew has retreated beneath the coffee table and folded herself into a small, trembling nub, but she is guilty by association. Jen digs her out from underneath the table by her elbows and tosses her over the gate with Pecan. She lands on her back with a yelp. Almond barks in solidarity.

"Shut up, Almond!" Jen squirts him in the face, effectively silencing him, so she squirts him a few more times for good measure.

"The booking system crashing was such an obvious sham," Jen says, resuming the conversation as though she didn't just skip a beat to actively terrorize three defenseless rescues. "She only said that to make everyone think SPOKE is *so* in demand."

Lauren and I are speechless a moment. I check over my shoulder to make sure Cashew is still breathing. Lauren clears her throat. "Well," she says. "She was in her spandex still."

"Why is she always in spandex?" Jen groans. "It's probably why her sister is so skinny. How could you *eat* looking at all that dimply flesh?" She blanches.

"Whoa." I laugh, though I'm thrilled to have Jen around to say it. I'm tired of having to pretend like Brett is some sort of war hero for having thighs that touch. Like she's a better feminist than the rest of us just because she's willing to expose the most unsightly parts of her body in a crop top. Though I suppose that's my contest to lose. Don't ever call me a feminist.

"Her sister is a smoke." Lauren holds another white finger to her nostril and sniffs. "In that trashy, *Barstool Sports* kind of way."

I've heard enough about Brett's hot, trashy sister. "How did the conversation about Morocco go?"

Jen and Lauren exchange toothsome smiles.

"God, I wish you could have been there," Jen says. "She was *insufferable*, bragging about her investors and how they were going to expense the entire trip."

"Jen was like"—Lauren makes moon eyes and her voice turns buttery—"it sounds like Morocco will be a really powerful moment,

Brett. I wish I could be there for it." She cackles. "Brett's *face* when she realized she was no longer *the darling one*. It really was priceless."

"Did Lisa say anything to either of you afterward?" I ask.

Jen and Lauren look at each other, then at me to shake their heads *no*.

"Why?" Jen asks.

I swirl the wine in my glass, surprised to realize there is not much left to swirl. "When I met with Lisa and told her why I couldn't make Morocco work, she straight-out asked me if we had made a pact not to film with Brett."

"Did she not buy your reason or something?" Jen picks at a cuticle. Why do women affect fascination with their nails when they are trying to appear as though they are not bothered by something that bothers them?

The space between my vertebrae elongates, ever so slightly. "Why wouldn't she buy my reason?"

"I mean . . ." Jen glances at Lauren, then back at me. "Are you really trying to get pregnant?"

I don't like this suggestion that it's not believable that Vince and I would want a baby. I know who my husband is, but I work hard to make sure no one else does. "I don't know how I'll feel in a few years."

"So you're not actually trying . . ." Jen trails off. This is an awkward conversation to have with someone who's not really my friend.

"Soon," I fib, which is what I've been promising Vince for the last year too.

The seam of Jen's nail reddens, and she sticks her finger in her mouth, sucking. Interesting. I had always assumed that Jen, like Brett and me, felt no stirring for motherhood. It's clear Lauren does, but that she has chosen the show over assembling the traditional family unit for now. At least Lauren has that goofy way about her. I could see her enjoying the mindless task of entertaining a cranially challenged being. But Jen is so aloof, so easily agitated, what part of having a child even appeals to her?

I can tell you what does not appeal to me. The very idea of motherhood feels like a hangman's noose around my neck. Just another set of hands, tugging at my hemline, a tinier voice hawing, *But what about me?* A baby is an emotional burden and I am emotionally burdened enough. I spent my childhood in service of my mother's anxiety, of pretending like it was unremarkable to be one of three black students in my graduating class. I've spent my marriage emotionally and financially supporting my husband's lazy ambitions to become the next Ryan Gosling. I've spent my life overprepared, overdressed, mostly sober, and voluntarily undersexed, because one phone call from an overzealous member of the neighborhood watch and I'm being dragged away in handcuffs from a bimmer that couldn't possibly be mine.

"Did Lisa talk to you about the SADIE party?" Lauren asks, pivoting the conversation for Jen's sake. Such a good hire, that Lauren.

I nod. At the start of every season, we need an event that brings all the *Diggers* together. Lauren has rented out the penthouse at the Greenwich Hotel to celebrate the launch of SADIEq, a version of her dating app that translates the experience for the queer community. The theme is slumber-party sexy. Oh boy, do *Diggers* love a theme.

"I think it's smart," I say.

"It *is* smart." Lauren grins wider. "I spent an arm and a leg on research that shows that in relationships between women, there isn't always one clear aggressor in the initial courting stages. Women are much more egalitarian in their approach to dating, and so the thing that sets SADIEq apart from SADIE is that we get everyone to meet offline."

I nod, pretending like that's what I meant, that her new initiative is the thing that is smart. "That *is* really smart. It's also smart that the first group event is your event. If it were my event or Jen's event and Brett wasn't invited, everyone would call us petty. But because it's you, our Switzerland, it sends a very clear message that the issue is Brett, not us."

Lauren rolls her diamond initial between her thumb and index finger, frowning. "Yeah, but I want to make it clear that the reason I didn't invite her is because she's the one who sent the video of me to Page Six. I don't want to look like I'm doing Jen's bidding. Or yours. I want everyone to know *I* have my own issues with her." We all have our *things* that get us dragged on Twitter. Lauren's is that she's the show's most malleable player. You can't so easily manipulate the rest of us. It would be like trying to crack a brick wall with another brick wall. We're strong, yet never stronger than each other.

"We have no doubt you will make it clear, Laur," Jen says, with a knowing snort. *My little pit bull,* Lisa calls Lauren with genuine affection. And truly, she's been trained to go for the throat. Don't be fooled by the lovable floozy act—when Lauren is told to sink her teeth into something, she holds on until she can no longer detect a pulse.

"Did anything come up about compensation?" I ask, knowing that if it had, it would have been the first thing discussed. I'm just looking to gripe that Brett was in the position to ask for more money and she took it.

"She had a Chloe bag," Lauren reports.

"I heard she negotiated low six figures," Jen adds.

I clutch my wineglass tighter. "Per *episode*?"

Jen snorts. "For the season. I would storm the streets if they were paying her that much per episode. It's not that much money, once taxes are taken out." She shrugs, trying not to appear bothered, but we are all bothered. I keep saying it's not about the money, it's about the principle, but I am starting to realize it is very much about the money. Five thousand dollars for 120 days of labor is not just criminal, it's despicable when pay parity is one of your major talking points on the morning talk shows.

"Did you see Jesse on *GMA* last week?" I ask.

"The one where she was talking about the second shift and all the emotional labor women take on for free?" Jen's eyes sail into the back of her head.

In perfect, unplanned harmony, all three of us repeat Jesse's hollow motto at the same time, "Women need to get their money."

We erupt into laughter, and I am surprised—surprised and pleased—to feel authentic warmth for these women. I could never disparage Jesse around Brett when we were friends, not when Jesse's doublespeak applied to everyone but her.

The dogs start to bark, and a key turns in the lock. Yvette stumbles through the door, front-loaded with two bags of groceries.

She steps on her right heel with her left toe, sliding one foot out of her shoe. Yvette Greenberg has to take off her shoes to enter Jen's apartment and I don't. Put that on my tombstone.

"Mom!" Jen cries, rushing over to help. Lauren and I are right behind her.

"I'm not an invalid!" Yvette pivots her body, cradling the shopping bags and showing us her back. Her shirt is split between her shoulder blades with a slash of sweat. "I can handle it. Go back to your wine. It *is* lunchtime."

"Would you like a glass, Miss Greenberg?" Lauren offers.

"I'm going from here to exercise, otherwise I would say yes."

Jen's face darkens. The only organized exercise Yvette partakes in is SPOKE.

"I thought you were coming tomorrow," Jen hisses, shadowing her mother as she steps over the baby gate in the kitchen.

"No," Yvette says, setting the bags on the island; Pecan and Cashew spring up around her knees. "I'm going out east tomorrow."

"But the cleaners came today."

Yvette groans, remembering something. "The open house."

"Yes. The open house. On Saturday. I told you *five times*, Yvette," Jen snaps, with a scathing intensity that sends Lauren and me searching for our phones, averting our eyes out of respect for Yvette. Because how *humiliating*, for your daughter to speak to you like that in front of her friends who grew up idolizing you. How *humiliating*, that this über-feminist icon has found herself in a place where she has no other recourse but to take it. Yvette is broke, running Jen's errands for pocket change now that commencement speeches at Sarah Lawrence don't pay like they used to.

Once Yvette had the Amagansett house as a cushion. But legally, Jen owns it. Jen's father, whom Yvette never saw reason to marry, left it in Jen's name when he died twenty years ago. Jen spent the entire winter overseeing an expensive and exhausting remodel. Last month, to Yvette's absolute devastation, Jen put the house on the market for 3.1 mil. I'm sure Brett has a less forgiving narrative for why Jen chose to sell her childhood home, but I have a sense that Jen will make sure her mother sees some of the money from the sale.

Yvette takes a long, hard look at her daughter. Pecan yaps, and she drops to her knees. "Hi, sweet girls. Yes," she coos, as they lap at her face. "Hello. Hello."

"You're giving them positive reinforcement," Jen complains, glowering over her.

"For being adorable?" Yvette laughs.

"They were jumping on the furniture."

Yvette stands with a sigh, brushing dog hair from her slacks. "Slacks" is the exact right word to use to describe Yvette's clothing. She dresses like Mary Tyler Moore at a march in the seventies, right down to the red, round glasses, lest we forget who she is and what she was up against back then. She has done a lot of good, I will give her that, but I find Yvette's belief system laughably shortsighted. Specifically this idea that we will succeed as women once we start to celebrate our differences, instead of pretending they aren't there. How convenient for her to say, this attractive Jewish woman born and raised on the Upper West Side and schooled at Barnard. What differences did she ever have to *celebrate*?

Not to mention, I think it's cruel that Yvette has taken to Brett so garishly, going so far as to offer to adopt her in season two. Yvette and Jen have always had a strained relationship. When I was Brett's friend I heard it from Yvette's side, which is that her desperate attempts to connect with her daughter seem to only push her further away. Now that I've gotten to know Jen, I see it differently. Yvette is woefully disappointed in how Jen has chosen to make a living, "preying" on women's body insecurities under the cover of blended-kale wellness. But here Jen is, a homeowner in Manhattan, a successful flipper in the Hamptons, a bicoastal business owner, all by her thirtieth birthday. There is much for Yvette to be proud of, but Yvette doesn't want to be proud. She wants Jen in her likeness. How dare she tell women to celebrate our *differences* when she can't even accept her own daughter for who she is.

"I'll come out Sunday." Yvette's voice is barbed. "So I'm not in your way." She reaches for the grocery bags with an impish smile. "Would you like me to unpack these for you as well, dear?"

Jen slaps a hand around her mother's wrist, stopping her. "How much do I owe you?"

"One thirty. It would have been ninety if you'd let me go to Gristedes but . . ." Yvette lets that hang, stepping over the dog gate and joining us in the sitting area. "Did I interrupt the powwow?" she asks, reaching for a vegan cracker. She takes a small, tentative bite and cries *Oh!* as the whole thing crumbles in her hand.

"We were just talking about this year's trip, Miss Greenberg," Lauren says, politely, hoping that this time she will be invited to call her Yvette, *dear*, please.

"I'm sorry to hear Morocco isn't going to work out," Yvette says, and Lauren dims, ever so slightly.

"It's not like Brett can't go just because we can't go," Jen says, reappearing to shove a fist of cash into her mother's pocket. "She wouldn't even have to go alone," she adds, her voice pitching with the risibility of it all. "She's got her sister and her niece to ride her coattails."

Yvette shakes her head, clearly disapproving of Jen's tone. "I think you should give Brett a chance. She's got a lot to celebrate this season and I know it hurts her not to be able to share that with her friends."

"No more than any of us!" Jen spits.

"Well . . ." Yvette presses her lips together, pained. "Maybe. I don't know." She fans her hand in front of her face, still sweating. "It's not my place to say."

We all look at each other, thrumming with curiosity. What is not Yvette's place to say? But we can't bring ourselves to ask. Asking implies that we care. Instinctively, I check my nails.

Yvette rests an elbow on the back of the couch. "Did you girls meet Brett's sister yet?"

"Kelly was at the prod meeting," Lauren says. She notices with a delighted little start that my wineglass is empty. Before she can get up to grab the wine bottle in the kitchen, Jen is behind me, topping me off.

"Do you think she will make a nice addition to the group?" Yvette asks.

"She's a mom," Lauren says, in lieu of *no*.

"I'm a mom," Yvette says. "So don't let Jesse tell you it's unfeminist to have children. You're all about that age where you need to start thinking about what you want to do."

There is a chorus of soft lies about our ages: thirty, twenty-nine, thirty-two and a half.

Yvette sighs, pinching the fabric beneath her arms and shaking it, trying to air it dry. "In any case. I hope you will be welcoming to this new woman. I know you think it's more interesting when you give each other a hard time, but I promise you are all interesting enough on your own."

Jen throws her head back and squeezes her eyes shut in blinding exasperation, and I can't say I blame her. Yvette likes to act like she left the show on principle, when what really happened is that she threatened to walk if they didn't give her more money, and Jesse called her bluff. I don't know why Yvette pretends like this didn't happen. Here she is, the ne plus ultra figure of gender equality, and she would rather the world knows she values her integrity over her wallet. Integrity is just the rock you hit your head on when you lose your fingerhold on power. The last thing the world needs is one more woman with principles. What we need is women with money. Women with money have flexibility, and nothing is more dangerous than a woman who can bend any way she wants.

Jen groans. "We welcomed her, Yvette."

Yvette turns to face Jen. "So you wrote her back?"

The question gives me whiplash. "Wrote who back?"

Yvette replies, over Jen's protestations that she not, "Brett's sister reached out to Jen and asked her to tea. She told her that she admires the way she's *scaled her product*"—Yvette throws a look to her daughter—"did I say that right, dear?"

Jen rolls her eyes, but she nods.

"You're not going, are you?" I set my wine on the table. I had been enjoying the taste up until now.

"Why wouldn't she go?" Yvette asks me, in the gentle, infuriating tone of a therapist prodding you to reexamine a preconceived notion that is patently false.

I squeeze my shoulder blades tighter together. The *hypocrisy* of this woman. "Because," I say, very slowly, as though Yvette *is* an invalid who may have trouble following, "Jen and Brett don't get along, and it would probably be very hurtful to Brett if Jen went out of her way to befriend her sister."

Yvette's posture improves as well. Appallingly, she says, "I very much doubt it. With the contributions Brett strives to make in this world, she doesn't have the bandwidth for such petty grievances."

Lauren pops a cracker in her mouth, watching the two of us anime-eyed.

"I told her I couldn't go," Jen says, slamming a cabinet door shut in the kitchen, startling us out of our standoff.

Yvette gives me a smile that says she hopes I'm happy (oh, I am), before rolling back the sleeve of her linen button-down. Jen has inherited her mother's love of linen. "Ah!" she exclaims. "I've got to get going if I want to make the twelve-thirty class." She heads to the door and plops down on the cane-backed settee while she stuffs her feet into her shoes.

"Be nice, girls." She stands, pressing her palms together, like it will require divine intervention for such a miracle to happen. "The whole world is watching."

Yvette really took the air out of our sails, and so we disband not long after she leaves. It's three quarters of a mile to the Canal Street station, the city a humid, gloomy fishbowl, but I decide to walk it anyway rather than get an UberBLACK, my usual move. My mood is not usual. I have the feeling of being both drowsy and frenetic, of yearning for and dreading the next season, all compounded by the email that arrived in my inbox while I was at Jen's. I read and reread the message from the private investigator on my walk. I don't realize that I'm covered in a film of sweat until I descend the stairs to the subway, swipe my MetroCard, and walk past three silent Christian missionaries who do nothing to try to convert me.

John Gowan from Spy Eye Inq. has responded to my latest panicked missive, assuring me that my mother's funeral was at St. Matthews, as I reported it in the book, and not at St. Mark's, as the friend of my grandmother's claimed at my event in Chicago. I look up from my phone sharply—the tunnel is coughing hot air in my face. I step over the yellow line and strain to see if that's the downwind from the express or the local. You always feel it coming before you see it.

The ground burbles beneath my feet, and a cast of headlights sends tourists scattering back, unlike the inured city roaches that hold their ground. I stay where I am too, like I always do when I rarely ride the subway, feeling one millionth of the train's impact as it cannons into the station. It's a blow at first, your hair sucked straight off your head, your dress, if you're wearing one, flying up to reveal your underwear, but once you get past the initial confrontation you find it's more of a pull, an invitation. Something you could almost imagine accepting.

Huh. For the first time in a long time, I might be a little bit drunk.

CHAPTER 7

Brett

How do you feel about your sister taking Jen Greenberg on a girl date?

Lisa's text stops me bone-cold. I read it again with a flu-like shiver. *Taking* implies that this *girl date* with Jen has already occurred. I was with Kelly yesterday, and I'm due to meet her at our warehouse on Long Island for our quarterly advisory board meeting in one hour. Was she planning on telling me?

"Please," Arch says, disappearing behind the door of the refrigerator, "no phones this morning. We promised." She reappears with a container of milk. Real milk. Milk that will grow a third arm out of your forehead, with hormones and fat and BPA leached from the plastic jug Arch got at the corner deli for $2.99, along with a loaf of Pepperidge Farm bread and some precut cantaloupe. Cantaloupe! She might as well eat jelly beans for breakfast. You don't understand; women like Arch are an endangered species in a city where a packet of powder and nut milk passes as a big breakfast on a *Grub Street* food diary. It's one reason I keep holding on.

My phone buzzes with another text from Lisa. *Jen invited her to Lauren's sexy slumber party party*

Then another. *See if Kelly can swing an invite for you lollololol*

I'm actually being serious BRETT

Need to get you in the same room with the others

No one wants to watch you peddling a stationary bike by yourself all fucking season long. BORING.

NOT EVEN JESSE

I raise a thumb to respond, but Arch plucks my phone out of my hand.

"Plates," she orders lovingly, when I start to protest, "to the left of the stove."

It's been nine days since Kelly and Layla moved into my old apartment downtown and I moved into Arch's one-bedroom on the Upper West Side, and, as Arch reminded me last night, nine days since we've had sex. *The place is a mess. My shit is everywhere. I'm stressed about Morocco.* (Don't think I'm giving up that easily.) Every night, we are on StreetEasy, searching for two-bedrooms in an elevator building by Arch's office on the west side, between $6,500K and $7,500K a month. I've raised $23.4 million in capital, and I still can't afford to buy in this town.

I set the plates on the counter and Arch drops a piece of toast on each, sucking a finger that's gotten scalded. We look at breakfast and then at each other with wrinkled noses. The toast is the color of Jen Greenberg's heart. Black, in case that wasn't clear.

"I have an hour before I have to reunite an incarcerated father with his newborn baby for the first time," Arch says.

"I have fifty-five minutes before I test-drive an electronic bike that will help twelve-year-old girls outrun rapists." This is our favorite game. Who will do more for the state of humanity today?

Arch slams a jar of Smucker's on the countertop with stoic resolve. "Charbroiled carbs it is then. Breakfast of champions."

We carry our plates over to the couch and settle in. Arch unfolds her disproportionately long legs—her thighs are normal, but her shin bones belong in the Museum of Natural History—and props her feet in my lap. Arch has skinny, knobby toes, like crab legs without any meat, and her nails are the same shade of red as the SPOKE logo. This was done to woo me, but it managed the opposite effect.

You're too much for me, I thought, guiltily, when she came home with the tissue still between her toes.

"Did you know Kelly and Jen Greenberg hung out?" I ask Arch.

Arch flicks a crumb off her top lip with the inside of a knuckle, unaware that she has left dark grit in the corners of her mouth. "Are you asking me or telling me?"

"Asking." Arch and Kelly are friends, which should make me happy. That the person you love meshes well with your family is all most people hope for in life. Instead, it makes me nervous, paranoid even. *What did you talk about?* I ask, my tone light, my heart racing, whenever Arch comes home from an outing with Kelly. Maybe I'm afraid of these two pairing off against me, the way Layla and I sometimes do to Kelly. Maybe I'm afraid that if Arch spends enough time with Kelly, she'll realize how little of an intellectual connection we actually have. Maybe. Maybe.

"I would have told you if I knew that," Arch says, to my relief. Now I get to just complain.

"How fucked-up is that?" I ask.

Arch mounts her long hair on top of her head, a ponytail holder in her teeth. I notice our age difference when she puts her hair up. Nine years. It's nothing sometimes, and then it's everything. "She's trying to get to know her new colleague at work," she says, the black elastic in her mouth bobbing. "She knows you don't like Jen, and she probably felt funny telling you about it." Arch lifts a shoulder, failing to see the criminal activity. "Give her a break, Brett. She feels like an outlier. She just wants to fit in."

"Well, she went and got herself invited to Lauren's party. She's fitting in *fine*." The group events are where it all goes down—the drama, the tears, the reconciliations. You are dead in the water if you don't attend the group events. Lisa is a monster but Lisa is right. No one wants to watch me pedal a stationary bike by myself all season long. NOT EVEN JESSE. A dizzying premonition suddenly kicks me in the head: My sister is in the opening credits for next season, but not me. *I'm raising the next generation of* Goal Diggers would probably be her tagline. I set my burned toast on the coffee table after just one bite.

Arch pokes my thigh with her bony toe. "Hey. You're going out to Yvette's to make peace with Jen today. Maybe she'll invite you once you smooth things over."

After we test-drive the bikes for the advisory board members, I'm headed out to Yvette's. There, butthole vehemently clenched, I will extend an olive branch to the Green Menace. Olives are vegan, right?

Arch checks the time on the cable display box. "You want to shower first?"

"You can," I say, removing her feet from my lap and going in search of my phone in the kitchen. It quickly becomes apparent that Arch has hidden it. I drill my fists into my hips and Arch laughs.

"I promise to tell you where it is after you shower."

In the bathroom, I turn on the water and plunk down on the toilet while it does the slow work of warming, unsure of what to do with my hands without a screen to manhandle. I flush and step under the spray, even though it's the temperature of forgotten tea. I wouldn't put it past Arch to try to surprise me in here, and I am so not in the mood.

I lather my hair with conditioner—the secret to my great hair is that I hardly ever wash it—and reach for my razor. Something small and shiny pings the tile floor, and I go very still, feeling each of the showerhead's individual strikes. With my big toe, I nudge the thing Arch sent me in here to find, as though afraid it may produce fangs and bite. Compared to my Standing Sisters ring, Arch's choice is thicker, sturdier, something my father would have worn. I realize Arch doesn't know what I want at all—this dyke would have welcomed a diamond. The sadness feels like a paper cut. Quick, non–life threatening, brutal.

I spin the faucet left without shaving. If I shave Arch will know I found the ring without . . . what? Shrieking? Crying? *Instagramming?* Maybe she thought she was going to come in here, pull her tank top over her head, and finally get some use out of this spa shower the size of a smart car . . . I shut off the water and practically staple my towel to my body.

"B?" Arch calls when she hears the door to the bathroom open.

"One second!" I call back, hurrying into the bedroom. I open my underwear drawer and rummage around inside.

Arch says something else, but I can't make it out.

"One second!" I repeat. My knuckles bump against the velvet box.

In the living room, Arch is on her knees on the couch, looking like a meerkat surveying her surroundings for predators, right down to the dark, fearful eyes. My skin is warm from the shower and cold with sweat, thundering with nerves.

"What are you doing?" Arch asks, nervously, when she notices my arm behind my back.

I inhale through my nose and exhale through my mouth, just like we remind riders to do in class. *Let it go. Whatever you're holding on to that's holding you back, let it go*. I present my hand for Arch. "I thought you would never ask. So I was going to."

Arch gasps when she sees the diamond eternity band, purchased last week from 1stdibs after I sent Yvette the link and she wrote back with her approval. *It's lovely. So SO happy for you, darling one.*

Arch jumps off the couch and makes her way over to me. She brushes my wet hair away from my face and lowers her lips to mine. Dread coils around my ribs when I close my eyes and return her kiss, when I think about how thin Stephanie's smile will be when she hears about this.

I am trying to focus on what our head engineer is saying, but Kelly has ripped off Lauren's crown braid from the other day and her single white femaleness is distracting. When we first walked in, Sharon Sonhorn, who Kelly has flown in from Alabama—*business class*—exclaimed in that accent so honeyed and Southern it sounds completely put on, "How precious are *you*?!"

Our advisory board is eight members strong, five men and three women, ranging in age from thirty-five to seventy-two. They live in New York, Texas, Alabama, Boston, Los Angeles, and London. We have one black person, one Asian person, and one gay person. Two have zero experience in the wellness industry and three have none in the B-corp world. Kelly put the whole thing together based on an article she read on Forbes.com that said advisory boards should represent diversity in its truest sense. You don't want to be paying a bunch of *yes* men and women for their time. You want people who challenge you, who offer a different perspective, who are constantly asking you to reexamine your vision. *This is money well spent,* she's always reminding me, when I see how much it costs to fly someone into New York business class just to hear that my ideas suck.

"Listen," Seth, my head engineer, says, flicking a switch on the e-bike. He had the model covered in a beige tarp when the board first walked in, allowing him the opportunity to rip it off as though we were at a magic show. He even said *ta-da!* Despite how mad I am at Kelly—for meeting up with Jen behind my back, for getting herself invited to Lauren's party, for that fucking braid—we exchanged a look. Seth is the nicest and most annoying person we know.

All kidding aside, my new bike does deserve an unveiling, a middle-aged man's dorky *ta-da! Bloody gorgeous,* our London guy said. *I'd quite like one for myself.* And everyone had laughed, because picturing stiff John Tellmun riding around Notting Hill Gate on this glossy red cruiser with the blush leather seat and plump pink handlebars is pure comedy gold.

"I don't hear anything," Layla says, her ear aimed at the ground. Girls as young as nine will be riding these bikes, so Kelly thought it would be a nice touch for the board to see that a twelve-year-old can easily and safely operate the machinery.

Seth points his finger at Layla, *ding-ding-ding*ing. "The little lady wins a 2016 Toyota Camry!" Layla looks confused, and Seth clears his throat, embarrassed the joke didn't land. "The electronic models sound like they are off even when they're on, so always make sure that you check the switch before you get on, okay, Layla?"

Kelly reaches up to tighten the chinstrap on Layla's helmet. Layla shot past me this year, which is not anything to write home about, but she's almost the same height as Kelly, who has a few inches on me. I don't remember Fad being especially tall, but maybe he had tall parents, tall sisters. We will never know.

"*Mom*," Layla groans, but she lifts her chin and lets Kelly fuss with the strap.

Sharon makes a sound that expresses how precious she thinks this is: Kelly's braid, Kelly's overprotectiveness, Layla's indulging of Kelly's overprotectiveness, all of it. Like Kelly, Sharon has a preteen daughter. Unlike Kelly, Sharon is practically fifty.

Layla swings her leg over the pink seat.

"Look at those stems," Sharon says, lowly, to Kelly, and Kelly beams. "And *that skin*. Like a latte. She could be in *Vogue*."

Kelly's smile fails like an old engine. "Not too fast!" she warns Layla.

"It goes, like, forty miles an hour." Layla directs her eye roll at me, the only other person in the room who could possibly comprehend the extent of Kelly's lameness.

"You kill someone if you hit them at forty miles an hour," Kelly says, matching Layla's sulky tone to make her point that this is nothing to be flip about.

We watch Layla pedal the SPOKElectric prototype deeper into the warehouse, the bike emitting a mild hum that's amplified by the concrete floors. I could crawl faster.

"Mine would have torn out the door going as fast as she could just to spite me," Sharon says to Kelly. "Top-notch mothering, honey." I used to think it was such a throwaway, whenever someone complimented a woman on her mothering skills. I didn't think it took talent to be a good mother—just don't beat them and take them to the dentist occasionally, and voilà!, you're a good mother. *Loving* them doesn't even take much work. Even the moms who beat their kids love them. Then Kelly had Layla, and I realized just how mistaken I was. Because Kelly's mothering skills were shaky at best that first year with Layla, neglectful at worst.

Do you know my father made two appointments for Kelly to skulk past the four angry men pumping posters of mutilated fetuses into the air at Kelly's behest? I flexed my biceps and spoke like Tony Soprano on our way out the door, *both times*, offering my services as bodyguard. I was trying to get her to laugh. Really, I just didn't know how to appropriately express to Kelly that it wasn't the end of the world. It wasn't the end of the world that she went a little nuts out from under Mom's watchful eye and it wasn't the end of the world that she hadn't had responsible sex and it wasn't the end of the world to undergo a safe, legal medical version of a procedure that has been a part of the human experience for thousands of years in every sort of society imaginable.

I wanted Kelly to laugh, but I also wanted her to *go*. Mom had just died, and although our relationship had been complicated, she was still my mom, and I still loved her. Our lives were in turmoil, and on some level, I believed that if Kelly could just go back to school, graduate, and became a radiologist like our mother had always planned, things would go back to normal too. Normalish. Never mind that normalish wasn't in my best interests, because normalish meant Kelly was the successful one, the pretty one, *the star*. But it was what was comfortable, and we're always drawn to what's comfortable, even when it hurts us deeply.

Kelly would need to face the angry men and their posters in order for things to go back to normalish, only she couldn't get herself through the clinic's door. *This is what I want,* she declared in the parking lot on two separate occasions, her voice an unconvincing whisper. Then Layla came along, and it was like she broke Kelly's legs instead of her vaginal canal. Layla would be wailing for her 2:00 A.M. feeding, sounding like she was being waterboarded, and Kelly would just lie in bed with her eyes closed, pretending to sleep through it. My father and I didn't have much of a choice but to take on those shifts, and so we did, trading off for the first few months. *Kelly needs her rest,* my father said to me. *She needs to recover.* I was never quite sure what he thought she needed to recover from, but it was clear to me that it was the shock of her new life. At first, I was resentful of having to wake up in the middle of my REM cycle every other night. But after a few weeks, I actually started to look forward to having Layla all to myself, our time together unrushed and uninterrupted. Those tiny little fists, flying up over her ears in outrage as I eased the nipple of the bottle into her mouth—*this is what I need?!* Her fingers unfurling, her eyelids drooping, lifting, drooping, lifting to check that I was still there, drooping again as she realized *this, this is what I need.*

They say that first year is critical to the bonding process, and I think it's why Layla and I are as close as we are. Kelly missed some special moments, and she can never get them back, all because she was resting, *recovering*. My sister has always needed someone to hold out her next life for her, like a coat she slips her arms into. Doctor, mother, CEO (in her mind)—these are more titles that have been foisted upon her rather than ones that she has sought out with purpose. My sister's major malfunction is that she is a doer with no vision. I suppose I have the opposite problem.

Millennial journalists are always asking me where the idea for SPOKE came from, a sort of attrition in their voices. I get it. It's hard to care about things that don't impact us personally, and I think that's what the *Bustle* staff really wants to ask but feels they can't—why do I care so much about a group of women I've never met, going through something I have never gone through? How can I be so selfless? Is there something wrong with them that they can't be that selfless?

The truth is that the idea for SPOKE didn't come from a selfless place at all. After my father and I tracked Kelly to Fad's apartment in the Hivernage district, our next stop was the hospital. She *seemed* fine, physically that is, but we just wanted to be sure. I was sitting in the waiting room, paging through a French tabloid, when the door swung open and in walked two sisters, one of them not much older than Layla is now. They spoke to the nurse at the front desk in soft French, and were given a series of forms to fill out. They came and sat down one seat to my right, the older one with the papers in her lap. Together, they pointed at words on the page and argued in a language that I know now was not French or Arabic. After a few minutes, the older sister spoke to me.

"Hello," she said, with a little circle of her hand. It sounded like *Halo*.

I glanced up and found the older sister waving the pencil at me.

"You can help?" she asked, haltingly.

My father leaned into me. "I don't think they can read."

I held out my hands, miming writing, my head cocked at a forty-five-degree angle. The older sister nodded, *Yes, you write it down.* The younger sister stared at her lap, stonily. I moved over one seat.

The forms were written in Arabic, then French, then English. It took fifteen minutes of stilted translation and signage just to get to the part that asked the reason for the visit that day.

"My daughter," the older sister said, and it took me a second to realize they were not, in fact, sisters. "She has go to the well. Three men have hurt her. We have seen doctor so she has not pregnant."

My father mumbled, three seats away, "Dear God."

I glanced at the daughter, who was still staring at her lap, her jaw clenched furiously.

"Rape?" I asked in a whisper. "Do you mean she was raped?"

"We have seen the doctor."

"I'm sorry. You have already seen the doctor?"

The woman nodded, both frantic and frustrated, misunderstanding me the way I misunderstood her. Later, I would learn that the English use of the present perfect tense is confusing for Arabic speakers. Many rely on the present perfect to describe things that have either already happened or have not yet happened. In this case, the girl had already walked to the well for water, had already been raped by three men. Seeing the doctor, preventing pregnancy, that was what needed to happen next.

Kelly didn't have to wait to be seen by the doctor, and all that was wrong with her was gross taste in men. I went up with the mother to deliver the forms to the French nurse, explained the situation in English, as though it would be more harrowing in English, more likely to spur urgent action. But the pair was still sitting there when we left an hour later, Kelly with a clean bill of health (it was too early for her pregnancy test to come back positive). I remember thinking in the taxi ride back to the hotel, *The world everywhere cares more about girls like Kelly than they do girls like that.*

So really, I'm not selfless at all. I've dedicated myself to a cause that feels entirely self-serving: helping girls like me who are not like Kelly. It's time we come first.

Layla makes a U-turn at the wire shelving on the far side of the warehouse. Facing us, she's all helmet and uneasy smile. She twists the handlebars back, speeding up for less than a few yards before Kelly starts squawking.

Layla parks the bike and climbs off to overblown cheers and applause from the board, like she's just qualified for the Olympics. She takes a slow bow and immediately turns the color of Jen's Power juice (beets + carrots + chia) when the applause thickens. "I didn't even max out, Mom," she says, unhooking the helmet and pressing it into Kelly's arms.

Seth shushes us. "Before we get too excited," he says, "I need to show you something."

He mounts the bike and releases the kickstand with his heel, sets his hands on the handlebars, and squeezes. The bike lurches forward violently. "Whoa!" Seth cries like a goober, bearing down on the handlebars, which only propels him faster. He comes to a dramatic stop just a few feet shy of a delivery van, looking back at us with gasping breaths.

"Most e-bikes make a rickety sound when they are at speed," Seth says, making his way back over to us. "But they all have one thing in common. They're silent when they're parked, whether they're on," Seth flicks the switch, "or off."

Kelly glances at me. "Is that a problem?"

"Most definitely," Seth says. "And one that Layla demonstrated perfectly."

"What did I do?" Layla asks, worriedly, going from feeling good about herself to despondent in a preteen second. She picks at a small pimple on her cheek. On our way out here, I listened to her narrate an Instagram story about the makeup products she used to cover up that very pimple. Instead of posting social media content that makes her peers feel as though their lives don't measure up, Layla uses her accounts to reassure girls her age that everything they're going through—the zits, the awkwardness, the malaise—is completely normal. That they are all in this together. She has nearly 30K followers now, and we haven't even started filming yet.

"You didn't do anything wrong," Seth assures her. "It's the design that's the problem. Since the bike sounds like it's off when it's been parked, it's easy for the rider to forget to power it down. The next person who uses it grabs it, intuitively, by the hand grip." Seth demonstrates the basic way everyone grabs the bike by its handlebars. "But because of the twist grip design, unknowingly, what the rider is doing is accelerating the bike—which is dangerous not only for the rider but for anyone who happens to be passing in front of the bike. A child, for instance. Then, because the rider is startled and off balance, the natural reaction is to do this," Seth grips the handlebars tighter, "which only accelerates the speed." Seth widens his stance and folds his arms across his chest. A good glitch makes Seth feel useful.

"Is there a solution to this?" Kelly asks.

Seth circles his workstation, pushes a few gadgets around, and holds up a small black lever. "Right here. This, ladies and gents," he swivels at his waist so that everyone has a fair view, "is called a thumb grip. It attaches to the end of the handlebar, which makes it much harder to accidentally activate."

I say, impatiently, "So attach it."

Seth levels his chin with Kelly. "I need your sister to loosen the purse strings on the direct materials budget in order to do that."

I turn to Kelly, my lips parted in outrage. She's flown six of the eight board members to New York business class, but we don't have the budget to outfit our bikes safely?

"Did you calculate the ROI with the thumb grips?" Sharon asks me.

The warehouse goes very quiet, as though it is the ninth member of the board, also awaiting my answer. It's a brutal few moments. I feel like I'm having one of those stress dreams, a nightmare really, where you're back in school, about to take your midterm final, and you realize with hot-cold-hot nausea you haven't attended a single class all semester. Because I have no fucking idea what the ROI calculation is with the thumb grips.

"It's three to one," Kelly says—bless and fuck her. "That will make costs prohibitive. We'd love to change our promise to riders. But *For every seventeenth ride we deliver a bike to an Imazighen family in need* doesn't have the same ring." Sharon *tsks*.

"I know," Kelly sighs.

"Where else can we hike?" Sharon wonders. "You know, the boot camp I attend charges for towels."

Kelly nods with a vigorous *mmm-hmm*. "Bike shoes. Water bottles. We can find it somewhere, I'm sure."

"Please do," Sharon says. "I wouldn't feel right letting a child around this thing in its current iteration." I notice for the first time that Sharon's neck is a different color than her jaw. It's very unattractive.

"Whatever it costs," I say, matching my sister's firm tone, "we'll make it right."

"Well," Sharon clears her throat, making bemused eye contact with Kelly, "not whatever it costs. That's the point, right?"

I can feel my ears getting hot. I know I should make more of an effort to understand the business side of my business. But every time I've asked Kelly to walk me through the figures and the projections, the accounting and the payroll, I end up cross-eyed, bored, and flushed with frustration. It's hard work to understand, and it's not that I'm afraid of hard work, it's just that I've already done so much hard work, and I don't think I should have to do this on top of it. I'm the one who came up with the totally original idea for SPOKE; I'm the one who won the entrepreneurial contest. I'm the one who landed a spot on the third most popular reality TV show in the highly prized nineteen- to forty-nine-year-old demographic on Tuesday nights. I'm the one who gets called a wide load but refuses to succumb to Whole30. I'm the one who gives hope to at-risk LGBTQ youth. I have done my part.

Sometimes, jokingly, when I can't understand something on the books that Kelly needs me to understand, I will flop onto the nearest couch and bring the back of my hand to my forehead like a Victorian lady with low blood pressure, gasping, *I'm the talent*. But there is a kernel of truth in the performance. I am the talent! Not everyone can be the talent, just like not everyone can balance the books. Except, here is Kelly, her hair in a trendy blogger-girl braid, signed on for the fourth season of my show, able to do what I do and also what I can't. She's the talent too. So where and what does that leave me?

Outside smells like melted dog urine and gasoline. It's the middle of May, but July hot. Kelly asks if we can talk before we get on the road. I'm dropping her and Layla off at the train station to head back into the city and taking Kelly's car to Yvette's house out east.

Now is when she's going to tell me about meeting up with Jen and explain, I think, and ready my anger and resentment and yes, paranoia that I'm about to be eclipsed by Kelly once again.

Instead, Kelly stares at me for a long time, like *I* have something to say to *her*. "What?" I ask, finally.

"You seriously aren't going to tell me?" Kelly shakes her head, her tongue pressed to the top of her lip in a mix of disgust and disappointment.

It can't be the engagement. I asked Arch if she minded if I didn't wear my ring for now. I wanted to break the news to Kelly in my own time, in my own way. I knew she would have a tough time with it. She thought shacking up with Arch after three months was moving too fast.

Besides. Whatever it is she thinks I'm not telling her, what she isn't telling me is worse. She watched Jen express *concern for my organs* in her talking head last year, the patronizing worry in her brow layered over a shot of me taking a SPOKE class in a crop top. *Waist circumference is directly tied to heart disease,* she'd added, her Popsicle stick neck somehow able to balance a head swollen with that much prejudice and misinformation. You know what is directly tied to longevity? The number of friends you have, but you don't see me going around insinuating that Jen will die early because she's an insufferable twat no one wants to be around. Jen has found so many ways to call me fat without actually calling me fat she should win an award. To be clear, it doesn't hurt me to be called fat; fat is not an insult to me. Fat is not who I am, who anybody is. But in Jen's world, fat is an abomination of womanhood, and it hurts to know that someone is *trying* to hurt me by aligning me with the worst thing she thinks a woman can be in our culture, which is anything over a few pounds shy of nonexistence.

"You seriously aren't going to tell me about meeting up with Jen?" I say to Kelly. "And you seriously did that? Behind my back? After everything she's said about me?"

Kelly's bitchy look falters. "How did you know about that?"

"Who knows you did that? Other than Jen, obviously?"

"Rachel," she replies, naming one of the field producers.

My laugh is full of genuine pleasure. After the ROI debacle, it feels so good to be the one who knows what she is talking about again. "Let me give you a little piece of advice, Kel," I say, lowering my voice as I glance into the back seat of the car, where Layla sits with the door open to get some air. I can hear snippets of the Instagram stories that aren't interesting enough for her to watch to completion: half a word, a streak of a song, a few dog barks. "The field producers are like high-end strippers. They're really good at getting you to spill your guts, and they're really good at making you believe they give a shit. But it's Rachel's job to run to Lisa with anything you tell her, and then it's Lisa's job to get everyone else all riled up about it."

Kelly nods, slowly, *flippantly*. When Kelly goes pious on me I am never more sure that I am capable of third-degree murder. I don't want to just wipe that smug look off her face; I want to annihilate it. "See, I figured that's how it works after Lisa texted me to ask how I felt about your engagement."

Layla's head pops out of the back seat. "You're getting married?" she exclaims. Then she squeals, drumming her feet on the ground excitedly. "Can I be a bridesmaid? Please, please, please?"

So she does know. I guess I could have crafted a more strategic response to Lisa's machine-gun spray of texts from earlier. But after Arch and I were done proposing to each other, I couldn't help myself. *How do you feel about your sister taking Jen Greenberg on a girl date?* she had written, and so I had responded: *It feels like not giving an F because I'm engaged!!!!* But the truth is, that's not what it felt like at all. It felt like someone had reached inside my body and turned my stomach upside down, shook all my organs onto the floor, and stomped on my spleen. By the expression on Kelly's face, I know she knows it too.

Like most houses *out east,* the three—no, *four* now!—bedroom modern saltbox looks like a place of worship for a cult. It's where Jen Greenberg was raised, so it would be the kind that spikes the no-artificial-sugars-added punch with arsenic. There is something about the Green Menace that is natural-born scary.

Last winter, Jen's architectural overhaul included knocking down walls, adding a fourth bedroom and a saltwater infinity pool, and outfitting the kitchen in gray-veined Carrara marble, which should have been the second warning shot for Yvette, after Jen's on-air claim that the reno was meant to make the house more comfortable for her mom. The thing about gray-veined Carrara marble is that it may look sexy, it may be *all* the rage on the home décor porn sites, but it's not recommended for people who actually cook in their kitchens because it stains, scratches, and chips like a wet manicure. (Source: Stephanie Simmons. I heard the word "Carrara" and had a craving for ice cream.) You would think Jen Greenberg, kale smoothie millionairess, would opt for quartz countertops—not as dazzling, but much more durable. Only Jen Greenberg never intended to use that kitchen to make her not food into food. Instead, her intention was to fix it up, jack up the market value, and sell it to some HGTV hornball for a cool 3.1 mil.

Jen has the legal right to do with the house as she pleases. Ethically, she should be fined for all she's fucking worth. She's given Yvette no say in the decision to sell even though, for the last twenty-some years, Yvette has paid the property taxes and utilities, taken care of the landscaping and the leaks and the clogs. She's replaced the roof, the kitchen appliances, and the crap furniture with gorgeous gray linen sofas and chairs. She taught Jen to swim in the ocean down the road, she's brined fourteen tofurkeys in the Tic Tac–sized oven, and she's shared gin and tonics on the back porch with Sir Paul McCartney. The house may be Jen's, but the home was always Yvette's. She's absolutely heartsick to lose it.

I park Kelly's car in front of the cheery red "For Sale" sign, by the flowering Japanese maple Yvette planted in honor of her late mother. The driveway is empty. The Greenbergs share an old blue Volvo station wagon, though Jen is "considering" the Tesla.

The sky is more white than gray, the sun illuminating the clouds from behind. It's been raining on and off all morning, and I had to keep the windows up on the drive out here. Kelly's car hasn't had working AC since Obama was elected for his second term and the back of my T-shirt is color-blocked with sweat. My feet slide around in my sneakers as I approach the front door and knock. I wait. Nothing.

I check my phone. 12:47. Yvette said to arrive at 12:30 *on the nose*, which was anal and unlike her, but I figured it was because she wanted me to get there before Jen. She's been out here two days already, trying to enjoy the peace and quiet before the weekend's open house. I wait until my phone says 12:48 to knock again. Still nothing.

I cup my hands around my eyes and press my nose to the panel of windows shouldering the front door. Jesus. The house is now a Tibetan fur fever dream: shag white carpet, shag white side chairs, shag white throw pillows on the blessedly un-shaggy white linen couch. All this distinctively fuzzy décor paired with cold white stone floors. Limestone is what Jen went with, I recall Yvette telling me. It's slippery when wet—which makes perfect sense for a beach house with a pool. *I'm afraid someone's going to crack their head open,* Yvette confided in me.

My sigh fogs the window, and I wipe it clean with my shoulder, searching in my bag for my phone.

"Hello," Yvette says, on the third ring. Her hello is always the same, a velvety *hell-low-ah,* managing to be both unrecognizing and deeply intimate at the same time.

"Hiya," I say. "It's Brett."

There is a pause. "Honey," she says, "everything okay?"

"*Ah,* yeah." I laugh. "Where are you?"

There is another pause. "What do you mean?"

"I mean." I slap away a mosquito on my thigh. I wonder if Stephanie will be avoiding the Hamptons this summer on account of Zika. Seems unlikely. "You told me to come at twelve-thirty." I wait for her to remember but she doesn't. "So . . . I'm here."

"Where?"

"Yvette!" I cry, exasperated. "The house in Amagansett!"

Yvette mumbles something to herself I can't make out. "I thought we said Sunday," she says. I can picture her squinting at the Imagined Desks of Historical Women calendar I gave her last Christmas, Mary Shelley with a glass of white wine next to her pen. "Is it Sunday?"

I suffer a spike of fear as I realize this isn't Yvette being flaky, this is Yvette being in her late sixties and having trouble with her memory. "No, it's Friday," I say, gently. "We said Friday."

"Honey, I am getting so old!" Yvette chuckles. "I come out

tomorrow. Jen was coming this afternoon to show the house to a listing agent. I must have gotten my days screwed up."

I squeeze my eyes shut and exhale hard. I'm stranded in the Hamptons with only the Green Menace to take me in.

"I feel horrible," Yvette says, though she doesn't sound horrible. She sounds like she's in the middle of plucking her eyebrows or some other banal but satisfying activity, like I've interrupted her pleasantly productive afternoon. "Jen should be there soon. Why don't you just wait for her?"

A smattering of raindrops cool my scalp. "It's about to pour."

"I don't mean *outside*. The key is under the rock in the second planter around back. Let yourself in. Make some lunch. Jen had scheduled a FreshDirect delivery for twelve-thirty." In an offhand manner that seems anything but offhand, she asks, "Is it there?"

FreshDirect. I wouldn't take Jen to be so *provincial*. I scan the front patio, spotting faster with raindrops by the second, but I don't see a delivery. "Nothing. No. It's really starting to come down again."

"Hmmm." Yvette sounds concerned. "They might have dropped it off by the back door. Would you check?"

"Yvette, I'm sorry, but I'm not staying. I don't feel comfortable being here without you."

"Would you at least bring the food inside so it doesn't spoil?"

I drop my arm by my side, shutting my eyes and taking a deep, calming breath. I return the phone to my ear and force a smile so that it sounds in my voice. "Sure."

I unlatch the gate and walk parallel to the house. I can see the new pool, its tarp littered with leaves and dead bugs and one lone Solo cup.

"The delivery's back here," I tell her, as I round the corner and spot the cardboard FreshDirect boxes, soggy from the rain, piled two deep next to the double patio doors that have replaced the sliding door with the screen that used to always jump the track. The rain has almost washed away the ink on the note taped to the top box: *two attempts to contact, left unattended per directions.*

"Oh, good!" Yvette says. "Well, help yourself to anything you want—"

"I'll just grab something at Mary's Marvelous on my way out—"

"It's fifteen dollars for a salad there!"

"Good thing I don't eat salad then." I locate the key and fit it into the lock. "I'm going now. I need both hands for this."

"You are a lifesaver!" Yvette says. "*Thank* you. I am *so* sorry about today. But you won't regret this."

"Thanks, Yvette," I say, hanging up and puzzling briefly over her last statement. What won't I regret, exactly?

I hear a car chewing up the pebbled drive and I brace myself, thinking it's Jen, but it continues down the road. Every crevice of my body is wet with sweat and the rest of me is catching up in the rain. I decide that's the only scare I need—I cannot be here when Jen arrives. We might both die of discomfort.

I squat and hoist a box into the crooks of my elbows. I've not taken one step when the waterlogged bottom gives out, like one of those commercials showing what happens to bargain paper towels when tested with too much blue detergent. Jen's groceries spray everywhere: on my shoes and bare legs and the fresh whitewashed oak porch. Mother. Fucker.

I step onto the lawn, wiping my feet on the wet grass like a dog, leaving behind what looks like yellow spittle. *Egg,* I realize, *gross.* It takes me a moment to connect the dots, because unlike Jen, I am not a masochist in a voluntary state of sustained primal hunger to meet the patriarchal-mandated beauty ideal. I eat eggs for breakfast and put cream in my coffee and cheese on my sandwiches and oh my God, bacon. That is a package of uncured bacon, seeping its pink bacony juice onto the new porch. It's like a puzzle overturned on the table: Only when everything is laid out in front of you can you really start putting all the pieces together. Jen's healthy, long hair. Her four-pound weight gain.

I hear another car approach, and I wait, unmoving, as its old engine fusses nearer. There is one short burst of hard rain, like someone has taken a cloud and wrung it out over my head, but I do not seek cover. The car door slams shut and Jen calls out, nervously, hopelessly, "Yvette?" My heart is banging like a gavel; hers must be too. She knows that's my car in the driveway.

I listen to the gate open, to Jen's careful footsteps on the slippery deck. I have to look away when she sees me. I can't bear to see her so vulnerable and exposed. I have *earned* each and every unkind feeling I have toward Jen after the way she's spoken about me to America. I get to feel vindicated by the discovery that the nation's most sanctimonious vegan has been skulking around ordering bacon off the Internet like contraband. It's turkey bacon. But still. She has no right to make that tragic face and make me feel bad, nearly empathetic, for her.

I make an intense project out of cleaning my shoes in the grass and speak casually. "I think it was from the rain. The boxes just fell apart when I picked them up." I'm quick to add, "Yvette told me to bring them inside."

I only look up when I hear Jen fit her key into the lock. She disappears inside, the door latching shut slowly but firmly behind her. For a moment, I think that's it. Jen is just going to stay inside until I leave, maybe even for the rest of her life, so that she never has to deal with the fallout from this. It's not the worst strategy.

But after a few moments, Jen reappears with a beach towel slung over her shoulder and some green plastic trash bags. She offers me the beach towel and shakes open a garbage bag. She picks up each grocery item and examines it for damage, setting it aside or throwing it out, depending. I don't know what else to do other than help.

"It doesn't look it but I think it's still good," I say, holding up a jacked-up wheel of Brie.

Jen holds out her hand, regally, as though I am a huntsman who has brought home the heart of a warring queen. I place the lump of cheese in her palm with a deep curtsy, playing along. I'm uncomfortable, and trying to act like none of this is that big of a deal, which I realize is very much in keeping with my nickname. Jen chucks the ball of Brie into the trash bag, *hard,* without bothering to examine it. Okay then.

"I had amenorrhea," she says, tightly.

"I don't know what—"

"I hadn't had my period in four years." Jen speaks over me without raising her voice. "My hormones were all out of whack. You can't have your hormones out of whack when you're trying to freeze your eggs, so that you can have a baby, which I would like to do, someday. My doctor suggested I try to go pescatarian to see if it would help. It's just *temporary,* while everything stabilizes."

I scan the groceries left on the deck. Not a piece of salmon in sight, but dairy and fatty cuts of animal hind legs for days. I can't help but feel a teeny bit vindicated—*See? Your way is not the healthy way.* "Good for you, Jen," I say. "You aren't a strong woman for denying your hunger. You are a strong woman for standing up to society's expectations of how we are supposed to—"

"Yvette sent you out here?" Jen demands, before I can say *look.*

I lift one shoulder in a vague non-answer, not wanting to betray Yvette, who clearly wanted me to discover Jen's illicit affair with breakfast meats and put her on blast. Jen tightens the strings of the trash bag with a scowl. "She's angrier than I thought that I'm selling. Or maybe she just actually hates me." She hurls a carton of hazelnut coffee creamer into a trash bag and it splatters back at her in retaliation.

"Your mom doesn't hate you, Jen. She hates that you are suffering and depriving yourself for an unjust cause. She hates that you see yourself as a body first and a person second. She just wants you to be—"

"I'll get Lauren to invite you to her party. That won't be hard. Getting Steph to film with you will be the real bitch." Jen's eyes are bright, unblinking. She looks away with a difficult swallow. "I'll do my best." *She's going to cry,* I realize. In fact, I think I mumble *Thanks* so that she doesn't cry. I can't think of anything I'd rather do less than wrap my arms around an emotional Jen Greenberg. I'd come away with thorns, I'm sure.

I know, on paper, that this looks like a bribe, and that bribes are measures only dishonest and despicable people resort to, but it isn't *like* that. (I also know *It isn't like that* is something only dishonest and despicable people say.) But it's *really* not like that! My investors are expecting a three-episode arc in Morocco with gratuitous placement of the e-bikes. I have gladly participated in all the other group trips for all the other women, who are older, more accomplished, and more established than I am. I arrived at the airport on time for Greenberg's trip, with a smile on my fucking face, the morning after she told me *Willpower is a muscle that can be strengthened* when I asked for more bread at dinner. I have shown up for these women. I have *ohh*'d and *ahh*'d over their expensive, rat-free apartments. I have read their four-hundred-page books and drank their chunky juices and downloaded their dating apps when I am in a relationship to help boost membership. I have supported them getting richer, more famous, and more important. Now, I get a little taste of that kind of success myself and they can't stand it. They have banded together to keep the little guy in her place.

So this bribe, which wasn't even my idea, really *really* isn't like that. If anything, it's a course correction. It's what is right. Still, I offer to toss the bag of spoiled food in the Dumpster at the end of Jen's street on my way out. A small act of penance. Because if I'm being really *really* honest with myself, it might be a little bit like that. I might be a little bit despicable. But I'm not ready to be that honest yet.

CHAPTER 8

Kelly: The Interview

Present day

"Jen and Brett reconciled because of you," Jesse says to me in a complimentary way that induces me to reply, almost involuntarily, *Thank you.* The gas fire is pistoling hotly behind us and the lights are searing my corneas. The effect is similar to that of the hot yoga classes that have recently become a part of SPOKE's new suite of services, how the heat allows you to sink more deeply into the poses. Jesse and I are warm now. We are plunged into our story.

"I don't know about you," Jesse goes on, "but I find some comfort in knowing that Brett left this world at peace with all of the women. When we first met Brett and Jen, they were friends, and one of the great joys I found in this season—and there were many, despite how it ended—was watching these two strong women overcome their differences and recommit to supporting each other. It seemed it was important to you to see your sister call a truce with Jen—why was that?"

A truce. Is that what it was? We've been at this for an hour or two now, and my mind feels melted and gooey. I wish someone would open a window, but they've been sealed with the crew's portable blackout curtains. I take a sip of the warm water on the end table between my chair and Jesse's, and I concentrate on the word "truce." No. It hadn't been a truce. It had been a deal. When Brett told me what happened, she had been very careful to phrase it as such—a deal—though Jen convincing the others to film with Brett in exchange for Brett keeping Jen's secret sounded like a bribe to me.

I did not facilitate the reconciliation, but I guess that's the spin production put on it. I can see how my actions would provide them with the raw materials. I did make a play for Jen's friendship, after all. And not just because I admired the way she *scaled her product* (and I did!), but because it was glaringly obvious that Brett didn't want me on the show—her show, is how she thought of it—and I had to do something that made me integral to the drama. Befriending my sister's sworn enemy was the sort of biblical betrayal that secured you a sophomore season.

"I've always admired Jen," I say, which is true. I admired all of them. Brett treated her castmates like old Barbie dolls she was tired of playing with. I was the less fortunate kid jumping up and down to receive her gently used toys for Christmas.

"I wanted to get to know the women on my own merit," I continue. "I went into this experience with an open mind. I didn't want to be influenced by Brett's relationships with the other *Diggers*." This is true too. I did want to stand on my own, separate from my sister, because I didn't feel like I could count on her. That is the hurtful but totally unsurprising truth about my sister. She did not have my back. Slowly, over the years, Brett had co-opted the concept of SPOKE as her own. Even though we were fifty-fifty partners, she used possessive vocabulary around the business—SPOKE was hers, the idea was hers, the seed money was hers.

Brett never let go of the fact that I only invested 2K of my own money into SPOKE when we were first starting out. The suggestion was that I was cheap, or that I didn't believe in the brand. But that's about what to expect from friends and family in the early stages of a startup. You don't go for broke with a new business. It's an inadvisable and rash strategy for anyone, let alone a single mother. Brett would have known that if she had bothered to do any research into what it took to incorporate SPOKE. And hey, at least I could write a check—Brett had squandered her portion of the money our mother left us in her will at a breakneck pace.

In the end, it worked to my advantage that Brett was too focused on the message of SPOKE than the nuts and bolts of building SPOKE. Before I put in my measly 2K, I spent half that on a lawyer to help me draw up a partner agreement that delineated me as her cofounder. I suggested Brett hire her own counsel to read the dense print over before she signed and accepted my check, but she didn't have the resources to do so and moreover, she couldn't be bothered.

My sister is very good at the ideas and selling stage, but there are so many uncreative, unsociable aspects to starting your own company. You have to write a business plan, come up with a mission statement (which I did and which Brett ridiculed mercilessly), secure funding, register your business name, file your papers of incorporation, set up account and tax records. All the unfun stuff. Brett gave me the brush-off whenever I broached anything vaguely resembling an accounting decision with her. She didn't want to hear it when I told her we had to diversify our revenue stream if we wanted to provide Imazighen women with e-bikes, which cost nearly double to manufacture than the first-generation bikes. I wrote out a break-even analysis, with charts and graphs and visuals that my sister's unique but easily distracted mind could compute, trying to get her to understand that if operating costs increased, then our profits needed to as well. Yoga studios have low operating margins and a successful history of throughput in New York City, meaning, they attract enough customers to cover the fixed and variable expenses of rent and personnel.

Sure, fine, yoga, she said in response to my painstakingly researched and thoughtful presentation on the matter. *Sure, fine, no thumb grips then*, she said, when I told her that if we wanted to upgrade the beta bikes with thumb grips they wouldn't be ready in time for the Morocco trip. I wasn't asking Brett to make a decision between giving the women bikes with twist grips or no bikes at all, I was suggesting we push off the Morocco trip entirely until we could provide these women *and children* with a safe and rigorously vetted product. But when I spelled it out for her, she pushed her jaw forward so that her bottom teeth protruded over her top, the same expression Mom used to make when you told her something she didn't want to hear (I'd rather take Spanish than Latin, I'm thinking about switching my major to art history, I was invited to the prom). *Just put a rush order on it.* Brett had sighed, irritably, as though this obvious solution hadn't been the first thing to occur to me. When I tried to explain how I had asked, but the factory we paid to meet our small-batch manufacturing needs simply didn't have the manpower, she had flung her hand across her forehead and performed her tired old line. *I can't deal with this right now. I'm the talent!*

It was funny when she said it in the beginning, until our roles became defined: I was to be stuck with all the slog work and none of the talent perks, like the show and the book deal and the 30K speaking fees. I was over it, and I was broke—something Brett continued to pretend she was long after she wasn't, because she hadn't figured out how to manage this new dimension of her image. She was not rich, not like the other women, not yet, but she could afford to gift Layla with a Mansur Gavriel bucket bag. To be clear, I wasn't angry at Brett for buying Layla that bag, I was angry at her timing. Layla had gone behind my back and disabled the app I use to limit her screen time just a few weeks prior, and the bag seemed a missed opportunity to encourage good behavior. Why couldn't it have been a carrot we dangled to motivate her to get her grades up? Or better yet, why couldn't she have set aside that five hundred dollars for the trip to Nigeria I've been saving for since Layla turned eight? Layla's hostility toward me for not knowing her father is natural and justified. Since I can't give her him, the least I can do is help her forge a connection to her country of origin.

Brett is always describing Layla as so perfect, an angel, a gift from above we don't deserve. Not only is that not true, I would worry if it was true. I'm *proud* that it's not. I'm proud that my daughter sneered *I hate you* when I took away her phone for a week. I'm proud that she fought me tooth and nail when I told her Mr. Gavriel would stay in his Barneys box until she pulled up her grades (being sure to remind me, once again, how embarrassing I am). These are things I never did as a kid because I lived in mortal fear of displeasing my mother. Truly, when I look back on my childhood, one emotion beats brightly and loudly above the rest: dread. I was shown love when I followed the rules, and I was deprived of love when I did not, and how I dreaded those times when I did not. Kids should be disciplined, but they should never be unloved.

Kids should also tell their parents they hate them, they should groan at their bad mom jokes. They should bang doors and push your limits and break your rules. Healthy adolescents use their parents to sharpen their arguing skills, to learn how to assert themselves, to advocate for freedom and autonomy. Healthy adolescents who know they are loved no matter what aren't afraid to use their voices. The ones to worry about are the quiet good girls who do everything mommy asks without complaint or question. I should know. I was one of those quiet good girls. I was the unquestioning, obedient daughter, in awe of Brett's complete and utter disregard of the rules. I know now it was because she already felt unloved, that she didn't feel she had anything left to lose by disappointing our mother—might as well have a little fun while she's at it. It crushes me to know Brett grew up feeling so neglected, but in a way I'm envious of her, because she developed a kind of resilience that was not in place for me when our mother died. Without her rules, without her militant disapproval acting as my North Star, I lost the road. And so, as Brett likes to say, *I went off the rails just a little bit.*

When I found out I was pregnant, I experienced the strangest sense of déjà vu. *I've been here before,* I thought, *I've done this before. But when?* It took me years of therapy to make the connection, to find words to adequately explain the curious combination of comfort and fatigue I felt holding that First Response stick in my hand five weeks after I returned from Morocco. Eventually, I stumbled on to it. When it came to becoming a mother, I felt the same sort of imposed purpose as I did when it came to being a radiologist. Neither were things I saw for myself, but there they were, provisioned for me like the perfect-sized shell in which to slip my naked hermit crab body. It felt like I only had two options: be a radiologist or be a mother, and I wanted to be a radiologist only slightly less than I wanted to be a mother. I could do it, and I would do it exceedingly well, though I had to warm up to the idea first. There was a rocky but brief adjustment period when I couldn't believe what I had done. I couldn't bear to face Layla in the quiet of the night, no one else around, to be confronted with the full weight of the titanic decision I had made. I was terrified to be that alone with her. Terrified too, of vocalizing such a thought to my father or Brett, because that is a horrible and unnatural thought to have about your newborn baby. And so I lay in bed, eyes closed, ears perked, while Brett got my daughter to stop crying, telling myself that I was protecting her by neglecting her.

I don't regret my decision to have Layla. Even when she's behaving like a hormonally ravaged monster, my primal love for her functions as a net. It catches the heinous thoughts that fall from my brain—*I could slap her! What would life look like if I had made it through the clinic doors? I could* fucking *slap her.*—shielding my heart from impact. Layla is my greatest accomplishment, which is something women used to be able to say without having to enter the witness-protection program. Because Layla isn't just a happy accident, or karmic compensation for a past life well served, Layla is a product of grueling and expensive work on my behalf. She is the direct result of my determination not to become my mother. It's the overachiever in me; it's my mother in me; it's exactly who I did not want Layla to become.

I took the money our mother left for us in her will and I invested it wisely—in the right asset classes, in Layla's education, and in self-care for myself. I found a good therapist, who referred me to a better therapist who specialized in intercultural parenting, who taught me that being a single mother to a biracial child is not the same as being a single mother. I learned to untangle love from hubris. I learned that I am wired to make my daughter feel less loved if she goes to a state school instead of Dartmouth, and while I can't change that instinct, I can learn to recognize it, and choose not to respond to it. I took notes on how to discipline with compassion. I signed Layla up for dance class, music class, horseback riding lessons, swim team, and Little League, and when she didn't take to any of these extracurriculars I didn't panic (outwardly) and I didn't force her to continue. I told her that she was allowed to quit anything, as long as she gave it a fair shot and had taken the time to think about what sport or skill she wanted to try her hand at next. When an Imazighen woman sent us woven welcome mats as a thank-you for her bike, Layla was the one who came up with the idea of starting an online store for Berber goods, and she executed the concept, soup to nuts. She has thrived in her position as "online shop coordinator," and above all, she is happy (for the most part) and healthy (which accounts for the times she is not). She is not beholden to anybody's expectations for her life but her own.

I am immensely proud of myself for raising a moody teenager with a passion, though that's not something I would ever say out loud to Brett. It's too dear a triumph for me to risk hearing her pooh-pooh it, or insist that she had it worse than me growing up, being the fat one, the dumb one, the lemon. Brett looks at most things through a binary lens—if she had it bad, I must have had it good.

I am always the first to say that my sister did not have it easy growing up. Our mother failed her, time and time again. But it was a pain that built Brett's character. She was forced to create a vision for her life and how she wanted it to turn out, because no one else was going to do it for her. It's why she's the talent, and I'm stuck being the Chantal Kreviazuk of the B-corp world. Do you know who Chantal Kreviazuk is? It's okay. I don't expect you to, and it's sort of the point. Chantal Kreviazuk is a classically trained pianist and singer-songwriter who has written hits for behemoths like Kelly Clarkson, Avril Lavigne, Christina Aguilera, and Drake. She's released a few albums along the way, trying to make it on her own name. One had moderate success in Canada.

I've been writing the hits, and I deserve credit, and not just in Canada. I am SPOKE's bookkeeper, ambassador, hiring manager, human resources department, janitor, publicist, and receptionist. I'm the duck's feet, treading furiously beneath the surface of the water, so that the Big Chill can appear to glide across the lake with no effort at all. It was true that Brett made a better face for the company. I have to give my sister credit—she forecasted the trend of authenticity and she engineered a way to monetize it. No one wants to hear the pretty, skinny girl's story anymore. They want the story from the slightly overweight, tatted-up though still camera-friendly girl who was tortured and made to feel like a freak because she liked girls. The girl who had no choice but to develop grit and spunk, to look out for herself. These are the stories we like to hear nowadays, so Brett enhanced hers, ever so slightly.

"Do you want to know what I think?" Jesse asks, and I nod before I even realize I'm nodding, feeling like a ventriloquist's dummy.

"The patriarchy survives so long as women are pitted against one another. It is a threat to a man's way of life when women gather, when they question the status quo, and when they inevitably start to resist it. That's what this season was about. Strong women apart, who were becoming stronger together. And it scared the shit out of him."

What is it to be a strong woman? I've been thinking about it a lot, recently, and I've decided it has to do with taking responsibility for your actions, even when it feels like you didn't have a choice in the matter, because you always have a choice. At the reunions, the women are always carrying on about owning it. You did this. You did that. *Just own it!* they harp, over and over, until they've beaten the catchphrase out of you. *Fine. Fine! I did delete your app to free up some storage. I own it!*

Owning it is better than an apology, better than retribution, better than an empty promise to change your ways. Because being forced to own it shows that you recognize how far you've orbited from a common and decent sense of self-awareness. And the longer you spend on a reality show, the more elusive the trait of self-awareness becomes, thereby increasing its intrinsic value. But a little-known fact about declaring ownership is that it's not just a victory for the person who has harassed you into submission. Those three words—I own it—also act as an astronaut's braided steel tether, preventing you from floating away into oblivion.

No one but Jesse knows that I have anything to own right now, but I do. How we're saying it happened is not how it happened. Everyone thinks Vince killed my sister, but he didn't. This is a fiction Jesse asked me to go along with, yes, but I fully acknowledge my part in it too. I want people to believe our story. Partially because I know Brett would have wanted it this way. Partially because if anyone ever finds out what really happened, I'd go away for eleven years. I looked up others who have obstructed a murder investigation in New York State and averaged the sentences they served.

Lastly, and I hope not mostly, I want people to believe our story because I was tired of standing in the dark while the spotlight shined on my sister unaccompanied.

There. I owned it.

PART II

Filming • June–July 2017

CHAPTER 9

Stephanie

The doorbell rings, and I try not to panic. I'm upstairs in my bedroom, *putting on my face* for Lauren's sexy slumber party. I have a strict policy against being filmed waking up or getting ready. I am not comfortable appearing on national television looking anything other than my absolute best. For this, Lisa and Jesse would lock me up and throw away the key. Confident women are cool women and evidently I am neither.

"Vince?" I call, when the doorbell brays a second time. He doesn't respond fast enough and so I have to raise my voice. "*Vince?*"

I listen to him plod to the front door with heavy footsteps—oh, the inconvenience of having to answer the door in the middle of a *Top Gear* rerun. There is low murmuring that I strain to make out but cannot. "Who is it?" I shout, batting away my makeup artist's hand. If it's anyone with a camera, I'll lock myself in the bathroom. They're not allowed to follow you into the bathroom. The bathroom is like the U.N.—generally accepted as off-limits, even in wartime.

Whoever was at the door is now on the stairs. I spring out of my seat just as Jen appears in the doorway with a pinched look on her small face. "It's Greenberg!" Vince announces, on a delay. "And she's wearing a flannel Snuggie!"

Jen and I are facing each other in a way that feels like we are squaring off. Her enduring scowl morphs into something worse as she takes in my face. It's the expression of a person who has just walked in on her boss going to the bathroom—mortified, *pitying*. Jason, my makeup artist, has only just finished "prepping" my face. Which means that my skin is bare, blotchy, and greasy with various serums and primers. I'm without my fake eyelashes, which means I'm without eyelashes entirely. In my twenties, I had my eyelash extensions replaced monthly at a small second-floor salon in Herald Square, until one day, the technician turned me away, declaring: *There's none left*. She refused to continue our treatments until I allowed my real eyelashes to grow back, no matter how much I offered to pay her. That was six years ago, and I'm still waiting.

Jen is not wearing a flannel Snuggie exactly, but rather a deep red and green plaid pajama set in silk. To a guy, it's a flannel Snuggie. To Jen Greenberg, this is stepping up her game. I suppress a sigh. I have no patience for people who refuse to help themselves. I don't care how cool the Fug Girls say she looks, she must know that she's not going to win back that guy—or girl—dressed like a little boy on Christmas Eve.

"Sorry," Jen says, twisting her Standing Sisters ring around her index finger. She's fidgety; nervous for some reason. "Didn't mean to barge in on you like this, but I need to talk to you before we go and I didn't want to put this in a text." We learned from Hayley to keep our digital footprints clean and our face-to-faces dirty.

"*Ohhh*." Vince leans against the doorframe, licking his heart-shaped lips. "Scandal at the sorority house?"

Jason snorts because my husband is hot.

"Vince," I say sweetly, "will you go downstairs and get us something to drink?"

Vince clasps his hands behind his back. "Red or white, *ma chéri*?"

"Water," I say, at the same time Jen does *white*. She grins wide, not because it's funny, but because she doesn't want to show up to

Lauren's party and film with purple teeth when she prefers to sell herself as a garden-fed teetotaler.

"I've got a trick for that," Jason says, smearing my face with foundation.

"Actually," I change my mind, "I'll take a . . . white . . . too." Why not? My ongoing *battle with depression* (Why do they say "battle" when it's always a massacre?) has been at a cease-fire long enough that there is no reason to continue slandering an innocent glass of wine in my mind. And not to borrow a problematic line of thinking from Lauren Fun, but tonight is a special occasion. It's the first group event of the season, a banner evening, and Brett won't be there. I just received word from my publisher that I am the first female author to hold four consecutive spots on the *New York Times* bestseller list. In just a few weeks, I'm flying to L.A. to have dinner with the Oscar-Nominated Female Director. I should celebrate when there are things to celebrate.

Vince turns from a waiter to a soldier with an official salute. At least he's inconsistent. "Hup-two-three-four," he chants, as he descends the stairs to complete his assignment.

"I don't know how you live with that," Jen says, in a shocking moment of insubordination. She pushes aside a pile of coffee table books from an ottoman and takes a seat without being asked.

"I do." Jason flutters his eyelashes, and I decide it's time to give Jason a raise.

"You'd have some competition," I tell him, trying not to move my mouth as he paints it nude. Smoky eye tonight. Neutral lip. "The gays *love* Vince."

Jen emits a doubting laugh, drawing her knees to her chest. Jen is always rearranging limbs, fixing herself into impossible entanglements, as if to say, *Look at me! I'm such an unconventional free spirit that I can't even sit normally!* I dare you to find one photograph of Jen Greenberg on the Internet where she isn't wound like a five-year-old in need of a bathroom. "Do you want to hear this or not?" she asks. "It's about Brett."

I'm dying to hear it. My rib cage feels like it's suffocating my stomach, but I don't want Jen to know that Brett still holds that power over me. "Who?" I quip. Jason snickers.

"You know she hired my ex to do her hair this season," Jason says, slipping a folded tissue between my lips. "Blot."

"She's such a scam artist," I seethe as Jason crumples the stamp of my kiss. Brett took great pride in anointing herself the air-dried one of seasons past.

"She's engaged," Jen blurts out, made impatient by my attempt to prove that whatever news there is about Brett, it can't be worth begging to hear it.

Jason speaks with his powder brush, thinking I'm still in the mood to kid around, "That bitch is even thirstier than I thought."

Brett is *engaged*? The last eight months flash before my eyes. Brett and me in the lingerie department at Bloomingdale's, because she had just moved back in and I couldn't believe she was still wearing that moth-eaten XL Dartmouth T-shirt to bed. Rihanna had taken a class at her studio. *Vogue* had profiled her. Time for a grown-up pair of pajamas.

Brett, accompanying me to a colposcopy at my gynocologist's office, because my body hadn't cleared HPV on its own and they needed to make sure I hadn't contracted a cancerous strain of the STD. I was sick with nerves, and Brett actually managed to sweet-talk the receptionist, and then the nurse, and finally the doctor herself, into allowing her to stay in the room with me while I underwent the excruciatingly uncomfortable procedure. She clutched my sweaty, cold hand while the doctor scraped tissue from my cervix, cracking jokes about how you weren't cool unless you had HPV. Women who have HPV are the women who have lived.

Brett and me, rewatching the first season of the show in my bed, hands in the same bowl of Skinny Pop, marveling at what apple-cheeked babies we had been just three years ago, how soft-spoken we all were. *We must have just been nervous,* Brett theorized, and I had agreed, but now I think differently. I think we were all just softer then.

The timehop of our friendship has caused the saliva on my tongue to thin and sour. I feel ill. I feel as though I might cry. I am painfully aware that I am sitting here with a greasy face and fewer lashes than a four-month-old fetus, that the person I loved the most in my life turned out to be a stranger, and a cruel one at that, that people are starting to openly question how I live with the annoying man downstairs. I swallow and try, desperately, to sound jaded and impersonal. "So none of us would film with her and she knew she needed a storyline." I nod. "Got it."

Jen shrugs, flatly. What a shoddy imitation of a friend—of Brett—she turned out to be. "According to Yvette, it's not staged. They're *soul mates*." Her voice is a gauzy impression of her mother's.

"Right." My laugh is rough. Brett wants to be married about as much as I want a child: which is a lot if a TV crew is willing to capture it. "I'm surprised I'm hearing it from you and not Page Six."

"Yvette says she's waiting until they tell Arch's parents before they go public."

"And yet," I say, rottenly, "Yvette knows. And now you. And me." I give Jen a long look, allowing the facts to speak for themselves. "How long have they even been together?"

"Long enough," Jen says, folding her heel into her plaid crotch. I'm suddenly furious with her for what she's chosen to wear to Lauren's sleepover-themed party. *That is the sexiest you could come up with?* I want to jeer. *No wonder there are cobwebs growing between your legs.*

"Not really," I say, lightly. I will not let Jen see that this news has gutted me. "Like three months."

"More like six."

"Jen," I say, an edge to my voice I can no longer smooth out, "six months ago I was in Miami, trying to help her get over her breakup with Sarah."

"Okay, so, three months. Whatever." Jen shivers, like the details of Brett's romantic life are icky. "I don't care."

There is a creak and we both look to the doorway. It's Vince, ascending the stairs.

"So how long until she's pitching a spinoff to the network, *Brett Buys the Cow*?"

Jen's face tightens. "Shouldn't it be the other way around?"

It's shameful, but hearing Jen disparage Brett for something as high school as her weight settles me ever so slightly. *She's still on your side. She still despises the same person who you despise.*

"You two actually hate each other, huh?" Jason says, taking a step away from me and examining his work on my eyes. "I wasn't sure if it was just for the show."

I give him a sharp, stunned look. "You thought we made it *up*?"

"Who hates each other?" Vince wants to know, appearing in the doorway balancing three glasses of wine in his hands, mine with a straw because, lipstick. Vince is never more the doting husband than during filming season. Forget crotchless underwear or piping my nipples with whipped cream, *filming* is the aphrodisiac of our marriage. Somewhere along the way, Vince decided that holding my handbag on the red carpet was still the red carpet, and that was good enough for him.

"Who else?" I say, as he sets my drink in front of me. I see that he chose the glasses that his friends bought us for our wedding, monogrammed VDS: Vince and Stephanie DeMarco, assuming, naturally, that I couldn't wait to take my deadbeat husband's last name.

"Aw, you guys," Vince chastises, "give Brett a break."

One nice thing I will say about the cad I married is that he stays out of our scraps. We've had significant others who try to get involved when *Diggers* butt heads, evangelizing the more forgiving politics of brotherhood, who are viciously edited into mansplaining donkeys when the time comes. *Diggers* have lost their places for less, and I've made it very clear to Vince, his opinion doesn't matter but it counts, it could cost us everything.

"Then you can be the one to congratulate her on her engagement when you see her tonight," Jen says, and I realize how artfully she's buried the lede. Because Jen didn't come here to tell me that Brett is getting married. She came here to tell me that Brett has been invited to Lauren's event. That the alliance is off.

Vince fumbles the pass, slopping some of Jen's wine onto the silk rug. "She's engaged?" He sets the glass down on my vanity and goes in search of a towel. "No shit," he says from the bathroom. "To that . . . that same woman? What's her name?"

"Arch," Jen says.

"*Arch*?" Vince repeats, rudely, appearing in the bathroom doorway with a roll of toilet paper in his hands.

"Use a hand towel," I snap at him, and direct my chin at the glass he's left on my vanity. "And put a coaster under that!"

"Welcome to New York, Vince," Jen cracks, as he disappears into the bathroom again, "we have people from lots of different cultures here. And obviously the white savior of African girls wasn't going to marry some corn-fed blonde from Ohio."

"You should have told me she was coming sooner," I say to Jen, waving off Jason's attempt to apply mascara to the falsies he's glued to my eyelids. "I just wasted a fifty-dollar strip of lashes."

"You're not coming now?" Jen spits, incredulous.

"*Babe,*" Vince implores of me, standing in the bathroom doorway with a hurt puppy-dog look on his face. He ordered a satin Hugh Hefner playsuit for this night weeks ago, monogrammed for seventy-five dollars extra.

"I agreed not to film with her," I remind Jen, icily. "And unlike some people, my word means something."

Jason returns the mascara wand to its bottle in consensus.

"Fine, Steph." Jen sets her wine on the vanity—*Put down a coaster, you animal!* I almost shriek. "She's going to get the good edit, you know that, right? She's going to Morocco to help little illiterate rape victims and she's planning a wedding to Amal lesbian Clooney. Yvette wanted us to know so we have the opportunity to make things right with her before she tells us. Otherwise, you know what it's going to look like? Like we're a bunch of calculating mean girls who changed our tune when it became clear Brett was going to be everyone's favorite this season because she's getting married, and guess what? Suckers like to see fat chicks get married. It gives their little artery-clogged hearts hope."

Vince sucks in a horrified breath. "Jesus, Jen."

Jen shoots him an eviscerating look, but her face is a shameful red.

"She's *always* the favorite," I mutter, sounding so petulant I can't stand myself.

"Listen to yourself," Jen says, and I am shocked when her voice nearly cracks. Is she close to tears? I stare at her in wordless disbelief as she swipes the heel of her hand across her face. What is *up* with her tonight? "Jesse's going to be pissed if you don't go. Do you know what they'll do to you in the edit room?"

Jen is not wrong about any of this, unfortunately, as it is a much more reliable characteristic of humanity that we're happier for people in love than we are for people in the highest tax bracket. Perhaps because we need to see ourselves in our heroines, and the modest accomplishment of finding a spouse and having babies is achievable by most of the general population, Green Menace notwithstanding. Our audience in particular likes nothing more than to see unconventional people getting to partake in conventional traditions. It's why Vince and I were so popular at first, it's why Jesse is taking a chance on Kelly and her mixed-race, non-nuclear family, hoping for a Cheerios commercial backlash, promptly followed by a Cheerios commercial defense.

"Guys, *relax*," Vince says, daringly. It takes a set of steel to chance on the r-word around two women with a combined net worth of *not in your lifetime, bud*, but my husband does not exactly conduct himself in a risk-averse fashion. "You're getting way too worked up about this. Just go and tell Brett you're happy for her and get on with it." Not waiting for my answer, Vince peels off his T-shirt and locates the top of his pajama set. The tier-three trainer at Equinox is doing an abysmal job of taming Vince's baby potbelly, I see. Jason pretends not to look anyway; those heart-shaped lips and that strong, scruffy jaw make up for that much.

The first time Vince ever had that effect on me, he was the bartender at a promotional event for a women's razor blade. My friend from college worked for the PR company that represented Gillette, and she brought me as her plus-one. The event was held at a windowless warehouse in the theater district, and I remember exactly what I wore: a DVF wrap dress and a pair of nude, patent leather Manolo Blahniks. I was twenty-six and he was twenty-four, a two-year infinity. He was an aspiring actor whose biggest break to date was biting into a BLT in a Hellman's commercial. His dark hair fell into his light eyes each time he looked down to mix up a fresh batch of the event's signature cocktail (a Hairy Navel—haha), and every woman in the room was imagining what he would look like on top of her, with that hair in those eyes. I still get weak in the knees remembering how, at the end of the night, he beckoned for me to come closer so that he could shout into my ear (the acoustics were poor in the windowless warehouse), "Your boyfriend is an idiot."

I made a dubious expression in an effort to play along. "But he graduated from Harvard Law top of his class." My boyfriend didn't graduate from Harvard Law top of his class. I didn't have a boyfriend.

"There's no way," Vince said, buffing a wet wineglass dry with a dish towel. "Because no one that smart would be so dumb to let you out of his sight for even a minute."

I rolled my eyes with brute force, but inside, I was jumping up and down, screaming, *Don't stop! Keep trying!*

"Seriously," Vince said, flinging the dishrag over his shoulder and going very still, so that he could be sure to take in every inch of me. "You are incredibly beautiful."

Do you know what I felt like saying in that moment? I felt like saying *I know*. All my life, people have complimented my looks, but nothing they said ever rang true to me. *She has a nice smile,* I overheard a friend of my mom's say when I was eleven. What does it even mean to have a nice smile? Hitler had a nice smile. Sometimes the girls at school would express an appreciation for my skin that they would never actually want to trade me for—about how lucky I was that I didn't have to worry about my "tan" fading in the winter. Then there were the guys who fetishized me, declaring, *You're hot,* with such lascivious fervor that I'd want to go home and take a shower. I'd look at myself in the mirror, perplexed no one else could see it. I don't just have a nice smile or nice skin. I'm not hot. I'm beautiful. *Incredibly beautiful.*

The fact that I believe myself to be beautiful—and talented, I might add—does not run counter to my deep-seated insecurities. If anything, it is salt on the ever-open wound that is going through life unseen. But for five minutes on a Tuesday night in a windowless warehouse in the theater district, I felt seen by someone who happened to be incredibly beautiful himself, and that part mattered. Because when we walked down the street holding hands, Vince acted as my conduit. *Oh,* people thought, making the jump after taking in Vince's good looks without needing to parse and qualify them first. *He's with her. She must be beautiful too. Come to think of it*—wow—*she is so beautiful.* And that's why Vince.

It must be said that we were *good* in the beginning. There is a picture of us on New Year's Eve, caught mid-kiss in the drunken crowd, unaware the lens was turned on us (those were the days, huh?). Vince had his hands on either side of my face, my lower lip pierced between his teeth. Passion had distorted our faces, made us appear tormented and deprived of some basic human need. *Oh, God!* I cried, slapping my laptop shut and covering my face in mortification when I saw the photo on Facebook. Something so private and primal should never be for public viewing.

The sex was no frills, constant, and torrid. Which makes the reality that we don't have any now—at least not with each other—all the more gutting. You know how couples rarely make it if they have a child who dies? It's simply too awful a reminder of the life that was lost to stay with the person who helped create it. Sex is the dead baby in my marriage. It rips my heart in two to look at Vince and be reminded of what has been lost. We will not escape the reality TV marital curse. The only question that remains is when. When?

"You're a good friend for coming over here and telling us this, Greenberg," Vince says, stepping in front of me and working some of my pomade through his thick, wavy hair. For a few moments, with

Vince's flat ass in my face, I'm at least spared the replica of my grief in the mirror.

No matter what anybody says, I know that Vince loved me once, *before* I was rich and famous. I will go to the grave knowing somebody saw me for who I really am, and he didn't turn away in revulsion. I don't think Brett could say the same.

The doors to the lower terrace of the penthouse are flung open, June at night like a bath you wake up in, lucky you didn't drown. Outside, lanterns illuminate wisteria-wrapped pergolas and Franny's hand-stretched dough chars in the wood-burning fireplace. Well, that would have been the scene, had the Greenwich Hotel been willing to sign the release form and had Franny's not pulled out as the caterers once they discovered they would have to cook their pizzas in a conventional oven. As a result, we are in a very gold bar at a four-star hotel in midtown, trays of oversalted tuna tartar shoved in our faces every seven steps.

Jen and I trade stiff compliments about the décor because we've been mic'd, and the cameras will pick up our audio even though they're not turned on us yet. *This is nice,* Jen says, with a half grimace, half smile. My contribution: *I never really get to this part of town.*

Natural Selection, the production company employed by the network, allocates three crews that rotate between the five of us for garden-variety home shoots, but for an all-cast event, the whole unit is deployed. Out on the small, cement terrace, catty-corner to a third open bar, two crews have staked out a space. Between the camera operator and the gaffer and the grip and Lisa, they appear like one big roving alien, stalking its target in a square of spotlight. Lisa notices me and raises her arm, wiping the air in short, frenetic waves.

I pause before our showrunner and she squints at me, yanking the tail of a Canal Street pashmina worn by a production assistant. "Can we maybe . . . ?" She goes to dab at my lips with the scarf, still leashed to a pop-eyed PA. I duck out of her way before she can touch me. Lisa and Jesse hate how much makeup I wear.

"What am I walking into?" I peer behind her and am relieved to see that it's only Lauren in the shot.

"Lauren trying in vain to convince us that she's not drinking," Lisa says. Next to me, blotting his forehead with oil absorbing papers, Vince snorts.

"How many glasses of prosecco have you snuck her in the bathroom?" Lisa asks the PA, who is carefully turning her scarf around her neck again.

"Four?" she guesses.

Lisa punches four fingers inches from my face. I gently lower her hand. "Four glasses of prosecco. I get it."

"Don't be shy about blowing up her spot." She reaches around me and pats my back, finding my mic pack between my shoulder blades. "Good."

"Is Brett . . . ?" I remove a piece of imaginary fuzz from Vince's shoulder. As if to say, *I'm asking about Brett but more concerned about getting my husband camera ready*. In a perverse way, I'm dying to see my former best friend. It's like a criminal who finds reasons to revisit the scene of the crime. I don't know the psychology behind that, and I'm not the criminal here, but I can tell you what I'm hoping to get out of an encounter with Brett is acknowledgment. I want to hear Brett say that I had every right to try to turn the cast against her. She's figured out a way to keep herself relevant by proposing to some woman she's known five minutes, and I get it, it's self-preservation. But since I'm stuck with her, I deserve, at the very least, to hear her own it. She knows what she did.

Lisa gives me a witchy grin. "Oh, Brett's around." She gives me a gentle push. "Don't worry, we'll find you," she adds in my ear. Vince goes to take a step forward as well, but Lisa's arm lowers in front of his chest like a safety bar on an amusement park ride. "Not right now, my Hungry Hippo."

Vince's pretty little mouth drops open. He's missed a greasy patch between his eyebrows with those blotting papers. "Whatever, Lisa," he mutters. He surveys the room, trying to decide his next move. "I'm getting a drink," he tells me, unpinning another button on his pajama top for all the women here to meet other women.

"I'll take a vodka soda!" Lisa cackles after him. "Go," she whispers into my ear, with a firm push this time. "Four glasses of prosecco. Thank me later."

—

Lauren is kitted out in a lace bustier and sweatpants rolled several times at her hips, pink furry mules, serving up terminally cool. She sighs when she sees Jen's chastity plaid. "Oh, Greenberg."

"I'm comfortable," Jen retorts.

"Comfortable doesn't get you fucked," Lauren says, with the vigor of someone who has drunk too much to enjoy sex anyway. "Comfortable doesn't get you *over that dickwad.*" Her anger is abrupt and embarrassing. Lauren realizes it and laughs, pretending she was joking. My adrenaline rouses, a static rustling the fine hair on my forearms. Between Brett's engagement and Jen's sudden willingness to film with her, Lisa's comment that I can *thank her later,* it doesn't take a veteran reality star to predict that things are about to go down.

"*Phewwww,*" Jen says to Lauren, releasing a long, cleansing breath and gesturing for Lauren to do the same. "Big breath. Your energy is too powerful to waste it on anger."

Your energy is too powerful to waste it on anger—sigh. I couldn't admit this before, because I was so desperate to see the good in Jen after I lost Brett, but Jen actually patents certain phrases before the season, then has coffee mugs and sweatshirts made with her inspirational sayings so that she can sell them from her Instagram page when the episode airs. I find myself wishing I had a drink in my hand to take the edge off her etheric drivel. This is a new sensation for me. I could never relate to those people who declare *I need a drink!* after a long week. I'd rather some stinky cheese, or a massage at the Mandarin. The desire for a cocktail stiff enough to make my eyes water should be a sign—get out while you still can!—but I'm not one to believe in signs.

Lauren pushes out a short, peppery breath for Jen's benefit, before staking a toe to swivel in my direction, nearly losing her balance in the process. "*You* look hot," she says, assessing me up and down. "I like your nightie thing."

"Thanks, it's Stella—"

"You know, I really admire what you've done. Telling your story. Helping women." Lauren yawns, flitting her hand around as if to say, *yada, yada*. "But it doesn't make you a saint."

I force myself to respond calmly. "I never claimed to be a saint."

Lauren burps silently, sending a whiff of hunger my way. "You claim to tell the truth, though, and you almost never do."

Welcome to reality TV, where duplicity is not just encouraged, but a survival skill. The last time I saw Lauren, she was my yessum woman. The last time I saw Jen, she was abusing an abused rescue dog. Now Lauren is an adversary and Jen is peace, love, and light.

"Why don't we discuss this at another time when you're more clearheaded," I say to Lauren in an undertone. It's both an offer to protect my skin (I've lied about so many things, I'd rather discuss when I'm prepared to address which lie) and her own (you're telling everyone you're not drinking, but I know how many proseccos you've had tonight).

"I'm completely clearheaded." Lauren makes her eyes wide and alert, as though this is undeniable proof that she is fit to operate a moving vehicle. "And I want to know why you told me Brett was the one who sent the video of me to Page Six when it wasn't her."

If I weren't on camera, I would sigh with relief. Telling Lauren that Brett was responsible for that item in the press is the least of it all. "I didn't tell you it was Brett. I said I *suspected* it was Brett because I know she has a line in to one of the editors there."

"So do you!" Lauren trills.

"And so do you!"

A few lesbians in imported polyester passing as satin sleepwear stop speaking to stare at us. It will make for some great B-roll.

"Why don't we go into the hallway to discuss this so we don't ruin Lauren's event?" Jen suggests, and I've been at this long enough to be able to translate that to *Brett is waiting for us in the hallway.*

I square my shoulders. I thought I was ready to have it out with Brett, but now that the opportunity has been presented, I realize I'm not, and that I don't think I'll ever be. I should not be the one who has to apologize to her, which I'll have to do if I see her tonight. "I'm fine right here."

"Of course," Lauren mutters. "It's not *your* event you're ruining."

I release a tinny, exasperated laugh. "You started with me!"

"Let's just . . ." Jen puts a palm in the middle of our backs and takes a step toward the doors, our Buddha bellwether, forcing us to follow her. I'm resistant at first, but as we step inside I notice something in the far corner that makes me a willing participant of the cavalcade. It's my husband, sitting on a love seat by the fireplace, too close to another woman.

I narrow my eyes and realize the woman is Kelly, wearing a white negligee that looks like it came with the sexy nurse costume from the Halloween store. Vince dips his head and murmurs something into her ear. Kelly plants her hand in the middle of his chest, restraining him with a kind smile. My heart is battering in my ears as I glance back at Lisa, fearful she will have Marc turn his lens on my scoundrel husband, but everyone is too focused on the impending confrontation between Brett and me to have noticed. *One less thing to worry about,* I think, momentarily relieved, but then I catch Jen's eye and realize she saw what I saw. Great. Just great.

Brett is standing by the elevators, wearing the silk pajamas I bought for her last year. This is no happenstance. The pants are wrinkled and if I get close enough to smell her, I'm sure I will discover that they're in desperate need of a dry cleaning, which is also strategic. She wants me to know she's been wearing these, that she's been thinking about me. The crew rings us and waits to see which one of us will speak first.

"I don't want to fight with you," Brett starts, which is a riot. That is exactly what she is here to do.

I laugh crudely in her face. "Why else would you be here, Brett?"

"I asked her to come," Lauren pipes up with glee. How thrilled she is to be the wounded bird at the center of this drama. "It's my event. I'm allowed to ask anyone I'd like to come. I don't need your permission, *Steph*."

Jen reaches for Lauren's hand and clutches it close to her heart. "Laur," she says, her voice deep and husky. "Remember what we talked about. Speak from a place of vulnerability, not vengeance."

"Christ on a gluten-free vegan cracker," Brett says, making eyes at the camera. When we were filming the first season, we were told to ignore the cameras. It was *drilled* into us. Then season one aired and we discovered that not only had Brett completely disregarded that rule, but that the viewers loved it, ordaining her the Jim Halpert of the show. Brett is incapable of seeing that private communication for what it is, which is a betrayal of her cast. Staring into the camera at moments like this is analogous to a laugh track. It's saying to the audience—yeah, I'm laughing *at* them *with* you.

"Do you want me to mediate or not?" Jen says to Brett, dropping the Dalai Lama inflection. Something passes between them, indiscernible to anyone who is not us. *They've seen each other since I was at Jen's apartment*, I realize. *They've agreed on something. I am the one on the ropes tonight.* I take a moment to gather my bearings—do they have something on me? Have they agreed to their own alliance? I decide, whip fast, that my best course of action is to show remorse.

"Lauren," I say, turning to her with my hands steepled in prayer. "I genuinely thought Brett was behind the Page Six article. That wasn't a lie. If Brett says it wasn't her, then it wasn't her, and I'm sorry to have created such confusion. Now, can we just go back in there and celebrate this important and necessary new chapter of SADIE?" Important. Necessary. These are the things every *Digger* would like to believe about herself.

Lauren runs a hand through her sunny hair, pluming herself. *She's going to work this conflict to the bone,* I realize with a slump. How could the tide have turned against me so quickly? How am I the one on the outs here? "I don't believe you thought that," Lauren persists. "I think you told me that to get me on your side and fight your battles for you."

I attempt to disarm her with a smile. "Laur, come on, you know me. I can fight my own battles."

"Or maybe you did it to try to distract everyone from your *marriage* issues." She cocks an eyebrow, lazily, but the trick does very little to assuage the regret on her face. She knows she's taken it too far by bringing up Vince.

"Laur," Brett gasps, disapprovingly, and the eyebrow falls completely. It's official. Brett is our new puppet master.

Thank you, Lisa, I think, as I remember what she told me earlier. "You're not making any sense," I say to Lauren. "Maybe it was the four glasses of prosecco you've smuggled tonight when you're telling everyone you're sober?"

Lauren thinks she lunges at me, but in reality, it's more of a slow, sad lean. She bumps her shin on the bench between the elevators, doubling over and yowling. Jen grabs her by her upper arm, helping to right her, and that's when I notice it. The bruising. The puncture wounds. Lauren has gotten her vaccinations for Morocco.

"Grow up," Lauren says, clutching her shin with her hand. "You're too old to be a mean girl."

Over Brett's shoulder, Lisa's lips form a grotesque *o.*

"Steph!" Brett begs after me as I hurry away, crew number two stalking me down the hallway. I'm done. I can't. I'm done.

Vince has disappeared, and with the camera crew unrelenting at my back, I don't risk looking for Kelly in case she might lead me to him. The last thing I need is a storyline that my husband is schtupping the new *Digger*. The second to last thing I need is for my husband to actually schtup the new *Digger*. I head for the bathroom, where at least I can sit on the edge of the toilet and not worry what my face is or is not doing in this new reality where I have somehow found myself the villain in the story.

The door to the bathroom is locked. I rattle the knob to let whomever is inside know there is a line, and then again a few seconds later, and then again. I can't get my face away from this camera fast enough. The door blows open with a *Jesus,* though the woman giggles an apology when she sees the cameras and realizes who I am. I step past her, pulling the door shut behind me, but it catches on something before I can get it to latch. I look down and find the dirty toe of a Golden Goose sneaker.

Brett turns sideways and fits her body inside, closing the door on the long snout of the camera. This has happened before—Marc stuck outside filming a slammed door, while our mics pick up a "private" conversation. Brett seizes me by the shoulders, pulling me toward her with her lips puckered. I can't tell if she's going to kiss me or spit on me. "I won't let you do this, Steph!" She shakes me, with dramatic effect but very little actual force. "You don't get to walk out like that. You don't get to decide when we talk and when we don't. I'm not your fucking subordinate." She releases me to bring two fists to her mouth, her shoulders quivering with silent church laughter. She jabs a finger at me, mouthing, *Go! You go!*

I stare at Brett for a few long, hard seconds. *Give me something,* I plead with her inwardly. *Give me anything.* Brett blinks back at me, the smile dropping away from her face. It seems like she might say something—something real—but instead she starts to cough, abruptly and violently. She coughs so hard she chokes. She coughs so hard tears stream down her face. "Wrong pipe," she croaks, clutching her throat with one hand, jabbing at the faucet behind me with the other. She means for me to turn it on so she can get some water. The most I'm willing to do is step aside so that she can see to her survival herself.

Brett folds at the waist, splashing water into her mouth with her hands, getting as much of it down as she can while coughing and sputtering, her nose running, her face a pleasing and unbecoming shade of red. Doubled over as she is, I have full access to my image in the mirror. I lean in, closer, scrutinizing Jason's work tonight. My skin is a flawless, even canvas, allowing my dark eyes to really pop. But still, I am thirty-four, ache in my heart.

It is not my age that stings, it is that my age decided to make itself known with very little warning. I have always looked so young. Then somewhere, midway through thirty-three, I looked into the mirror and *saw* that I was older. Ever since then, I've felt apologetic and guilty, exposed as a fraud, like a prominent evangelist pastor busted in a tawdry sex scandal. *I deeply regret my last birthday and beg for your forgiveness.* I've been skulking around the *Forbes* thirty under thirty crowd, aged out for a while now, but at least looking the part. Then thirty-three-and-a-half kicked in the door, seeming to bring with it the decade's full wallop overnight.

Every year, I have looked back on my last birthday and yearned to turn that year again. Twenty-eight was so young, twenty-nine was still so young, thirty was a baby! But thirty-four felt different. There will never be a time when I look back and think I was young at thirty-four. Young was left on the doorstep of thirty-three. I am sure of it.

Sometimes I think Jesse sniffed out my fear of aging, the way abusive men have a nose for women who grew up feeling undeserving of love. What did I say in my memoir? *Feeling less than was wet wood for a termite like A.J.* That was a good line. Jesse, like A.J., must have sensed my expiring sense of self-worth and thought to herself, *That one. That one won't think more of herself when I subject her to my mind games, that one will just take it.* All of the *Diggers* are damaged in some way. We must be. Why else would anybody sign up to be tossed out? Reality TV is like driving drunk. You know it might kill you, but there is something rakishly sexy about tempting the fates.

Brett straightens, gasping still, thumping her chest with a fist. "Wow," she rasps. "Wow. I don't know where that came from."

I know exactly where that came from. It came from Brett's subconscious, from the latent desire to come clean, to get something off her chest. The ego quashed it in her throat, strangling her, really, but knowing it resides within her—guilt—gives me the conviction I need to move forward with our original plan, hatched eight months ago in my kitchen on my thirty-fourth birthday.

I turn my back on the mirror, hoisting my butt onto the sink's ledge. I need to sit down for this. "I never thought of you as a subordinate," I say. "I thought of you as my friend. And me?" I tent my fingers lightly over my heart. "I go to the ends of the earth to support *my* friends. I took you in when you had nowhere else to go, and I guess I thought it was a given, that if ever an opportunity presented itself to return the favor, that you would take it. But you didn't. You had an opportunity to get my book into the hands of a major celebrity, whose support would have been huge, and you flat-out refused to help me. You wanted to keep that relationship all to yourself."

Brett's breathing is still labored, but I manage to detect a sigh of relief in the pattern. So far, I'm on script. I've said exactly what we always planned for me to say. "That's so not fair, Steph," she says, with a dopey, upward tug at the corners of her mouth. "You didn't lose anything by allowing me to stay at your house." She seems to realize that this line, which we practiced months and months ago, no longer applies, because her lips straighten once again. "I don't know," she says, eyes downcast. "Maybe I could have found a way to bring it to her attention. I could have at least tried." She looks up at me, her big eyes bigger. "I'm sorry, Steph. I'm so, so sorry."

I raise my eyebrows, and a valve in my heart thinks about opening. Because Brett is the one who is off script now. The plan had always been for me to apologize to her. Brett was to have come out of this scuffle smelling like roses.

"I miss you," Brett says, thickly. She might mean it. "It's killed me not to be able to congratulate you on all your success, which is so *so* well-deserved. And it's killed me not to be able to share with you what's going on with my life. Can we just—I don't know. Meet for a drink? Coffee? Catch up. I miss you," she repeats. "Every single day."

I am silent. Brett prompts me with a slow roll of her finger. It's my turn. "I miss you too," I force myself to say.

Brett hops up on the counter, so that we are thigh-to-thigh, shoulder-to-shoulder, conjoined twins. She covers my hand in her own, and I feel the cold metal on two fingers, instead of one. "Oh yeah," she says, holding up her hand with a wry smile. "I got engaged."

The band is plain, gold, and a little too thick. The signet I bought for her has so much more style.

"I'm happy for you, Brett," I say, with feeling, but everything in my body language is rigid. This does not deter Brett from draping an arm around my shoulders, from the assault of her warm touch. Does she actually believe me? If she does, she is so far down this rabbit hole of our perceived reality I almost feel sorry for her. Almost.

"We can make this right, can't we?" Brett pleads. "Come on. You know I always support you. Real queens fix each other's crowns."

My disdain takes my breath away. *Real queens fix each other's crowns?* This is the equivocating claptrap that passes for feminism these days. An Instagram idiom that places the burdon on the less effective party. Men get to go about their lives, paying women less and black women even less than that, unencumbered by cutesy demands to fix a problem *they* created. Telling women to help other women in a society that places us in a systemic competition with one another is a fool's errand. Two percent of the world's CEOs are women, and yet we are expected to treat each other like sisters and not rabid hyenas thrown a carcass picked to the gristle by lions. Malnourish me, undervalue me, humiliate and harass me when I try to *get my money* anyway, but don't you ever tell me to go about it nicely.

I say none of this because I am not here to be a truthsayer. I am here to capitulate. Brett isn't the only one acting out of a sense of self-preservation. I lean into this changeling's embrace, even though the stink of the French perfume I bought her tangled with the body odor in the pajama top I also bought her makes me queasy. "Yeah," I say. "I think we can make this right."

But touch my crown and you will lose a fucking finger. Put that on a coffee mug and hawk it.

CHAPTER 10

Brett

It was last year. Steph's thirty-fourth birthday. I had moved back in with her for the second time, after breaking up with my very needy ex-girlfriend. Sarah and I had lived in a newly constructed high-rise on North End and Murray that cost us forty-five hundred a month. The apartment had one hundred and fifty more square feet than my first place on York and Sixty-seventh, with a dishwasher and a view of a better high-rise across the street and nary a rodent nor a kitchen drawer wide enough to accommodate a utensils divider, and in New York City, that is the height of luxury living. No rats and no room. It was the nicest place I had ever paid to live in, almost nice enough for me to pretend like the relationship was working, but in the end, I couldn't take one more drunken accusation that I wasn't *all in*. The process of breaking a lease on a New York City apartment is more soul crushing than lunch hour at the DMV, so Sarah and I worked out a deal where if I moved out, I only had to pay a quarter of the rent until our lease was up in the fall, just a few months away. Sarah wasn't totally wrong about me not being *all in*, and I felt I owed it to her to let her stay in an apartment neither of us could have afforded on our own, at least for a few more months. Meanwhile, like a Pew Research statistic come to life, I was forced for financial reasons to move back in with my surrogate parents at twenty-six years old.

Steph had declared that for her thirty-fourth birthday, all she wanted was a quiet night in and Vince's killer coq au vin, which was very unlike Steph. But later, over dessert, she admitted the truth, which was that she didn't want proof of a birthday celebration on anyone's social media or in the press. She was afraid to remind Jesse that she was another year older.

"You are . . . ridiculous," I said, catching myself in time. I *wanted* to call her insane.

"You're too young to understand," Steph said, hysterically, toppling her untouched slice of Milk Bar Birthday Cake onto its side with her fork. She told me once that her medication makes anything sweet taste like cardboard.

"Try me," I said, thinking about reaching for her plate, but I didn't want to look like a pig, having already cleaned my own. *Why can't you just be normal* came my mother's voice. *I'm not saying to not eat dessert, I'm saying don't eat your dessert plus everyone else's.* I'd sneak down here later tonight and eat it straight from the box, I decided. If I polished it off, which was likely, I'd just tell them I noticed roaches in the kitchen and I threw the cake out before it could attract more. The plan had soothed me at the time.

"So," Steph said, resting her fork, tongs down, on her plate, "there's this German word, *torschlusspanik*. It literally translates to 'gate-shut-panic.' Are you familiar with this?"

I pushed a pair of imaginary Coke bottle glasses farther up the bridge of my nose. "Intimately."

On the other side of the table, Vince dropped his head with a soundless laugh.

"Forget it." Stephanie's shoulders tightened, and she clutched her water glass to her chest defensively. There was wine, but only Vince and I were drinking it. *Alcoholism runs in my family,* she has said to me enough times that I've started to suspect there is more to it than that. Like maybe Stephanie is someone who lubricates life's edges by staying in control at all times.

"Aw, babe. Come on." Vince reached for the hand that was pinned beneath his wife's armpit and settled on holding her wrist when she wouldn't give it to him. Stephanie never could laugh at herself. People say that I'm quick to make others the butt of my jokes, but I am the first one to recognize when I'm being too Brett-y. Stephanie doesn't have that ability, and I never realized before I moved in how delicately Vince had to tread around her. He seemed to not mind it, but later I learned he was exhausted.

"*Please*," I begged. "Tell us. I didn't graduate from college. How else am I supposed to learn about . . . *tushy* . . . *spank*?" I glanced from Stephanie to Vince with big bimbo eyes, my palm flipped up by my shoulder—*is that right?* Vince tried not to laugh again, but even Stephanie couldn't hold a straight face.

"I hate you." She laughed, despite herself.

"But in direct proportion to how much you love me, right?" I stole one forkful of her dessert and immediately regretted it. It only made me want to pick up the piece of cake in both hands and bite into it like a sandwich.

Stephanie drummed her fingers on her forearm, taking her time being convinced to share. "*Torschlusspanik*," she said finally, resting her water glass on a white marble coaster, "is the sensation—*the fear*—that time is running out." She jabbed at her heart with a finger. "I have that. With this birthday. Thirty-three was my last *something* birthday. The last year your success is special. It's the last age anyone can call you a wunderkind, if we're sticking to the German theme."

I cleared my throat and chose my words carefully. "Um. Okay. Go on." I raised my eyebrows at Vince, who sighed wearily.

"It gets better," he said, gesturing at his chin, meaning I had frosting on mine. I wiped my face with their lattice-woven linens. *Japanese, sixty bucks*, Stephanie had told me when I said they were pretty, which is something Stephanie always does, volunteer a brand name or a price when you pay her a compliment, as though you don't even know the half of how nice her things are.

Stephanie bowed her head, as if summoning the patience to explain a very advanced concept to very advanced imbeciles. "After the obvious markers—sweet sixteen, you can drive, eighteen, you can vote, twenty-one you can drink, there is a whole chunk of time where you are presumably getting your ducks in order as a young adult. If you're going to do something exceptional with your life, it takes until twenty-seven to get society to notice. Unless"—she silenced me with a hand before I could object—"you are Brett Courtney, girl wonder of the boutique fitness world."

"Damn right," Vince said, topping off my wine.

"Damn right," I agreed, raising my glass in what turned out to be a solitary toast.

Stephanie waited for me to set my glass on the table before continuing. "So that brings us to the twenty-seven club, of which icons like Kurt Cobain and Janis Joplin and Amy Winehouse are members. The club *romanticizes* the very idea of the young virtuoso, taken from us too soon. Next we have the thirtieth birthday, your dirty thirty, which is an overtly sexy birthday that doesn't need much explaining. That's when all the lists start, the thirty under thirty most powerful, most influential, wealthiest, yada, yada. And everyone gets to say, oh my God, she's only thirty? You don't believe me now but you're such a baby at thirty. You are," she said off my skeptical look. "And then thirty-one is the year women peak in their beauty and then thirty-three is your Jesus year. Your next special birthday after that is thirty-five, when the medical community categorizes your pregnancy as geriatric."

"I'm sorry," I sputtered, "a *Jesus* year?"

Vince tossed his napkin onto his plate. "Talk some sense into her, Brett," he started, collecting our dirty dishes, "because I've tried."

"Leave it, Vince," Steph said.

"It's your birthday, babe." Vince came around to Steph's side of the table and kissed the top of her head. "Sit with your friend."

"I gotta find myself someone who cooks *and* cleans," I said, in a blatant attempt to get Stephanie to warm to her own husband, to recognize how much he'd done for her today, to appreciate it. Some days I was Vince's publicist and some days I was Stephanie's, depending on who was the one who needed to be pitched to the other more.

"I'm a man of the millennium, Brett!" Vince said from the kitchen, turning on the faucet and running his fingers under the water, waiting for it to warm. "You should come over to our side. We cook and clean and fold your thongs into adorable triangles."

I emptied the bottle of wine into my glass. "Great! I need more rosé, millennium man!" I drew a knee to my chest and addressed Steph. "Okay, so, Jesus year . . ."

Steph paused long enough for me to stop smiling. "The Jesus year," Stephanie said, with such reverence I cleared my throat to cover my laugh, "is a year of great historical precedence, given that it's the age God decided his son had accomplished everything he needed to accomplish on this earth. Your Jesus year is the year you realize it's now or never. You cash in your 401(k) to open an ice-cream shop in Costa Rica. It's the last year you're ever young enough to make a major career change, and it's the last year anyone can fawn over how young you are if it hits."

"Steph," I said, giving in to the urge to laugh, "you're a *New York Times* bestselling author with a major Hollywood studio paying you a lot of money to turn your books into movies. You're on a TV show with two million viewers. You have *stairs* in your New York City apartment and three Chanel bags—"

"And bae is ridiculously good-looking," Vince said, appearing tableside with a fresh bottle of rosé, so chilled his thumbs left translucent prints on the fogged bottle.

I made a gesture of support toward Vince. "Who also talks very cool! How much better can you do?"

"I can't do any better—that's the point!" She slid a coaster under the rosé bottle and with her Japanese linens mopped its wet ring from the oiled oak table. Vince responded *Sorry*, as though a verbal exchange had taken place. "I've already peaked. Thirty-four is a nothing year. It's your done year. I'm not getting asked back for next season. No one has survived the show past thirty-four."

Vince and I shared an incredulous look across the table. But then I actually thought about it. "That's not true, is it?"

Stephanie readied her fingers to be counted. "Let's examine the evidence, shall we?" Tapping finger number one, "Allison Greene, season one, thirty-two." Tapping her middle finger she continued, "Carolyn Ebelbaum, seasons two and three, aged thirty-two. Hayley Peterson, seasons one, two, and three, aged thirty-three." She set all her counted fingers on the table, as if to rest her case.

I shook my head, refusing to believe any of this was purposeful. "It's a coincidence. It's not, like, a height cutoff at an amusement park ride. You don't have to get off this ride at thirty-four."

"Well maybe I don't want to take that chance," Steph said, folding her dinner napkin into a prim square. "I need to make sure I'm asked back for season four. The last book came and went with a whimper. I can't go out like that."

Oh, god. The desperation on her face. It will never not break my heart to remember it.

"Get ready," Vince said, back in the kitchen now, exfoliating a soaked pan with a Brillo Pad, the sound of steel on iron making my teeth ache.

Her voice smaller than I'd ever heard it, Steph said to me, "Don't say no until I'm finished, okay?"

Across the room, Vince worked his finger around his ear, as though he were spinning cotton candy onto a yarn, mouthing, *Crazy*. In that moment, I hated him.

During those weeks I lived with Steph and Vince, my empathy was like a transferable property right, something I leased out, depending on who was shitting harder on whom. I had heard the rumors about Vince before I moved in, of course—everyone had—but I chose to believe Stephanie when she said they were just that, rumors, and that she and Vince were still madly in love. I've thought a lot about the difference between believing her and in choosing to believe her, and why I was so gung ho to participate in such an obvious sham, and it must have been because I idolized her. I couldn't reconcile my fangirl image of her with the clichéd reality that she was just another little wife at home, waiting up for her husband past midnight.

I was fifteen and Stephanie twenty-three when she published the first book in her fiction trilogy. I remember stealing my mother's copy from her nightstand while she was out of the house, memorizing the page number after each reading because if I folded a corner, Mom would know I had been reading a book with a lot of sex in it and *ew, ew, ew*. Stephanie's author picture was a stunningly perfect glamour shot, with lipstick, honking diamond studs in her ears, and a dazzling smile. Her bio was terrifically cosmopolitan: *Stephanie Simmons lives on the Upper East Side* (Not in New York! Not in Manhattan! *On* the Upper East Side.) *with her dearly beloved collection of Jimmy Choos*. The wit of her! The beauty! *Stephanie Simmons is when I found my vagina*, I once joked to a reporter who asked me how it felt to have her take me under her wing. Stephanie tweeted a link to the interview twice. She loved how much I adored her, and that turned out to be the root of all our problems.

Living with Steph and Vince, I couldn't help but notice I played a role for Stephanie not unlike the one Vince had taken on. She had a tendency to gravitate toward people who were below her station in life, to build you up to a certain point but never too high. She did not react well as I started to close the gap between us. She became needy, suffocating, jealous. Why couldn't she host the fourth hour of the *Today* show with me? Why couldn't I bring her as my date to the *Glamour* Women of the Year Awards? She could keep Vince under her thumb to a certain extent, but she didn't have the same jurisdiction over me, and she started to resent me for it.

Steph clings to the fact that Vince *chose* her before the show was even a twinkle in Jesse's eye, but she had two books published before she got married, and one movie *based on the novel by Stephanie Simmons* already made. She may not have been movie-star recognizable when she met Vince, but clearly, he took in her clothes, her jewelry, and her doorman apartment *on* the Upper East Side and fell in love with her lifestyle. I do believe he fell in love with her next. But marrying someone who falls for what you have first and who you are after does not a healthy marriage make.

So, yeah, Vince is sort of scummy for that. But Stephanie isn't off the hook either. She knew what she was getting herself into when she married a guy like Vince, and she still registered for all the crystal stemware from Scully & Scully anyway, because she liked the idea of a trophy husband. And Vince is the *quintessential* trophy husband—a little skinny-fat—but this is New York, not L.A., and it is nothing those eyes won't make you forget. Had he been too ripped, a certain grassroots rumor might have picked up more steam, which is that Vince and Stephanie are covering for each other in a Will and Jada Pinkett Smith–esque arrangement, if you know what I mean.

It's hard to feel bad for either one of them and it's hard not to feel bad for both of them. It depends on the day. Throughout *that* day, leading up to Stephanie's birthday dinner, I had been firmly in Vince's camp. He had waited on us hand and foot from the moment we woke up, starting with a heavenly batch of homemade blueberry ricotta pancakes served to us in bed, but nothing could lift Stephanie's spirits. Stephanie suffers from a sort of dysmorphia when it comes to her success, and good luck to anyone who attempts to convince her that her talent and tenacity have been recognized. Clearly, Vince sensed my exasperation with her, and that's why he felt emboldened to make that gesture, to break the cardinal rule of *Goal Diggers* by mouthing *Crazy*. I crossed party lines again in that moment, over to Stephanie's side, as I watched Vince wash his white Le Creuset pans that his wife bought him in the beautiful kitchen his wife paid for. I may be engaged to a woman but I know this much to be true about hetero relationships, and that is that men who call women *crazy* are always the men who have first pushed them to the brink.

"I'm listening," I told Steph, and the gratitude in her smile made me look away in secondhand embarrassment. The worst part about getting old has to be asking people younger than you for their help. God, I pray that will never be me.

"Do you know the highest-rated episode of reality TV of all time?"

I thought about it for a moment. "Talk shows don't count, right?"

"Don't count."

"What about that WWE shit?"

"This tied WWE Raw."

"Holy shit." I laughed, genuinely intrigued. "What was it?"

"*The Hills*. Season three premiere. 'You Know What You Did.' "

I instantly saw Lauren Conrad in my mind, cast red by West Hollywood lights, berating Heidi Montag, *You know why I'm mad at you. You know what you did!* "I remember it," I said.

"Of course you do. Show me a woman under the age of thirty-five who doesn't remember the Lauren and Heidi feud. The Lauren and Heidi feud was a thing of beauty. So was the rivalry between Katy Perry and Taylor Swift, Tonya Harding and Nancy Kerrigan, Bette Davis and Joan Crawford. Female aggression is curtailed, and therefore taboo, and therefore ratings gold. Did you know that toddler girls are just as inclined to roughhouse as boys, but we teach them to blunt those instincts?" She sees the recognition on my face and says, "Yeah." I was thinking about Kelly and me: biting, scratching, strands of her hair in my hand, from root to split end.

"We learn to channel our aggression passively from a young age," she shrugged, as though this were old news, "and that's why woman-to-woman combat is spectator sport. Women have to get creative when we fight. We're professionals. No wonder people line up to see us do our thing."

"Jen and I fight," I point out.

"But you've always fought. There's no room for treachery when you've never gotten along. Viewers don't want a fight, they want a betrayal."

"And how do we give them that?"

"We pull a Lauren and Heidi." She stole my glass of wine and took a walloping gulp. "I'll even let you be Lauren Conrad. I'll be the heel," she said through that puckering face we all make when we drink something too cold too fast. Stars, they're just like us.

The fight, Stephanie said, had to be serious enough that viewers wouldn't accuse us of being petty, wouldn't tell us in the comments on our Instagram posts to put our *big girl* panties on and sort it out.

(If birth control doesn't give her a stroke at thirty-five, it will be a grown woman in Minnesota telling Stephanie how to conduct herself using the language of a kiddie diddler.) The fight also couldn't be so irreparable that we wouldn't reconcile in time for the Morocco trip. We would end the season in Morocco, she promised. Nothing we were doing was ever meant to be permanent.

The heart of this serious-but-not-irreparable fight would be this: that Stephanie had come to me and asked me to push her book on Rihanna, with the thought that she was perfect to play her in the film adaptation should the rights be optioned. She was working on a new book about her childhood, opening up about some things she'd wanted to talk about for a long time. *What things?* I had asked, intrigued, but also feeling a little queasy. I could tell by the look on her face she was not talking about happy childhood memories.

"Just some stuff I went through when I was young," she'd said, glancing at Vince furtively. "But when I ask you to push it on your new star client, you say you aren't comfortable doing that, and I flip out. I claim you *owe me*." Stephanie lowered her eyes sadly. "I'm going to look crazy. But," she raised her shoulders and thinned her lips, "if Jesse finds out we're fighting, she'll have to ask me back next season to see it all play out. And I'd rather be hated for a few months than fast-forwarded."

"Fuck that guy," I said, meaning the writer at *New York* mag who had taken to calling Stephanie *Sleptanie* in his recaps of season three. But suddenly, as if her fear were an app with a share feature, I felt it too. There was a very strong likelihood that my closest ally on the show would not be asked back. She had been a bore to film last season. Marc had made that crack about timing his Ritalin dosage to Stephanie scenes, and Lisa was always coming at Stephanie's face with a Starbucks napkin in hand, calling her Miss New York, not kindly.

And sometimes, when Stephanie stops smiling but the lines around her mouth remain, she does look like she's starting to get old.

The fight was supposed to have happened off camera, between seasons, and, like method actors, we were to commit. As soon as my lease was up in the fall and I was through paying rent to Sarah, I could afford to move out, and that's when we would cease all communication. We couldn't put on a front to the media, to the other castmates, to *Jesse,* if at home, late at night, we were texting each other goofy emojis. We'd seen what happened to Hayley when she was hacked, and we couldn't chance anyone figuring us out. It's why I didn't reach out to Steph to congratulate her when the book came out and caught fire, even though I was dying to. Even though I was actually hurt. She had been choked out, spit on, and raped, and she never told me? She was supposed to be my best friend.

It's also why I was unable to give her a heads-up about the lunch with Jesse and my sister. Maybe I would have found a way to get in touch with her if I thought Kelly was anything more than a Green Party candidate. But I truly saw it as a mercy meeting for my sister, which was completely naive in retrospect. Of course Jesse would see my niece, nine-foot-tall mini mogul, with stars in her eyes. And of course Steph would read the decision to cast two of my family members as me trying to make a grab for the spotlight when we'd manipulated an arc that was meant to split it. I allowed myself to believe that was when the fight became real for her, though deep down I knew that wasn't it. Deep down, I knew what it was really about.

It took me until the all-cast prod meeting to realize that the fight was no longer fake. Steph and I are the only castmates who keep in touch off camera. So it was normal that I hadn't seen Lauren or Jen until the prod meeting. That Stephanie had seen them was not. And when the women simultaneously turned their backs on Morocco, I knew it had nothing to do with me "refusing" to slip the book to my celebrity rider.

I don't know what would have happened if Yvette hadn't taken pity on me and exposed Jen's back-alley protein habit. Once I obliterated the alliance, I figured I had two choices. I could expose Steph's scheme, but in doing so, I would have to admit to my role in it, and Jesse, whose nonnegotiables are no fashion bloggers except Leandra Medine and no fake storylines, would have been irate. Or, I could play dumb. Pretend like this was all a part of the plan, that Stephanie wasn't trying to ice me off the show, that she didn't sincerely despise me now, and proceed with the reconciliation as we had originally conceived, cumulating in the trip to Morocco. To my great relief, Steph played along when I cornered her in the bathroom at Lauren's event.

Only now, it feels like instead of pretending to be in a fight, we're pretending to be friends. In my wildest dreams I never would have imagined that the fight would become real and the friendship the charade.

CHAPTER 11

Stephanie

My best friend is meeting me at Barneys, to help me pick out shoes for the dinner with the Oscar-Nominated Female Director. I reread Lisa's reminder text from earlier this morning: *REMINDER, this is the first time you've seen Brett since you made up in the bathroom at Lauren's party.* This CliffsNote is necessary as she assumes we've seen each other since Lauren's party, three weeks ago. And why shouldn't she? We "made up." Things are "back to normal." I'm going to Morocco. How I wish I could put negating quotation marks around that.

Lisa sends us these reminder texts before most scenes out of chronological necessity. We are not a scripted series but we are a corralled one. We shoot out of order, sometimes filming a coffee date after a big blowout between two of the cast members to "set up" the confrontation, which will appear to have taken place later in the hour on your television screen. Lisa used to text me before I met Brett, *REMINDER, the last thing you talked about was Lauren's arrest,* when we'd spoken about a million different things since then, some on camera and some off. You start to pick out threads as filming progresses, the reminder texts serving as headline beats for all the intersecting storylines. Clearly, the Brett and Steph reconciliation is going to be a big one this season, just like we planned it.

Ever since Lauren's event, I've waited for . . . something from her.

If she texted me, I would have said she should have called. If she called, I would say she should have done it in person. She couldn't have done it right, no matter what she did, but anything to acknowledge the real thing that happened between us would have been something.

I have lost friends before but it has never felt like this, like having a stroke and having to relearn how to walk, which hand is left and which hand is right. Brett nuked my instincts, coaxed my most vulnerable secrets out of me by dangling her own, which turned out to be artificial bait. I told her the painful details about things of which I've only given Vince the broad strokes, most notably, the extent of my struggle with depression. I hate that word. "Depression." I hear it and I think of that black lab in the commercials, toy in his mouth, whimpering for a walk, his owner too flatlined to get off the couch. I hate it because it's true. When my depression is at full strength, it doesn't roar, it yawns. I have wet my bed, wide-awake and sober, because the effort of getting up and taking ten steps to the toilet has felt like an insurmountable summit. That Brett knows this and more—much more—and that I have now lost her loyalty feels like my secrets have sprouted legs and are out there in the world, wearing short skirts and hooker heels to solicit listeners. The threat of exposure menaces me constantly, but the fear is always secondary to the pain of the breach. I left my heart open around Brett. I turned around for one second and she burgled it.

Lately, I've been thinking that we challenged God by machinating our storyline the way we did, and he did not appreciate it one bit (we all know it's a man). Like he got wind of our small-potatoes stakes and scoffed down at us, *Oh, you're looking for something to actually fight about?* If I'd never proposed it, if I'd never messed with the order of the universe, would it still have happened? *Wait a minute,* I think-gasp, as I glide above a mannequin outfitted in so much velvet Prince would take offense. Does she think it's my fault? Has she been waiting for *me* to say something to *her*? The softness I was feeling toward her stales as I ride the elevator the rest of the way to the shoe department. That would be typical Brett, who I am convinced does so much good in this world just to absolve herself of any wrongdoing.

I get to the fifth floor and discover I am the first to arrive. *No matter,* I think, pacified by the image of Brett showing up sweaty and frazzled, knowing she will find me coiled and rattling. I hate being made to wait. The minutes tick by and I realize, not only is she not early, she is late. Very late. Ten minutes late. Seventeen. Twenty-two.

"If she's not here in five minutes I'm leaving," I say to Rachel, our field producer who could not be bothered to find something other than rubber flip-flops for a morning at Barneys. I know Rachel earns about 38K a year and I'm being an almighty snob, but my mood is decomposing by the second.

"Let me see where she's at," Rachel says, stepping away to call her. But then, as though summoned, Brett rounds the corner, not a stride harried and wearing an expensive-looking T-shirt and weird jeans, a nice watch and those blocky white sneakers that cost more than a laptop. She looks good, I realize, breathlessly, she looks young and rich. *But is she pretty?* I find myself wondering, pettily. She's a bigger girl, downgraded from *big girl,* which was how she identified herself in season one. Oh, the Big Gulp–swilling biddies came for her on Facebook: *The average American woman wears a size eighteen. If you're "big," what does that make us?* (Edited for clarity, spelling, and punctuation. The discourse did occur on Facebook.) I was tempted to fire back on her behalf, *What that makes you is enormous, Deb,* but Brett can't stand to be unliked or less than thoroughly understood. She responded to each and every plus-sized crybaby and apologized, explaining that in New York there is a premium placed on thinness, and so she often feels like a *big girl* compared to her peers. She thanked them for this teachable moment, this reminder that she moves in a true bubble of privilege, and vowed to be more thoughtful about the language she used to talk about bodies in the future. What a spectacular waste of everyone's time.

I have no idea what size Brett wears, though it's not a size eighteen and it's not a four, which is what I am, and I'm a *bigger girl* than Lauren and Jen combined. I do know that her shape is proportionate and the skin on her thighs and stomach—of which I've seen too much, alas—is impressively smooth, unpocked by dimples or cellulite. It is a bigger body but it is not an unconventional one, and I haven't even gotten to her face, which, with her cartoonish big brown eyes and clear olive skin, is undeniably lovely. It would seem then that the answer is obvious—*Is she pretty? Yes, she is.* But I can't quite get there. Perhaps because Brett behaves in a way that suggests she doesn't even think it is true. She talks a loud game about self-compassion, about how women need to develop the neural pathways to access kind and loving self-talk (self, self, *self*), then turns around and maims her skin with all those seedy tattoos. And I've seen the way she "nourishes" herself. Brett was a violent eater during the time she lived with me, housing boxes of frozen waffles still frozen, spooning strange concoctions of sugar and flour and vanilla flavoring into her mouth like soup in the middle of the night. There was nothing kind or loving about that. It was the secretive, shifty behavior of someone downright ashamed of herself.

Brett smiles at me, shyly, but not apologetically. I am walled in by a fort of shoeboxes at this point, a pink-bowed Aquazzura sandal on one foot, a suede Isabel Marant bootie on the other. I get up to examine my lower legs in the short fitting mirror, and Brett mistakes it for an invitation to embrace. I cannot reject her, not with the cameras here. And so against my will, I wrap my arms around her and tuck my face into her shoulder. As I inhale the keen powder scent of her Moroccan oil shampoo and compare, breast to breast, her mellow heartbeat to the rabbit's pace of my own, I wonder, indulgently, *Has she gotten fatter?*

"Did you have trouble finding it?" I ask her when we pull away.

"Finding what?"

"The shoe department. I know there's the other one on the seventh floor and you don't get up here much."

Brett seems confused. "I mean, I don't. But I found it fine."

"Just late then." I grin at her, savagely.

Brett checks that nice Cartier on her wrist. Looks vintage. How cool is she? "I was five minutes early for you."

For a moment, the last eight months never happened. We both turn and glare at Rachel. "I was told eleven!" she says, sounding guilty.

Occasionally, Lisa has production supply varying arrival times for the cast. It's a dirty trick, designed to load us with resentment before we even walk onto the set. You make an egomaniac wait, make her feel like her time hasn't been respected, and you work her into a state. Even if she puts it together, which I just did, I'm glowering. I will be cordial but gruff toward Brett, and everyone will think I'm a bitch for saying I'm over it when I'm really not, and it will make for a delicious two minutes of television.

Well, if I'm going to be portrayed as a hag I may as well make my money. I reach into my purse for the gift I wrapped for Brett earlier. I had second-guessed myself up until now, unsure if I should give it to her or not. That nasty production hack cemented my decision.

Brett laughs.

"What?"

She reaches into *her* purse and offers me a small, long box in wrapping paper. "I got you something too."

We open them at the same time. Mine is a pair of red Wayfarer sunglasses with the word SPOKE in white along the temple. Brett's gift is my memoir, signed. Could we be any less subtle?

"Damn, we are thirsty bitches." Brett laughs, directly into the camera. I take it back—we couldn't be any less subtle, but Brett could. I have placed my books into scenes sparingly over the years, knowing that the Internet stops and frisks women for being too self-promotional. Unless you are Brett, who can't sneeze without wiping her nose with a SPOKE embroidered hankie. The Big Chill always manages to get off without even a warning.

"The sunglasses are to wear in Morocco," she tells me, then clutches my book, cover up, to her chest. "And I will display this in my new apartment with pride."

"How's it going?" I ask, my eyes twinkling with obligatory curiosity. "Totally different than living with Sarah, I imagine. I mean, you *are* engaged." I laugh as though we have just shared some sort of inside joke.

"We're both so busy we hardly see each other," Brett says, neutrally. It is a smart answer. A politician's answer.

"That's not necessarily a bad thing," I return. "Time apart makes time together exciting. Vince and I can't keep our hands off each other after I get home from a book tour." I curl one side of my mouth into a suggestive half smile. *You're not the only one in a hot relationship, honeybuns.*

Brett is visibly uncomfortable, as I'd hoped.

Victorious, I turn my attention to my feet. "Which ones for dinner with the Female Director?"

"The sandals," Brett says, without hesitation. "Definitely."

"The pink ones with a *bow*?" I hoot. "That girl has made you soft."

Brett stands up straighter. She didn't like that. I knew she wouldn't. "They look beige to me."

I sit down and thread the ankle strap through the buckle. "Blush," I say with a tiny little smirk. Brett is far girlier than she lets on. "They're blush." I look up as the saleswoman approaches. "I'll take the Isabel Marant boots and the Aquazzura sandals—but the Aquazzuras in a size eight."

"Do you want to try them on first to be sure they fit?" the saleswoman asks.

"No," I tilt my head in Brett's direction, "but she does."

Brett chops the air with her hands, refusing. "No," she says. "Absolutely not."

"Absolutely yes," I say, firmly. I cannot let my book be my present, not after we were both caught on camera gifting each other our own swag. "This is my engagement gift to you. I'm going on a book tour again, and then I have this dinner in L.A. obviously, and I feel bad I can't make your . . ." I stop. Brett's engagement party is meant to be a surprise. "I mean, I feel bad I haven't gotten to celebrate with you yet."

Brett gives me a quizzical look, but she doesn't probe, just stoops to pick up the sandal and check the price tag on its arch. She gasps and sets it back down. "Get me a candle or something," she says. "This is too much."

"Give me a break," I scoff. "They're not much more than those ratty things." I raise an eyebrow at her sneakers. Brett turns her toes inward as Marc lowers the lens, as though trying to conceal the incriminating label on the tongue. All it takes is one Google search to find out that our hopeful young striver paid five hundred dollars for a pair of gym shoes.

The saleswoman returns with the sandals in Brett's size and reluctantly, she slips off her sneakers and buckles them on. Everything about her changes with those vampy four inches. It's as though her appearance finally matches what I know about her. I cast about for some kind of veiled insult.

"Giving your upper appendages a break?" I comment, noticing her latest tattoo along the inseam of her foot, some word in another language, looks like Arabic. The ink is SPOKE red, of course.

Brett rolls her eyes. "For now, Mom."

I blink, protectively, as though she has aimed a laser pointer at my eyes. Whether she meant to highlight our age difference or not, how dare she.

"You are one of the most generous people I know, Steph," Brett rushes to say, hearing how the joke landed. "But I can't accept. Putting your baby-making on hold to come to Morocco is more than enough of an engagement gift."

I rummage around in my purse for my wallet. She is leaving with those shoes, if I have to stake them in her eyeballs. "My doctor said Zika isn't even in Morocco right now. There's really no sacrifice. Besides," I find the steel-colored card I intend to use, "they're bridal-looking. You'll have plenty of events to wear them to in the near future." I lock eyes with her. It feels like the moment in a wedding ceremony when the priest addresses the crowd: *If anyone can show just cause why this couple cannot lawfully be joined together in matrimony, speak now or forever hold your peace.*

"I still can't believe you're going to have a baby," Brett says instead.

"I still can't believe you're getting married," I reply without missing a beat. We smile out of formality, both of us holding our peace for now.

CHAPTER 12

Brett

"New Year's Eve?" I vault a puddle in the street, barely clearing its littered shoreline. I'm feeling wildly precious in the shoes Steph bought me, which I'm only wearing because Arch asked so nicely. *With the lace dress*, she suggested. The last time Arch was in L.A. for work she brought me home a tea-stained, bell-shaped floral paneled caftan. It looks like something straight out of the Green Menace's closet, but I must admit, it does look rather fetching on me. I think it would have paired cutely with my sneakers, but what's that old sexist adage? *Happy wife, happy life.*

I need to say something here, which is that I didn't set out to own a pair of five-hundred-dollar sneakers. I ended up with them by way of bad weather and distracted walking. I stepped into a puddle on my way to check out the construction at the Soho studio one morning, and I popped inside the first store I came across that featured sneakers in the window display. I didn't even think to check the price—how much could a pair of sneakers cost?—and the salesgirl had been so sweet and helpful, with nothing but wonderful things to say about SPOKE. I wasn't about to kill her commission when she rang me up, though I almost fainted when she announced the damage. *You'll wear them every day*, she promised when she saw my face, and so to justify the splurge, I have, to the point that Arch has asked me to stash them in the hall closet so that they don't stink up our bedroom.

The truth is, five-hundred-dollar sneakers are not a splurge for me anymore. I can't afford to spend like that every day, but to occasionally treat myself and those I love to some big-ticket items without breaking a sweat? Yeah, I can do that. I am in a different tax bracket this season than I was in previous years, and I haven't figured out how to square that with my role as the "low-income one." I am proud of how far I've come, but I don't want to alienate the women who relate to my former financial struggles. Unsurprisingly, my colleagues seem dead set on outing me before I am ready to address the discrepancy. They want to punish me for their own cowardice. Yes, I asked the network for more money and I got it, okay? That doesn't prevent my castmates from stepping up and doing the same.

"I always pictured myself getting married outside," Arch says, bearing down on the hand I've offered her and stepping off the curb like a praying mantis. She's wearing high sandals too, only hers tie at the ankles with two furry pom-poms.

"We could do New Year's Eve destination," I say, looking both ways before crossing the street. "Anguilla?"

"It's already going to be such a haul for my family." Arch slips her thin body sideways between two parked cars. "Thank you." She smiles at me winningly as I hold the door for her.

"We don't have a reservation," I tell the hostess at L'Artusi. "Anything at the bar?"

She *hmmms*, jamming a fist beneath her chin as she scans her tablet. "Actually, we just had a cancellation." She punches various coordinates on the screen with her finger and locates two menus, pinning them under her arm. "I have a table open upstairs."

My eyebrows practically fly off my forehead. No wait at L'Artusi on a Saturday night? Money!

Arch steps ahead of me, grabbing my hand and leading me through the restaurant. I pass a girl who drops her bread knife in recognition. "Brett!" she calls, waving drunkenly. "I love you!" Her friend seizes her hand, groaning, *Oh my God, Meredith.*

"Have a good night, Meredith." I laugh over my shoulder, and Meredith rips her hand away and gets in her friend's face as if to say, *See? She liked it.*

"What about a destination wedding at a midway point?" I shout over the Saturday-night racket, clomping up the stairs behind Arch. *Pick up your feet, Brett,* Mom used to complain as I shuffled into the kitchen, wondering what low-carb nightmare she was making for dinner that night. There are countable moments of silence between Arch's steps. Another reason my mother probably would have preferred her to me.

At the top of the stairs, Arch pauses, waiting for me to catch up. My first reaction is that there is a glitch in the reservation system, because there are absolutely no tables available up here. There are no tables, period, only people standing around, champagne flutes resting at their hips. Then I see the cameras and Lisa, Arch's parents, Kelly and Layla and Jen and Lauren and Vince and most staggeringly *Jesse,* and the collective congratulatory cry is the last piece of the puzzle.

"Arch!" I clasp my hands over my nose, tears springing to my eyes.

"Mom and Dad wanted to surprise you," Arch says, laughing a little, but her eyes are misty too. "Oh my God, come here." She grabs my wrist and tugs me into her chest. Everyone *aws*, and Arch's parents approach us first, Lisa, Marc, and the rest of the camera crew steps behind.

"You are really surprised?" Arch's mom asks, sweetly skeptical. Her smile makes me feel like a hot, hair-covered turd. *I don't deserve to have you or your daughter in my life,* I think as I wrap my arms around her neck.

"I am so surprised," I promise Dr. Chugh, sinking into her warm, plump body like a cushion. This is how my mom would have felt if she had let me hug her more. This is how a mom should feel—soft but solid, with some weight on her, some permanence. Arch gets her stature and long limbs from Satya, her father. I wasn't sure how the parents of a first-generation Indian woman would react to their daughter dating a tattooed American with a nose ring and nipples that lactate, but Arch pointed out that she introduced her first girlfriend to her parents when she was twenty-three years old, that she's thirty-six now, and have I seen her ass? Do the math; there have been many who came before me.

The filthy family money comes from Satya's side and the progressive female ambition from Dr. Chugh, a retired surgeon at Lucile Packard Children's Hospital who thrust scientific literature onto her wary husband when Arch first came out. *There is no medical cure for homosexuality and we have one daughter,* Dr. Chugh said, extracting tolerance from reason. She has offered to talk to my father the way she talked to Satya, but the problem is, my father has two daughters.

I release Dr. Chugh and lean back to get a better look at her. Dr. Chugh wears the same uniform whether it is day or night, summer or winter: a dark blazer, dark soft jeans, red or navy loafers, and always, a colorful silk scarf that starts exactly where her gray-streaked bob ends. "Thank you so much," I tell her. "You planned this?"

"We suggested Per Se but Arch says that is not *your style*." Dr. Chugh deploys the bunny ears after she finishes speaking, though it's clear the words they are meant to bracket. "We are *not cool*." The bunny ears come after, again.

"I said *Per Se* is not cool, Mom," Arch says, planting a kiss on the top of her mother's head.

I laugh. "You are the coolest, Dr. Chugh. You too, Satya." I rise up on the balls of my feet to hug Arch's dad. His hug is weak; but it is a hug.

"We are happy for you both," Satya says. He pats me on the shoulder and his hand gets tangled in my hair. We laugh, awkwardly, as I weave him free.

Arch rests her elbow on her mother's shoulder. Like Kelly, she's a head taller than the woman who bore her. "Mom and Dad want to know if there is any way they can convince you to have the wedding in Delhi."

"We were married at the Roseate," Dr. Chugh says. She swoons, remembering. "Beautiful."

Satya nods, eyeing the boom pole above our heads uncertainly. "It really was."

Arch walls her face with her hand and speaks out of the side of her mouth to me. "We're not getting married at the Roseate."

"What did you just say?" Dr. Chugh swats her daughter.

"We'll think about it!" Arch laughs. "Oh, Brett," she says, as the crowd starts to press forward. "I think you need to make the rounds." I look up in time to see Jesse, moving through the room like an ambulance blaring. Women step out of her way as though lives depend on it.

"I can't believe you're here!" I cry, as she jumps into my arms and—*oh, God, no!*—straps her legs around my waist. I check quickly to make sure my future in-laws aren't looking, but they are gawking. I pretend to stumble under the double-digits of Jesse's weight, hoping she will take a hint and unravel herself from me.

"It was that or plunge headfirst into a bottle of Casamigos." Jesse sets her feet on the ground, to my great relief, and locks her elbows around my ribs so tightly I grunt, like I'm being given the Heimlich maneuver. "You're breaking my heart, woman." She sighs, peering over my shoulder. I don't have to turn my head to know she's eyeing my fiancée. "If I had to lose you to anyone, I'm glad it's to someone as special and, honestly? As camera friendly as Arch." She rests her forehead against mine and whispers, loudly, "You are going to bring in a shit ton of wedding advertising dollars for me on your spinoff show and for that reason I am supremely happy for you." She lays a kiss on the tip of my nose. "What do you think about *Bride Pride* as the name of the show? We could time it to Pride month."

I wave a hand, unenthusiastically.

"We'll work on it." She turns to the camera and addresses Lisa. "Obviously this does not make final cut."

"It doesn't?" comes Lisa's sarcastic, piercing voice. It's impossible to see her on the searing side of the Fresnel.

Jesse lays her hand on my shoulder, in a departing sort of gesture.

"You're not staying?"

"It's my only night off from the aftershow this week," Jesse says. "And this, Miss Bride, is work." She spins me and steers me toward the crowd. "Please clock in now."

I shield my eyes and scan the crowd that has formed a small circle around me. I'm looking for Layla, but I lock eyes with Lauren first. "Congratulations, gorgeous!" she cries, throwing her arms around my neck and sort of collapsing against me. She smells like an old blowout and a bender, and she's wearing short jean shorts and a prissy white top. It makes no sense, but she looks incredible.

The Green Menace, on the other hand, greets me looking asexual as ever in a sack the color of an old Band-Aid. She tells me she likes my dress and it's the meanest thing she's ever said to me.

Vince is right behind them, with a hug that lifts my feet off the ground. "Steph is so sorry she couldn't be here but she asked me to take a picture of your shoes to see if you're wearing the ones she bought you."

Vince slips his phone out of his pocket and turns it sideways at my feet. There is a burst of bright light, my blush shoes the star. "Whoa, Brett," Vince says. "Those are a little sexy for you."

"Thanks, *Dad*."

"Sorry. I've just never seen you in shoes like that before."

Lauren sets down her glass of water (questionable) and takes my left hand in hers, swinging it like we are two schoolgirls turning a jumping rope for a third friend. She is rougher than she realizes—I feel like she might pull my arm out of the socket. "Have you seen the woman she's marrying? Of course she's feeling sexy." She brings my knuckles beneath her nose, examining my engagement ring at cross-eyed length. "Were you *so* surprised?"

"No. Not really surprised."

"Not really, huh?" Lauren smirks. "That's the problem with relationships today. There's no mystery. No spontaneity. You have a mature talk about where you are headed and then you go to Cartier and buy classic yellow-gold bands together." She doesn't just drop my hand, she slams it down, like you would an old-timey phone into its cradle after a heated conversation. "Where's the *romance*?" Her voice catches on what she pretends she doesn't want.

I laugh at the cameras as though I am confused by Lauren's angry, despairing reaction, although I'm not. Lauren is tired of being defined by her colorful sex life. She's getting older. She's getting lonelier. But she has a role to play. I feel for her. "The reason I wasn't surprised," I say, "is because I was the one who did it."

"*You* did it?" Vince gapes.

Technically both Arch and I did it, but for whatever reason, I've found myself telling people this version of events when Arch isn't around to fact-check. Taking ownership of the decision is helping me feel more confident about the decision. *Leap when you're almost ready* is an idiom in the business world, because you will never actually be ready to do something that has the power to change your life for better or for worse.

"Yeah," I punch Vince's pecs, playfully, "don't sound so shocked."

"It's just, I don't know. She's the older one." Vince runs a hand through his hair, distraught. "I guess I thought she was the . . . you know. The man in the relationship."

"The man in the relationship?" I look at Lauren and Jen, assuming they find this stereotypical understanding of same-sex relationships just as offensive as I do.

"Mmm-mmm. Mmmm-mmm," Lauren says, shaking her head in vehement agreement with Vince. "Arch is definitely not the man in the relationship. She's so thin."

I guess I should have known better than to have expected an enlightened rebuttal from Lauren when her eyes are approaching half-mast and her jaw is dangerously still. Tonight, it's Xanax and whatever is masquerading as water in her glass.

A server penetrates our group with a small silver tray. "Sorry to interrupt. But dayboat scallops with lemon, olive oil, and espelette?"

"Bless your heart . . . what's your name?" I raise my eyebrows in wait.

"Dan," he says.

"Dan the man." I knight him, spearing a scallop with a toothpick and popping it into my mouth in one bite. "Don't apologize, Dan," I say, chewing. I hold up a finger, chew, chew, chew, and swallow. "Interrupt me *anytime,* Dan. Especially if I'm still talking to this crowd the next time you see—" Before I can complete my sentence, a piece of scallop wedges in my throat, triggering another one of those goddamn coughing fits. I thump my chest with a fist, pointing desperately at Lauren's "glass of water," but she holds it out of my reach.

"I have a cold!" she exclaims.

Jen is staring at me, dead-eyed and comically unconcerned. Had Vince not been there, willing to thrust his glass of red wine into my hands, I might have died at my own surprise engagement party. I manage three sputtering sips. "*Ahem,*" I declare, "*Ahhhh-hem.*" My fist expands into a palm, covering my heart. I release a long, centering sigh. "Thanks, *Vince,*" I say pointedly to Lauren.

"You just got engaged," Lauren says, lamely. "I wouldn't want to get you sick." She sniffs, twice.

"Aunt Brett!" I hear from the sidelines, and I see Layla, wearing the graphic tee I recently bought her from Zara. The ends of her hair are a lighter color than her roots, which is new. Also new is Kelly's decision to leave the house without wearing a bra. Vince checks to be sure. Twice.

"What's this?" I tug on a piece of Layla's hair. Layla has been begging for ombré highlights for the last year, but Kelly has been adamantly opposed.

"We went with Jen to get her hair done and they had dye left over," Layla explains. "It's all-natural so Mom said okay this time."

A knot forms in my stomach. *Kelly and Layla went with Jen to get her hair done? How did I not know about this?*

"Layla signed up for lacrosse tryouts this year," Kelly adds. "And I'm proud of her for trying something new."

"Why not basketball?" Lauren asks with remarkable oblivion.

"You don't have to answer that," Vince says to Kelly, laughing awkwardly.

"I know I don't have to answer that," Kelly snaps at him. It is the exchange of two people who know each other better than I thought they did.

Vince's eyes get very big and he puffs his cheeks, actively holding his breath. He digs his hands in his pockets, rocking from the balls of his feet to his heels and back again, trying to think of a way to change the subject. "So. Um," he says to me. "When is the wedding?"

"No date yet. But sometime within the year for sure. Neither of us has any interest in planning a wedding for too long."

Kelly makes an inflammatory sound.

"What was that, dear sister?"

"I didn't say anything," Kelly says, but she doesn't have to. She thinks I'm rushing into this. She doesn't understand what our *hurry* is. A freeze settles upon the group, everyone stiffening, compacting their shoulders.

"Steph and I had a short engagement too," Vince offers, idiotically.

"Well, in that case," Kelly says, and Jen covers a cruel smile with her hand. Her compassion for all living creatures does not extend to turkeys or to me, evidently.

"Layla's here," I remind my sister in a low voice.

"What do you want me to say?" Kelly sighs.

"Um, how about congratulations?"

Kelly regards me for a brief, mean moment. "You have red wine on your new dress."

Dan the man is taking too long to bring me the club soda I requested, so I head downstairs and ask one of the bartenders at the back end of the restaurant. I'm blotting out the stain when I feel my phone buzz.

Not sure where you are but it's late so taking Layla home, Kelly's text reads. *See you at Soho tom?*

I'm just about to respond that I'm on the lower level when I see Kelly and Layla descend the stairs. I'm behind them, near the kitchen, so I know before they do that Vince is following them. He catches up to Kelly by the hostess station, reaching out and brushing her elbow, tentatively, almost as though he knows he shouldn't be doing this. I'm too far away to hear them, but I watch as Kelly points out the bathroom in the front of the restaurant for Layla. Layla disappears inside, leaving Vince and Kelly alone.

Vince's back is to me, but he must be speaking, because Kelly's lips are still. Puckered but still. When she finally opens her mouth, she jabs a finger at Vince's chest, never actually touching him, and I'm able to read her lips because she's speaking slowly for emphasis, punctuating each word with her finger, Leave. It. Alone.

Suddenly, Kelly drops her hand by her side. She sees me. She says something dismissively to Vince, before rapping on the bathroom door, yelling at Layla to hurry up. I spin on my heel, giving Vince my back as he turns and retraces his path through the restaurant and up the stairs. I'm fast enough that he doesn't notice me, but not so fast that I don't take a mental snapshot of his expression. He is dejected, I realize, my chest ablaze with panic. Because if Stephanie finds out that her husband is chasing my sister down darkened stairwells, having what appears to be a lovers' quarrel in the middle of the West Village's sceniest restaurant, I don't know what she would do. Worse, I don't know what she would say.

CHAPTER 13

Stephanie

When Vince hazards on the bedroom door, I am awake with my eyes closed. We go through seasons of sleeping together and sleeping apart. A lot of it is allergy related. In the spring, when the pollen count is higher, Vince tends to snore and it keeps me awake and—oh, I don't care enough to lie anymore. We only sleep in the same bed when we're filming. It's easier to slip into the skin of wedded bliss when we're dueling over the same linen top sheet. The closer you can get to believing your own lies, the more palatable they become for mass consumption. Brett doesn't even know it, but she taught me this.

Sometimes I wonder if Vince and I would still be having sex if I hadn't made another cent. I think about all the chaste space my money has created in our marriage. A bi-level home that allows us to spend the better part of the day on unobstructed planes, if we prefer. (Turns out, we prefer.) A living room large enough for two couches, one for each of us should we ever agree on a show to watch. A master bedroom that fits a California king in which we can sleep diagonally, upside down, and inside out without ever so much as grazing a limb. We never touch anymore because we never have to touch anymore. In the first apartment, we were on top of each other. We spooned on the single couch out of necessity and if we got into a fight right before bed, Vince didn't have the option to hermetically seal himself into the guest bedroom. We didn't have a guest bedroom. So I wonder, if my success had plateaued, if we had never been able to upgrade to our current conditions, would this coerced contact have saved us? Or was it only ever a palliative treatment for something that was ailing from the start?

"How was it?" I ask him without opening my eyes.

"Oh." He stumbles, probably over my suitcase, which is packed for the next book tour and the dinner in L.A. "You're awake."

I open my eyes to find Vince shirtless, his lower belly more pronounced than usual after too much free champagne, drunkenly grappling with the buckle on his belt. Not exactly a view to get the motor running. Vince has never tried very hard to have a great body, and there is something so arrogant about all those times he's blown off the trainer he begged me to hire, as though he has decided someone with his face doesn't need a six-pack too.

He spreads onto the bed in his boxers, the stench of him spilling over onto my side, despite what feels like a full Manhattan avenue between us. If he were an air freshener, what would we call him? Partially Metabolized Champagne Breeze. Radiant Herpes. "It was fun, babe," he says. "You should have come."

I told Brett and Lisa that I left for my book tour today, but I actually leave tomorrow. I'm stopping in three cities, making my way across the country to L.A., the trip culminating in the all-important dinner with the Female Director. I always make my own travel reservations (production won't fly us business—the show features women so successful they should already fly business), so no one has any idea that I was actually in New York on the night of Brett's surprise engagement party.

When I received Arch's Evite with the bossy, bubble-lettered *Shhhhhhh!*, I RSVP'd *Will attend!* for two. But as the date approached, a special cocktail of venom seemed to pool in my glands. I could not bear the thought of raising a glass of champagne to the happy couple, one half of which is a nasty cold-blooded animal, the same temperature of whatever her environment happens to be that day.

I mash a fist into my pillow, carving out a view of Vince's profile in the bright city dark. "Did everyone think it was weird that you were there without me? I just thought one of us should represent. I don't want them to think I'm, you know, holding a grudge."

Vince shuts his eyes, and not because he's tired. "No, babe. No one thinks that. They all believe you made up."

This is the perfect opening to address something that has been eating away at me for months but that I haven't had the pluck to ask. Does Vince know? "Do you believe we made up?" I ask, my voice going hoarse. It's a chickenshit way around it, but it's better than the willful ignorance I've been affecting since Brett moved out.

Vince takes his time, choosing his words wisely. "I don't think you should have to make up with her if you don't want to," he says, which is an answer not nearly as ambiguous as it sounds. It's the closest we have gotten to the truth in a long while. My breath feels like acid in my nostrils and there are tears in my eyes, but I hide it from my voice.

"I appreciate that. I'm relieved no one said anything. I thought for sure Lisa might."

"Lisa didn't say anything. Brett didn't say anything. Jesse didn't say anything. You're good. I promise."

I hurl myself upright, my weepiness expunged, my heart like a jumping fish in my throat. "*Jesse* was there?"

Vince flings a forearm over his eyes with a groan, regretting the admission instantly. He knows Jesse only makes an appearance on set if the scene is of paramount importance. Jesse will be meeting up with me in L.A.—a first for me, and something I was immensely proud of. Now an engagement party—to celebrate the most banal of life achievements—is on par with a dinner with an Oscar-Nominated Female Director? I can't believe I'm saying this, but Yvette Greenberg was right. The show has lost its way.

"She stopped by for, like, five minutes," Vince says, trying to make it sound as if it's not as big a deal as it is.

"Did she say anything about doing a spinoff with Brett for her wedding?"

"Oh my God, babe." Vince flops onto his side, punishing me with his back. "She was there, like, two seconds. I don't know. Maybe. But I doubt it. That wedding's never going to happen."

I am still sitting up in bed, chewing on a thumb, but my panic tapers ever so slightly. "You think so?"

Vince answers with a short, confident laugh. "It's all for a storyline. You know that."

I remove my thumb from my mouth before I ruin my L.A. manicure, suddenly flush with appreciation for Vince, that he looks at Brett and sees what I see: an overhyped, overfed grandstander who's cozened women's empowerment into a brand for money and fame. Appreciation and something more: determination to make this charade less of a charade, to embark on the next venture designed to maintain my relevancy. I curl into my husband's pale, hairless back, slinging an arm over his narrow hip. "Well. Thanks for representing us tonight. I just worried what it looked like to back out at the last minute. But I couldn't bring myself to go either."

"It's fine," Vince says, voice as taut as his body when he feels my roving hand. It takes some effort to weasel it between his thighs.

"Jesus," he gasps, "your hands are cold."

Seven years ago, even three years ago, Vince's rejection would have flattened me. But I have developed a tolerance for my husband's apathy. I rise on all fours, grit overpowering dignity, and stake a hand on either side of Vince's face, a knee on either side of his hips. He does nothing for a few agonizing moments, before releasing his knees and straightening out to face me on his back.

"You have to get up early," he tries.

I kiss him. His breath is putrid.

I worm a hand beneath the elastic band of his boxer shorts and capture him in my thumb and index finger. His penis is baby soft and pliable, spineless in its faithful state. Is it just in my mind or has he gotten smaller? Like the opposite of Pinocchio—every time he lies, it shrinks.

Vince wraps his fingers around my wrist, removing my hand from his boxers and setting it on the mattress with a consolatory pat. For a few long moments, that is that. I'm about to retreat to my side of the bed when Vince changes his mind, flipping me onto my back, then waiting, unhelping, while I wiggle out of my pajama bottoms. He does lean down to kiss me—there's that—but it's a wet, cold kiss, too many front teeth, and we abandon pretense to focus on getting his dick inside of me, which hasn't happened since I went off birth control three months ago.

Vince is humping the seam of my inner thigh, wheezing, working dutifully for an ember. This outlives my capacity for dirty talk, and there are only so many times one can say, *I want you to fuck me,* before its rehearsed timbre incurs the opposite of its intended effect.

Vince slams onto his back with a sharp cry of frustration. He pounds his temple, a caveman's show of self-flagellation. His angry breathing moderates into soothing neighs. "It's not you," he assures me. "I just drank too much tonight." He drags me onto his pale, wimpy chest, nuzzling the top of my head and rubbing my back, like I'm the one who should be upset, even though there is nothing wrong with *me.* I should be the one consoling *him. Yes, dear, it's perfectly normal that I have cashmere sweaters harder than your dick.* "You're so beautiful," he continues, moronically. "I want you so much."

"Thank you, babe," I say. I prop my chin in my hand, my elbow sharp above my husband's fickle heart. "You tell all the girls that when it doesn't work?"

Vince doesn't even call me *crazy* as I roll onto my side, my turn to punish him with my back. My intelligence isn't worth insulting anymore, apparently. *I can say anything,* I realize. I can really be crazy now.

—

"No reservation, you said?" The hostess consults her seating plan. She's the only other black person in the lobby besides me.

"Right," I tell her for the second time. "But I just want to eat at the bar."

"We take reservations for the bar."

"There's nowhere that's first come, first serve?"

The hostess looks up at me. She is wearing no makeup except

for goth lipstick, no jewelry except for a jade bangle. "You can see if there's anything open."

I tip my head at her. "So the bar is first come, first serve?"

"Only if it doesn't have a place setting. If it has a place setting it's being held for a reservation."

"Eleven Madison isn't even as tough as this." I smile easily, letting her know I'm no stranger to the vagaries of posh restaurants.

The hostess is unbelievably annoyed. "Huh?"

"It's in New York," I say, pathetically.

The little bitch shrugs. As if New York is over and the dining room at this four-star boutique hotel in Phoenix is where it's at. She looks like someone who would watch the show, but she certainly doesn't recognize me. I find myself wishing I told the camera crew to follow me to dinner (they went back to their hotel—a three-star chain—after my reading), so this haughty newborn would realize she should be clamoring to make nice with me. Not that I have any right to complain. I avoided the other two black kids in my class studiously. On my own, I was a refreshing breeze. Two would have been a twister, everyone in my town hiding in the basement.

I remember my Chanel bag as I follow the hostess's unhelpful directions to the bar, adjusting it on the chain so that it rests flush against my pelvic bone. When in doubt, lead with Chanel.

The bar isn't immediately visible at the foot of the stairs, and I walk around a second dining room space like an asshole, wondering if Brett would have gotten an escort, and if it would have been for her star or for her skin. When I finally locate the bar, it's empty and unset.

"This okay?" I ask the bartender, hoisting myself onto a stool.

"You drinking or eating?"

"Eating." I rethink my answer. "Both."

He smiles in a way that makes me feel stupid for asking. His hair is slicked back and his beard is unkempt. His bow tie is baby shower pink. "Then this is okay."

I'm set up with a placemat and menu and silverware, then ignored for several minutes until a red-faced man in a rumpled suit takes the stool two empty seats over from mine. He is immediately given the bartender's full attention; to his cocktail order I manage to tack on a request for a glass of white wine. *What kind?* the bartender asks, and I shrug, because I have no idea, only that I am desperate to feel the way I felt that day in Jen's apartment, like nothing could ever go wrong again. *Surprise me,* I tell him, kittenish. *But, like,* he says, all business, *dry, fruity, what?* I weigh my options before telling him fruity. Who wants to drink something *dry*?

The bartender tends to our drinks in the order that they are placed, though I know from Vince's bartending days that you are almost always supposed to pour a glass of wine or beer before assembling a more complicated cocktail. The man gets his beverage and the bartender retreats to the other end of the bar. I'm forced to raise my hand to remind him I'm still waiting. He waves back with a patient smile that says, *Don't worry, I haven't forgotten you.* After drying a rack of wineglasses steaming from the dishwasher, he opens a bottle of fruity white for me. He fills a glass to the top and empties the bottle into a mini wine carafe that he presents to me on the side with a *Don't tell anyone* wink.

"Sorry about that. I'm the only one back here tonight and we were out of clean glasses." He flings a bar towel over his shoulder and folds his arms across his chest. His shirt cuffs are rolled to his elbows; his thick, veiny forearms say farmhand, his watch says Trust Fund Baby who dropped out of SMU sophomore year to start his own T-shirt line. He has warm, green-flecked eyes. People whose licenses list their eye color as *hazel* are usually reaching—they're brown, just say brown—but in his case, I'd allow it. What are the genes needed to produce a child with eyes like that? I uncross my legs, thinking just how far Phoenix is from New York, how unlikely it is that this not-brown-eyed gentleman watches Saluté.

"What can I get you to eat, miss?" he asks.

Just as I'm no stranger to the vagaries of posh restaurants, I'm also no stranger to poor service with a smile, that ensuing whiplash of indignation and clemency. The moment you are sure this is *it* is always the moment you're brought a free glass of wine, the moment that the handsome bartender offers his heartfelt apologies, *miss.* So you adjust your blinkers and you say, "The beet salad to start and the salmon."

"Excellent," the bartender says, forgetting to collect my menu before he walks away.

I find my phone and open my email. The glass is hot from the dishwasher and the wine tastes like a wedding bouquet, nothing like the crisp elixir poured for me in Jen's apartment a few weeks ago. No matter, tomorrow I will be in L.A., where I'm *all set for dinner with the Oscar-Nominated Female Director at 8pm at Bestia. Exciting!* my motion picture agent's assistant added.

Next is an email from Gwen, my editor, *Re: Stephanie Simmons's AQ.* Every writer fills out an Author Questionnaire pre-publication. It's distributed to different departments to help develop publicity and marketing plans. *Steph, I need you to pull the AQ on Stephanie Simmons's memoir first thing tomorrow morning. Thanks.* I have to read this several times before I remember that Gwen's assistant is also named Stephanie, and that she must have sent this to me in error. Still, what does she want with my AQ?

I hear "Beet salad?" and half raise my hand to claim it, but the plate is set in front of the man to my right. I turn my attention back to my email. Vince has forwarded me the details of my flight to Marrakesh. 5:47 P.M. out of JFK, three days from now. We've arranged for him to meet me in the airport with a suitcase packed for Morocco; this way I didn't have to pack for my book events, the Female Director dinner, and Brett's trip. I wince. It's going to be a brutal day of travel. But backing out of Morocco is not an option, not like backing out of Brett's engagement party was, especially since I've recently come to the conclusion that now is the opportune time to extricate myself from the show. You may think such a shift in mind-set would give me carte blanche to bail on all the events I would never attend if the cameras weren't there, but if anything, I'm under even greater obligation. I need to make it clear that I was an integral part of this season, that nobody phased me out. I want to quit while I'm on top, as they say. The top is like Mars, hostile to human life.

The gentleman to my right is now cutting into a small steak, grilled a diligent brown, just as he ordered it. That's what the bartender called him, indicating to a busser where to place the plate, "The filet is for the gentleman."

I move on to the mini carafe of wine. Also the temperature of soup, but nonetheless helping to fuel the bold fantasy I've nurtured since before my memoir came out; *The Site of an Evacuation* is a number one *New York Times* bestseller (done), I am both a massive commercial success and a critics' darling (done), and a very famous and timely director or actress is committed to adapting my memoir for screen (almost done). I'm of course asked to return to the show, even though I will be a crusty thirty-five next season, but I demur, because I've got a better idea. Lauren Conrad crowing at Heidi—*You know what you did!*—may be the highest-rated reality TV episode of all time, but did you also know that *Keeping Up with the Kardashians* peaked in popularity when the sisters had babies? A motherhood storyline may sound heretical, but remember, our audience loves seeing unconventional women caving under the pressure to do the conventional thing.

With this in mind, I pitch a spinoff where I get pregnant and move to Los Angeles to oversee the film project. I'll live in a house with a yard and have a meltdown trying to put together a crib. A storyline about the comic discordance between having a baby and having zero maternal instincts is a classic knee-slapper. *Is this right?* I can imagine myself saying in the trailer, holding up my baby with her diaper on inside out and backward. *Stephanie Ever After*, Jesse would probably want to call it, and I would tell her, laughing, *absolutely* not.

"Excuse me, you had the salmon?" A lonely filet is placed before me, but before the server can set down the accompanying plate of sautéed spinach, I stop him.

"I never got my appetizer."

The server extends an unsympathetic "Oh."

"Excuse me." I wave down the bartender, and this time he doesn't dare give me a cute smile back. "I never got my appetizer."

"Oh no. Really?"

"Really."

The bartender flags down a passing waiter. "Nathan," he says. "This young lady had ordered a beet salad. Can you go back in the kitchen and check on that for her?"

Everyone seems appeased by this, and the server attempts to set the side plate of spinach down again. "I would like my appetizer first," I say, firmly, "then I would like my fish."

The gentleman to my right sets his steak knife down. A few people in the dining area break off their conversation, eavesdropping, but I have no problem standing up for myself when it's clear I've been wronged. It's the nebulous, middle-of-the-road disrespect where I can't find my footing.

"Of course. Of course," the bartender says, removing the plate before me and dumping it into the trash so I can be sure they won't try to reheat and reserve. "We are so sorry about this." He disappears under the bar for a moment and reappears with the bottle of fruity wine, topping me off.

"And can I get a glass of ice?" I ask, fearlessly. "The glass was a little warm."

The bartender does me one better and switches out my wineglass. "Again," he says, "so sorry about this."

When the bill arrives, all I have been charged for is a single glass of wine. I leave a fifty-dollar tip and something else, holding tight to the merchant's copy as I place my dinner napkin on the bar and reach down for my purse, hanging on a hook by my knee. It's only when the gold chain strap is over my shoulder and I'm on my feet that I slip the signed receipt, upside down, into the check holder. I hurry out of the restaurant like I've just hidden a bomb in a trashcan, like I will be blown to smithereens if the bartender makes the discovery before I board the elevator to my room.

I wake to a noise in the dark, like the sound of someone shaking open a new garbage bag, the way the plastic gasps for air. I am very still, waiting to find out if my broken brain has produced this track or if a maid is simply emptying the hallway trashcan. The last time I was in Phoenix, five months ago on my first book tour, a man chased me down after I passed through security.

"Ma'am? Ma'am?"

I refused to respond to "ma'am," and so he had to say it twice.

"I think this fell out of your bag," he told me, giving the pill bottle three shakes, the world's glummest tambourine. I about fell over thanking him, explaining that I need to be better about latching my purse, my husband is always on my case about latching my purse. And God, wouldn't my husband die to hear me tell a stranger that he is right?

The man laughed, his face shiny, like his smile had stretched his skin to its tearing point, the way men's faces get when you let them believe that they are of any use to you anymore. "I know my wife can't step foot on an airplane without her Xanax." He gave me a neighborly wave good-bye. "Safe flight."

"Thank you," I said, watching him go the other way, thinking how nice it was to be mistaken for a silly woman with a silly fear of flying.

The next stop on the first book tour, five months ago, was Nashville, and there I decided I would again "forget" to latch my purse before sending it through the CT scanner, and I did the same thing in Milwaukee and Chicago too. I could have just tossed the prescription for Cymbalta into the trash, but that felt too intentional. I'd been using a pill cutter for the last few weeks anyway, under doctor's supervision, and, well, my book tours are the ten days out of my year when I'd really rather not feel so . . . dampened.

It took me ten years to admit to a doctor that occasionally, I hear things. Not voices, well, I suppose it is *a* voice, but it isn't speech I hear. It is a word, sometimes a first name, sometimes a familiar sound—shaking open a garbage bag, or revving the engine of a lawn mower.

Before I told my doctor about the voice, my blood pressure was one-forty over ninety. After my doctor told me that hearing things is not synonymous with schizophrenia or manic depression, that some 13 percent of adults will hear voices at some point in their lives, and that the cause can be anything from bereavement to stress, I clocked in at one hundred over eighty. I was predisposed to depression, that much was likely true, but my symptoms were dull and textbook, easily managed through sixty milligrams of Cymbalta daily. I have weaned myself off the drug once before, when the second book in my fiction series sold one million copies and the show was in its newlywed phase with fans, long enough to remember that *oh,* I do like sex as enthusiastically as I appear to in my books.

The noise does not repeat itself, and I remind myself of what my doctor told me, that success is a stressor too. Although it's a stressor I might enjoy, it's a spotlight nonetheless, shining on things I thought I'd jettisoned on the therapist's couch when—surprise!—all I did was stuff them into a coat closet before the company arrives. The reassurance fails to soothe, and I turn over in bed and locate my phone, charging on the nightstand. It's 4:40 A.M., and Gwen has responded to my email. I read the exchange in its entirety, twice.

Me: *Gwen! I think you meant to send this to your assistant, Steph! Not me, Steph. But why do you need my AQ? All okay?*

Gwen: *So sorry, honey! Yes, meant to send this to Stephanie my assistant. How is wherever you are?*

I compose a response.

Phoenix, but Los Angeles in a few hours!! For the Female Director dinner. Will let you know how it goes. Then I go from there to JFK to Heathrow to Marrakesh for the trip. Crazy few days! It's so confusing that I have the same name as your assistant! Just curious, though, why do you need my author questionnaire for the memoir? You know me—I worry! Everything okay?

I hit send and swallow, dislodging the sweet film of that bad wine. I hear the noise again and I realize it is not the maid, emptying the trash in the hallway, and that it is not in my head, a result of going cold turkey on my medication somewhere over the Rocky Mountains five months ago.

"What time is it?" the bartender groans, kicking off more of the covers. His rough skin scraping the cheap sateen sheets—that was what woke me up.

"Almost five."

"Jesus. Go back to bed." The bartender raises his forearm and shields his eyes against nothing. The room is practically invisible, though my eyes have adjusted enough that I can make out his empty wrist. Last night, after he read the note I left him on my check (*Room 19. Only here tonight.*), he had shown up and removed his nice watch, leaving it on the nightstand before we got into bed, something Vince used to do when we used to have sex.

Boston, 2014, was the first time, though I thought about how easy I could get away with it at a hotel bar in Atlanta, considered it with a yoga instructor in L.A., and nearly called the number my black car driver slipped me after he picked me up from the airport in Tulsa. Looking back, I realize that after traveling all over the country for the second book tour, Boston felt familiar, and therefore like the last in my series of attempts to prove that I was too good to fit in anyway. I finally felt prepared for this particular challenge: The blooms hadn't fallen off the show yet and the book was selling so well I had just gone on an antique Persian rug spending spree with money to spare for an Alhambra earring and necklace set from Van Cleef. I was thirty but I looked twenty-six. I was on *TV*. If I failed, there were plenty of affirmatives to cushion the blow to my self-esteem.

The men in Boston did not feel like the hipster men of New York—rather, they felt like the WASPy guys who told me I was *hot* in high school and college but were too afraid to actually sleep with me. What were they afraid of? That they might like it? That they might like me? That they might have to take me home and explain me to their mothers? I could relate to that, at least—not knowing how to explain a black partner to a white mother. I dated a few black guys in college, and while I met some of their families, I never introduced them to mine. I had grown up reassuring my adoptive mother that although I was one of a handful of black members of our community, I didn't feel like an outlier. I dressed like the popular girls and I played the sports the popular girls played and I spoke like the popular girls and I ultimately became a popular girl to prove to her that I felt welcomed and included, to soothe her lingering concerns over my adoption. People warned her that despite the privilege she could afford me, she could inadvertently make my life worse by raising me in a place where I would always feel *out* of place. On some level, I worried that if I brought home a black guy, she would interpret this to mean that she had failed at creating a home where I felt like I belonged. Like what she had to offer me in terms of connection and love and empathy had never been enough. Like I might have been better off without her—always her greatest fear.

I knew Boston guys, the ones whose families had summer places on the Cape and degrees from small liberal arts colleges. But I had only ever known them through the lens of wingwoman or platonic friend. When I was younger, I had been quick to take my sexuality off the table before they could do it for me. It's true that I didn't neuter myself for Vince, but Vince had no pedigree. He may have been better-looking than the guys who rejected me growing up but as a struggling actor from a second-generation Italian family on Long Island, he was always a cut below. His degree didn't say Colgate or Hamilton, and he didn't have a long line of blond ex-girlfriends with pearls the size of jawbreakers in their ears. Who was I beating, really? Gia from Holbrook, studying for her nursing degree? It's not an accomplishment to take men from the Gias, it's an accomplishment to take them from the Lauren Bunns of the world, who would have slept with a guy like Vince, but married him? Not even blacked out in Vegas, something she did once, with a guy she met at the craps table.

Jamie was the name of the first. Sort of fat. Really tall. He was funny, bearded, and jobless, drinking a Bud Light at the bar at Mistral. Vince hadn't had sex with me in two months. That is a different thing than saying Vince and I hadn't had sex in two months. Do you understand that? My husband couldn't get hard for me but he could for everyone else, and I was still so young. Thirty. A baby. This couldn't be it for me. Yes, both Vince and I have had sex with other people in our marriage, but I am not a cheater. I am an outsourcer.

Jamie and I ended up back in my hotel because I was staying at the Taj and I wanted him to understand that he knew me too. A guy who occasionally serves Bloody Marys at his parents' country club probably thinks he doesn't have much in common with a woman who looks like the sassy sidekick to the hot girl on his favorite TV show, but money catches that trust fall. The sex was sloppy, neither of us finished, and when I woke up in the morning all that was left of Jamie was a few congealed specks of his urine on the toilet seat. But I had succeeded—or so I thought at the time. Because looking back, I'm now able to ask—but at what? Fucking an unambitious slob with decent breeding? *He* was my prize, and one I only felt worthy of collecting once I had amassed the advantages of fame? What happens when that goes away? And it would go away. That, or turn on me and last forever. I knew this from the start, but only in the most abstract of terms. The way anti-tobacco campaigns that attempt to deter kids from smoking with lung cancer horror stories don't really work. It's too far in the future to worry about having to talk through a hole in your neck now. That's what I thought when I signed on to The Show. Yes, this will end, and maybe even badly, but not for many, many years. I always thought I had more time before someone punched a hole in my neck.

I pay for the half hour of in-flight Internet on the way to L.A., but after the first thirty minutes I still haven't heard back from Gwen, and still nothing after an hour. I film a few clips of myself on the GoPro camera production gave me to use on the plane.

"On my way to meet the Oscar-Nominated Female Director,"

I whisper, so as not to disrupt the other Mint passengers, and the line works like an affirmation. I'm on my way to meet the Oscar-Nominated Female Director. Gwen isn't avoiding me. It means nothing that she has requested my AQ.

It's not until I've shelled out $7.95 for the fourth time that Gwen gets back to me.

The director dinner!!! You must tell me how it goes!! Don't worry about the AQ—just wanted to check on something! Did you see your piece in the Times*?! That picture—you look like you're twelve!* I think Gwen has hit her yearly exclamation-point quota in a single email to me.

Of course I've seen the *Times* piece. I've seen the *Times* piece and the *People* piece and the *HuffPo* piece and the piece on *The Cut* and in a few months there will be the *Vogue* piece and an interview with *Vanity Fair*. There are so many pieces coming out that when I land and listen to the voicemail from a reporter fact-checking a story, I don't even pay attention to what publication he says he is from. I call him back and when he tells me he's with *The Smoking Gun*, I apologize, telling him I didn't put this interview date into my calendar.

"We didn't have one," he says, as I pass under a sign that reads "Yoga Room This Way." Definitely in L.A. "I was hoping to confirm that your birth date is 10/17/82 and that the date you graduated high school was May 2000."

I stop walking. "Why?"

"Are those the correct dates?"

"They are correct, yes," I say, and they are, so why do I immediately regret my answer?

"Thank you," he says, and hangs up.

I dial Gwen, who is in a meeting. "Can you please tell her it's urgent, Stephanie?"

"I will," Stephanie promises, dutifully.

"Stephanie, do you know why *The Smoking Gun* would be calling me?"

"They called you?"

The alarm in her voice turns my stomach. I am right there with her, but I can't bear to hear it echoed in my own. I make it sound like it wasn't a big deal. "They just wanted to confirm my birthday and the year I graduated high school."

"What did you tell them?"

"I confirmed it." Silence. "They had their dates right."

"I'll let Gwen know they're calling you now," Stephanie says.

"Calling me now? What . . . have they been calling you? Does this have something to do with Gwen asking for my AQ?"

"I really don't know all the details, Stephanie," Stephanie says, softly. But of course she does. She's the receptionist at the oncology unit, telling you not to worry while looking at your lab results that say *stage four*. "I'll have Gwen call as soon as she's back at her desk, okay?"

I'm in my tiny corner room at the Sunset Tower Hotel, *House Hunters* failing to attenuate my anxiety, when my phone seizures on the nightstand. It's my motion picture agent, not Gwen.

"Hi," she says, then, "so."

The Oscar-Nominated Female Director has to head to Chicago unexpectedly. She sends her deepest regrets. It means nothing, my agent assures me, and we will find a time for us to get together sometime soon. The good news is that I still have the reservation at Bestia if I'm up for going, just her and me. Or maybe Jesse and I want to go? *Jesse*. I glance up at the ceiling. She texted me earlier to let me know she had arrived, and we'd worked out that she is in the room directly above mine. *I'll refrain from doing my step aerobics then,* she'd joked. The thought of harpooning her good mood with this news plunges me deeper into the mattress.

I thank my agent for the update and we hang up. I don't risk asking if the cancellation is in any way connected to my conversation with the reporter from *The Smoking Gun*. Asking would be akin to flaunting symptoms of a flesh-eating plague, like if anyone were to hear me cough, I'd be brutally exiled from mankind's last surviving community.

I hold the ceiling in contempt, knowing I need to get up and go upstairs and tell Jesse not to bother breaking out the good Dr. Martens, but upstairs feels far enough away to require a passport. I bargain with my eyelids—*five minutes*—as the sunset pinkens the smog on the 405.

I wake to a gaveling on the door. My room is dim and cool, perfect sleeping conditions really, and when I eventually creak to my feet, walking feels like a new skill. Jesse is on the other side of the door, looking like the model-dating member of a boy band in a blaze orange beanie, tight black jeans and a black leather jacket, black Converse sneakers and black socks. "Steph!" She laughs, admonishingly. "We're going to be late."

"Oh my God, Jesse." I grope the wall for the light switch and flip it on. The bright burst feels like a million hot needles in my eyes. "I fell asleep. I'm so sorry."

"Well . . . let's go! Splash some water on your face and throw on those Jimmy Choos." She claps her little hands: *Chop-chop!* "I'll meet you downstairs." She starts for the elevator.

"No, Jesse, no. Wait. The dinner is rescheduled." I cannot bring myself to say *canceled,* although that's what it is.

Jesse stops and turns, looking forty-whatever again when she furrows her brow. "To when?"

"I'm not sure. She had to go to Chicago unexpectedly."

Jesse exhales through her nose, a single hot puff, like a bull. She lolls her head in a slow arc, the physical embodiment of the words "of course." *Of course* she canceled on you. *Of course* this was going to be a waste of my time. You're Stephanie Simmons, not Brett Courtney. "Were you going to tell me?"

"I just found out."

"But you were sleeping."

"I mean, I found out an hour or so ago. I was going to tell you. I don't remember falling asleep. I guess I'm more jet-lagged than—"

Jesse raises a hand, silencing me. "Is this your way of trying to stretch this storyline into another season?"

It's not. "It's not."

"Because frankly, Steph, the abuse stuff is too depressing to warrant a two-story arc."

I know. "I know."

Jesse smashes the elevator button with the heel of her hand.

"We still have the reservation at Bestia if you want to go," I try. "I actually do have something to talk to you about. Something *not* depressing." It hurts to smile.

Jesse tugs off her beanie, spiking her short hair with her fingers. "No, well, I actually have work to do."

"I think I'm pregnant," I call out into the hall. The words feel like the bell lap of a race, like emptying the tank; they *wind* me.

Jesse checks the panel above the elevator, watching its protracted climb. "But you're not sure."

"I mean, I'm so *tired*." I gesture at my disheveled appearance for proof. Sometimes, I think I'm too quick on my feet. I've gotten too good at this game.

Jesse regards me as though I am the last cupcake in the box, left on the counter in the office kitchen overnight. I'm sort of dried out, my buttercream swirl smooshed. But she has a sweet tooth and I'm still a cupcake. "Let me know when you're sure."

She takes the stairs.

I pass out in my clothes during a *Seinfeld* episode and when I wake, Kathie Lee and Hoda are drinking wine and my cell is buzzing. I slide my thumb right to answer. "Gwen," I croak.

"Did I wake you? I forgot it's early out there." There is a raised-eyebrows pause. "Well. Not that early. Want me to call back?"

"Don't call me back," I say, struggling to sit up in bed. "I'm freaking out." My stomach is screaming and I remember I couldn't stand the thought of dinner last night.

"Don't freak out. This happens all the time with nonfiction."

"*The Smoking Gun* calls up authors to validate their birthdays and the year they graduated high school?"

"Normally they go through the publisher. That's why I was pulling your AQ. I wanted to be the one to give them those answers so that they wouldn't call you and make you worry."

"But what are they even planning to do with that information?"

"You know, cross-reference to make sure it all checks out."

I need water as a matter of life or death. I clomp a hand around the nightstand, finding the Dasani I took from the airplane yesterday. "What if it doesn't check out?"

"You wrote a memoir, Steph, not an autobiography. If some of the dates or details are screwy, it's really not a story, and they'll let it go. Like I said, this happens all the time with nonfiction. I doubt it will come to a head."

The Dasani bottle is empty. I throw it across the room in despair. I don't want anyone to make me feel better. I want my misery shared; I want *responsibility* shared. "I said in the AQ that the book was fiction, Gwen."

Gwen is silent so long I pull the phone away from my ear to make sure the call didn't drop. "I know," she says, at last.

"You were the one who said it would have so much more impact if we could package it as a true story. And then when I wouldn't agree to that—because I'd have to be a real fucking Judas to womankind to lie about being *raped!*—you said"—and here I do my best impression of a dumbass white girl—"well, like, how about we call it creative nonfiction, not a memoir? So that, like, I could explain to people that the abuse never happened but was a metaphor for, like, how the subtle racism I dealt with growing up was as painful as a physical assault?" I drop my voice. "And I am the fucking weakling who agreed to that, to assuage my guilt just a teensy bit knowing neither of us would correct anyone who assumed it was real, and I am the monster who also agreed to make him black because you said a white kid in a black neighborhood could be more easily traced.

So, Gwen, don't you *ever* leave me hanging for over twenty-four hours like that again. If I go down, I will do everything in my power to make sure you are right there with me." I hang up, feeling like I shouldn't have done that and also like I could have chewed her out for another hour and it wouldn't have been enough.

I labor into the bathroom and stick a glass under the tap, examining myself in the mirror while I gulp down aluminum-flavored water. God, it is so much work to be a human being. Eight glasses of water a day—no wonder I look like shit, life is utterly demanding even on the best of days. I turn away from the mess in the mirror and limp back into the room, timbering into bed. I don't have to leave for the airport for a few hours; I should probably get up and do something. Take advantage of the fact that I am in L.A. Go on a hike. Meditate on a mountaintop. Eat an egg-white frittata. I think about closing the curtains, but the bed is quicksand. I sink into sleep with the sexy SoCal sunshine aging my face.

Vince is waiting for me in the Air France departures gate at JFK, sitting on my extra-large rose gold Rimowa suitcase in line to check in. When he sees me, he climbs to his feet, guiltily, knowing that I hate it when he treats my nice luggage like a beanbag chair in a dorm room. He threads his fingers through his hair and gives me a *busted!* smile.

"I tried to check in for you," he says. "But apparently that's a security issue." He laughs and tosses a flap of hair that is not in his eyes.

"No shit it's a security issue." I send the carry-on I've been living out of for the last few days wheeling his way.

Vince stops it with his foot, his pink pouty lips ajar. He's been using my Fresh sugar lip scrub while I've been away, I see. "Babe?"

"You can't *check in* for somebody else, Vince. Not even someone as devastatingly handsome as you." I balance my foot on my overturned suitcase and rest my Fendi power bag on my knee, pushing aside old plane ticket stubs and Quest Bar wrappers in search of my wallet. The inside of my purse has never looked like this before in my life. I am not one to take my nice things for granted. I have lived the good life since I was six months old and yet I somehow always knew it would be temporary.

Vince crouches at the knees so that his face is below mine and he's gazing up at me. His hair flops forward, skimming his searching, soulful eyes. How he imagined he would look on the movie posters outside Regal Cinema one day. "Steph. Babe. You okay?"

I have shuffled all of my credit cards and medical ID cards and Sweetgreen rewards cards and I still can't locate my passport. I tip my head back and tears spill into my ears.

"Babe," Vince says, gently, reaching into his back pocket and pulling out my passport. "Is this what you're looking for?"

I forgot my passport and Vince suspected I forgot my passport. He looked in the drawer where I keep it before he left for the airport just in case I had. I feel suddenly, overwhelmingly grateful for him, and suddenly, overwhelmingly certain that it is a bad idea I go to Morocco.

"Come here." Vince straps his arms around me. "I know you're disappointed about the dinner with the Female Director. And it's a lot of travel. You're tired."

I hook my chin over his shoulder, remembering the bartender, and the regret is as express and dangerous as a flash flood, water-logging my heart. Not regret because I love Vince and I broke our vows—I am so far past that kind of regret—but regret for doing something so careless when there are already so many cracks in the façade and I am running out of caulk. "I am tired." I sigh, tearfully. "But I'm also scared." Admitting this turns my tears into physical, silent sobs.

"But Gwen said not to worry, right?" Vince rubs circles into my back. "This sort of thing happens all the time with nonfiction?"

"It's not nonfiction, Vince."

Vince's hand dies between my shoulder blades. He pulls away from me. He takes a step *back*. The look in his eyes—like he has turned over his meal ticket and realized *Oh, shit, she has an expiration date.* I shouldn't be surprised, but still it twists. We loved each other once. I think.

"*Steph,*" Vince groans, bringing his hand to his cheek, his revulsion exemplary in case anyone is eavesdropping. Someone is always eavesdropping on this termite mound of a life I've built out of my own saliva and dung. "Jesus. You made that *up*?"

I look into my husband's guileless eyes, showing off the acting chops he honed playing *cute guy in a bar/elevator/towel* in so many CW pilots that never got picked up I've lost count. My contempt for him is superhuman. I could pick him up and throw him through the plate glass revolving doors, send him all the way back to the Joey Bag o' Donuts town where he came from. "*Aw,*" I say, with pitying scorn, "poor, innocent Vince. Just another victim of his fame-hungry wife's desperate grab for her sixteenth minute. You must be shocked. *Appalled!* I'm sure that's how you'll try to sell me out to *TMZ* once the divorce is finalized and you're searching between the couch cushions for quarters." I shake my steepled hands at the heavens. "Thank you, Mom, for talking me into signing that prenup before you died."

Vince checks over his shoulder. Yes, the couple ahead of us in line is listening. In a stage whisper, he says, "Steph, I actually am appalled. You lied about being assaulted? That's a new low. Even for you."

I snort. "You knew none of it was true after chapter five."

The memoir is a memoir for the first seventy pages. I did hear things. I did have what felt like an unquenchable thirst for sleep. I did immediately jump to the worst-case scenario, as most teenagers do, that I was showing early signs of a debilitating case of schizophrenia. I did become convinced that if I could get in touch with my biological mother and understand my mental health history, I could somehow outsmart my genes.

A few months after I heard my first voice, I did pay to run a background check on her. At seventeen, I did gather the courage to drive my baby blue BMW to my biological mother's residence in a banal middle-class suburb of Philadelphia. As I parked my car across the street from the townhome where my mother lived with my grandmother, on a circle preposterously named Kensington Court, a boy about my age happened to be walking by my window. He looked like he had just come from some sort of sports practice, the smell of grass and dirt and sweat clinging to him, alluringly. I was quick to call out to him.

The boy stopped. He looked at my car, eyebrows cocked in appreciation, before registering me and doubling back in surprise. I don't think he expected to find someone like me behind the wheel.

"I'm looking for somebody," I said. I read my mother's name, written in blue pen at the top of the MapQuest webpage printout. I'm prehistoric, remember.

The boy made an indeterminable face. He had pretty, curled eyelashes and a strong jaw; the combination of hard and soft was extremely appealing. There were no boys like him in the magazines my friends and I read, but if there were, I would have cut out his picture and taped it to the wall, over the tear of Leonardo DiCaprio dragging down his lower lip with his thumb. I never got the Leo lust, but as a matter of survival, I performed it.

"I have her address as fifty-four Kensington Court. But this is Kensington Court and there is no fifty-four."

"This is Kensington Square," the boy explained. "Kensington Court is over there." He pointed.

"That's confusing!" I laughed. He was *so* cute. "Thanks." I started to roll up my window, but he took a step forward, motioning for me to lower it again.

"Wait," he said. "That woman you're looking for? Sheila Lott?"

I nodded.

"You know she killed herself, right?"

My vision went spotty. I gripped the steering wheel tighter, like the stress balls they give you when you donate blood. "When?" I managed, thunderstruck.

"Few months ago." He shrugged, like the specifics weren't important. "Something like that."

"Do you, um . . . do you know why?"

He actually laughed a little. "Who knows. She was a little, you know . . ." He wound his finger next to his ear. Like Vince would later do whenever I asked him why he took his phone into the bathroom with him to shower. *Stop being crazy*, he'd laugh.

"Got it," I said, weakly. "Thank you." I pressed the gas pedal and the engine blustered. I'd forgotten that I was still in park. I yanked the gear stick into *get the fuck out of here* and lowered my foot.

And so that perfectly average and helpful boy, who was admittedly a little insensitive in his language around suicide, became A.J., even though he never laid a hand on me. Even though I never saw him again.

Vince snatches my wrist and draws me close. "I can destroy you if I want," he says, not very loudly, but the cavernous Air France departures terminal amplifies the threat. His eyes dart over my shoulder, bulging, and he releases me at once. I turn to see Brett, Kelly, and a girl with Didi braids rolling some truly disgraceful nylon luggage our way. Lisa and Marc trail a few steps behind, Marc gripping the little handheld camera by the stabilizer like a pitchfork.

"*Bonjour!*" Brett does a little skip. "*Bonjour, amis et—*" She stops with a gasp when she gets close enough to see my splotchy face. "Steph. Are you okay?"

I wipe my wet chin on my shoulder. "I'm fine."

"You *look* fine," she laughs, because she can never be fucking serious, not even when it *is* serious.

"Stay the fuck out of it, Brett," Vince snarls. "You'll regret it if you don't."

Lisa gasps, positively delighted.

Brett lowers her head and presses her lips together, which is smart. Cowardly, but smart. Kelly steps in front of Layla like a soundproof shield, as though Brett Courtney's niece has never heard anyone say "fuck" before.

"Well," Vince says, with demented cheer, "have a *magical* trip, everyone!" He takes off, my suitcase clattering smoothly behind him, his knuckles white on the handle.

"Nice guy," Brett quips, but there is a wobble in her voice. I feel queasy when I look at Lisa and find her studying Brett with ruthless curiosity. *Does she suspect?*

Brett turns to Layla and forces a smile. "We should get in line to check in, Layls."

I gesture to the sign before us that says "Air France First-Class Check-In." "We are in line to check in."

"Layla and I are flying coach," Brett says, chest puffed. She directs a quick, sanctimonious glance Kelly's way.

"We're donating the difference in a first-class ticket to the Imazighen women," Layla says. The little do-gooding bitch extends her hand. "We've met before but I'm not sure if you remember me. I'm Layla. I'm a big fan of your work."

Oh! How *adorably* creepy. How scientifically miraculous! I did not know that doctors had succeeded in transplanting the brains of thirty-year-old women into the skulls of twelve-year-old children. I take this Girl Boss Borg's hand with unease, finding some comfort in the fact that next to her leggy niece, Brett looks like Shrek with nicer hair. Layla is tall and thin, yes, but this—*this?*—is the "runway model" I've been hearing about for the last few months? She has a fresh whitehead on her chin and an old angry one on her cheek and not a stitch of makeup to soften the blow. And for this, she gets to hear she is beautiful. Get me a cane to shake grouchily into the air, because in my day, not even actually being beautiful was enough.

I squeeze Layla's hand until she grimaces, thinking, *You have no idea about pain, girly. You have no idea what I've been through to get here. You don't want to know what I'll do to stay.*

CHAPTER 14

Brett

"The weak are always trying to sabotage the strong."

"Huh?" Layla shouts.

"*Shhhhhh.*" I can't help but laugh, slouching farther down in my seat. I tap the ear of Layla's headset, reminding her that on a plane she has to speak at a volume she can't hear. Layla has never been on a plane before. The passengers around us don't seem at all bothered. A few actually chuckle. Because even on a red-eye to London in seats that don't recline all the way back, Layla beguiles. How could she not? She looks like an off-duty model on her way to walk her first runway at London Fashion Week, and unlike her mother, she chose to fly coach so that an Imazighen woman could afford a loaf of bread to feed her children tonight.

"It's a quote from this movie," I tell her, touching the screen of her airplane TV. "You should watch it. It's about female ambition, and the lengths people will go to extinguish it."

Layla's lips travel the synopsis of *Election,* silently. She mumbles an intrigued *huh,* and selects the play now option. Thank God. Aunt Brett needs some adult talky time with her ole buddy ole pal Marc, who is stomping his foot in the aisle seat, trying to get the blood circulating.

"This sucks," I sympathize, tearing open a bag of sour cream 'n' onion chips and offering it to him first.

Marc sticks his hand in the bag and rustles around. "I can't believe you're not in first."

"I can't believe *they* are. We are about to meet some of the most disenfranchised women on the planet. It's like"—I explode a hand by my brain—"total disconnect."

Marc snorts, popping a chip into his mouth. "Did you really think Queen Simmons was going to slum it in coach? She's probably allergic to cloth seating." He dusts his hands together, sending onion powder into the air.

I slide a chip into my mouth, unsure if a white guy calling Stephanie a queen is racist but unwilling to go to bat for her even if it is. I need something from Marc right now. I twist my Standing Sisters ring with slippery chip fingers, trying to figure out the most artful entry into this conversation. As director of photography, Marc sees and hears everything on both sides of the lens. If there are any rumblings, and if anyone is willing to share them with me, it will be Marc. "What, um. What do you think was going on with Steph and Vince back there?"

Marc sighs, sounding disappointed.

"What?" I ask, wide-eyed and innocent.

"Don't do that, Brett," Marc says. "If you want to have a real conversation about this, then let's have a real conversation about it. But don't pretend like you don't know what Vince and Steph were fighting about back there. You're not like that. That's why we're friends."

Something about Marc that everyone knows but not everyone appreciates is that on the weekends, he plays bass in an eighties cover band called Super Freaks. This detail is traded mockingly by the other *Diggers*, but what they don't know—because they would never deign to ask the crew *anything* about their lives—is that his band used to regularly sell out the Canal Room, and that twenty-two-year-old girls line the stage whenever they open at Talkhouse in Amagansett. My ex and I went to see them once, and afterward, we'd eaten slices at Astro's with Marc and his boyfriend, who plays drums. I did all of this because I like Marc. But what if I didn't like Marc? Would I still have sought him out like I did, knowing the producers can't edit, for better or for worse, film that doesn't exist? The answer floors me: Probably. Definitely. I am exactly like that.

"You're right," I say. "I'm sorry. I'm just . . . I don't know what you know. What anyone knows. And, well," I glance at Layla, making sure she's watching the movie and not listening to us, "something happened that shouldn't have happened, and I'm not sure what to do about it."

Marc smiles at me, kindly. "Everyone makes mistakes, Brett. That doesn't make me love you less. It makes me love you more." He reaches for my hand and I let him hold it for a few moments, smiling back at him gratefully, marinating in my full stink.

Marc cranes his neck, making sure the passengers in our immediate vicinity are asleep or otherwise occupied. Determining that we have our privacy, he says in a low voice, "Lisa doesn't think that you and Stephanie were fighting about you not passing on her book to Rihanna or whatever it is you're saying."

I swallow, tasting bile in my throat. I can barf in the chip bag if I need to. "What does she think it's about?"

Marc bites his lip, checking our surroundings again. This time, he reaches into his pocket, pulls out his phone, and opens up the Notes app. I am practically in his lap, watching as he taps out the answer: *She is starting to think you and Stephanie had a thing while you were living with her and it ended badly.*

The words on my tombstone blur and come into focus, blur and come into focus. This is bad. This is really, really bad. I'm *engaged.* Steph and Vince might have the sort of marriage where they trade hall passes every other week, but Arch thinks more highly of herself than that. She will leave me if she gets wind of this.

Marc is opening the camera icon on his phone now, thumbing through pictures of his niece at the beach and expertly captured sunsets, arriving finally on a grab of what appears to be a page in a book. He offers me his phone, and I spring my thumb and index finger apart, zooming in.

It's the title page from Stephanie's third novel. The one I thought

I had trashed in the clean-out of my old apartment. *To the love of my life,* she had written to me. *Sorry, Vince!*

"Where did you get this?" I ask Marc, my ears roaring.

"Lisa sent it to me. It was on the bookshelf at your old place. Where Kelly and"—he signals Layla with his chin—"are living. We were there to film and Lisa noticed it. She thought it was weird it was there, and she opened it, and then, well, she read that, and it just got her thinking and then—"

I hold up a finger to Marc—*press pause* on that thought. I motion for Layla to remove her headphones.

"Layla?" I ask, in a quiet, stern voice. "Remember that copy of Stephanie's book that I put in the recycling bin?"

Layla swallows.

I nod. "Tell me the truth."

Layla looks like she wishes she could disappear. "I was curious," she whispers, her cheeks blazing. Curious about sex, she means.

I return her headphones to her ears, cursing my sister under my breath for banning Layla from watching *Game of Thrones*. Jon Snow could have sated that curiosity. This could have been avoided.

"Go on," I tell Marc, digging my fingers into my armrests.

"Lisa started to think about it more, and she asked me to show her the film I took of you and Steph meeting up in Barneys." Marc waits for me to remember. "And she noticed that Steph brought up your new tattoo on your foot."

I feel my face contort into a confused scowl. "*So?*"

"So it had been a month since you and Steph quote unquote *made up* in the bathroom at Lauren's event, and you got that tattoo just a few days later. We filmed it, remember? That means when you and Steph saw each other in Barneys you hadn't seen each other in a month—but why? If you had really patched things up, and if it had been over something as insignificant as what you said it was about, why wouldn't you two have been hanging out all the time again? But the nail in the coffin is that she bailed on your engagement party."

"She was *traveling*."

"No," Marc says to my surprise. "Lisa checked her flight info. She was in New York that night. She chose not to come. Maybe because she's in love with you and it would have been too painful for her to attend?"

I tip my head back, resting it on the seat, wishing I was asleep and this was all just a bad dream. "Has Lisa told anyone else about this yet? Other than you?" I hold my breath.

"I don't think so," Marc says, and I exhale, audibly. "I think she's waiting to see if her theory has legs before she brings the others into it."

I sigh, feeling unjustifiably sorry for myself. I've waited four years to take everyone to Morocco and a secret lesbian affair storyline is going to overshadow all the good we've come here to do.

"I will say," Marc adds, "that it's definitely another post to the pile that she saw Steph and Vince arguing like that. She thinks Vince knows and is pissed. Which is hypocrisy of the highest order given the way he's been sniffing around your sister."

"Oh, great." I laugh, helplessly. "So I'm not the only one who's noticed that."

After my engagement party, I had to have a serious sit-down with Kelly. *Did something happen with Vince?* I asked, my throat tight, because I really was afraid to hear her answer. Kelly doesn't date. She won't allow herself to devote that much of her time and energy to anyone other than Layla and the business. Occasionally, she uses Tinder to screw. I've babysat for her on those nights. *Have a good orgasm!* I call after her as she heads out the door in a tight dress. Vince would have happily provided her such a service and saved her the effort of dragging her thumb across the screen. Kelly is all about efficiency.

She had responded to my question with hostile disdain. "You have problems," she scoffed, and walked out of the room. No *yes*. No *no*.

"Jesse can call this episode 'Incest Is Best,'" I mutter to Marc.

Marc raises his eyebrows. He's never heard me take a jab at Jesse before, but I'm not so googly-eyed that I haven't noticed her sense of humor, which all too often tries to appeal to the youths and all too often falls abysmally short. And her pun-y captions on Instagram—*cringe*.

Suddenly, the plane gets caught in a nasty ripple of turbulence. Layla, first-time flyer, seizes up in fear. I put an arm around her, tucking her into my side and assuring her this is normal, even though it feels like a shark has the pilot's cabin in its mouth, like we are being shaken to death. I promise her that this is nothing to be afraid of. Nothing I haven't seen before. I'm talking to her but I'm talking to myself, and I'm lying to both of us.

It's early afternoon by the time we land in Marrakesh and taxi to the hotel, Marc swallowing yawns while trying to hold his handheld steady in the front seat. I'm in the first row of the van, squeezed between my sister and Layla. Steph and Jen are behind me and Lauren shares the third row with an arm looped over her luggage, which she insisted come in our van. Something about her grandmother's silk scarves. Something none of us believed. I'm assuming she did her research and knows that in certain establishments in Morocco, women are barred from drinking alcohol, and took her own precautions.

I warn everyone against napping. The best thing to do is power through the day and let sleep snatch you only when you can't run any further. I suggest that once we get to the hotel, we freshen up and meet in the lobby for a ride through the Jewish quarter on the SPOKE electric bikes, which have been shipped to the riad in anticipation of tomorrow's field trip to the village of Aguergour in the lower Atlas Mountains. I do think this would make for a nice outing and my investors will be pleased with the prime product placement, but a part of me wants to keep the group together, under my paranoid eye. I don't know who has heard what—about me and Steph, about Kelly and Vince. The last thing I need is the women splitting up, saying God knows what about God knows who on camera.

"Actually, there's this spice shop I wanted to check out," Jen says.

I close my eyes, briefly. Of course there is.

"The Mella Spice Souk," Jen reads off her phone. Kelly twists in her seat, ears perked.

"*Très bon*," the driver chimes in. "*Est célèbre*."

We all turn to Lauren, who says to him, "*Est-il*?"

He rattles off something else in French, and Lauren raises her eyebrows, nodding, making it clear she understands. "He said that market is like a famous market. Where the locals go. Tourists too, but *not* a tourist trap."

Jen gets this smug smile on her face, as though she has bested my plans. "My yoga instructor told me about it," she says. "There's a Moroccan blend that's supposed to increase the restfulness and renewability of sleep. I may integrate it into a new tonic." She beams. "Rest is the new hustle!"

Oh.

My.

God.

"I think Steph agrees." Lauren laughs, and Steph's eyes pop open at the mention of her name. She had been dozing next to Jen, her forehead suctioned to the window.

"Sorry." She wipes away some drool with the back of her hand, "What?"

"I was just talking about what we should do between now and dinner," I repeat for her. "I wanted to take the SPOKE bikes for a ride through the Jewish quarter to test them out. Everyone is welcome to join."

"I want to ride the bike again!" Layla declares, sure to let everyone know she already got to do it once.

Lauren leans forward in the back seat and addresses me. Already, she is making an impression on Morocco, as much for her aggressively blond hair as for her not-so-sly innuendo. *No one has ever handled my bags like that,* she purred to the driver when he met us at the curb. "They, like, do the work for you, right?" She grins at the driver in the rearview mirror. "I'm loyal to one kind of cardio and one kind of cardio only."

Jen groans.

"You won't even break a sweat," I promise her.

"Then I'm in." She gives me a flirty wink. Just a few months ago, Lauren stonewalled the trip to Morocco, convinced I was the one who sold her out to Page Six. But *Digger* alliances are like New Year's resolutions—made to be broken. She even seems to have softened on Steph, her new projected mole, though her gentle ribbing doesn't necessarily mean all is forgiven. She could just as easily be lying in wait. In some ways, Lauren is the most dangerous. A butcher with a blowout. You never know when she's going to come for you.

I turn to Kelly, my expectation that she will want to stick by me apparent. Instead she says, "I'll go with Jen. So she's not alone."

"Kel," I say, annoyed, "don't you think we should make sure the bikes are working properly?"

"I don't think it takes both of us to do that." She leans around me and taps Layla's knee. "And Layls, I'd prefer it if you came with me too."

Layla whines, "*Why*?"

"Because it's different riding the bikes here than it was in the warehouse. There's traffic and people walking and I don't want you or anyone else to get hurt."

"I thought *nine*-year-olds could ride them."

Kelly glances at me, but I refuse to meet her eye. I don't want Layla riding the bike on a busy city street either, but that's Kelly's fault—for begging to take on the responsibility of the manufacturing process, for being the cheapskate who said *no* to thumb grips. The next shipment of bikes will arrive in the fall with a safer design feature, but in the meantime, we're here with the prototypes. It's not the end of the world, necessarily. Plenty of early model electronic bikes were designed without thumb grips and plenty of people have ridden them without incident. We just have to impress upon the villagers how easy it is to unwittingly accelerate with a twist grip, that you can kill a person going only forty miles an hour.

Kelly says to Layla, "Well, when you have to walk ten miles to collect water for your family I'll let you ride it again, okay?"

Layla appeals to me with her eyes stuck in the back of her head.

"Sorry, Charlie," I tell her, pursing my lower lip to assure her that her pain is my pain. "But I'm with your mom on this one." I glance over Layla's shoulder. "Steph? You coming with?"

Steph speaks to the window with glazed eyes, lulled by the rolling portrait of brown earth and blue sky. "I have some calls to make when we get to the hotel."

"You sure?" I ask her. "This is the only full day we have in Marrakesh. Don't you want to see the city?"

Stephanie shuts her eyes again. "It's beautiful."

When we arrive at the hotel, the hits keep coming. Lisa informs all of us, in her creepy little-girl voice, that there has been a change to the rooming assignments. I am no longer staying in the suite with Kelly and Layla. Jen will be taking my place, and I am to room with Stephanie.

"I'm happy with that." Jen bumps Kelly's shoulder with her own, and I try not to gag.

"And I'm happy to be on my own." Lauren beams. I eye the luggage that hasn't left her side. I'll bet she is.

I'm also betting that this is a setup, so that Lisa can see if her theory *has legs*, and that there is a very real possibility she may bug my room. I am alone in that concern, it seems, as Stephanie appears indifferent to the fact that we have been stuck together, and that there is only a single, king-sized bed for the two of us to share—*not* a coincidence. When we get to the room, she drops her things, kicks her nice shoes across the room, and heads for the privacy of the bathroom.

"Steph, wait," I say to her before she can shut the door.

She pauses without turning to face me. I put my phone in front of her face so that she can read the unsent text message to her: *Marc told me Lisa thinks we SLEPT TOGETHER! That's why she wants us in the same room. She might have bugged it so we have to be careful what we say.*

Stephanie reads and rereads the message, her face eerily blank.

She takes my phone and composes a response, handing it back to me and shutting the bathroom door without waiting for me to read it. I look at my screen to find that she didn't write me back in words. Instead, she selected three emojis, the ones with the screaming faces and hands clasped to the jaw.

"She's definitely not coming?" Lauren asks when I meet her by the elevators.

I shake my head. "I think she's pretty tired. She's probably jet-lagged from being in L.A. right before this."

The elevator doors open and Lauren and I wait patiently while Marc backs in with the camera first.

"Is she tired?" Lauren asks when the elevator doors have trapped us inside. "Or is she upset?"

The hair on my arms prickles. "Why would she be upset?"

"I don't think it's escaped her that Vince has a little crush," Lauren teases, and I instantly regret giving Lauren this opening on camera. "Did you not notice at your engagement party?" she continues, to my complete horror. "He followed her everywhere."

I steady myself against the gold ballet bar lining the inside of the elevator. "I didn't even get a chance to *eat* at my engagement party. So no, I didn't notice. And anyway, Kelly would never."

Lauren slaps a hand over her mouth, capping a *gotcha!* laugh. She is wearing the most impractical biking outfit I've ever seen. To not exercise Lauren wears head-to-toe Nike and to exercise she wears a gown rimmed with rainbow-colored tassels that the wheels of the bike are going to gobble alive.

I glare at her. *"What?"*

Lauren drops her chin to her chest with an infuriating giggle. "I didn't mention Kelly by name."

A cold sweat surfaces on the back of my neck. "No," I insist. "You did."

"Nope." Lauren says the word with a pop of her lips: no-*pope*!

She grins, adjusting the gold beaded tikka splitting the part of her baby blond hair.

"That's Indian, you know," I tell her.

"I *know,*" Lauren huffs in a way that makes it clear she didn't. She lifts her chin as the elevator door opens on the ground level. "Africa is trying to improve relations." I follow our self-appointed U.N. representative into the lobby, making *did she really just say that?* eyes at the camera.

"And by the way," Lauren says to me over her shoulder. "I would never either. Doesn't mean he hasn't tried. This slut has standards."

I accidentally land on the heel of Lauren's sandal, and she snaps backward. "Fuck!" she cries, and when I look down, I realize I've torn her ankle strap.

"Oh my God, Laur. I'm so sorry."

"I just got these," she moans, crouching down to examine the damage.

"You're supposed to bike in closed-toed shoes anyway."

Lauren scowls up at me from the brightly tiled floor of the riad and I laugh. "I'll buy you new ones at the Tanneries, okay?"

"*Américain maladroit,*" Lauren mutters, standing.

"I'll wait for you down here," I tell her, as she hobbles back toward the elevator. Marc stays with me.

I plop onto a sand-colored linen couch in the lobby, scrolling through my phone and rereading reminder texts from Lisa. *REMINDER: talk to Lauren about how you feel about Jen and Kelly pairing up today. I know you and Jen have made peace, but she has talked so much shit about you over the years. Kelly is your SISTER. How does this not bother you??*

I drop my phone into my lap, running my hands over my face and sighing. Of course it bothers me that Kelly is under the spell of a holistic hack, but I have bigger things on my mind. Like the fact that Lauren has noticed Vince's fixation on Kelly, and that Stephanie seems very much on the verge of defecting.

On the other side of the lobby, there is a bit of commotion that catches my attention. Kelly, Jen, and Layla appear beneath an olive arch with a second camera crew in tow. Kelly and Jen are both wearing flesh-colored pillowcases that Jen probably had commissioned from her own exfoliated skin cells. I start to lift a hand to get Layla's attention, but I'm stopped cold by what I witness next. Kelly, noticing that the tag on Jen's dress is sticking out, reaches out and tucks it in, her fingers grazing the back of Jen's neck. Jen, walking a few steps ahead of my sister, is clearly startled by my sister's touch. Startled and something else that changes her face in a single, sneering flash: repulsed. She wrangles her reaction not even a second later with a grateful smile.

The axis of my world shifts, just enough for me to review everything I know about Jen and Kelly's infuriating friendship in a new light. *I'm happy with that.* Jen had said to Kelly when she found out they were rooming together. Why, then, did my sister's touch just cause her to recoil in disgust? It makes no sense, unless it is not that Jen is happy to spend more time with her new friend—but that she's been coached to spend more time with her.

And who would coach Jen to spend more time with my sister? I wake my phone and reread my reminder texts. *Lisa.* Lisa must have shared her suspicions about Vince and Kelly with Jen. *Of course* she did. Lauren knows, and if Lauren knows, her overlord does too. I watch Jen wind the diameter of the lobby's central fountain, wondering what her reminder texts from Lisa say. *Ask Kelly how she's getting along with the other women. How are things going with Steph? It doesn't seem like Steph has taken to her—any thoughts as to why?* My best friend's husband and my booby sister—it would make for a luscious storyline.

Marc says, "Check out the Bobbsey Twins." He zooms in on Kelly and Jen, who are now swishing out of the lobby in their long, shapeless dresses. Kelly doesn't look like the new girl anymore. She looks like an original. Like she could be wearing my ring.

I didn't know it could be possible, but I feel worse after Lauren and I get back to the hotel. Based on our conversation as we roamed the market with our guide, it's clear that she has been instructed to ask me questions to help shape Kelly's impending storyline as a husband-stealing harlot.

"So, what's the deal with Layla's father?" Lauren had asked as we perused the stands of leather slippers and Moroccan saffron and tin lanterns.

"He's not in the picture," I'd replied with a friendly note of finality in my voice.

"So, like, has anybody *been* in the picture for Kelly over the last—how old is Layla?"

I took my time examining a SPOKE-red beaded gandoura. I asked how much in my spotty French. The merchant rattled a response too quickly for me to understand.

"He said four hundred and forty dirham for one, eight hundred dirham if your sister wants one too," Lauren translated for me. Lauren speaks French like a rich college girl dripping in Patagonia and Van Cleef, which is who she was once. Even I can hear that her accent is a travesty.

"Rude," I joked, hoping for a pardon.

"Right?" Lauren agreed, playing along. "Like *we* could be sisters."

"Mother, daughter, maybe," I said, grinning, and Lauren gasped, truly stricken I would say such a thing on camera.

We continued on our way after bargaining down to seven hundred and sixty dirham for two caftans, red for me and virgin white for Lauren.

"So how old again?" Lauren asked.

I stopped to admire a pair of sandals. "How old again what?"

Lauren smiled at me, patiently, while the camera looked on. "Layla."

"Twelve." I held up the sandals. "What do you think of these?"

"Cute," Lauren said without looking at them. "And so, has Kelly been with anyone in all that time?"

I bartered with the vendor before answering her. "I really don't like to think about my sister *being* with anyone, Laur." I shuddered as if to say, *Kelly? Naked? Ick.*

"She must be pretty lonely then."

I shrugged, counting out thirty dirham.

"She must be pretty *pent up*. I can't even imagine going that long without the D."

I handed the money to the vendor without answering, trying not to think about what happened the last time Kelly felt *pent up*, right here in Marrakesh.

When I open the door to my hotel room, the lights are off, an episode of *Keeping Up with the Kardashians* on but muted. It's an old one; Khloe still has her original face.

Stephanie is asleep on top of a creamy, sequined Moroccan wedding quilt, barefoot but dressed in the same clothes she's worn from L.A. to New York to London to here. The pink polish on her toenails is chipped, which brings me to a full stop. I've only ever seen Stephanie with a perfect pedicure. She wraps her toes in plastic before going to the beach in the Hamptons, to keep the sand from dulling the topcoat. It used to drive Lisa crazy. *Cut the princess off at the feet,* she'd tell Marc, at a pitch dogs could hear.

Steph's phone is charging on the floor next to the bed. I check my battery—16 percent—and drop to my heels. When I unplug her phone, the screen lights up long enough for me to read a text message from Vince. *If anyone asks me about it, I'm telling the truth. I'm done lying for you, Steph.*

The hair on the back of my neck stands to attention, as though summoned. I look up. Stephanie is in the exact same position she was in when I entered the room, only her eyes are wide open, watching me.

"Steph!" I fall back with a startled gasp. "Sorry. Can I . . . ? Do you mind?" I hold up the cord of her charger because the way she is looking at me has rendered me incapable of speaking in complete sentences.

Stephanie reaches for her phone. She skims the message from Vince, then regards me, coldly. "Help yourself."

"I was going to shower," I tell her, standing unsteadily. All the blood rushes to my head, blinding me for a moment. I put my hand on the cool lime wall until my vision clears. "Unless you want to first?"

Stephanie closes her eyes. "You go." She slips her phone under her pillow, like you would a gun.

The women are sitting cross-legged on a smattering of quatrefoil-printed pillows, facing the cameras with their backs to the fire. When I came to Morocco for the first time at fifteen—twelve years ago now!—I was surprised to find that a fire would be necessary at night. When I pictured Morocco, I pictured rolling orange dunes, wavy in the heat, men in turbans hallucinating pools of fresh water. Basically, a dumb American's caricature of a country that I found later to be as diverse in geography and climate as my own. In June, in Marrakesh, the weather is what my mother would call *pleasant*. A far cry from New York, right now a festering septic tank of loogies and dog piss and two million colony-forming units of bacteria per square inch. Bless its yucky heart, I miss it.

The clover-shaped windows are open, calling the flames west. Maybe north. I'm such a girl when it comes to directions, though I know better than to say so out loud and perpetuate such a stereotype. Lisa holds up a hand in question, wanting to know where Stephanie is. I mime applying mascara while one of the sound guys mics me up.

Lisa rolls her eyes. "So another two hours then?"

I spread my palms—*what do you want me to do?*—and enter the shot. "*Salut, les filles*," I say, tugging on Layla's pony and wedging myself between her and Jen, who, I shit you not, is wearing a red fez like she's motherfucking Aladdin. "How was today?"

"Oh my God. We walked, like, ten miles," Layla says, leaning forward to dunk a cracker into a bowl of hummus. The fire sets off a sterling flash at her neck.

"This is new," I tell her, pinching the charm between my thumb and index finger.

"Oh, yeah." Layla tucks her chin. "What's it called again?"

"Hand of Fatima," Jen answers, and I realize she's wearing one too. I don't need to look at my sister's neck to know they got a three-for-two deal at the souk today.

"It's supposed to keep anything bad from happening to you," Layla tells me.

I reach for something that looks like lamb. "Is there enough food here for you?" I ask Jen, at the same time deliberately scraping the meat off the bone with my teeth like the top of the food chain savage I am. "I told them we have a vegan in the house." I stick a greasy finger in my mouth and suck off the juices. Definitely lamb. Lamb has such a distinct taste—pure animal.

Jen buries her face in a mug of tea, her words parting the steam. "It's plenty."

"Are you sure?" I say, scooching closer to the table to examine the spread. "What can you even eat here?"

Jen indicates her paltry options because I did not, in fact, call ahead and warn the hotel we had a vegan guest in our party, because we do not have a vegan guest in our party. "Olives, carrots, naan, hummus."

"There's egg in the naan and feta in the hummus," I tell her.

"You're so thoughtful to worry so much about me." Jen means to smile but only shows her teeth. "I ordered some veggie kabobs to the room earlier so I'm not very hungry." She sets her tea on the low table, linking her hands around her knees, her beady eyes alighting. "Is Steph coming or did you two have another fight?"

"We had so much to catch up on we lost track of time," I return, easily. "But, I'm sure any minute now."

I watch Lauren make eye contact with Lisa over my shoulder. "Maybe I should go check on her," she says. She climbs to her feet, holding tight to her water glass. A lot of lime in that water.

I do not want the second camera crew following Lauren upstairs so she can grill Stephanie—*Have you heard the one about your husband and Brett's sister?* I stand and offer to go with her.

"Brett," Kelly says, tugging on the hem of my dress, "we actually want to talk to you about something." I stare down Lauren a moment, but what can I really do? I can't be everywhere at once. Reluctantly, I return to my seat on the floor, watching Lauren sashay out of the room, her caftan grazing the black-and-white medina floor, the assistant cameraman weaving the same unsteady path behind her.

"We were talking," Kelly continues, tucking her hair behind her ear and glancing at Jen to make it clear who she was talking to, "and we thought that maybe when we get back we can throw you a bachelorette party at Jen's Hamptons house."

I point a lamb rib at my chest, looking both ways over my shoulders, as though she couldn't possibly be talking to me.

Kelly *har-hars* at my put-on bewilderment. "Yes, you. Jen was saying she'd like one last summer weekend in the house before it sells."

"And I think it's important to continue to feed this good energy between us," Jen says. "Celebrating joy builds walls that keep animosity out."

Jesus, hold my earrings. We both know this is a production-driven move—there is always "one last hurrah" before the end of every season, an event that brings the women together to kiss and make up before we tear each other to shreds at the reunion. I had been the one to suggest a bachelorette party to Lisa, I just didn't think Jen would be the one hosting it.

"Are you going to have guy or girl strippers?" Layla asks, already red-faced, mouth covered, waiting for Kelly to scold her.

"*No* strippers." Kelly wraps her arm around Layla's shoulder and kisses her forehead while Layla squirms. Kelly says something quietly into Layla's ear that stills her.

We pick at the food and make safe observations about the weather and the people and the time change, and I go over the plan for tomorrow. The vans are leaving at 7:00 A.M.—one for us and the crew, one for the bikes. The village of Aguergour is only twenty-one miles away, but as the last ten miles are a dirt track on the edge of a treacherous mountain range, it will take over an hour to get there.

The waiters come to clear the platters and bring out coffee and tea. Layla stops them from taking her plate. It's full of bread and dips and meat that she hasn't touched. "I put it together for Lauren and Stephanie," she says, and Jen's *aw* maybe would have duped me had I not seen how she looked at my sister earlier.

I tried to get Kelly alone before dinner, to share with her my suspicions that Jen is not her friend, that she has only glommed on to her to push a narrative that Kelly has slept with Vince. I was also hoping to finally get a definitive response from her regarding whether or not she actually slept with Vince—because on that, I am still not clear—but Kelly hasn't left Jen's side since we arrived this afternoon, and I'm too smart to put this into a text message.

"Here we are!" Lauren peals.

When I look up, it appears to be only Lauren in the doorway, holding that same glass of heavily limed water. But then Stephanie steps out from behind her, her wet hair in a bun at the nape of her neck and a shocking amount of makeup on her face, even for her.

"Sorry," Steph says, unapologetically.

I make room for her on my pillow. "It's fine. It's all very casual. Layla saved you a plate."

"You are such a sweetheart!" Lauren cries.

Stephanie mumbles something that I can't quite make out, ignoring the spot I've opened for her and sitting next to Kelly, on the other side of the table across from Layla and me.

Kelly turns to her, which is a lot more confrontational when you are shoulder to shoulder with someone, sharing a bright pink pillow. "What was that?"

Stephanie reaches for an olive. At a slow, thunderous volume, she repeats herself, "I said, she's been *raised* so well."

Kelly purses her lips, disbelievingly. I'm pretty sure Steph said *trained*—not raised—too.

"What are you drinking?" Steph helps herself to a sip of my wine. "Mmm." She rubs her lips together. She points at it and barks at the waiter stationed in the corner, "Get me a glass of that."

Stephanie reaches for a piece of naan. Instead of tearing off a bite-sized piece, she folds it and shoves the whole thing into her mouth like a taco. "Mmm," she says. "Thank you for not eating carbs, Laur. This is *heavenly*." She reaches for another piece of naan, though her jaw is still working like a baseball player's on chewing tobacco.

"I eat carbs," Lauren protests with a laugh.

Stephanie spells out, "L. *O*. L." I can see all the food in her mouth when she pronounces the "O." She glances around the table, her eyes wide and unfocused, herbs tacked to the thick coat of gloss on her lips. "How was everybody's *day*?"

The question is mockingly curious, clearly not meant to be answered, and we fall silent, unsure of how to handle this Joan Crawford–shellacked Stephanie before us.

I clear my throat and take a stab. "Well. Lauren and I rode the new bikes down to the Jewish—"

Stephanie interrupts me. "Lauren partook in *physical* activity that was not—?" She glances at Layla, clasps her lower lip in her teeth and performs a slow, sexy body roll, crooning, throatily, "Bow-chick-a-wow-wow."

I open my mouth to object. Stephanie shoots me a look that makes me close it.

"Subtle," Kelly snaps.

"This is an adult trip," Stephanie says, matter-of-factly. "If you didn't want your daughter exposed to adult language, you shouldn't have brought her."

Layla looks fairly heartbroken. I reach for her hand on the floor.

"I'm glad you're here, little mama." Lauren winks at Layla. Lauren may be a drunk pitbull but at least she's kind to kids. Turning to Stephanie, she responds, "And for your information, I don't mind partaking in physical activity when the piece of equipment is, like, the Hermés bag of the fitness world."

"What a ringing endorsement!" Stephanie cries, her tone swinging from nasty to bubbly faster than I can think, *how many milligrams is she on?* The waiter returns with her wine. "Sir," she addresses him formally as he sets the glass in front of her, "could you go into the basement or storage unit or mummy tomb or whatever and look for our bikes? You'll know they're our bikes because they're SPOKE bikes. They are the most beautiful bikes in the whole wide world. They came in first place at the Omaha county bike beauty pageant in '09. They beat out Christy Nicklebocker and she motorboated all of the judges, including the three-hundred-and-seven-pound church lady who is related to her through marriage."

The waiter turns to me, dumbstruck. "Madam?" he asks.

Everyone is looking at me, waiting for me to do something, to say something. "Just a joke." I laugh haltingly to the waiter, offering him the plate of food Layla put together for Stephanie and Lauren, so that he has an excuse to take it and leave the table. I have to keep nodding at him as he backs away, *you can go, it's okay*.

"I'll make sure you're the first to ride one tomorrow," I say to Stephanie, desperate to placate her. *Just hold out on going completely crazy until the trip is over*. "When we get to Aguergour."

"When we get to A-grrr-gorrrr," Stephanie repeats with ridiculing concentration. "*A-grrr-gorrrr*."

"Yeah," I say, pretending like she isn't making fun of me. "It'll be better anyway. We'll have more room to see what the bikes can really do in the country."

Layla sighs longingly, turning to my sister with big, pleading eyes. "If I promise to stay under a certain speed limit, can I try them?"

"Layla," Kelly says in her scary mom voice, "what did I say?"

Stephanie works a back molar with her tongue, dislodging a lump of wet food, her eyes darting from Layla to Kelly, Layla to Kelly. "My mother never let me do anything either," she says, her gaze settling on Layla.

"Excuse me," Kelly laughs, testily, "but she is in Morocco."

Stephanie rises to all fours, trying to untangle her legs from her caftan to get into a more comfortable position, but for a moment, I think she might spring across the table and attack Layla. "I hid everything from her," Stephanie continues, leering at Layla like a lecherous old man. "You'll learn how to do it too. You'll have to because your mother will never truly understand what life is like for you. You'll become little negro Nancy Drew." She giggles, queerly. "I should do a children's series. Negro Nancy Drew."

"Hey!" I say, more startled than angry. I have never heard that kind of language from Stephanie before.

"Don't use that word about my daughter," Kelly says, voice quivering with indignation.

Layla grumbles, looking absolutely humiliated. "*Mom.*"

Stephanie only laughs. "You don't get to tell me anything about that word, Miss Teen Mom."

I gesture desperately at the riad's butler, who has been waiting on the sidelines for a moment to intervene. *Now is the time,* the wave of my hand says. *Now. Now. Now.*

"Ladies," he says, his hands clasped in prayer, "dessert is served on the Atlas rooftop, along with a special treat." He holds out an arm, leading the way. "If you will."

The Atlas rooftop is so named for its unobstructed views of the High Atlas mountain range, its djebels brown and snowcapped in the winter, but only brown now. I stay close to Layla as the rest of the *Diggers* fan out on the quiet, twinkle-lit rooftop. I can tell she's reeling after what happened downstairs.

"That's where we're going tomorrow," I tell her, pointing at the mountain range. Tucked into the crests and valleys are mud-thatched Berber villages where the women sing as they weave pom-pom rugs and knead dough for bread, celebrating their emancipation from the walk to get water, their freedom to work.

Layla aims her phone at the view width-wise, snapping a picture for an Instagram story. She attempts a few different captions before giving up with a dispirited sigh.

"You okay?" I ask her.

"Why doesn't Stephanie like me?" Her mouth tightens and

twists to the left, a sign she's about to cry. Kelly and I used to take videos when she was a baby, her mouth a little raisin on the side of her face, the veins in her temples straining against her skin. You can hear us giggling in the background, *Oh, oh, there she blowwwwws.*

I lean against the clay ledge of the rooftop, so that I'm facing her. Under the fat Christmas tree lights, Layla's face is arresting save for a humdinger of a pimple in the corner of her chin. Marc electric-slides around us, capturing us in a profile shot. "It hurts when it feels like someone doesn't like you, especially someone you might admire." I rove my head around, until I find an angle where I catch her eye. "Right? You admire Steph?"

"I do admire her, but I thought . . ." She exhales with enough force to blow out the candles on a birthday cake, as if frustrated she can't find the words to explain.

"What?" I ask gently, reaching out to smooth her hair.

Layla ducks out from under my hand. "You wouldn't get it." There is something on that word—*you*—that I have never heard before, at least not directed at me.

I blink, stung. Kelly is the one who loves Layla but doesn't get her. That's my job. That's what I *do*—I get people. I try to make her see that I understand. "I admired Stephanie too, and it was important to me that she liked me," I say. "But something I realized, Layls, is that—"

Layla doesn't let me finish. "Stop telling me you understand because you don't. You don't know what it's like not knowing anyone who looks like you."

The statement feels like a concrete barrier erected on a previously open border. I'm shook to my core realizing that Layla feels like this and didn't tell me. Of course I have worried about her, being one of a handful of black students at her school, but Layla is so far from an outlier. She's one of the most popular girls in her class. Everyone who meets her falls in love with her. I guess I assumed that being liked was the same thing as belonging. I never stopped to think how meaningful it would be for Layla to meet someone like Stephanie, someone who would understand what life was like for her better than anyone, but who instead has taken a visceral dislike to her. "I feel really stupid for not realizing you might feel like that," I tell her apologetically. "And for assuming you would just volunteer those feelings if you did. I'm the adult. I'm the one who should be asking if you're doing okay."

Layla gives me a half-hearted shrug. "It's fine. Mom is always asking me anyway. It gets annoying." But she doesn't sound annoyed at all.

On the other side of the rooftop, where white benches pen in a short table set with a platter of sour fruit tarts and a mosaic-styled ice bucket, Lauren cries, "A *fortune*-teller? Maybe she can tell me which one of you hussies planted the *Post* story."

"Shut the fuck up about the *Post* story," Steph roars. "Everyone is so fucking bored of the fucking *Post* story."

I can practically hear the air being let out of Lauren's sails from across the rooftop, but I ignore the heated exchange for Layla's sake. I will do anything to cheer her up. I pop my eyes at her as if to say, *A fortune-teller? Fun!*

"Come on," I say, leading her over to the sitting area, where the evening's *special treat* has turned out to be a plump, fifty-something woman with a sheer yellow scarf draped loosely around her head, shuffling a deck of tarot cards.

As we approach, I hear the butler explaining, "Jamilla only speaks Arabic and French, but I'm told we have a translator for the group."

Hmm, I wonder who told him that? I study Lisa, my enthusiasm for this *special treat* waning. There are very few people I trust on this rooftop right now.

Lauren thrusts her hand into the air, thrilled to provide such a critical service for everyone here. She introduces herself to Jamilla and listens intently to the woman's response.

"She says that the person she is reading should sit next to her," Lauren says.

Kelly addresses Layla with a buoyant smile. "Want to go first, Layls?"

I know Kelly is just trying to make up for what happened downstairs, but I don't want Layla anywhere near this crystal gazer.

Even if she isn't a producer plant, I don't trust Lauren to translate truthfully.

Layla sidesteps the bench, taking a seat to Jamilla's left. Jamilla pats the pouf of Layla's hair, exclaiming delightedly, and poses a question to Lauren, who claps her hands together, hooting at whatever it was Jamilla said to her.

"No," she says, shaking her head. "No. *Elle est sa fille.*" She points to Kelly, saying to Stephanie, "She thought Layla was yours!"

"Why is that funny?" Stephanie wants to know.

"Jesus, you are in a *mood* tonight." Lauren reaches for a sour fruit tart, checking to make sure the cameras are watching. *I eat carbs.*

"Let's let Jen go first," I intervene. "This is more her *beat* anyway."

Jen purses her lips in what could be considered a smile. "I believe that wellness of mind and body is the best predictor of the future, but sure," she shrugs, "okay."

Jamilla shuffles the deck, fanning it out for Jen and motioning for her to pick one. She pats her chest, instructing Jen to press the card to her heart.

"Fermer les yeux et penser à ce que vous derange."

Jen turns to Lauren.

"Close your eyes and think about what troubles you," Lauren translates for her. Jen complies with a gamely sigh through her nose, clamping both hands over the card as though trying to smother it.

"Ouvre tes yeux."

Jen arches one eyebrow, eyes still shut.

"Open your eyes," Lauren says.

Jen flutters her eyes open. Jamilla motions for her to reveal the card on the table: The Lovers. Jen runs a hand through her longer hair with a laugh. "Okay," she says. She's *nervous,* I realize.

Jamilla begins the reading.

"The Lovers do not always symbolize love," Lauren says, when Jamilla pauses to take a breath. "Especially when somebody places the card upside down like this."

The group leans forward, elbows on thighs, to get a better look.

Jamilla rattles off a long spiel that Lauren seems to have trouble with.

Seems to.

Seems to.

"Can you say that again?" Lauren asks.

Jamilla repeats herself, and Lauren nods along, brow cinched, in a commendable effort of trying to understand. "She says that a reversed Lovers card can indicate that you are at war with yourself, and that you are struggling to balance your own internal forces."

Jen produces a polite *hmm!* As though Jamilla's reading is interesting, but doesn't resonate.

"That's all?" I say. "It sounded like she spoke for a lot longer than that."

"That was the *essence* of it," Lauren says with a celestial smile.

"*Toi,*" Jamilla says, suddenly, beckoning Stephanie. "*Je veux te parler.*"

"She wants to talk to you," Lauren says.

Jen gets up—almost eagerly, I note—but Stephanie makes no move to trade positions. "Why?" she asks in a surly way.

"Get over there and find out!" Lauren places a hand between Steph's shoulder blades and shoves. The plane of Stephanie's back hardens in response.

Jamilla says something else that sounds urgent.

"She says it's important!" Lauren exclaims.

Stephanie sighs irritably. We all watch, collectively holding our breath, as she decides to finally get up and move into Jen's spot. She plunks down next to Jamilla with category-five attitude and, without awaiting instruction, pulls a card, holds it to her chest, and shuts her eyes. She'll do this on her own terms.

She opens her eyes and places her card on the table at Jamilla's untranslated behest: The Hanged Man, upright. Jamilla says something short and unemotional.

"So," Lauren says. "The Hanged Man is a willing victim. He makes personal, financial, and professional sacrifices in order to accomplish a higher goal. You are the ultimate martyr."

"No shit," Stephanie says, and, just like the pink chipped polish on her toes, this response is pronounced and out of character. We have a funny contest at the end of the season—which *Digger* required the most bleep censors in the editing room. It's usually a toss-up between Lauren and me, but Stephanie, the group's wordsmith who prides herself on more thoughtful articulation, has always come in last place.

Jamilla is speaking again. When she finishes, Lauren takes a moment before translating. "You are giving too much of yourself to someone. Someone who doesn't give enough of himself or herself back to you. You let him or her hurt you time and time again."

Steph leans back, getting comfortable, a dangerous smile pulling at one corner of her mouth. "Is that so?" she asks, nodding, thinking it over. She strokes the underside of her chin, ruefully. "Ask her to narrow it down for me, Laur. Is it a him?" She looks directly at me. "Or is it a her? Because really," her laugh tinkles, "I could go either way."

My hands and feet go numb. It is chilly up here, so close to a woman I thought I knew so well. Because the Steph I knew cared deeply about the dog and pony show. She was hell-bent on protecting her pride. If I wanted, I could turn to the cameras and say *you can't use this* or *fuckshitfuckshitfuckshitfuckshit,* which we do sometimes to blemish the shot if it isn't to our liking. But doing so would only draw more attention to Stephanie's oh-so-unsubtle insinuation that we had a thing. It won't make Lisa let go of that theory, it will only make her latch on harder.

Lauren translates Steph's question for Jamilla. Jamilla closes her eyes, thinking about it—is it a him or a her? *Lui,* she says to Lauren, after an airless moment.

"Him," Lauren says to Steph.

Stephanie pouts. She *wanted* this to be about me, I realize, feeling dizzy.

Jamilla continues to speak.

"You let him hurt you because you believe, in your heart, that he loves you," Lauren says. "But he has given his heart to someone else."

Stephanie sidles up closer to Jamilla, her lips parted in absolute elation. "Is that *someone* sitting here tonight?" She wiggles her fingers, spookily.

Jamilla looks to Lauren for assistance.

"Go on," Stephanie whispers, at a silly, horror-movie pitch, "ask her."

Lauren moves an inch away from Stephanie, but she does ask Jamilla the question.

"*Oui.*" Jamilla nods, and Stephanie claps her hands and *woot-woots.*

"The person *is* here?" Stephanie cries. "Oh, goody goody gumdrops! Wait, okay." She shimmies in her seat, excitedly. "I'm going to point, and I want her to tell me to stop when I've pointed to the person my husband has given his heart to."

Stephanie raises one arm without waiting for Lauren to communicate her request to Jamilla. For a moment that feels incalculable, she rests an arrow-straight finger on Kelly.

Kelly starts to say, "This is"—but before she can finish, Steph directs her finger around the circle, stopping for a fraction of a second on Jen, then me, then Lauren. When she's finished implicating all the *Diggers*, she raises her arm and points above our hairlines at Lisa, Marc, and the rest of the crew. Stephanie explodes with a hoarse laugh, one that sounds like it's skinned a layer of tissue off the back of her throat.

"I have to tell you," Stephanie says, wiping away tears of joy, "I was skeptical, at first. But this is the most accurate reading ever. She didn't stop me on anyone—which is the God's honest truth. Vince is the *Goal Diggers'* bicycle. Everyone take a ride! We should have brought him instead of your fancy new electric bikes, B. Kel, would you have let Layla ride *him*?"

"*Steph!*" I say, horrified.

Kelly hooks her hand under Layla's armpit, standing, forcing Layla onto her feet with her.

"Mom!" Layla cries, trying to find her footing.

"On that note," Kelly says with a thin, ferocious smile.

Layla rips her arm away from Kelly.

"We're going to bed," Kelly hisses at her, and Layla skulks ahead, her long legs outpacing my sister's, clanging open the heavy wooden door without bothering to hold it for Kelly.

"That was fun." Stephanie sighs, contentedly, leaning back and resting her hands on her stomach, like she's just finished a fabulous meal. "Who's next?" She turns to me. Her makeup is truly insane. She's extended her dark charcoal eyeshadow far above the arch of her brow. "Roomie?" Her eyes glitter nastily. No, seriously, they glitter. That smoky neutrals eye palette she favors was always too heavy on the shimmer.

I watch the dark above me, listening to my sister breathe like Darth Vader in the next room. No fucking way was I shacking up with my *roomie* after that little scene on the roof of the riad. I'd rather not be shanked in my sleep.

I'm on the short couch in the living room, Jen in the bedroom to my left and Kelly and Layla in the one to my right. I assumed Kelly would sleep in the bed with Jen and I would bunk down with Layla, but apparently my sister and the Green Menace aren't *there yet* in their friendship. I flop onto my stomach, sighing, jet-lagged, uncomfortable. My feet are hanging off the arm of the love seat and I'm only five foot three.

I'm considering moving to the floor when I detect movement behind me—bedsheets thrown off, a soft bump, a softer *ow*. I figure Jen is just getting up to pee out all that mint tea, but then the door wheezes open, and Jen's feet are making a sticky sound on the tile floors.

I squeeze my eyes shut and go very still. Jen pauses next to the couch, watching me. Goose bumps flare across the back of my arms. I'm sure my eyelids are twitching but I'm hoping her eyes haven't adjusted enough to notice. After a few moments, she continues her tacky trek toward the door. I crack open an eye and in the brief flash of light from the hallway, I see that she's clutching her phone in her hand. I count to twenty-seven—my age—then I get up and follow her.

The second floor of the riad is outfitted with a small balcony at the end of the hallway, just past the stairwell. Sheer curtains snap in the cool breeze, providing a sound cover. I stay flat against the wall, side-stepping my way closer to Jen. The breeze stops, and I stop. It turns a sort of quiet that makes Jen's voice the star, a clear, bitchy three-in-the-morning solo.

". . . to hear your voice tell me it's okay," Jen is saying, as I hold my breath and starfish the wall. The pious camera tenor is gone, replaced by something I've never heard before: something like tenderness. Is she on the phone with Yvette?

"Yes, she pointed at everyone. But she started with Kelly. And sort of, like, lingered on her."

She's talking about Stephanie.

"No, no. I believe you. But I thought you should know. They're trying to set it up as a storyline. So maybe try to stay away from her."

There is a long stretch of *mmm-hmm*ing while the person on the other line responds. I no longer think she's speaking to Yvette, but I can't think of who else it might be until . . .

"Yeah, I'm rooming with her. I asked Lisa as soon as she told me about it. I'm giving her all kinds of opportunity to deny it. I don't want you to look like a jackass either." Her pause is uncertain. "I miss you." This one too. "Baby."

Baby. The word is a peach pit in the back of my throat. *Baby.* I can't swallow. *Baby*. I can't breathe.

Jen suddenly makes a shushing sound. I hold everything in my body still, lungs burning, as a trolley trundles in the lobby below. There is an exchange in Arabic, and a shared laugh.

"Nothing," Jen says, "just the concierge. I should get back, though. The Big Chill is sleeping on our couch."

Pause.

"Because she doesn't want to sleep in the same bed as your crazy . . ."

I slide back along the wall with wide steps, crisscrossing ankles. I slip inside the room, dive onto the couch, and shut my eyes. A minute or so later, the door opens and Jen ducks inside.

She's watching me again. I can feel it. My slow, deep breathing is a mismatch for my heart, hauling blood to my organs like it is under a time constraint. Can she hear it? I don't know how she couldn't.

"Brett," Jen whispers.

I breathe. I pray.

Jen tiptoes into the bedroom and shuts the door. I don't move for a very long time. Not until the sun starts to squint into the room. Then I get up, stuff my feet in Kelly's sandals, and head downstairs.

—

The lobby is illuminated, the fountains whistling dark water. A single attendant sits at the front desk, reading French *Harry Potter*, Selena Gomez playing softly from the computer. It's still too early for most of the guests to be awake. I caught Kelly's eye up in the room when I said I was going downstairs to wait for everyone. *I need to talk to you in private* is what I hope she took from my expression. I couldn't very well have this conversation up there, with Jen padding about in her towel and humming happily into her first mint tea of the morning.

I know Kelly understood me, but as the minutes tick by, I am worried she chose to disregard me. She's upset about last night, the way Stephanie went after Layla, and I'm sure she's found a way to illogically blame me for it.

I'm just about to give up hope and go get breakfast when Kelly and Layla appear at the bottom of the stairwell.

"Layls," I say to her with a mischievous wink, "they have a latte machine."

Layla murmurs an adolescent, "Cool." She's mad. At me for being a racially insensitive dunce. At Kelly for embarrassing her in front of Stephanie.

"You know I don't like her having caffeine, Brett," Kelly says to me.

"She's on vacation," I say.

Kelly takes her time, deciding. Finally she jerks her thumb in the direction of the dining room: permission to imbibe caffeine, granted.

Layla perks up, ever so slightly.

"Will you see if they have to-go cups for us?" I ask her. "I want to talk to your mom for a second alone."

Layla nods—*Sure, sure, sure*—just short of skipping to the dining room.

"What's up, Brett?" Kelly folds her arms across her chest. Yup, she's definitely mad at me for last night.

"Something happened after we all went to bed. I heard Jen leave the—"

"They don't have to-go cups!" Layla shouts from the dining room's arch.

"I'm coming, sweetie," Kelly calls back, and starts to turn away from me.

"Kel, wait."

"No. You know what, Brett? I don't want to hear it if it's about Jen. I'm so sick of listening to you bad-mouth her. She's been the only one here who has been a decent person to me."

"She's using you! She thinks you—"

"I mean it, Brett," Kelly says with a murderous edge to her voice. "Shut the fuck up about Jen. And if Stephanie ever treats Layla that way again, I will come at her with what I know. On camera. Make sure your *best friend* knows that."

Kelly turns and walks away without giving me a chance to respond. Without giving me a chance to explain that Vince is the one who broke Jen's heart, that Jen calls him baby and is probably still in love with him, and that she sidled up to Kelly because she wanted to make sure Vince wasn't in love with *her*. Worst of all, she's walking away without giving me the chance to demand an answer to the question that has been burning a hole in my throat for the last few weeks. Did you sleep with Vince, Kel? Yes. Or no.

CHAPTER 15

Stephanie

The tea here is a punch to the heart, a shock from a defibrillator, a towline out of my benzo muck. Who says I'm a penny-a-liner all out of decent metaphors? Oh right, *The Smoking Gun.*

"I take one during the day and sometimes two to sleep if I'm traveling," Lauren had said last night, shaking seven Valium into my palm. The triggerman *herself* had come to my room with the cameras, glassy-eyed, straight tequila in her cup. *What's wrong?* she asked, almost sounding sincere. *Is it Vince?* I so longed for the days when the only thing I had to worry about hiding from the cameras was my husband's wandering Willie that I actually said *yes. Yes,* I think he's cheating on me. Lauren got all excited, thinking she was about to deliver the scoop of the millennium on national TV: *Some of us think it might be Kelly,* she told me, reaching for my hand to comfort me. *You dumb twat,* I would have said if I wasn't busy savoring every last ounce of her sympathy. I'm about to become too repugnant to touch—might as well enjoy these last dregs of human contact.

Lauren said she takes two at night when she's traveling, so I took three, figuring it's like when a new partner swears they've only slept with eight other people before you. Multiply by two or three or four (in my case) for a more accurate count. Fifteen minutes later and my brain felt like a tube of toothpaste oozing out of my ear. I'd slumped on the edge of the bathtub while Lauren jammed a wand into a tube of lip gloss and applied what felt like too much. Even to me.

The van hits another pothole and all of our heads lurch left. I'm sitting in the last row, party of one. My erratic behavior's gotten me *quarantined*. I feel like I'm being treated to a private preview of season five with Kelly, Jen, and Lauren seated in the row ahead of me, Brett and Layla in the row ahead of them. Layla has released her braids, reminding me that it's been twenty years since I've seen my natural hair texture. I take another sip of tea.

I started with the straightening treatments my freshman year of high school, not long after I had the bright idea to dress up as my best friend for Halloween. Ashley had big red hair, freckles under her fingernails, and pale blue eyes. It would be hysterical, we decided, if I came to school as her and she came to school as me. Despite the obvious differences in our coloring, we were roughly the same height and build, and in profile, our long curly hair almost matched. We just had to swap clothes and buy that hair spray paint from Hot Topic. We even went as far as to order non-prescription colored contacts from a dicey-looking "online pharmacy."

I showed up to school on October 31 wearing a long-sleeved waffle shirt underneath a short-sleeved piped crew neck—one of Ashley's signature stylings. I had used my mother's foundation to lighten my skin—something that did not ring any of my mother's alarm bells when I told her why I needed it—and my hair was stiff and passably red from the temporary colored spray. It took forever to get the contacts in. I hated touching my eyeball, but in that scene from *The Craft*, the black girl had used magic to make her eyes light and I thought she looked *sooooo* pretty.

I lent Ashley a pair of my loudly printed Lilly Pulitzer cigarette pants and a complementing kelly green cable-knit sweater. My mother barred me from loaning out my real pearl earrings and so we had provisioned a pair of plastic bulbs from a jewelry kiosk at the mall. We had then gone to CVS and purchased "tan" foundation for Ashley, so I was even prepared for that. I was fourteen and knew nothing about the offensive history of blackface—who in that town could have possibly educated me?

In short, I thought I knew what to expect when I saw Ashley at school. I had helped to appoint every defining detail of her Stephanie Simmons Costume. So when I met her at her locker that morning, I was unprepared for both what I saw and what I felt. Ashley hadn't just sprayed her hair my color, like I had done that morning in our garage, standing on old newspapers at my mother's behest. Ashley had used a comb to tease and rough up her texture to within an inch of its life. She looked like a troll. She looked like she had lice. She looked heinous. *Pretty good, right?* she asked, patting her rat's nest. And that was the part that hurt the most. She hadn't done this to hurt me. That was just how she saw me. I wanted to die.

I pretended to have bad cramps so that I could go home early. I went straight to the shower to rinse off the remnants of the costume, the way women do after they've been raped in a Lifetime movie. The slight had been unintentional, but it hurt like a physical assault. Maybe I would have preferred a hit, to have had my underwear torn off. At least then there would have been evidence for forensics to collect, a bad guy to catch, my uncomplicated pain.

Later that evening, my mother knocked on my bedroom door. I'd told her what happened in the car ride home, and she had fallen silent. When I looked over at her, I saw that her cheeks were streaked with tears, and I had rushed to comfort her, to reassure her that it was just a stupid misunderstanding, that I knew I would be able to laugh about it in the morning. A few hours later, she had arrived at a solution: Would I like to go into the city that weekend to have my hair styled at a salon she read about in *Glamour*? They offered a service not yet available anywhere else in the United States. Some chemical treatment from Japan. All the girls in New York were crazy for it, she said. It would make me look *so* polished.

It feels like the van is tightrope-walking the crag after a few beers. Lauren has her eyes glued shut in terror and Brett is laughing at her, telling her this is nothing, just wait until we get to the apex. I tried to get out of going this morning. I care fuck all about these bikes. Why are we giving them bikes? How much does it cost to make these bikes? Would it not be more economical to send a year's supply of Poland Spring? I guess a bottled water studio wouldn't attract twenty-something million from investors. Wouldn't attract *Rihanna*. You know what should have happened when I outlined the terms of the fake fight to Brett? Brett should have told me to come up with something else, because of course Brett would never refuse to pass along my book to the perfect person to play me because she does fucking owe me. In fact, Brett should have gotten on the horn that minute and made it happen. Brett didn't know Van Cleef from Van Halen before she met me, and now look at her, protecting her eyes from the splendid North African sun in the limited edition SPOKE sunglasses designed by Thierry Lasry. Don't make me feel guilty for flying first-class when the money you're charging for a pair of plastic sunglasses could feed a family of drumbeaters for a year.

I'm racist. I'm elitist. I'm a liar. I'm going to hell, but even hell will be better than today. Today, at some point, *The Smoking Gun* plans to publish a report regarding the "multiple" discrepancies between my life and the account in my memoir. Gwen learned this information ahead of the public after promising *The Smoking Gun*'s copy editor she'd read her lousy manuscript.

I told Lisa that I couldn't leave the hotel today, that I had an important phone call I was waiting to receive and I couldn't be without service, but Lisa showed me her MiFi and threatened to call Jesse in a voice that could shatter the glass ceiling. So here I am, trapped in this van with a weak signal and five type-A lunatics in caftans, myself included.

"That's Mount Toubkal," Brett says to Layla, pointing out the window. "It's the tallest mountain in North Africa."

Layla takes a video with her phone and thumbs a red caption.

I lean forward and speak between Lauren and Jen. "Did you just post an Instagram story?"

Layla doesn't respond to my question, and I repeat it, crankier.

"Oh, sorry!" she says, looking over her shoulder skittishly. Apparently, I *traumatized* the holy babe last night. Something about a Negro Nancy Drew? I'm a hoot when I'm on thirty milligrams of someone else's prescription! Serves her right for assuming I'd talk to her just because we share the same skin color, which is as presumptious and offensive as assuming all gay men are attracted to one another. "I didn't know you were talking to me."

"Did it load?" I ask, impatiently.

Layla looks down at her phone. "Um. It's load*ing*."

"Lisa," I grouse, "what the fuck, man?"

That turns a few more heads in my direction. I don't normally speak like a twenty-year-old frat boy whose buddy puked on his pillow last night, but here we are.

"Too many of you are trying to get on the connection for it to work," Lisa says without looking up from her own inbox.

"Can we take turns on airplane mode?" I pose the question to the group, but no one bites. "I'll go first," I volunteer, holding up my phone and showing everyone as I drag the button right. "Lauren?" I ask. "Please?"

Lauren groans, but she closes out of Instagram, swipes left, and taps open the Settings icon.

"Done," Brett adds. *The least you could fucking do,* I think. Yesterday's scrumptious memory returns to me: the optimistic panic on Brett's face when she showed me the message on her phone: *Marc told me Lisa thinks we SLEPT TOGETHER!* She was *so* sure I'd flip out too. What did she think—we'd put our heads together and figure our way out of this, Thelma and Louise style? The truth is, I hope Arch hears about it. I hope Arch leaves her fat ass.

I stare at Brett's Pantene commercial hair that she claims is *wash and go*. When we lived together, her Conair 2000 wasn't the only discovery I made about her. With a wolfish smile, I say, "I knew I could count on you, Brett."

Everyone lapses into silence again, with these phony looks of appreciation for the dusty geological wreckage outside our windows. I make an *ooohhh*ing noise as we pass another patch of burnt-out wasteland. Then I wake my phone and connect to the MiFi when no one is looking.

—

From far away, the village looks like it was built out of mountain-colored Legos. We pass an ancient man straddling the neck of a white donkey, two rattan bags attached at the flank. Why don't they just ride the donkey to the well?

"It's a mule, first of all," Brett says, and I'm startled to discover I voiced the thought out loud. "Only the wealthy families can afford to own them and it's tradition that the men use them to transport food and supplies." Brett turns around in her seat and adds, "'Wealthy' being a relative term."

A revulsion bucks me, that I am expected to care about these poor village women denied a mule. I am not heartless. My heart is enlarged with caring thanks to the mess my mother made out of raising me. My mother loved me, and she didn't mean to ruin me, but she did, by teaching me that I am responsible for how other people feel. Between her and Vince and Brett and the twenty-four-year-old blond viewers who don't want to be made to feel guilty that their ancestors owned slaves because they don't even, like, *see* color, I have performed my job so well I deserve a raise and a corner office.

We descend slowly to the lowest tier of the village, where the stone-stacked huts are squat and windowless. Brett explains the *gites* are grouped politically by association, and asks Layla if she notices anything as we pull into what is going to have to pass for the village center.

"There aren't any guys," Layla says, after a minute. Brett reacts to this glaringly obvious observation as though Layla has just defined a parabola.

"That's *exactly* right. Most men between the ages of sixteen and forty temporarily emigrate to North African cities to find jobs, and send the money back home to their families."

Then who is raping them?

We come to a running stop in the hard dirt, attracting a ring of filthy, curious children. A woman approaches the driver's-side window, wearing a headscarf and sweatshirt, both sound-the-alarm red. The color choice is not a coincidence.

Brett unbuckles her seat belt and squeezes between the driver and front passenger seat. "*Salam*!" she calls through the open window, and I think about swallowing my fourth Valium in fourteen hours. There is only so much of Brett's ham-fisted Arabic I can take. "*Salam*, Tala!"

"*As-salam alaykam*, Brett!" she returns. She rattles off directions in rapid-fire Arabic to the driver, pointing and waving like a crossing guard with tiny balls and a big blowhorn. I thought women here were oppressed little wallflowers who spoke only when spoken to. I thought these bikes were built to save the hymens of preyed-upon preteens.

We reverse into a narrow sod alleyway, deep enough so that the second van can plug us in. Through the front windshield, I watch Marc push open the back doors and blunder to his feet, rolling his neck and stretching his arms above his head. All warmed up now, he hoists the F55 onto his right shoulder. I take one last sip of tea. Wait for the jump.

Oh, it's exhausting. Meeting all these grateful women. Watching happy children be happy with so little, the way they pogo in front of Marc, their scalps momentarily clearing the lens. We visit a hut where women weave rag rugs, where Tala explains the spirit of creative reuse, how when a rug is old or torn, the women cut it and sew it into colorful wool and cotton scraps. *They never throw anything away*, she says, and I glare hotly at Layla. For a time, these rugs were only considered fit for local homes, a practical solution to chilly mud floors in winter. Today they sell for thousands of dollars in a store on La Brea Avenue in Hollywood. Layla takes hundreds of pictures of toothless smiling women holding up their tatty designs, while Brett explains to Tala in pidgin Arabic that Layla is the curator of Qualb, an online boutique that sells home goods made by Berber women.

"The heart?" Tala curves her hand around her breast.

Brett nods. "We have an expression in the States: Home is where the heart is."

Tala parts her dry lips with an *ah* of understanding. "That is very clever."

Layla is on her knees, fingering the fringe end of a rag rug in progress. "Thank you," she says in a courtly voice that sets my teeth on edge. Who does she think she is, repaying a compliment with a thank-you?

On a sunny stoop we come across an older woman, her face ravaged by the sun, and a young girl with her knees around a pottery wheel. They look like they've dunked themselves in a mud bath at an expensive California spa. Layla cries out a name—*Kweller?*—and the girl glances up, shading her eyes.

"Layla," she determines. The girl allows the potter's wheel to come to a stop and stands, clasping her wet hands at her pelvis, unsmiling. She's tall and angular, like Layla, and what she's wearing is the closest I've seen to an *outfit* since we've arrived: a long-sleeved navy and white top, bulky bright blue jeans, and a burnt orange headscarf, pushed far enough back from her head that I can see she parts her hair deeply to the side. Nautical top, denim, pop of color, hair flip. I had no idea the basic hos of Starbucks had such far-reaching influence.

Layla squeals. "Can you believe I'm here?"

I set my molars to work again. *Can you believe* I'm *here*. Starting her young on the *make it about me* train, which is all reality TV is. Narcissist training.

Kweller closes her eyes and nods, she *can* believe it. It's like watching two people meet off Tinder for the first time when one of them is so clearly out of the other's pay grade. Kweller has more composure in the tip of her dirty pinkie than the entire hoodwinking Courtney family.

Layla slides her eyes to the left—*I see it! She's checking to make sure Marc is getting this!*—and approaches Kweller, arms flung open like Kate Winslet on the bow of the *Titanic*. Kweller doesn't look like she wants a hug, but as a pawn in the shoddy SPOKE empire, she's getting one.

"Kweller is one of our top sellers on Qualb," Layla tells us, her arm around Kweller's waist. "She makes the most beautiful painted vases."

I expect Kweller to blush beneath the dry clay on her cheeks and pass the compliment to the elderly woman who taught her everything she knows. But like Layla, all she says is, "Thank you." This is the new guard of girls. They take ownership of their accomplishments. They don't cover their zits in concealer. They like themselves. We hate them because we ain't them. That's something they say too, right?

I cannot take one more second of the Layla and Kweller show, so I slip back to the van while the rest of the women go on to meet the bread makers and olive oil pressers. The driver is perched on the front bumper, smoking a cigarette. I start to explain to him that I'm looking for the MiFi router because I'm expecting important news from back home, before realizing he doesn't understand me nor does he give a shit.

I haul myself into the front passenger seat and turn on the router. I'm sweating so hard my sunglasses keep sliding down my nose, and I set my face with powder, watching and willing the signal light to stop blinking.

At long last—a *connection*. I refresh *The Smoking Gun* report on the screen of my phone, and there it is, top of the page. *Digging Deep into* Goal Digger *Stephanie Simmons's Bullshit*. I actually laugh. That is some *New York Post* levels of puniness.

An Oscar-nominated female director has been had.

A few months ago, she anointed the *Goal Digger's* memoir "her next great passion project," calling it "shocking, heart-breaking, and important."

But an investigation into Simmons's number one bestseller, which has sold close to one million copies in just five months, reveals that the most shocking thing about Simmons's memoir is that it's not a memoir at all.

Hospital records, police reports, and interviews with personnel at the rehab center where Simmons claimed to have checked her mother in after pawning her adoptive mother's diamonds have called into question many key sections of Simmons's book. After months of diligent fact-checking, *The Smoking Gun* can be the first to report that the thirty-four-year-old embellished and, in some cases, wholly fabricated details of her relationship with her birth mother, and the Pennsylvania neighbor she claims she entered into an abusive relationship with while searching for her.

Simmons appears to have gotten away with sweetening her backstory given the fact that she is an orphan herself. Her adoptive mother passed away in 2011. Earlier this year, Simmons was quoted in the *New York Times* as saying, "I felt I was finally able to unload my story after I was no longer saddled with protecting the feelings of my adoptive mother. She would have been horrified to know the truth."

While Simmons claims that her birth mother passed away in her arms when she was just seventeen years old, hospital records show that Sheila Lott died at the South Ridge Rehab Facility in Newark, New Jersey, in 2003, when Simmons was twenty and enrolled in her sophomore year at Colgate.

> Another whopper of a discrepancy involves "A.J.," the eighteen-year-old neighbor of Sheila Lott, whom Simmons alleged was her lover and abuser. Simmons claims that on the day she first sought out her biological mother, she met and began a tumultuous eight-month affair with the local high school football star who lived on her mother's cul-de-sac. Simmons has been widely heralded for her bravery in coming forward as a survivor of domestic abuse when black women are both statistically more likely to suffer at the hands of a romantic partner and less likely to report their abusers. Thus far, *The Smoking Gun* has been unsuccessful in our efforts to identify "A.J."

I reach a scroll of ads and click next. There are six more pages to go, and the screen goes white for too long. I glance at the MiFi. The light is red. The battery is dead.

"There are your friends," the driver says, gesturing with his cigarette at our moving spectacle, like one of those Chinese dragon parade floats, Brett the flamboyant head and Lisa the stinger tail. Marc films Kelly and Jen as they start to unload the bikes from the back of the cargo van, Lauren looking on, helpfully. Brett plays bouncer, her hands spread wide to keep jumping children at bay. *Be patient.* She's laughing. *You'll get to ride them. Just be patient.*

On a plot of young grass, framed by the old craggy bluffs, I spot two girls in orange headscarves taking a selfie. It's Layla and Kweller, who must have gifted her pushy American friend a matching wrap. From here, they could be sisters. On any other day, it could be sweet.

I set to work making a happy place lunch out of a Valium and Lauren's traveling handle of vodka. I'm too close to caring.

Slightly north of the village, we come upon a brindled valley, studded sparsely with the sort of Christmas trees that pass as status symbols in New York City. You should see Whole Foods in December, everyone chomping at the bit to get to the front of the line and declare their need for an eight-footer, their ceilings are *that* high. The *Diggers ooh* and *ah* over the mountaintops, which loll before us, flexing an occasional dirt road, not that great. We could be on Mars, everything so brown and dry.

"Isn't nature majestic?" Jen marvels at my shoulder. I turn to her with flared nostrils. I decide against informing our sole Jewish castmate that there is a Hitler smudge of dust above her lip. Lane-swerving bitch.

It was only a ten-minute walk to get here under the mild-mannered sun, but I'm heavy-footed with malaise, greased in a gritty solution of sweat and dust. There is no place to rest but on a bike. I puncture the dirt deeper with the kickstand and swing a leg over the seat. I wish I could say the SPOKE electric bikes look like every other bike I've ever seen, nothing special about them, but it wouldn't be true. The body is a glossy, lacquered red, the seat baby pink leather, with a rear rack designed to transport two jerricans of fresh water. The handlebars look like stitched leather ram horns, like something an old Texan oil baron would hang above his fireplace after a luxury safari. Fuck me, they're gorgeous.

"Okay!" Brett claps her hands twice to get everyone's attention. There is a gaggle of children surrounding her. Periodically one will reach out and wind her fingers in Brett's long hair, and Brett will gently untangle them without losing a beat. "I thought it would be fun to have a race! Who can make it to the river, fill up her container, and get back here the fastest."

Tala translates, and the kids titter excitedly. One girl raises a grubby arm, and another clamps it down with a bucktoothed laugh, waving her arm wide. *She* wants to go.

"Grown-ups first," Brett says, and there is a collective outcry of disappointment when Tala translates.

"Looks like Steph here is our first competitor!" Brett says, noticing me slumped on a bike.

I yawn without covering my mouth. "Nah."

"But you said you couldn't wait to ride one last night!"

I did? I try to remember last night as I dismount the bike, but it's as though the memory has been placed in a cement-sealed file.

"Scared you'll lose to me?" Brett's smile is playful and infuriating.

The bolt of competitiveness is absurd, vehemently childish, but it's in my lungs, sharp as if I had just sprinted to the best, fullest, tallest Christmas tree. I reclaim the pink leather seat with aplomb. "Winner gets her book given to Rihanna," I say, because I can be funny too.

Brett plunks a helmet on her head, and in a voice so serious she can only be joking, says, "You're on, sister."

I don't like things that go fast. I don't like Jet Skis and I don't like Vespas. I don't even like speed intervals at Barry's Bootcamp, which I took up again joyfully once Brett and I were no longer friends. (SPOKE might make you cool but it will not make you skinny.)

Lauren starts the race, ripping off her new headscarf and throwing back her chin like she's Cha Cha in *Grease*. Brett zips ahead of me, too fast too soon. The Big Chill's got no strategy. She has to keep slamming on the brakes to avoid crashing into the trees. After a few hundred yards, I catch up with her by maintaining a steady pace. The idea of a race is mostly fallacy, as we don't have any idea where we're racing to and we have to follow Tala—at least on the way there.

It's a rocky, uphill climb, the elevation subtle then ungracefully steep, and I can't help but imagine what it would be like to walk this, day after day, year after year of my life. At least it's downhill with the jugs of water, though I remember the older women I saw as we wandered the village, their backs curved like boomerangs. How bitter they must be, watching these young girls with the bikes, going to school, making their own money. Why wasn't there a better way in time for them?

I have barely moved my legs to get here and yet this film of sweat has turned cold, has drowned gnats in the creases of my elbows. Maybe I'm a little bit sick. Maybe I'm a little bit dying. There is something waiting for me on the other side of these mountains, something happening back in New York that will not leave me unscathed. I should never want to leave, and yet I'm dying to know how bad it is. I'm dying to know what I'm going to do about it. It's past time to locate my spine.

"Careful!" Tala calls ahead of us, and then she drops off the horizon.

The descent is straight out of a stress dream. Something seasoned hikers would consider rappelling. Even Brett idles at the top, removing her feet from the pedals and stemming the earth for a moment.

"She's doing it," I say to Brett, unsure, as we watch Tala bump around boulders and sparse, scraggly bushes.

"It's amazing," Brett says, watching her, and I realize she hasn't stopped because she's scared. She's stopped to take it all in. "You lose touch, back in New York," she continues. "You know you're doing something that matters, but it's never more real than when you come here and see it with your own two eyes."

With that, she twists her handlebars and navigates her way downhill fearlessly, her hair flipping sweetly in the wind. I wonder what would happen if I bumped her tire on the way down. If the back would flip over the front, if her top teeth would go through her bottom lip, as easily as a knife parting hot butter.

It's greener by the river, obnoxiously, Irishly so. Brett expresses her disappointment that the camera crew was unable to follow us down here. "This is Morocco," she declares, sucking in a torrent of fresh air, and I want to tell Tala that I won't say anything if she holds Brett's face in the shallow river until she stops struggling.

"Oh, come on, I'll do it," Brett says, when she notices me daydreaming her death at the river's seam. Tala has already waded up to her waist and has her jerrican submerged, the water at her side bubbling greedily.

"I'll *do* it," I say, but Brett has already snatched the jug out of my hand and joined Tala. She doesn't bother to take off her five-hundred-dollar sneakers, which, if you want a tell that someone is newly flush, watch how they treat their expensive things.

I'm about to remove my sandals and join them, prove to Brett that I'm not too much of a priss to get wet, when my pants pocket purrs once, shortly, before going off like a pager at some godforsaken Cheesecake Factory.

My cargo pants are thin silk, adhering to my damp skin like Saran Wrap to Saran Wrap. There is a horrible moment when my phone gets trapped in the lining of my pocket, and my hand writhes like a cat trapped under a bedsheet.

"Oh my *God*," Brett judges. "Look where we are! Ignore it!"

"There is a mobile tower over that hill," Tala says.

"*Stop* it." Brett clucks, making apparent her disapproval that underprivileged people should be able to make a call that won't drop.

"It's true. There is a well closer to home than this, but everyone comes here because they can find a signal."

"I left my phone in the car," Brett boasts as I free my own and open my email. It was as if I'd set a Google alert for "weight loss." Try it sometime. You'll see what I mean. My screen is a scroll of vitriol, hit after hit, a greatest collection of pun-y insults. Goal Digger *"digs" her own grave?* The New York Times *removes Stephony Simmons's "memoir" from bestsellers list, citing fraud. Simmons's life story is fake news,* Fox is the most happy to report.

"Who died, Steph?" Brett laughs, tipping her head back and wetting her hair.

Gwen is coming, Vince has texted me. *Call me when you can.*

Why is Gwen coming? Where is Gwen going? I open the conversation and thumb back, feeling faint.

At 1:16: *A reporter from the* Daily News *just knocked on the door. I said you weren't home. Just wanted you to know.*

1:47: *Okay. A few more have knocked on the door. I didn't answer. But now there is a small crowd gathered outside the apartment. I'm assuming you are somewhere without service.*

I call him immediately, but the connection fails, again and again. I text back, *What's going on? Is Gwen there? I won't have service much longer.* I hit send, but the message doesn't go anywhere. I growl a curse.

"Can we ride the bikes closer to the tower?" I ask Tala.

Brett wrings out her hair, watching me concernedly. "What's going—"

We both freeze, terror-eyed, when we hear the ominous rustling in the brush. In an instant, I've catalogued every gruesome talking point of Brett's cause célèbre: the fourteen-year-old girl raped and murdered by four men, the twelve-year-old girl who escaped her rapist only to deliver his baby nine months later, the young mother raped and tortured by a gang, leaving four children behind. At least the Internet will remember me kindly. These days, a woman is forgiven everything when a man kills her.

Tala, shouting a bizarre chant, charges out of the river and joins me on the shore, stomping her feet ferociously.

"Hey-hey. Hoo-hoo!" Tala shouts, and motions frantically for me to mimic her odd dance. But I cannot move a muscle for fear that my brain may stop changing shape, that my synapses may stop spinning this gossamer: A woman is forgiven everything when a man kills her.

"Oh my God." Brett doubles over with a laugh when a ferret-looking thing sticks his whiskered nose out of the shrubs.

"Jesus," I say, relieved, and maybe a little bit disappointed. "I was thinking about all those women who have been raped and murdered out here."

Tala is picking out sharp-edged shells from the soles of her feet. She stops. "What women were raped and murdered here?"

Brett sloshes out of the water, her caftan melded between her thick thighs. "Shouldn't we go? I thought wherever there are little animals there are bigger animals tracking them."

I look down at my phone. The text still hasn't been sent to Vince.

"It's only a weasel," Tala says, as Brett plops her big dump on the bike. I'm tempted to go over there and rip her dress from shoulder blades to ankles, check to make sure there's no butt pad under there. Not a thing about her has turned out to be true.

—

I smoke Brett on the way to the top, but she gets me on the down, even though we're both creeping. The other side of the hill is unduly treacherous with a couple gallons of water at our backs, like shooting down a water slide attached to an anchor. A few times I grip the handlebars out of fear, causing a sudden surge forward. *How counterintuitive*, I think, smug at last knowing Brett has been running game too. Brett upped the stakes of SPOKE's mission—the bikes will certainly improve the quality of life for the women of this village, but they aren't the getaway vehicles for fourteen-year-old virgins she made them out to be. But you know what? Of all people, *I* get it. It's not tragic enough that boys get to travel to big cities to learn and work and experience life while illiterate women mule tanks of water on their backs in their third trimesters. The truth won't make people listen unless it is sufficiently awful.

It wasn't awful enough that I grew up fearing every day would be the day I wouldn't find my mother's car in the school pickup line, would be the day she decided it was all simply too complicated. It wasn't awful enough that I used to change the channel when *Family Matters* came on after *Full House* on Friday nights, telling my mother, *I don't really like this one* because I was afraid it would hurt her feelings if I showed any interest in the mores of this nice, normal black family with the pretty daughter just a few years older than me. I put that memory and others like it on the page—the constant, small indignities and my constant, asphyxiating silence. It didn't feel like lying when I said I was choked, though I only said that later, after I handed in those first few honest chapters and my editor's response was unequivocal: *It's a little slow*.

So I self-inflicted some battle wounds, no worse, no better than my best friend.

The valley resolves, revealing the outline of the group, cheering us on, so far and so miniature I could contain them between my thumb and index finger and squish. I roll the handlebars forward another turn, arcing around Tala. Brett appears at my hip, and for a few seconds, we stay parallel but staggered, on a collision path with a clump of wooly evergreens. To be safe, I should lean right and Brett should lean left. To win, I should play chicken and stay the course, force Brett to go wide.

"Steph!" I think I hear Brett call, but the wind has its hands cupped around my ears. I spin the handlebars until they catch, heading rock-ribbed for the trees. Brett swings a wide left, exactly like I hoped she would, leaving a narrow slit between her bike and the trees. I zip through, brakeless, so close a branch cat-claws my arm. I release a wild laugh, glancing over my shoulder, expecting to see Brett in my dust. But she's not far behind at all. She's coming up on me, which is impossible, because I'm at max speed. The group is just a few yards before us, forming a chanting, dancing finish line. The cameras track Brett as she crosses half a body before me. She jams a fist into the air; *the victor.*

We swing around and park our bikes, noses facing the direction from which we came.

"I never took you for such a *daredevil*," Brett says, releasing the chinstrap of her helmet and shaking loose her wet, gnarled hair. She round-kicks one leg over the handlebars, walking over to me with her hand outstretched. "You almost had me."

"I would have if I'd gotten the faster bike," I say, refusing to shake.

"Steph," Brett drops her hand with a laugh. "Be serious."

"You were behind me," I say. "I was going full speed. How could you pass me if you were behind me?"

"I don't know what to tell you." Brett's fingers get stuck trying to flip the rat's nest she's made out of her hair. No woman should flip her hair past the age of sixteen. "Then you weren't at full speed. Full speed is really fast."

"I was going really fast."

Brett picks a few of her long hairs out of her engagement ring with a small, discrediting smile. "Well, for you, yeah."

For you. The uptight, rule-abiding, scared-of-her-own-shadow princess. I abandon my bike without staking the kickstand. It topples on its side, clipping the backs of my ankles as Brett yells after me, "These are expensive bikes, *Steph.*"

You know what else is expensive? The lava stone in my guest bathroom, which Brett—au naturel Brett—stained dark with hair dye. Oh yeah—that glossy brunette mane? Not real, but Brett can't risk going to the hair salon and being found out so she DIYs it. Also expensive, the antique silk runner in the hallway, which Brett spilled coffee on and attempted to clean using soap and water, which got the coffee out but tie-dyed the pattern. And the candy dish that belonged to my mother's mother, which Brett shattered, drunk, trying to take off her shoes? That wasn't expensive. But it was priceless.

I aim my big toe at the kickstand of Brett's bike, flinging my leg over the saddle, determined to prove she gave me the lemon. I assumed the motor was off, and I'm ill prepared when it bolts forward before my feet have even touched the pedals. Instinctively, I tighten my grip on the handlebars, and before I know it I'm careening toward that cluster of trees again, my heart flung between my shoulder blades.

I don't know why I don't pull back. I think about it later and it's not a blur. It doesn't happen so fast. If anything, time seems to slow down as I speed up, according me an infinity during which to make a different choice. But still I choose to drive straight for the trees on Brett's winning bike.

At the last moment, I make another choice. I lean right, even though the right path is not the clear one. Layla is standing in my course, witless and unmoving, a jerrican in her hand, no doubt on her way to the river by foot just so she can say on Instagram that she lived like a poor little village girl for two measly hours of her life. She is her aunt's niece. The force of the impact throws her onto my handlebars so, for a moment, we could be one of those pictures that already comes in a frame on the top floor of Bloomingdale's Fifty-ninth. A black-and-white stock photo of an adorable mother-daughter outing, the girl riding the handlebars in peals of laughter while her mother pushes the pedals in discomforted joy. Because that's what it takes to be a good mother, right? *Relishing* your unhappiness. They thought we were related, when we got to the private hospital in the Gueliz district, because anyone who is not white must be related. The nurses and the doctors, they were all wondering why my daughter was bleeding from her ears and I wasn't crying.

CHAPTER 16

Kelly: The Interview

Present day

"I'm okay," I tell Jesse, my heart swelling in my throat.

"I think it might help," Jesse says, motioning to someone off camera.

"No, really," I insist, no, I beg. "I don't need to see it again. I was there. I remember." The pitch of my voice crests in direct proportion to the position of the AP, who is in front of me now, proffering the travel-sized C300 camera, a freeze-frame of the dramatic cloud formations that hung low in Morocco's blue skies that day. Jesse has suggested I review the clip of the accident, to refresh my memory before we discuss it. It reminds me of something Brett warned me about before she died—something the producers do to the women during their confessional interviews. Like a confessional, we're filming this interview last but speaking about the accident in the present, to weave together the narrative the producers have constructed in the editing room. Brett told me that sometimes, production will show you a clip of your "friend" *throwing shade* at you, to make you angry enough to *throw shade* at her, even though you promised to have her back. But I've never heard of anyone having to review footage of a woman trying to kill herself and changing her mind, going after an innocent child instead. I'm confident this is a first for all involved.

I have come to conclude that the "accident"—as it was reported in the press at the time it occurred and as we are continuing to refer to it now—was Stephanie's first attempt at suicide that turned, only somewhat successfully, homicidal. My suspicions were raised when we got home and I found out that the collision occurred on the same day *The Smoking Gun* report was published. Always the diligent student, I spent hours researching *suicide by driving* and *family history suicide*. I knew from Stephanie's memoir—the part that was true—that her biological mother committed suicide, and I turned up a rash of studies that suggest a person is more likely to complete suicide if a family member has taken his or her own life. I then came across a figure that put the percentage of vehicular fatalities that are actually suicides between 1.6 and 5 percent. The number is impossible to calculate because it is impossible to determine intent, which is the reason people choose this method. They would rather their friends and family believe their deaths were accidental.

That suspicion cemented into certainty after Brett died. What Stephanie did in Morocco was merely a test run. *Can I really go through with this?* she must have asked herself right before she took aim at Kweller, who she mistook for Layla, something I can't prove but am sure of. The girls are the same age and height and build, were wearing identical orange headscarves, and Stephanie had acted so strangely, so *aggressively*, toward Layla the night before.

And what the viewers don't know, will never know, is that on the ride to the hospital, Stephanie had asked repeatedly if Layla was okay. Her clavicle had been slick with sweat, but her face was dry, her immaculate makeup preserved somehow. It was a bright summer day, too sunny for her pupils to be that dilated. God knows what she was on. "You hit Kweller," we had to keep reminding her. "Layla's friend. The pottery girl."

The AP has hit play without my consent, and because Jesse is watching me, and because I am under her thumb until I no longer draw an audience, I pretend to relive the horror of that day. Really, though, my eyes are focused on the black plastic corner of the camera, the same way I pretend to look when the technician sticks a mirror between my legs after a bikini wax—*Yup, looks great!* I always told her, without looking, before heading out on my bimonthly Tinder date while Brett babysat Layla. I discovered long ago that I have needs, and bad things happen when they are not met. Still, no matter how hard up, I never would have turned to Vince for a reprieve. The suggestion is unbelievably offensive.

"God." Jesse sucks in a sharp breath next to me, watching, I assume, Stephanie scoop Kweller onto the handlebars. I mutter something indeterminable, but similar in feeling.

"Thanks, Sam." Jesse smiles at the AP, which is his cue to exit the set.

"Jesse," I say, "I really want to address one of the interview questions in this segment. About Vince and me."

Jesse sets her lips together.

"I don't want to answer any questions about us."

"But we're giving you the opportunity to dispel the rumor that something happened between you two."

"I don't even want the suggestion out there that something happened, though."

Jesse doesn't say anything, pointedly.

"Because it *didn't*."

Jesse half smiles. *She might not believe me,* I realize.

"We don't have to use it," she says. "Let's just get through this set of questions and we can reassess from there. Okay?"

No. "Okay."

PART III

Tequila Shot • August 2017

CHAPTER 17

Brett

A pink boob sways from a branch of the Japanese maple on Jen and Yvette's front lawn. Kelly cuts the engine and squints. It's eight o'clock in Amagansett in August, roads steaming, sky the color of shark skin. "Is that . . . a piñata?" She releases her seat belt and puts on her Dad-joke voice, "Or is it a *tit*ñata?"

I groan at the bad joke, but it's a loving groan, an *oh my God you're so corny but I love you anyway* groan. I'm making an effort to be nice to my sister this weekend. Things haven't been easy for her since we got back from Morocco last month, and they're about to get so much worse.

We climb out of the car, our feet sliding around our wet sandals as we make our way to the trunk. We both make a stab at chivalry by trying to pass the other her weekend bag. Kelly ordered the same duffel as mine—an army print from Herschel—but at least her outfit doesn't irritate me to my core. *Net-a-Porter,* she told me proudly when I asked her where she got her cute white romper, pronouncing it like a person who carries your bags at a hotel.

"*Por-tay,*" I corrected her, which was me, still being nice! The not-nice thing to do would have been to let her make a fool of herself on camera. *Oh shit,* she said, covering her eyes, cringing too much. It wasn't *that* embarrassing, but I'm not the only one making an effort to be nice. Kelly is scared, and that chinks my resolve a little, but I'd be lying if I didn't admit that it mostly feels like standing on a mountain of cocaine with a machine gun slung over my shoulder and two hot bitches on either side of me. Being right is a hell of a drug. And it's for that reason that I've held off having the conversation with Kelly that I need to have. Because what if my judgment is clouded by these *being right* goggles?

My sister and I climb the three steps to the front porch, wobbly with the weight of our weekend bags. Jen has strung a banner across two tall topiaries: "Welcome, BrideS!" It's curling at the corners and wrinkled by the humidity, making it look weathered and forgotten, like it's been there for months, like my bachelorette party already happened and this is some sort of weird coma dream in a *Sopranos* episode. Am I already married? Did I really go through with it?

Kelly ducks beneath the banner and pauses before the red door. "Is this . . . ?"

"She says it's Rectory Red."

Kelly peers closer. "Looks a lot like Blazer."

Blazer is the shade of Farrow & Ball paint used in all my studios. I can barely bother to shrug. That I am an object of imitation for some women is old news. "She says it's Rectory Red."

"Well, I mean," Kelly says, knocking, "we should take it as a compliment."

We. It's like a guy you are very obviously blowing off, very obviously getting ready to break up with, who sends you flowers in a last desperate attempt to rekindle the flame. *We.*

I can hear laughing and revelry inside. A Chainsmokers song that will be dubbed over with some nondescript track. (Production music libraries are much cheaper than licensing commercial music.) I can smell food Jen pretends to eat browning on the stove. It's a decent imitation of a fun summer party, but it's the difference between a cardboard cutout of your favorite celebrity and having him rescue you in his big strong movie-star arms after you've fainted onto the subway tracks. Usually, by the last group shoot of the season, we're like rubber bands that have been snapped too many times, all the bite of wet spaghetti. The Martini Shot is an old Hollywood term to describe the final setup of the day—because after that, the next shot is out of a glass. This crew has a taste for a different spirit, and thus, this weekend Lisa is here to get her Tequila Shot. It's a spectacular display of senioritis, the few days of the year Lisa really earns her paycheck. She circulates the room in an attempt to get a current going, whispering in our ears to remind us of all the season's petty slights, trying to livewire the action. But tonight feels different. Tonight feels like the start, the music and the laughing a trap when they only used to be a trick.

Maybe it feels that way because we've never been upended by a bombshell this far into the season. Stephanie, man, what were you *thinking*? In this day and age of digital espionage, you do not tell a lie before you *become* the lie. If Stephanie wanted to peddle a triumphant survivor's story as her own, she should have gotten herself invited to dinner at Bill Cosby's house first.

She's been in hiding for the last month, ever since we got back from Morocco. She won't open her door for anyone—not even Jesse, who knocked two days in a row. I heard she's still selling a lot of books, but the *New York Times* has removed her name from *The List,* as has her agency's website. Both outlets extended their heartfelt apologies to women of color who are survivors of domestic and sexual abuse. The Oscar-Nominated Female Director publicly denounced *The Site of an Evacuation* on *Jimmy Kimmel,* calling it a cowardly appropriation of survivor culture, and everyone cheered and clapped. Search *Stephanie Simmons* and Google will vomit-spatter all the scorched-earth headlines you can imagine. *Is Stephanie Simmons the most hated woman in America? Stephanie Simmons is the reason no one believes abuse victims. Four black women will die today at the hands of their abusers and Stephanie Simmons has made millions off their backs.*

I don't know how you come back from this.

I thought about knocking on her door. About sitting with her in her mostly white living room, the Roman shades pulled flat against the photographers still skulking around outside. I still love her, though I have no right to.

In the end, I didn't have the stones. I still don't know what she knows and doesn't know about Vince and Kelly and Vince and Jen, and I'm deeply disturbed by what she did in Morocco. An *accident*, we told the reporters who asked about it, but I watched it happen, and she was clear-eyed. Kelly is convinced Stephanie thought Kweller was Layla, but I think the only person Stephanie was aiming for was herself, and at the last moment, she reneged.

The red door swings open on an exuberant Lauren Fun in shredded white jeans and a shredded white tee, braless, barefoot, toenails black. "Happy bachelorette!" she cries, offering me a rainbow-tiered Jell-O shot from the tray she's balancing on her right palm. She backs up so that we can enter and the crew surrounds us like a rival gang.

"Vegan and alcohol free," she makes a point of saying, because I guess we are still pretending like she's not drinking, even though the shot is so loaded with Tito's it leaves grill marks on the back of my throat. "And also Greenberg's organic sex sprinkles!"

"So that's why I'm hard," I deadpan as I follow her into the kitchen.

"I'm hard for your sister in that adorable little playsuit," Lauren returns over her shoulder.

"Net-a-Porter," Kelly says correctly, rubbing the goose bumps out of her arms. It is Siberian in here. The house is designed for indoor/outdoor living, but every window, every double French door is latched shut against the summer. My nipples feel like knives. Good thing Jen's tree-hugging brand doesn't advertise its intent to reduce the impact of climate change or anything.

In the kitchen, Jen is shaving corn off the cob with a serious butcher knife. Behind her, three hopeful dog noses press against the glass doors from outside. Yvette told me Jen makes them sleep in the backyard now that the house is done. She is paranoid about dog hair and dog urine, dog laughter and dog joy.

"Our guest of honor is here," Lauren says, presenting me like the evening's entertainment, and for a moment we pause and regard each other somberly. It's the shaking of the hands before the duel.

"How was traffic?" Jen asks, civilly.

"Not bad." Kelly drops her bag at her feet. "We just got a late start. I had to get Layla to a friend's in New Jersey."

Jen looks at me. "Where's Arch?"

"She's going to come out tomorrow," I say. "Stuck at work."

Jen nods, running a finger along the steel plane of the knife.

"May I offer you a beverage?" Lauren asks us formally, trying to be funny.

"Whatever you're having," Kelly makes the mistake of saying.

"I'm having club soda," Lauren says laughably, "but we have a bottle of Sancerre chilled."

Bottles of Sancerre, it appears, as she tugs open the refrigerator. Sancerre and Tito's and Casamigos and a carton of almond milk that's been turned on its side to make room for more booze. Lauren shuts it quickly, before the camera responsible for the wide shot tells on her.

On the stove, a pot boils over. "Want me to . . . ?" Kelly offers, heading for the utensils holder by the sink. She lifts the lid and something puke-colored spits at her. My stomach grumbles. I haven't eaten since noon and I need a real meal, not a mushy plate of ancient grains.

"Oh!" Jen cries, like she just remembered something. She steps around Kelly and brings out a platter of chips and dip. "I picked up that guac I know you like from Round Swamp, Brett."

Kelly gives me a little smile over her shoulder. *See! She isn't so bad!*

Kelly still doesn't know about Jen's middle-of-the-night conversation with Vince, on the balcony of the riad in Marrakesh, or about my suspicions that he is the one who broke her heart last season. I tried just that once, the morning of the accident. Then came that nightmare of a day, and my focus was on damage control for SPOKE. After speaking with my shareholders and having a lawyer review my partnership agreement with Kelly, I figured she was in for enough of a kick. No need to add insult to injury by telling her that Jen was only pretending to be her friend to find out if she was having an affair with Vince, because she might still be in love with Vince herself. Let Kelly believe the friendship was real. Who could it hurt?

Jen wipes her hands on an apron that reads *Viva Las Vegans!* "So. The plan for tonight is dinner, then Lauren has organized some bachelorette games—"

Lauren blows into a party horn, immediately whispering *Sorry* when Jen glares at her for interrupting.

"And then, I don't know?" Jen continues, using the base of her wide knife to rough-chop raw walnuts for the salad. "Maybe Talkhouse if everyone is up for it?" She glances up, mischievously, and for a moment she is not the drippiest drip I know. Jen can be fun when the cameras are not around, and Talkhouse is the fraternity rager you go to after having dinner with your family when they're in town for parents' weekend. The network has never been able to obtain the permit necessary to film there, which means everyone can take as many shots of piss-colored tequila as they'd like without record.

"You are here until eleven," Lisa squeaks from behind the camera. It's like a reverse curfew—we have to stay home until a certain time, deliver some decent footage, and then we get to go out and paint the town red.

"Yes, Mom," both Lauren and Jen say at the same time.

"Call me that again and you're fired," Lisa says, touching the drooping skin on her neck. "And for the love of God, someone bring up the elephant in the room."

Jen sets down her knife and inquires with over-performed concern, "Has anyone heard from Steph?"

We all pooch our lips—*No*.

"What about Vince?" I don't look directly at Jen at first, so as not to be obvious, but when I do, I find she's picked up the knife again and is chopping those nuts into sawdust.

"I *heard*," Lauren hinges at the waist and sets her elbows on the counter, chin in hands, voice gossipy, "she served him with divorce papers but he's refusing to sign." She rubs her thumb and three fingers together, indicating *money*. "He gets nothing in the prenup."

There is a glitch in my heartbeat. "She's divorcing him?" Steph divorcing Vince means that she no longer cares enough to keep up the façade of their happy marriage. It means she can go public about the things that happened in that house, if she wants to.

Lauren smirks at me. "Don't sound so surprised. You of all people should be well aware the wheels had fallen off that marriage."

I feel like I swallowed Jen's big butcher knife. I need to stop doing that—giving Lauren openings to contribute winky commentary to further the Brett and Stephanie lesbian affair storyline.

"Brett." Jen turns to me in a way that makes me think she's about to accuse me of something. My breath catches in my throat. "I made up the downstairs guest bedroom for you and Arch. Laur and Kelly, you're in the upstairs guest room."

I exhale and steal a glance at Kelly. Disappointment streaks her face that Jen doesn't want to share a room with her again. It's because Jen no longer feels like she's got some detective work to do on Kelly, but Kelly doesn't realize that.

"Thanks, Jen." I give her a warm smile. In this group, niceness is power-saving mode, and I may need to reserve my strength too. Hoisting my weekend bag higher on my shoulder, I say, "I'm just going to drop my stuff in my room and freshen up."

"Dinner in fifteen!" Lauren calls after me, my buddy once again.

I take my time in the hallway, waiting for the conversation to resume before quickly opening the door to the garage and stepping inside. I hit the switch on the wall and blink a few times, my eyes adjusting slowly. Things used to scatter when you turned on the light in here. There were beach chairs and old bikes and pool toys, plenty of cobwebby places for creatures to hide. All that's left in the garage after the gut is a collage of fuse boxes on one wall and the old popcorn-textured refrigerator that never kept anything cold. It looks like a fossil humming next to Jen's new metallic Tesla, charging from the flank. I yank open the freezer door and angels sing when I discover long-expired bagels and pizza inside.

"I'll be back for you later," I whisper, before turning off the light.

With its blue-and-white-pinstriped wallpaper and toile linens, I feel like I should be wearing pearls to sleep in the downstairs guest bedroom. Closer, I realize that instead of a pattern of regal-looking people and animals in a classic landscape setting, the sheets are covered in skulls and skeletons, and that those aren't stripes on the wall, they're femur bones. I zoom in with my phone and send a picture to Arch, flicking a low-battery notice out of the way. *This is where Jen has stuck me to sleep. Creepshow.*

Almost immediately three typing dots appear. I plop onto my back on the bed, stretching an arm behind my head, too lazy to find my charger in my bag. Arch responds with three monkeys covering their eyes. *I wish I could see the creepiness in person but I don't think I can make it after all. Up to my elbows. Do u mind?*

I pull a face that is much more disappointed than I feel. In truth, I'm happy to keep Arch as far from this circus act as possible. *I'll miss you!!! I'm not mentioning it to anyone, though. They all think you're coming so I get my own room. I don't want to get stuck with Kelly. I'll probably let it slip in my sleep.*

My screen is white and judgmental for a few moments. Then, Arch lets her real feelings be known. *She deserves to know.*

I type with a sigh, *I know . . . but if I tell her before we're finished filming it will be a part of the show. And I owe it to her to keep it from being a storyline. I don't want to humiliate her any more than necessary.*

Arch texts back, *Any chance you haven't told her yet because you're not sure this is the right decision?*

I close a second low-battery warning and text back at righteous speed, *It's not UP to me. A girl almost DIED after being struck with one of our bikes. And it wouldn't have happened if Kelly had agreed to pay*

THIRTY-SEVEN DOLLARS EXTRA for the thumb grips. The investors want a blood sacrifice, or they're going to pull out. And Kelly is the one who is accountable. She's got to go.

Arch doesn't respond for so long my attention wanders to the lights prod has taped to the corners of my room. When I check my screen again, I realize my phone has died.

"Kids!" Lauren calls down the hallway. "Dinnertime!"

I find my charger in my purse and plug my phone into the wall. Outside, the rain returns, as immediate as a gun going off at the starting line of a race.

—

A fire chews wood in the sitting room, because that makes sense on an eighty-degree evening with 95 percent humidity. The low-for-effect coffee table is covered in a tray of desserts that, like dinner, have to be explained before consumed. I tune out while Jen moves her hand around the board, listing ingredients, but a lot of dates and cashews are involved. Kelly grabs a black bean brownie and pops it into her mouth.

"Mmmm," she lies, getting to her feet. "So good. Just running to get a sweater real quick." She makes a *brrrrr* noise as she trots up the stairs.

Lauren is on the floor, her back against the raised white brick hearth, laptop on her thighs, blond hair cast orange by the fire. Marc circles the perimeter of the room to zoom in on her screen when there is a brief burst of a familiar voice. Lauren rushes to lower the volume.

I lean over the arm of the sofa. "What is that?"

"Just your Mrs. and Mrs. quiz." Lauren sets the laptop on the coffee table, turning it so that the group has a view of Arch paused on the screen, eyes wide and mouth agape, the most unattractive I've ever seen her. Outside, thunder grumbles softly—or is that my unhappy stomach?

"What the fuck is a Mrs. and Mrs. quiz?"

"It's to see how well you know each other," Lauren says. "You both answer the same set of questions about the other and then we see if they match."

Answering questions about my personal life in front of Jen Greenberg sounds about as much fun as replacing my toilet paper with kale. "Why don't we just do this tomorrow when Arch is here so you don't get electrocuted?"

"*Please.*" Lauren presses her palms together and repeats the word in quick little puffs, like a child begging for ice cream before dinner. "Come on!" she demands when I groan my reluctance. "What else are we going to—"

She jerks her head in the direction of the front door opening. My stomach plummets as I take in the figure in the classic Burberry raincoat. Stephanie removes the hood of her slicker and shakes free her hair, which is as perfect as it ever was. Her pedicure is fresh and her hips look like two towel hooks, holding up her white jeans. Her face is carefully made up and haggard.

"Oh my God," Lauren says, getting up to greet her. "You look amazing."

"I'm on the most hated woman in America diet," Steph says, returning Lauren's hug, grateful someone has seen fit to give her a warm welcome. The rest of us are staring at her in stunned silence.

"Lis, is it okay that I'm here?" She seems to hold her breath.

Lisa assesses Stephanie for a few suspicious moments.

"I just wanted to close out the season with a little bit of my dignity still intact." Stephanie laughs, self-deprecatingly. It is a rare thing to see—Steph laughing at herself. Maybe what happened to her has humbled her, slightly.

"Do you want the makeup person to paint on a black eye for you?" Lisa jokes, and Stephanie's face drops. "Jesus," Lisa rolls her eyes, "I'm *kidding*. Just steer clear of motorized vehicles, please." She snaps her fingers at one of the audio guys to mic Steph up.

Jen, little weasel, adds, "You can room with Laur."

Lauren looks panicked. "But Kelly is—"

"She can move her stuff into my room," Jen says through a hard smile.

"Or you could stay in Brett's room?" Lauren suggests, her voice high. Stephanie may seem subdued, but you'd be a fool not to sleep with one eye open next to her. "Arch doesn't come out until tomorrow."

"Guys," Steph says, holding her arms straight out for the audio guy like she's being patted down by a TSA officer, "I'll sleep on the couch. I'm just grateful you're willing to let me stay." Stephanie addresses me directly, "How is Kweller doing, Brett?"

"Um," I say, not really sure how to respond. I am unaccustomed to dealing with such a deferential version of Stephanie. "She's good. She was released from the hospital last week."

"I'm so relieved to hear that," Stephanie says, sincerely. The audio guy clips the mic to the collar of her blouse and fans her hair over it, telling her she's good to go. Steph comes and takes a seat next to me on the couch. "I'd like to reimburse you for the cost of her care."

"That's really not necessary," I tell her.

"Please let me do this, Brett."

"Really, it wasn't even that—" I turn my head at the sound of footsteps, padding down the hall.

"Kelly," Jen says, "look who's here."

Kelly stops when she sees Stephanie sitting next to me. She's wearing a long chunky cardigan over her romper. "Wow. Hi."

"Hey," Stephanie says, shyly. "I was just telling Brett that I want to cover the cost of Kweller's hospital stay."

"We don't need you to do that," Kelly says, in a clipped tone. She starts toward the far couch. Before she takes a seat, she chucks my phone into my lap, a little harder than she meant to, I'm sure. "All charged up."

"You were in my room?"

"I accidentally grabbed your weekend bag and you grabbed mine." She slaps the arm of the couch and says, without laughing, "Isn't that funny?"

I press the home button of my phone with my thumb. The screen comes to life, Arch's response to my last message beneath an alert from *Huffington Post* that Houston is bracing itself for new rainbands from Hurricane Harvey.

What is Kelly supposed to do if you fire her? Arch had texted me after my phone died. *The only job she's ever had has been working with SPOKE. She's your partner!*

I look up at Kelly, who is smiling at me, foully. My blood runs cold. She's read Arch's text.

"Let's start the game!" Kelly cries, spiritedly. She leans forward and collects the printed-out quiz from the coffee table. She raises her eyebrows as she reads the questions to herself. "Oh, this is going to be *fun*."

"First question," Kelly starts. She demanded to be the one to cross-examine me. She's pissed and she's going to make me squirm, so I just have to suffer through ten minutes of this juvenile game and her tortuous innuendo. That's it. She's not going to blurt out the real reason she doesn't think I should be marrying Arch, which has nothing to do with us "moving too fast" and everything to do with the woman sitting uncomfortably close to me on the couch. She wouldn't do that to me.

Would she?

"What's the one thing—apart from you, dear *precious* sister—Arch would save in a fire?" Kelly looks at me, expectantly.

"The one thing . . ." I do my best to picture our apartment, but the question—would she do that to me?—is flying around the projected image of the room like a trapped bird, banging beak-first into windows, wings knocking over lamps. "Her French press," I manage to pull out. "She packs that thing on business trips and vacations."

Lauren hits play. Arch is pensive for a moment. "Hmmm." She ponders. "I guess I would say the oil portrait of my grandmother from when she was my age."

Lauren pauses the video. "Arch has a fucking soul, Brett. You thought she'd save a coffee maker?" Her laugh carries her tangy breath my way. The butcher with a blowout has something on me, and she's four glasses of "water" deep already. *Oh God, Oh God, this is going to end in disaster.*

"Now *you* go," Kelly bosses me. "You say what you would save."

There is a skylight above us, the rain pounding so hard it's revving my anxiety. I have the irrational urge to scream at it—*Shut up! I can't hear myself think!* "Other than Arch?" I struggle to come up with something. I will say anything to bring this game to a close. "My cell phone."

Lauren hits play. On screen, Arch rolls her eyes. "Her cell phone. She'd probably save that before she saved me."

"Ha!" Lauren cries, pointing a black fingernail at me.

"She knows you pretty well," Stephanie remarks. I turn to her, but there is no trace of snark in her expression. If anything, I only recognize sadness. "It's special," she says when she finds me looking at her, askance. "You should hold on to that."

"Next question!" Kelly barks. "What is your betrothed's favorite sex position?"

Jen snuffs her disapproval of the question.

"Now we're talking," Lauren says, rubbing her palms together lustily. "I bet you're a sixty-niner, you little equal opportunist, you."

Next to me, Stephanie shifts, like she's uncomfortable for me. I start to sweat in this freezing-cold room.

"Let's consult the tape," Lauren says.

"Favorite sex position?" Arch makes a face like she's absolutely stumped, then answers, cuttingly, "Asleep."

"Brett!" Lauren scolds. "No bueno, girlfriend. You've got to keep a woman like that, you know . . . *satisfied*."

"She gets home after midnight and she's up at five!"

"So do it and go back to bed!" Lauren says, unmoved.

I practically beg Kelly, "Next question, please."

Kelly scans the question first, to herself. A slow, depraved smile spreads across her face. "What were the exact words she—she being you, Brett—used when she proposed?"

"Oh, come on," Steph says, surprising me by coming to my defense. "That's private. Don't make her share that."

"I thought you said nothing was private," Kelly says, tossing my own arrogant words back in my face. "I thought you prided yourself on being open and transparent."

"You must have said something amazing to get *her* to say yes to you." Lauren sticks her tongue out at me.

"I don't remember," I say, quietly.

"Yes you do!" Lauren laughs.

I chew the inside of my mouth for a few moments. I have to say something to get them off my back. "I guess, *I love you and I want to spend the rest of my life with you*. Something to that effect."

Lauren hits play. Arch furrows her lovely brows. "She told me that I was the only woman who had ever made her consider marriage, and that together she thought we could run the world."

Lauren whistles. "I am woman *hear me roar*. Why wouldn't you want us to know that? It's good. Assertive." She shivers. "Assertive is sexy. Damn. I'd marry you, Brett."

"I wouldn't want anyone knowing that," Kelly says, ironing out her posture so that the superiority of her next statement really lands. "A proposal like that sounds more like a business proposition."

"I'm attracted to Arch *for* her ambition," I say, my heart booming both with indignation and the risk I'm taking in challenging Kelly in her current state. "And vice versa. It's not something I'd expect someone like you to understand."

Kelly tenses, wild with restraint. "Because I have no ambition, right?"

Don't say it. Don't escalate it. But I can never help myself. "You have regrets."

Kelly launches herself off the chair, her hands clawed in the practiced shape of my neck. Lauren gasps and skitters onto the hearth, moving out of her way. But Kelly only stands there, dragon-breathing, the quiz stuck to the lap of her romper. *Chocolate or cheese?* is the next question. "You are out of line, Brett. Keep pushing me. I fucking dare you. Because I am not going quietly."

For a few moments, I am almost resigned. *Just say it, Kel.* The fallout will be painful, but covering my tracks is exhausting work.

She might have said it. I'll never know, because Jen suddenly shrieks Lauren's name. I smell the very distinct smell first, and I know without having to look at Lauren that she got too close to the fire, and it took a lick at her hair.

"It's me? It's me?!" Lauren leaps to her feet, beating the back of her head, and the unmistakable stench fills the room. We jump up to help, looking and wincing, assuring her it's not that bad when she demands to know how bad it is. She pushes us away and flees up the stairs to see for herself. Who could blame her? None of us deserve to be believed.

CHAPTER 18

Stephanie

Jesse Barnes knocked on my door two days in a row, and on the second try I texted her to come back after six, when the reporters leave their empty Starbucks cups on my front steps in retaliation for my downed blinds. I take solace in the fact that mixed in with the vermin from *TMZ,* there are journos from the *New York Times, Vanity Fair,* and *New York* magazine. My scandal is news fit to print.

Jesse brought me flowers, like someone I loved had died. I was fleetingly touched—*Wow, she gets it*—before realizing that was what made her choice so deplorable. She got it, and still she would disavow me.

Because death was all around me. My love for the page? For those mornings the alarm of creativity woke me early, the way my fingers played the keyboard like a concert pianist sight-reading inspiration? Dead. My romance with my phone? Also dead. No more thunderbolts of excitement every time I open my email or Instagram, no more prestige interview requests, fawning mentions from fans, from *celebrities.* Who knows what lies in wait for me on that handheld fieldstone now. I know better than to charge it.

My marriage is dead too, but that was a funeral that should have been held long ago. Vince and I are the two losers from *Weekend at Bernie's*, everyone laughing at our bungled attempts to convince them our love is alive.

Jesse's flowers were potted in a long, narrow glass box, a series of hot pink orchids. Very modern. Very Jesse. I set it between the two of us on the kitchen counter like a fragrant dividing line and grabbed her a beer from the depths of the meat drawer while she laid out a proposal. She wanted to not pay me and a bunch of black survivors of abuse to go on her aftershow and talk about how deeply my deceit has damaged the community. To talk about the fine example I've provided for the men's rights activists who say women lie about abuse for attention and sympathy and book sales. To acknowledge the *Stephanie Simmons effect* I've created in the publishing industry, which rarely takes chances on black women writers, and when they do, and when their books hit, it's not like *Gone Girl,* a sign that the consumer wants a million more domestic thrillers with the word "girl" artlessly thrust into the title. When a black woman's book blows up it's an anomaly, and there can only be one of you, and that the one of us it got to be was a dirty, filthy pretender who hurt not just black women with her lies but black men too is the ultimate injustice.

After I am appropriately dressed down on national television, after we've turned this into a *teachable moment,* I will apologize to the public and make a gracious donation to a local women's shelter. Then? I take my garden leave. *We'll stage a comeback together,* Jesse lied to my face. I'll write my next book and she'll document my rise from the ashes, call it *Return of the Stephi,* proving that not even a faux-hawk can resuscitate your cool once you hit your forties.

I walked Jesse to the door, where she gave me a long hug. *Think about it,* she said to me, and also, *Orchids need light.* So I gave them none. They're sitting right where I left them, their neon limbs lost to the floor.

But I did think about it. And I would rather have my ears surgically attached to the insides of Brett's thighs so that she can ride me like a SPOKE bike than give Jesse the mea culpa ratings boon she's after, to pardon her of the supporting role she played in all of this. Jesse Barnes is the heroin dealer stationed outside the middle school whose bedtime lullaby is *But I didn't stick the needle in anybody's arm* every time a thirteen-year-old is found purple-lipped beneath the bleachers. Like the seventh-grader, I had a choice: feel like every other normal loser in his class, or feel so extraordinary that you almost believe you are extraordinary.

For her role in creating such an obvious, fatal option, Jesse must pay. So must Lisa, and Brett, and our whole coterie of Janus-faced feminism. I will not be their straw man. I will not be tarred and feathered in the town square for gaming a game that gave me an unfair start. They want to hold me responsible for an endemic culture of not believing women while at the same time telling me my story is "a little slow" without mention of crushed windpipes and torn arteries. They want a black woman on their "diverse" show, but only if I have been through something sensational, and all those times a white woman has mistaken me for her waitress, her hotel cleaning lady, her salesgirl at Saks? Unfortunate, but not sensational. I don't know who "they" is—Jesse, Lisa, my publisher, men, women, you.

So here I am, the second to last weekend of summer, a bounty hunter on behalf of personal responsibility. For the time being, I am how we like our women: contrite, trussed, eyes on the floor. But know I'm doing it through clenched pelvic floor muscles. (Where are you now, Vince? Oh right, the Standard on my dime while we move ahead with the divorce proceedings.) I just have to keep up this yes, ma'am and no, ma'am act through the night so Lisa allows me to attend the brunch at Jesse's tomorrow. And that's when I drop the motherfucking nuke.

You should have seen Brett's face when I came to her defense during the asinine Mrs. and Mrs. game! She's actually buying what I'm selling. I'm sure she's twisted the whole thing in her head, managed, impressively, to fashion herself as the victim in this sordid tale. And now here I am, catering to that delusional fantasy. Brett's biggest blind spot has always been her willingness to believe her own hype.

Lauren is locked in the upstairs guest bathroom, crying animatedly about the back of her head, and I can't say I blame her. Haha. It's totally charred. Kelly, her rhinestone-studded Victoria's Secret thong (probably) in a twist, marched up the stairs to Jen's bedroom, chin held at a righteous angle, Greenberg behind her, repeating her name in consolatory tones. I've always wondered how much Kelly knew. Clearly, she knows enough to know that Brett has no business marrying Arch. I'll make her suffer too.

I turn to Brett and laugh a *wow everyone is crazy but us* laugh. "Talkhouse?" I suggest. Because you know, if I'm going to do this, tequila wouldn't hurt.

—

"I can't believe I said that to Kelly," Brett says to me in the cab, her long hair hanging in wet panels over her ears. We waited until the crew packed up and left, even going so far as to change into our pajamas to make everyone think we had called it a night, then put on ho clothes that show our ankles and snuck out without telling Kelly, Jen, and Lauren where we were going. The minivan Lindy's sent over takes a glacial left at the end of Jen's drive, the rain pummeling the windshield harder than the wipers can keep up. "About having regrets," Brett says. "What if they use it? Layla will see that."

God forbid Layla know she's not the reason Kelly was put on this earth. "She already knows," I say, pulling my ponytail out of the collar of my shirt. I tucked it in to protect it from the dash from the front door to the cab but it did no good, which is a shame. My nails are done. My toes are done. I dropped eight hundred bucks on a new pair of Aquazzura wedges and I had a hydrafacial yesterday. I plan on looking absolutely fucking perfect when I do what I am planning on doing tomorrow.

Brett turns to me. "Knows what?"

"That Kelly regrets having her so young." I put my phone back into my Chanel. For the last few seasons, I've tried to make those raffia woven clutches from Roberta Roller Rabbit work out here. I've tried for the low-maintenance, beachy look, but as I packed for the weekend, I decided I couldn't spend another night in an ikat print skimming my shins. I packed clean white jeans and sleeveless tops and red lipsticks. I packed things that make me look like a classic beauty.

Brett is mulling over what I've just said, rolling her bottom lip in her top teeth. "You really think she's picked up on that?"

I prop an elbow on the back of the seat, shifting so that my knees point in her direction. It's like the Wonder Woman pose but for empathy—if you put yourself in the position for it, maybe actual empathy will come. "*Of course* she's picked up on it. That's why she's so lucky to have you in her life. You are the one who makes her feel loved and wanted. You are setting an example of hard work and perseverance."

Brett waves me off bashfully—*You don't mean that but yes of course you do because I am the ne plus ultra aunt, businesswoman, lesbian, human being.* I swallow repeatedly to force the acidic truth back down: *She's twelve going on twenty-eight for a reason, you half-wit. When I was twelve, I was painting my friend's nails and making up dances to Boyz II Men songs, not attending staff meetings with my aunt and running her company's social media campaign. She feels like she has to contribute or you won't love her. That she can't just be a kid because being a kid is a burden on you.*

Brett tips her head back, running her fingers through her wet hair. I can smell her Moroccan oil shampoo again. Mixed in with the Febreze and cigarette smell of the cab, my brain marches in olfactory protest. "Steph," she says, "are we okay? I mean, real okay. Not TV okay. I know you have a lot going on right now so I can't tell if it's that or if it's something . . . something I did."

The almost-admission makes me hold my breath. *Keep going,* I urge her, *exonerate yourself.*

"Because." She takes a shaky breath. *It's coming! She's going to do it!* "I miss us," she continues, "but it's never going to go back to the way it was. I'm not the runt of the group anymore. I'm not going to stop being successful because you're uncomfortable with my success, Steph."

It is all I can do not to laugh in her fat, beautiful face. They should list *impaired hearing* as a side effect on the bottle of fame. There are so many people clapping for you all the time, for walking, for breathing, for wiping your own ass, that it drowns out what I like to call your *not that* inner voice, the one that says you're not that smart, you're not that talented, you're not that funny. Some may confuse this gag for progress, as women come out of the womb hearing we are not enough. But having been on both sides of the fence I can tell you this: If you don't hate yourself just a little bit, you are intolerable.

In any case, I am back in touch with my *not that* inner voice as of late. No one is clapping for me anymore. I'm probably a lot more fun to be around for everybody else, but when I lie in bed at night I can't help but wish that this human suit of mine came with a zipper, that I could hang it in my custom white oak closet with the Chanel spotlights and take a break from myself, even for an hour.

I have been saying I am too old for Talkhouse since before I was too old for Talkhouse. The crowd tonight is twenty-one years old or fifty, no one in between but the two of us. It's the first time I've ever been where there is room to rest my elbow on the bar in the main room, with a clear view of the empty dance floor and the stage, where a few roadies are busy assembling a drum set. The rain has kept it quiet so far. My new wedges are squeegeeing water with every step and I don't dare release my ponytail for fear of the shape my hair will take on its own, but the cameras aren't here, two fingers of tequila are playing the tendons in my throat, and downwind, a pack of fraternity brothers in pastel shorts are debating how old to tell us they are.

"Girls?" The bartender places two plastic cups in front of us, half-full with something clear. *Vodka* shots. Shit. They might not even be twenty-one. "From the gentlemen down the way." The bartender indicates with a thumb. That two adult women with multimillion-dollar empires between them are referred to as girls and this group of rosy-cheeked pussy grabbers as gentlemen—even facetiously—is the problem with the world in two words.

The boldest one calls over the Pool Party 2017 playlist, "You were looking too serious over there!"

Brett turns to me, mouth agape, and I match her outraged expression—time to have some fucking fun.

Brett shouts back, "You basically just told us to smile. It's been illegal to tell women to smile since 2013."

He takes the rebuke as an invitation to approach, which, of course it was. Closer, I see that his baseball hat is from a sailing regatta he attended in Newport two summers ago when he was ten. "Yeah, 'cause no one ever tells men to smile. It's only women who are expected to be pleasing and accommodating at all times."

Brett makes a raspberry sound with her lips. "Ex-fucking-cuse me?"

The kid tucks his hands in his back pockets, broadening his hairless chest, ever so pleased with himself. "We watched that short *Stop Telling Women to Smile* in my women's studies class." He dips his head and looks up at us with a debilitating smile. "We watched your show too."

Brett flips her hair to the other side of her shoulder. It's drying in gorgeous, wild waves. I'm still thinner.

"So?" I rest a hip against the bar and fold my arms across my chest, scooping my breasts so that my top pulls up, exposing a sliver of lean midriff. "Which one of us is your favorite?"

"Oh, man." He laughs, twisting his hat around backward, smearing his thick blond hair across his forehead. If we were all in college at the same time, he wouldn't bother with either of us. "Lauren, probably."

"Shocking!" Brett rolls her eyes.

"You asked me who my favorite is. Not who's hottest." He looks right at me, and goddamnit if his shit-eating grin doesn't impale me from my inner thighs to my sternum.

Brett says, "Because it's 2017 and women care fuck all if a bunch of whiskey dick frat boys think they're hot." She twists a hair around her finger, her brown eyes huge and nonthreatening. Oh, she cares. We all care. Women sexually attracted to socks are not impervious to the male gaze. The difference today is, we have to say that we are. Feminism doesn't emancipate us, it's just one more impossible standard to meet.

Brett leans in closer, her voice greased with charm. "But for shits and giggles, if you . . ." She flutters her eyelashes up at him and waits.

"Tim," Tim supplies after an unsexy moment of confusion.

"*Tim,*" Brett speaks his name with comic seduction, soft on the "T," long and yummy on the "m." "If you were to pick the hottest, *Tim*. Who would it be?"

He gestures at us with a startled expression on his face, like he can't believe we even had to ask. "Either one of you. And I swear I'm not just saying that because you're both here. The other girls"—he shows them the exit with a sideways scoop of his hand—"I know a million girls who look like that. You two are different."

Different is good, Instagram tells you. Conformity is boring. Be you because everyone else is taken. Easy to repost in earnest when you haven't labored under the duress of different all your life.

"A *tie*?" Brett pouts.

"Yeah, Tim," I cosign, "girls like us? We don't do ties. Someone has to lose."

Tim points his chin at the ceiling with a groan, as though we have tasked him with settling something as complex as the national budget.

"It's honestly a tie," he says. "But if I'm hedging my bets . . ." He looks from me to Brett from Brett to me, oscillating between two sets of pleading *oh, please, pick me!* eyes. "I'd go with you." He shrugs one shoulder half-heartedly in my direction.

Brett covers her heart with her hand and crumples a little.

"You don't like *guys*," Tim reminds her.

"You're into the cougar thing." She sips her drink. "I get it."

The word "cougar" hits me like a fist wearing brass knuckles. My heart is pounding in my brain, clobbering my intellectual capacities, making only high school mean girl ripostes accessible. "Or he's into the thin thing," I say.

"See," Brett directs her plastic cup of vodka at me, jovially, "thin" failing to deliver the body slam I hoped it would, "the thing is, Steph—I could be thin if I wanted. You can't be in your twenties. No matter how disciplined you try to be."

Brett raises her vodka shot and knocks it back, her face twisting gruesomely like a Salvador Dalí portrait. Tim watches us, a little nervously, unable to tell anymore if we're joking. We're deadly serious, but we can't let him know that. He came over here to make us smile.

"In that case," I say, raising my shot, "to women being in their sexual prime in their thirties." I knock back the warm vodka, gagging. Tim wasn't wrong. We were looking a little too serious over here. And I'm not ready to get serious. Not yet.

The nineties cover band comes on at midnight and we have no problem securing spots in the front row. The children who frequent this place are just wrapping up cocktail hour at their squalid summer shares. The rain stops at some point, and when a bead of sweat trickles down my spine I turn and realize it's the next day, that the entire room has filled to its usual capacity, which is whatever one body shy of suffocation is. Brett and I are holding hands, dancing and screaming the lyrics to No Doubt and Goo Goo Dolls songs, making lewd Tim sandwiches to R. Kelly covers while the floor swipes at our feet with warm toffee gloves. A constellation of cell phones hangs in the air, capturing our every move.

The lead singer is not much younger than me, her hair in high pigtail buns, and I do the math to figure out if she is closer to Gwen Stefani now than Gwen Stefani then. Then. Though, just barely. If she can be here, I can be here, I decide. As she sings the final verse of "Spiderwebs," a girl in the crowd tugs on Brett's arm. I can't hear what Brett says when she turns to her, but her eyes light up in recognition and she throws her arms around her neck. Someone she knows. Someone to distract her. I gesture for Tim to crouch down so that I can shout in his ear, "Drink!"

I take his hand, pulling him through the crowd, but I don't stop at the bar in the main room, or the bar in the back room, or the bar outside. We keep going, into the loud, spongy night, past the bouncer standing beneath the white wood arbor, punching entrance stamps onto the backs of hands, and around the side of the bar and into the strip of grass between the outdoor patio and the next building, which I've never bothered to identify. There, I close Tim's arms around my lower back and slip a finger under his chin, guiding his mouth toward mine. The first kiss is long, soft, and without tongue, leaving me bow-kneed and swollen.

"Aren't you married?" he asks, the noble question a gurgle from deep within his throat.

"We can stop if you're uncomfortable," I offer sweetly, releasing the buckle of the needlepoint belt his mom bought for him. Tim groans. It's not a *no*.

We reenter amid protests from the peons who have been waiting in line for the last forty minutes. At the outdoor bar, we find Brett stuffing a lime down the neck of a Corona.

"I have been looking for you everywhere!" she cries. She jumps up and gets behind us, herding us like a flock, ordering, "Inside, inside. I have a surprise for you."

We get stuck in a jam at the door, and Brett takes the opportunity to dust the wet leaves and grass and crud off our new friend's back in a dramatic, sweeping motion. "Steph," she chides, slyly, "way to not be a dead fish, girlfriend." I'm both incensed by the implication that I don't have interesting enough sex with my husband to keep him faithful and pleased that Brett has noticed that I am desirable enough to have pulled a guy like . . . shit. I've forgotten his name.

"If only Arch could be as lucky." I tousle her hair, the way I've seen Kelly do to annoy her. Brett slaps my hand away, hard enough to be heard over the music.

The three of us—the world's most beat ménage à trois—push our way inside. At the bar, what's his face runs into his friends again. *Tim!* they cry, and I silently thank them. Tim waves at me to go on with Brett, who continues to drag me onto the dance floor, holding one of my hands in both of hers for extra leverage. I glance back at him before the crowd swallows me whole—two newborns with tits have joined their group, are squealing, *Oh my God, Tim!* and reaching up to hug him because they are just *so* little and *so* pretty and so very, very young. It's like the weight of the universe has suddenly settled on my eyelids. I could fall asleep standing up in this drunken, dancing crowd.

Brett has forged a path to the stage, and she's waving her arm at the lead singer, who points right back at her, as though she knows her. "So," the singer says into the microphone in her loud, clear veejay voice, "you know I don't usually take requests." The crowd hollers, incoherently. "But there are special circumstances tonight, because we have two *Goal Diggers* in the *houseeee*!" This announcement is greeted with cheers that could be cheers for anything, and booing that is very specifically for us. Brett jams both middle fingers into the air.

"And one of these bitches," the singer continues, "has been screaming at *this* bitch to play 'Bitch' for the last hour. So what do you say we three bitches sing a song about bitches together?"

More vague cheering. More intentional booing.

A stagehand ambles toward us, sticking his hand into the crowd and hoisting the two of us over the large speakers. The stage lights are bright lie detectors, and I realize with a start that despite her twee pigtails, the lead singer might actually be older than me.

She cups her hand over the mic and speaks to us. "Please tell me you know the fucking words."

"I dominated this song at middle school dances," Brett says. "Steph, what was that? College for you?"

The lead singer gives me a look—*oh no she didn't*—and makes a grand gesture out of pressing the mic into my hands. "She can sing backup," she tells me with a wink. The act of camaraderie frames the moment as two old broads taking back the night from the young buck. I am struck brutally and repeatedly with a blunt-forced thought: *I never should have come here.*

The song starts, that bouncy pop beat laced with a few warning strokes of the guitar, gearing up for the title profanity that Brett screams into the mic with adolescent glee. Brett wasn't in middle school when this song came out. I was. I remember my mother hanging up the phone with shaking hands, turning to me and asking if I had used street language at Ashley's beach house after they were kind enough to host me for an entire week. That was the word ginger, golf-shoe-wearing Mrs. Lutkin had used. *Street.* I had washed the dishes after dinner and hung the towels to dry on the outdoor line and made the bed every morning, but what Mrs. Lutkin remembered most of my stay was the night she came home early from dinner and found Ashley and me in our pajamas, dancing around the family room to *street* music.

Brett is having a hell of a time, whipping her long, wet hair in circles and hogging the mic only to screw up the order of the lyrics. *I'm a bitch, I'm a mother, I'm a child, I'm a lover*. By the second verse, Brett decides to personalize the song and shout, *I'm NOT a mother*, which no one thinks is funny but doesn't seem to embarrass her.

We're at the part in the music video that involved a heavy lift from central casting. Black women, wacky women, butch women, old women, pretty women, all dancing together in the same room, proving that the bonds of sisterhood are stronger than cultural and generational walls, than the beauty standards that try to tier us. *Whoo-oh-ohhh whoo-oh-ohhh*. Brett turns to me, and in a moment of passion, reaches behind my neck and slips her hand under my ponytail. I think she might kiss me—put on a display of faux lesbianism to ruin the very last of our feministic cred—until I realize she's sliding off my hair tie. Before I can stop her, she tosses it into the crowd with a mirthful laugh. "Let your hair down for once in your life!" she screams at me, forgetting—or not forgetting—that there is a microphone in her hand.

It's as though she pantsed me. I scan the crowd for Tim, hoping he isn't watching this. I hope for something different when I locate him, surrounded by his friends, laughing and shaking his head. Why is he shaking his head? Is he *denying* that he hooked up with me? He says something in a defensive posture to a member of his group. Whatever it is only incites more teasing. He is. He's denying it.

The band plays the main chord, again and again, softer and softer, until we can hear the crowd cheering again. Brett passes the mic to me to take a deep bow, which is just another opportunity to flip her hair over her back like Ariel the Fucking Mermaid.

"How about a round of applause for these two?" the lead singer says into the backup singer's mic. "That was terrible," she says over the jeers and cheers. "Terrible! Stick to spinning and making up stories, you two."

A low *ohhhh* travels the crowd and the lead singer brings her hand to her mouth, mortified. I don't believe she was being malicious, but it doesn't matter, because that's how it was interpreted, and I have to say something. I have to *defend* myself. One of the bouncers is helping Brett scale the speakers, but I still have the mic in my hand when her feet touch the ground.

"I am good at making up stories," I say into the microphone, before I can think about it too hard. "But this one"—I point to Brett—"she's the master at it."

Brett looks up at me from the crowd, laughing a little, because I've kowtowed to her all evening and she has no reason to believe I'm about to turn on her. "You heard we had a falling-out, right?"

Brett's mouth drops open a little.

I continue with a rictus grin. "You'll see it all play out on TV. But when you do, you should know it's fake. The whole thing was fake. We made it up for the ratings."

"Get off the stage!" somebody yells.

Brett is now trying to scramble back over the speakers like an obese mountain goat.

"Oh, and no little girls are raped in the mountains of Morocco. Brett lied about that too. And *oh yeah*, they're going to try to make it look like Vince fucks Brett's sister this season. But that's not who he—"

Brett tackles me before I can finish. It is a real, honest-to-God football player tackle, a hug around my ankles that cripples me at the knees. I fall back on one hand, raise one filthy heel into the air for balance. It could be a dance move: Do the cover-up, and kick it like this.

"Girl fight!" the singer cackles into the mic, like the fucking traitors we all turn out to be as soon as the opportunity presents itself. I hurry to my feet, furiously embarrassed, clenching my fists at my sides to keep from whaling Brett across the face, which is what I'm dying to do, though not here, not yet. I trundle over the speakers, refusing anyone's help on the way down. It's farther than I expected and I feel my shins in my pelvis when I hit the floor, stumble ungracefully, and stride out, as dignified as too many vodka shots will allow.

We get stuck with a van again, Brett in the left middle two seats and me in the back row. The driver had waited after we'd gotten in, sure more of our friends were coming since we'd sat so far apart. "It's just us," Brett finally had to say. She doesn't speak again until the cab has made a U-turn in the middle of Main and we have passed the old Presbyterian church on our right, and then she swivels in her seat to face me. She's paled considerably in the last few minutes. "Everyone is probably too drunk to remember what you said anyway."

Somebody is *scared*. I hold her eye, a half smile on my face, my head grooving in gentle, unconcerned rhythm with the road. "I wrote it on the bathroom wall in permanent marker just in case," I say. I didn't, but I'm having too much fun, watching Brett quake in her sneaks.

Brett turns away from me. "I never should have agreed to this," she mutters to herself. Then louder, for the people in the back, "I didn't *need* to agree to it. I'm not the one who's past my prime."

I stare at her Cousin Itt hair for a hot minute.

"Your sister is gorgeous," I tell her, finally.

Brett snorts. "She's single. Go for it."

I find my lip gloss, dab some on. I must look a *fright*. "But I never worried about Vince around her. Not for a second. You know why?"

Brett's head bobs back and forth with the motion of the van. She doesn't answer me. I grasp the back of her headrest with both hands and stick my chin over her shoulder. "Because she's too smart for him. We all know Kelly's the brains behind the operation. Vince likes his side pieces dumb. Dumb and not ugly, exactly—I mean, look at me—but, you know, like the castoffs. The lemons."

Brett takes out her phone and at first I think this is some sort of sister strategy that I never learned, being an only child and all—ignore her and she will get bored and give up. But then I see she's texting Jesse. *Steph just got on stage at Talkhouse and told everyone that the show is fake and scripted. She's badmouthing all of us and I just wanted you to know before we film at your place tomorr—*

I rip Brett's phone out of her hand, drop it on the floor, and smash the screen with a single stomp from my new wedges. This next part, this *does* happen so fast. Brett throws herself at me, all claws and wet lashings from her hair. She slashes my face, drawing three lines of blood along my jawline.

My fury is swift and deafening, makes outrageous demands: break her nose, blacken her eyes, bite off an ear. With a battle cry, I comply. The two of us are a twister of limbs and low base insults, rolling around on the floor between the two middle seats, scratching, biting, wailing at each other to *stop* even while our fists blur in motion, because stopping feels about as impossible as sneezing with your eyes open. It is the most conventional catfight you've ever seen, and it feels like doing heroin for the first time. The pleasure center of my brain must look like a club in Ibiza during spring break. Lit. I cannot control much anymore, but I can control how hard I hit, how much I hurt this unrepentant impostor. The cabdriver swerves to the side of the road, shouting at us to stop or he'll call the cops. We pull apart, gasping, exhilarated, and when I look down I realize I'm holding a hank of Brett's hair in my hand. No, wait. Not Brett's hair. Brett's *extensions*. I actually bow down to her. At last, someone to whom I can cede the moral low ground.

"I should sell this on eBay," I say, dangling the pelt in front of her face.

Brett wipes her lower lip and pulls her thumb away to check—yup, it's blood. She stymies the cut with her tongue and says with hangsman good cheer, "Might help pay for your divorce. I hear they get expensive."

That's *funny*. For a second, I actually think about sparing her.

Nah.

CHAPTER 19

Kelly: The Interview

Present day

It could be late, time to go to bed, but it could also be time for lunch. The blackout shades are still drawn and Lisa has pocketed my phone. The dark, hourless room has sedated me, lowered my inhibitions like alcohol, weakened my judgment, made me say things I never would have said sober.

"You didn't hear them come home from Talkhouse?" Jesse asks.

"I slept through it all," I say, grateful for a question I can answer honestly. After Brett and Stephanie snuck out, Jen had gone into Lauren's room and returned with a light blue oval the size of a stud earring. *What is that?* I asked, when she offered it to me. *It's only five milligrams,* she said. *Enough to take the edge off.* I had taken Xanax before in college, but I was already drunk, and I didn't remember feeling a difference. I got it into my head that pills just didn't work on me, that I was too Type A to be felled by such a diminutive capsule. *Never trust a first impression,* came the gooey, giggly thought right before the benzo dropped me into sleep like a stone into a stream. Plunk. Bye.

I wish I could say that I told Jen the truth in a mentally altered state, but it was in the opposite order. The Xanax was administered to calm me down after I told Jen the truth about Brett. I am always so levelheaded, so restrained, until I'm not. It's the reason Layla exists.

Following the near-violent end of the Mrs. and Mrs. game, I was relieved to hear Jen behind me on the stairs. I needed to vent to someone who didn't see the good in Brett. Sometimes you just have to bitch about someone you love to someone who really hates her, okay? My hands were still clawed in the shape of my sister's neck and throbbing with the unmet need to strangle her. I opened my mouth to say the things I almost said before Lauren's hair caught on fire but Jen had raised her finger to her lips, lifting her shirt to display a rib cage that looked like a ladder of sharp elbows. She pointed at her mic, reminding me that it was strapped beneath my bra band too. She picked up my duffel (I ordered the same one as Brett because I'm unoriginal. Is that what she wanted to hear me say?) and gestured for me to follow her, down the hall, to her bedroom. There, we took turns unwiring the other, and then Jen stuffed the mics under a European sham and sat on top, to be sure.

"I could destroy her if I wanted to," I said to Jen, finally free to speak. "With just a few words on camera, I could destroy her. But I haven't. I have been loyal, thinking I would be rewarded for it." I laughed bitterly at my own naiveté.

"What was that about?" Jen asked. "Did I miss something? I don't get what happened down there."

I told her about the text message I read on Brett's phone.

"She wouldn't actually fire you, would she?"

She saw my expression and said, "Right." She rubbed the thin skin on her forehead, thinking. I was about to tell her to stop, she'd give herself wrinkles, when her eyes suddenly flared. "Oh my God!" She slapped the upturned sides of her thighs with both hands, as though she had it. "You can come and work for me! Think about *that* storyline. I poach you from my number one frenemy."

"I don't give a fuck about a storyline!" I thundered. "I care about what's right and what's fair. SPOKE wouldn't exist without me! It's so *arrogant* of her to think that she could get rid of me and that I wouldn't even put up a fight! With what I *have* on her." I wanted to go on, but I bit my tongue, like I always do.

Jen crossed her ankles in her lap, perched lightly on the pillow as though she were about to levitate. "Does what you have on her have something to do with her and Steph? Because everyone thinks they had an affair."

I shook my head, more to myself than to her. *No. You've kept it this long. Don't tell it now.*

Jen had shrugged. Not a *whatever* shrug. There was understanding in her narrow brown eyes. Brett never missed a chance to describe them as beady, but to me Jen always looked focused, like she was listening to what you had to say. "I get it," she said. "She's your sister. You love her and your loyalty is to her. I just want you to know, Kel." She had stopped, blushing a little. "Look. I'm a pretty solitary person. You know, you run a holistic-minded company and people expect you to be this sort of soft, nurturing earth-mother type, but it is serious business what I do. Do you know that at the first advisory meeting for Green Theory, eight out of my ten shareholders passed me the résumés of *qualified* men who could take over as CEO? One told me I had developed a great product but I had taken it as far as I could take it. I learned early on to say I didn't need help. It felt like a sign of weakness if I admitted that. And it's made me lonelier than I'd like. I was really excited when I was asked to be a part of the show. I really thought I had found *my tribe*." She rolled her eyes and made a sound that was not quite a laugh. "I couldn't wait to meet everyone and swap war stories. But Steph, she's a writer and she didn't really get it. And Lauren, I mean, she's fun to hang out with, but we all know her rich dad put up capital and she's not doing any of the heavy lifting. Honestly, I was most excited to get to know Brett. But it quickly became apparent to me that Brett was a very good self-promoter but she had no idea what she was doing. I tried to have a conversation with her once about the new state tax law and she was clueless. I always thought she was hiding something, and now I realize it was you."

I felt as though I had just been proposed to by the man of my dreams. It was the validation I had been waiting for since the inception of SPOKE. Finally, someone saw me. Not only that, but someone had been looking for me all along. The only way I could think to repay this kindness was with the truth.

It starts, as it always does, with what seems like a harmless white lie, only it became the foundation on which to lay larger beams of deceit. When NYU pays my sister's 50K lecturing fee, Brett tells the Stern students that she read about the entrepreneurial contest that ultimately funded the first phase of SPOKE in a doctor's waiting room. She tore out the page from the magazine and brought it home to show me, and I laughed at her. The truth is, Brett didn't vandalize a magazine in a doctor's waiting room—she vandalized a magazine at the nail salon, where she was getting a pedicure on a Tuesday morning, because she wasn't in school and she didn't have a job, but she did have her cut of our mother's life insurance policy to blow through and endless time to while away.

Something she didn't lie about? My reaction. I *did* laugh at her, but not because I didn't believe in Brett or her vision, which is how she likes to spin it now (Look at all the people who doubted me along the way, kids!). I laughed because my sister had no business applying for a grant reserved for aspiring LGBTQ business owners given the fact that she is not lesbian, gay, bisexual, transgender, or questioning. My sister very much likes the D. No questions about that.

I told her not to do it. I begged her not to do it. And so of course Brett went ahead and entered the contest anyway, penning a heartbreaking application essay about what happened when she came out to our mother her freshman year of high school. She woke up the next morning to find her hair had been sheared off in her sleep. *If you want to be a dyke, then you can look like a dyke,* our mother told her when she stumbled downstairs, clutching her hair in both hands and crying.

It was fiction. Bad fiction that the judges devoured.

The grant covenant stipulated that twice a year for the next three years, Brett had to host aspiring LGBTQ business owners at the studio. She would listen to their stories, help them shape their ideas, and dispel her wizened advice. I always found reasons to stay away from SPOKE on those days. I couldn't bear to face these struggling, hopeful hard workers, knowing that my sister had robbed them of an opportunity designed to increase their parity. I thought we just had to get through those three years, ride out the contract, and then Brett's counterfeit sexuality would cease to be one of her defining qualities. But then the show came calling.

A magazine editor at *Cosmo* had taken a class at SPOKE, and she invited Brett to be a part of a package she had pitched: "Twenty-Five Boss Women Under the Age of Twenty-Five." The article caught the attention of a casting director for Saluté, on the hunt for a gay woman to round out the diversified cast of *Goal Diggers*. The show had so much to offer our nascent business—exposure, connections, *growth*—that it almost justified Brett borrowing an identity from a historically oppressed group of people.

I was complicit. I lied to the cast and to Jesse, which is why Jesse hates me and also why she needs me. I participated in a pyramid scheme that recruited her affections and played her like a gullible desperado, and she would die of embarrassment if anyone ever found out. I know by the way she looks at me—a little bit ashamed—that she imagines Brett and I laughed at her behind her back, called her a dirty old man for slavering over my sister the way she did. Brett tried to once but I shut her down quickly. There is nothing funny about what we did. The deception made me sick, especially when Imazighen girls would whisper to Brett that they thought they might be like her and they were scared that their families would no longer love them if they were, and Brett would comfort them with the made-up hardships she had endured when she was their age. But the sword in my heart was always Arch, who deserved so much better than someone who may have loved her, but wasn't *in* love with her. *She's thirty-six,* I pleaded with Brett after they got engaged. *She wants kids. Don't waste her time. Don't plan a wedding only to call it off or divorce her in a year for the storyline.*

I don't think Brett would have proposed, or accepted Arch's proposal (however you want to slice it), if she hadn't done what she did in the break between seasons three and four. My sister is not cruel by nature, but she made a bad decision, and she needed to make a grand gesture to cover her tracks. Proposing to Arch was a form of lifestyle insurance.

I could have told Arch the truth. Scratch that. I *should* have told Arch the truth. But if the viewers found out that Brett was lying about her sexuality, commodifying the gay community's plight, they would have turned on her (and rightfully so). SPOKE would be done. Her role on the show would be eliminated. *My* role on the show would be eliminated. Brett told a lie from which we both profited, and I let it live. I own it. But I also worked so hard to make SPOKE what it is today. The thought of walking away from everything I've built fills me with despair.

"It must be so painful to know the truth," Jesse says cruelly. "To know that your sister died while you were sleeping just above her. We know now that after Stephanie and Brett came home from Talkhouse, Vince arrived at the house, and he attacked Brett in the kitchen."

"That's the timeline the police are working with," I say, carefully. That *is* the timeline the police are working with—but it's not the correct one, and Jesse and I both know that.

"Do you also believe their theory that Vince killed Brett in a jealous rage after finding out about her affair with Stephanie?"

"It makes sense," I say, again, carefully. I flinch when I see the blip of anger in Jesse's eyes. I'm not here to play word hockey. I'm here to conclusively push a narrative that serves the show better than the truth. "It wasn't just an affair—Stephanie and Brett were in love," I say, and Jesse's face softens with forgiveness. "The humiliation of that was clearly too much for Vince to take."

There was a humiliation, too much for one person to take, but that person wasn't Vince, it was Stephanie. Jesse and I both know that Stephanie killed my sister, and we both know that it has nothing to do with Brett and Stephanie "being in love." But the tape shows otherwise. We've made sure of it.

CHAPTER 20

Stephanie

I thought I would lie awake all night, charged with loathing and second-guessing, but my sleep was straight out of a fairy tale, replete with a wake-up call from chirping birds and soft sunlight on my inarguably lovely face. Perhaps I slept so well thanks to the memory foam mattress in the downstairs guest bedroom—Brett's room, which I claimed from her like a birthright when we got home. I punch my fists into the air with a gratifying yawn, the kind that distorts your face with pleasure, like sex. Good sex. Not Vince sex. Vince. Why am I thinking about Vince on this morning of *all* mornings? I swing upright and then go very still, listening. It's after eight and the house is already smug with doing things, and that is Vince I hear in the living room.

I get up and follow his voice without washing my face or brushing my teeth, which is not how the day was supposed to start. The day was supposed to start with Jason and my team here at the crack of dawn (where are they?), my Starbucks order hot and my hair in rollers. I wasn't to leave my bedroom until I was spit and polished, my wits properly caffeinated. Leave it to a man to fuck up *this* day, the day I plan to cement my legacy.

In the living room, Kelly and Lauren are sitting on the couch, drinking coffee across from Vince, who sits in one of the hairy white chairs, a plastic Duane Reade bag at his feet. Outside, Jen is holding a warrior pose in the shade. The puddles on the porch are evaporating and the sky is a tragic, September 11 blue. What a beautiful day to ruin these bitches.

Lauren raises her mug in greeting. Her hair (what's left) is stiff and her face is red and shiny, like she just had surgery. *I'm not even hungover,* I realize. It's like a clear seventy-degree day—the temperature so optimal for the human condition that you don't even notice the air around you. I feel alive and fresh and happy, but not so alive and fresh and happy that I'm thinking about taking up yoga and cutting out caffeine and spending less time on social media or whatever it is people do when they decide to self-improve.

"How was *Talk house*?" Kelly says the name of the bar as if it were two distinct words. Like Burger King. Or Nordstrom Rack, which is probably where she got that dreadful cold-shoulder maxi dress she is wearing at the moment. God, she is embarrassing.

I ignore her and address Vince. "Why are you here?"

"I mean, Steph. Everyone is calling me. My mom is a mess."

"A mess about what?"

"You seriously don't know?" Lauren asks, her voice froggy and hungover. She must have knocked herself out last night through some combination of booze and pills, because she did not stir when Brett and I got home. No one did. God bless all these highly functioning addicts.

"Someone tell me what the fuck is going on before I lose it." I hear myself and smile, demurely, softening my tone. "I mean—please?"

Kelly reaches for her phone. She calls up something and tosses it my way. I have to wait a second for the screen to right itself, but when it does, I realize I'm looking at a video post from *TMZ: Drunken Stephanie Simmons does not hold back on her soon to be ex-husband.* I hit play. In case it isn't clear what I'm saying, they've taken the helpful liberty of adding subtitles: *They're going to try to make it look like Vince fucks Brett's sister this season. But that's not who he*—boom.

Brett plows into me, her huge hips eclipsing the frame. The video cuts off right before I jump offstage. Thank God. I already had monsoon hair. I didn't need everyone to see me land like an American gymnast with weak ankles.

I face my firing squad. "That's all?"

Vince folds his hands behind his head and tilts his face to the ceiling. "Great." He laughs, sarcastically. "There was more?"

"I'm keeping your name alive in the press, babe," I say to him, sweet as candy. Vince turns away from me, his jaw clenched. Across from him, Kelly is gripping her mug of coffee so hard I'm waiting for it to shatter. She knew. She had to have known from the beginning. That's why Vince found any opportunity he could to corner her. He wasn't trying to fuck her; he was trying to get information out of her.

"What are you all so upset about?" I say. "I said Vince *didn't* fuck you, Kelly. I did you a favor for when they try to make it look like he did. Which they will do."

"Steph," Vince says evenly. He clears his throat, glancing at Lauren and Kelly for their little nods of confidence—*You can do this, Vince!* "I think we should head back to the city together. I called Jason and the whole glam team and told them not to come."

I feel like a troubled teen who has come downstairs to find two former Navy SEALs in her living room, about to be shipped off to one of those Wilderness Therapy Camps where they sodomize you with a flashlight for cursing. I *cannot* go with Vince.

I head into the kitchen to pour myself some coffee while I land on a strategy: *Be agreeable.* "I wouldn't mind heading back with you after brunch." I stir steamed almond milk—my only option—into my mug. It immediately clots, forming a puke-textured scum on the surface. I don't care who or what has had to suffer to provide real milk for my coffee all these years, their sacrifice has been worth it. "Beat the afternoon crush."

Vince skims a hand through his hair, slowly, *sensually* exposing the belly of his bicep and a few underarm sprigs that have escaped the sleeve of his thin white tee. *Ugh,* it truly is a sight to behold, that hair move, something every girl needs to see before she dies. It makes Vince seem so troubled, so brooding. It makes women willing to do anything to make him smile. Isn't that the secret sauce of seduction? First the snare of mystery, then the distinctly female instinct to rehabilitate.

"Stephanie," Vince says, more patiently than he would if not for Lauren and Kelly's presence, "I think you should head back now. Just quit while you're ahead."

I curl up in the armchair next to him, bringing my mug to my mouth. Panic is streaking through me—*No, no, no, don't make me go*—but I have to remain calm. "We have a scene at Jesse's today," I remind him in a forgiving tone, like it is perfectly understandable that he could have forgotten given everything else that's going on in our world.

"For Brett's bachelorette, though, and Brett left." Lauren rubs out the leftover mascara from underneath one eye. Her dark nails have chipped between last night and this morning.

"Brett *left*?" I say, with pretend surprise and genuine disappointment. The surprise is for Lauren, Vince, and Kelly's benefit. They have no idea how the night ended, of course. But the disappointment is actually real. The plan had always been for Brett to be at Jesse's house today, but, well, plans change. Successful people are the people who find a way to roll with life's inevitable setbacks.

Kelly passes me her phone. Before the sun rose, Brett had texted her, *Called a car to take me back to the city. Over this shit.* I thought I had smashed the screen of her phone hard enough to destroy it, but turns out, it was still possible to send a text. Kelly wrote back early this morning, asking if she was okay. Thus far, there has been no response.

"I feel like I saw Brett last night," Lauren says, not to us, but to herself. As though she is just remembering this herself. She visors her eyes against the sun spilling through the skylight and squints at me for a long moment. "Did you . . . were you with us?"

I arch an eyebrow at Vince as if to say—*I'm the one who needs to quit while I'm ahead?* "I think you maybe dreamt that, Laur," I say.

Lauren's gaze drifts over my shoulder. I turn to see what she's looking at: Jen, balanced on one leg with a foot tucked into her crotch. "I guess so." Thank goodness for pillheads, and their easy suggestibility.

Vince gets up abruptly and starts down the hallway, taking that Duane Reade bag with him.

"Where are you going?"

"I'm packing you up."

"Vince," I say, but he continues on his way. "Vince!" I yell, sharply, but he doesn't stop like he used to. I jump up and follow him. Chasing after my estranged husband. Not the look I was going for this morning.

Vince is tossing my products into my toiletry bag in the downstairs guest bathroom, chucking glass bottles at glass bottles, like he is trying to break them.

"Vince," I say, closing the door behind me. "*Vince.*" I put my hand on his arm. "Please listen to me for a moment."

Vince stops with an anguished cry, reaching into the Duane Reade bag and producing a Jimmy Choo shoebox. *For Gary,* I'd written in black marker across the top before leaving it on my front stoop for—plot twist!—Gary, the photographer from the *New York Times* who has been staked outside my window for the last few weeks. Not only is Gary from the most reputable publication of the lot, but he's the one who has so far displayed the highest degree of professionalism. No, he doesn't work weekends. None of them do. I'm not that big of a story. (That's about to change!) But he is always there, bright and early on Monday morning, before the rest of the pond scum trickle in for normal business hours. Monday served my purposes better, anyhow. I needed Gary to discover the package and watch the clip in question after I did what I am planning on doing today. If this got out before the brunch at Jesse's, I don't know if I'd ever be in the same room with these prostitutes again. The scene today would be canceled. What is on that tape is that much of a bombshell.

I can tell that Vince has watched the footage by the injured expression on his face. "I saw you leave on the Ring," he says, referring to the security camera we have for our front door, "and I thought I'd try to get some more clothes out of the house while you were out. But then I found this and—" His voice breaks off, emotionally. How dare he. How dare *he* be hurt by *me*.

"You were going to let this get out?" Vince continues, woefully. "You were going to let my family see that? My mom?"

I eye the hot curling iron on the sink, which I forgot to unplug last night. Bring up that red-hat-wearing bitch one more time and I'll—

"You know," he goes on, "you were not an innocent bystander in this marriage either, and I'm not going around flapping my mouth about it onstage at Talkhouse. I'm not shilling videos of your affairs to the paparazzi."

It's the most honest thing he's ever said to me. There is an honest thing to say back, in an iron, *don't fuck with me* tone, but it is not time to be honest yet. I have to say whatever it takes to get me to Jesse's house. I take a deep, fortifying sigh, steeling myself for the industrial load of bullshit about to come out of my mouth. "I know," I say, making my voice as gravelly as his. It doesn't take much. After my stage performance last night, my vocal cords are shot through. "You wouldn't do that to me." You would just fuck the one person who I thought was safe, and so I told her everything—about feeling so invisible and so unmistakable, about neurotransmitters, about how hard it was to be a daughter to my mother, about what Vince does when I'm not around and how I did it too but only to keep the deep and abiding feelings of inadequacy at bay. I showed that bitch my belly because I thought I never had to worry about losing her. I thought Vince couldn't be attracted to that and even if he was, it wouldn't matter because *she* wasn't attracted to that.

"I miss our life together," Vince whispers, wiping away a crocodile tear. He presses his back against the wall and sinks to the floor of the bathroom, hooking his arms around his shins and dropping his forehead to his knees with a contrite moan.

Well, of course you miss *our life together,* you dolt. You are a thirty-two-year-old failed actor living in a brownstone on the Upper East Side with a megababe. You hit the jackpot with me and you fucked it up something fierce.

Eyes on the prize, Steph. So I lower myself to the floor alongside Vince, slowly, as though I am settling into a hot bath. I rest my head on his shoulder, mostly so he can't see my face, which is warped with revulsion for him. "I miss our life together too." I eye the Jimmy Choo box in his lap, the GoPro still inside. How am I going to get that back from him? And who am I going to give it to now?

Vince lifts his chin, his face full of promise. "Then why are we doing this?"

I raise a hand for his benefit, *I don't know anymore.* "I was angry, Vince. My ego was bruised. I guess I was just trying to hurt you like you hurt me."

Vince reaches for my hand, stroking my palm in a gentle motion that makes me want to rip my skin right off. "Do you really want a divorce?"

I clench my toes and grit my teeth. "I want to make it right. All of it. Us. The book. The show. That's why I came out here. This scene at Jesse's—it's my last chance to redeem myself. I have to go. And you should come too. We can tell everyone we're calling it off. We're going to stay together. Prove to everyone that we are stronger than the show."

Vince hooks a finger beneath my chin, the way I did to what's his name from last night. I learned that move from Vince, come to think of it. How sweet. "I would like that," he says, right before he leans in and brushes his lips against mine, teasingly, as though to say—this is what you've been missing. My hangover makes itself fully known.

And then—like a very good gold digger, using sex to get what she wants—I do my husband on the bathroom floor, one last time. As I dutifully hump that little jalapeño pepper, I say a prayer that what's his name gave me crabs, or something really nasty, like syphilis. Not that Vince would have long to suffer.

—

There is a funny standoff in the driveway. Jen is adamant that we not take her car to Jesse's, and I am absolutely adamant that we do. Kelly's car is a hunk of junk, and not in the intentional, nineties army green Defender way, the car Jesse bought off eBay and drives out here, her dyke hair not blowing in the wind. I need Jen's emissions-free douche-mobile that goes from zero to sixty in four point two seconds, that starts without having to press a button or put a key into the ignition, but when Vince approaches the passenger-side door, Jen makes a lame excuse.

"It's just." Jen falls silent a moment. "I feel a little dizzy today. From the heat. I really don't feel up to driving." She clamps a hand to her forehead, overselling it.

"I'll drive," I volunteer, impatiently. While I was "showering," I shared the GoPro footage to the app on my phone, then I hid the GoPro in the back of a closet in the guest room. A tasty treat for Jen to find one day! I smell like a party bus after the party and two different men's loads. Not the aromatic memory I'd like to leave behind, but I couldn't risk taking the camera with me and having Vince discover it on my person. He hasn't been able to keep his hands off me since we consummated our "reconciliation."

"It handles differently than what you're used to," Jen says to me. "We should really take Kelly's car."

"Ummm." Kelly laughs. "I don't think we want to do that. My car doesn't have AC."

"I'd rather go in Kelly's car too," Lauren says, slowly, staggering into the shade of a tree. The sunlight is relentless this morning, as if furious about its captivity yesterday. I say a little prayer it doesn't blind the shot. That would be the real tragedy.

Vince leans onto the hood of Jen's car, resting his palms on the curve of the trunk. "You look like you could use some AC," he tells Lauren with a wry, empathetic smile, assuming she's hurting from the night before. But I've seen Lauren hungover before, and this isn't Lauren hungover. On another day, I'd think harder about why it is she's acting so weird.

Lauren is wearing tiny round sunglasses, pushed low on the bridge of her nose, full-throttle nineties nostalgia. Above the thin wire rim of her shades, she stares at Vince's hands on the trunk of Jen's car, her lips parted in confusion. "I don't want to take Jen's car," she says, again sounding as though she's speaking to work out something for herself more than to any of us.

I toss up my hands—*Fine, I can make this work even in Kelly's car*—and lead the charge, planting myself in the middle so as to avoid another tantrum from someone whose legs are too long or whose ego is too inflated to sit in the bitch seat. Lauren gets in to my right and Vince to my left, grumbling, *This makes no sense.* Jen takes the front-passenger seat next to Kelly. The car smells like chewy, fruit-flavored candy. I look up to see a Strawberries & Crème air freshener dangling from Kelly's rearview mirror. But of course.

Kelly sticks the key in the ignition and turns. The engine bears down, wheezing, *trying,* before giving up with a woman's cry. Kelly drapes her arm around the back of Jen's chair and regards us over the brim of her neon blue sunglasses, the kind that everyone was wearing last summer. "Well," she says solemnly, "she lived a good life."

If that's not God telling me to go for it, it's Lucifer.

I could cartwheel to Jen's car. But just as I'm about to climb into the back, I notice that Jen has stopped in the driveway. She's examining her hand, holding it up to the sunlight. Something is caught in her Standing Sisters ring. A hair, it looks like, from the way she pinches it between her fingers and pulls—and pulls—flicking her index finger on her thumb, making that panicked face all women make when they find a bug crawling on them and they need to get it off but they don't want to touch it. She watches the hair float slowly to the ground, her eyelids fluttering, woozily. She stumbles, leaning into the side of the house, swaying a little, then spins and vomits all over the base of the Japanese maple Yvette planted in memory of her late mother. Some of it even gets on the bronze plaque Yvette had made: *For Betty "Battle Axe" Greenberg, who would rather die than rest in peace.*

"Jen! Oh my God!" Kelly cries, rushing to her aid. Is Kelly the new Lauren? "Are you okay?"

Jen straightens enough to wave a hand over her shoulder—*shoo, Kelly*—before lurching over and retching again. Vince, concerned for the well-being of others as always, turns away, his face crinkling in disgust, like he might be next. For some strange reason, Lauren's eyes fill with tears, though I doubt even she understands why.

I watch Jen's bony back expand and contract, expand and contract, as her equilibrium returns to her. She stands, wiping the side of her hand across her mouth. Is she hungover? Is she sick? Is it contagious? I have that visceral, germaphobe *stay away from me* reaction, before remembering with a dry chuckle to myself—*Someone could stick me with an AIDS-coated needle right now and it wouldn't matter.*

"Jen," Kelly says, as Jen heads for her car, "maybe you should stay home and—"

"I feel better now actually," she says.

"At least let someone else drive if you aren't—"

"I feel better now!" she cries, sounding fully hysterical as she climbs behind the wheel of the car and slams her door shut. This group is made up exclusively of whack jobs, but the Green Menace has always been the wackiest.

I've been to Jesse's house only once before, as a guest of Brett's, who is such a regular you could pick out her preferred lounge chair. Hint: It's the one with the slightly sunken middle. We drank Casamigos by the pool (I got Jesse's hydrangeas very drunk) and ate swordfish prepared for us on the grill by Hank, who Jesse refers to as her friend but everyone knows is her Jeeves. The Montauk community was sure Jesse Barnes would demolish the original Techbuilt home when she bought it in 2008, but she ingratiated herself when all she did was remodel the kitchen and add a pool.

We park in the dirt driveway, next to the white crew van and Jesse's vintage Land Rover. Jen's Tesla looks downright villainous on the humble property, the car of a collector come in from Gotham to repossess the land from farmer Ted, blithely unaware he's sitting on a multimillion-dollar lot. Thanks to the *New York Post*'s steadfast reporting, I know that a rolling meadow used to separate the end of the drive from the seventy-foot drop to the sea, but that the bluffs have eroded, little by little some years, in honking wet chunks during others. Jesse has had to file an emergency application with the East Hampton Planning Department to have the home moved one hundred feet back from the abyss. Lucky for me it has yet to be granted.

The crew has moved the picnic table from the shallow end of the pool to the deep, in an attempt to game the sun's position and mitigate the glare off the water. Marc is covering all of the cameras with beach blankets, keeping them out of direct sunlight so that they're not too hot to handle. The PAs are setting the table with platters of food and Lisa is halfway through uncorking a dozen wine bottles so that we do not lose a moment to our drinking, which is a production trick to keep the cast from realizing they've had too much. The act of stopping to open a new bottle can make you take stock—How many have I had? Might be smart to drink a glass of water. Anything smart is bad, when it comes to production purposes.

Jesse does her part by reading *A Little Life* beneath an SPF-coated umbrella—clearly, she has been expecting me. It's a dexterous insult, I'll give her that. The same month *The New Yorker* called out the *subversive brilliance* of Hanya Yanagihara's novel, *Kirkus* likened the third book in my fiction series to a *Lifetime movie-of-the-week, right down to the contrived dialogue.*

Jesse notices us and bends the page. Her Bettie Page paleness and black jeans swan in the face of the beach babe aesthetic that rules out here, and I think we are all grateful for it. Imagining Jesse in a swimsuit is like imagining your parents having sex. Her bare feet are embarrassing enough.

She walks over to meet us, removing her sunglasses in a way that implies I should do the same, so that we can have a proper gal-to-gal chat. I leave my big black Pradas right where they are.

"I don't know what you hoped to accomplish by coming here," Jesse says.

Lisa sets down the wine opener and joins Jesse at her side, a punky *yeah, what she said* expression on her thin, jowly face. All that weight loss only to look ten years saggier in her eHarmony profile picture. Being a woman is like the lottery. Yes, some sad sack is destined to win it, but the odds are very against that sad sack being you. No matter, most of us will continue to try, and most of us will continue to hear someone else's number called, year after year.

"You know you can't be here," Jesse says to me. "We were willing to let you try it last night but you've proven yourself to be untrustworthy and honestly, Steph? A little bit unstable. I hope you are getting the support you need for your mental health."

From the person who has stomped all over my mental health in steel-toed Dr. Martens. How does she not *hear* herself?

Vince slips his hand into mine in an act of courageous spousal support. Even his hand feels like it's been in another woman's hand. I turn to him with a brave smile, though I can feel my contempt for him in my fingernails. "Vince?" I ask in a tiny brave voice. "Will you just give me a moment to speak to Jesse and Lisa in private?"

He doesn't let go.

"I need to do this on my own. Please." I give his hand a measured squeeze, stifling the urge to bend his fingers back until they snap.

Vince sizes up Jesse and Lisa like schoolyard bullies, with a look that says if they try anything, he will be *right over there*. He lets go of my hand and wanders off. Dumb fuck. Pretty fuck. But so, *so* dumb.

"I'm just asking for an opportunity to take ownership of what I did," I appeal to them when it is just the three of us. "Please. Brett's not here so I can tell you everything that really happened. Do you want to hear about that or do you want to hear whatever vanilla lie Kelly has come up with to protect her sister?"

I know Jesse has heard the whisperings—insulting, frankly—that my fight with Brett was really about the affair we had while she lived with me. Ha. Maybe if she lost thirty pounds. Didn't seem to bother Vince.

Jesse stares me down, torn. She doesn't want to see Brett hurt, but she also wants her money shot for the season. She turns to Lisa to recruit her ever-valuable second opinion.

"It could be a powerful moment," Lisa says, to the complete surprise of nobody. Nothing would make Lisa happier than seeing me lay bare Brett's lies on camera. She will be thrilled, then, to learn that Brett's lie is so much worse than what she thinks it is. *Just hand over my mic pack*, I think, *and everyone gets hurt.*

Jesse sighs. Her decision is obvious, but she has to act a little bit pained so as not to look like a total turncoat to her very best vagina. She nods at Vince, over my shoulder. "And what is he doing here?"

"I thought we might address the rumors about him and Kelly," I say. "That could be a powerful moment too, right?"

Lisa snorts, genuinely tickled. "Someone found her ballsack."

Jesse returns her sunglasses to her face so that I can't witness the childlike excitement in her eyes. Christmas morning has come early for Jesse Barnes. "Let's just do it. We're here. Why not? We don't have to use it if it doesn't work."

As the kids are saying these days—*yas, queen.*

Everything settled, we wait by the car until Lisa gives us the cue to approach and greet Jesse.

"Oh, Jen!" I smack my idiot head. "Pass me the keys. I left my lip gloss in the cup holder."

"Your lips look—"

"Pass me the fucking keys, Greenberg!"

Jen does so, begrudgingly, and I dive back into the car, climbing around on all fours and reaching under the seats in a one-woman search party for an unmissing tube of Rouge Pur Couture. I time it perfectly, waiting for Lisa to give us the go-ahead before I shut the door, so that Jen loses her opportunity to ask for her keys back. I am wearing a darling, tropical-printed Mara Hoffman wrap dress with deep pockets—I bought it for today, figuring pockets always come in handy—and I slip the keys inside. So far, everything is going off without a hitch. I do wish Brett could have been here, but just because things don't go according to plan doesn't mean they can't work out for the best. *Done is better than perfect* is something my editor used to say to me when I needed more time with my manuscript but she wanted it *now*, so she could publish it *now*, so that she could make money *now*. Apparently, it's a Sheryl Sandberg quote.

Jesse greets Jen first with a hug, commenting on how clammy her skin feels. *Are you feeling okay?* she asks her. Jen mumbles something about just needing to get in the shade.

Jesse doesn't go on to hug everyone, but she makes contact in some form. Kelly gets a pat on the tush—groping your underlings is edgy when the groper is a woman!—and Lauren an arm around her shoulder while Jesse whispers something into her ear, probably about her not even noticing she burned off the back of her head because Lauren's hand flies to her choppy ponytail. Vince and I are the only ones who don't get any Jesse DNA on us, and I'm glad for it. Turn me away from the lunch table where the cheerleaders and football players feast. Sign your own death sentence.

"Where's our girl?" Jesse asks. She's thought for hours that "our girl" "went back to the city," but we have to have the conversation on camera for the viewer. That's one thing I won't miss, having conversations two, three, sometimes four times. Each take was a turn in a maze, leading me further away from myself.

"Brett had some work to take care of back in the city," Kelly says, making a beeline for the seat next to Jesse on the white picnic bench. The table has been set with natural cut wildflowers and purposefully wrinkled linens. On top of a mound of fresh-caught shrimp, a black fly sits like a king. Jen stares at him, turning green.

"*Work*?" Jesse is incensed. "I thought this was her bachelorette party. What happened?" She begins to pour wine for everyone, though she is drinking Casamigos on ice. For a long time, I assumed Casamigos was an actual spirit. Having taken a newfound interest in the drink, I've recently learned that Casamigos is tequila and that it is George Clooney's.

I shove my glass in Jesse's path. "I'd rather have what you're having," I tell her, and she sets the wine bottle down and obligingly starts me on my way to tequila-wasted while Kelly chews the inside corner of her mouth, undoubtedly sorting out her story for Jesse. For all Kelly knows, Brett *went back to the city* because the two of them nearly came to blows last night. She knows nothing of the blood shed on the floor of Lindy's van.

"It's such a bummer," Kelly says, "but our manager at the Flatiron studio had a family emergency and so Brett went back to fill in for her today."

Jesse peers at Kelly over the brim of her sunglasses, skeptically. "Why wouldn't you have gone? It was supposed to be her weekend." She serves me with a look that encourages me to jump in at any time.

I pull back my shoulders and run my tongue over my teeth to be sure I don't have any gloss on them. My financials are in order, all my money going somewhere that gave me a good, wicked giggle. I wanted to make sure Vince didn't see a cent, having no idea at the time that he would be able to join us here today. And though I haven't showered or had a pass by the glam squad's hand, I wrangled my hair into a pretty braid just before we left. I'm wearing my new dress and I will never be more ready than this. "Kelly doesn't think Brett should marry Arch and they had a fight about it," I say. On the other side of the table, Kelly bores a hole between my eyes, furious.

Jesse swivels her head in Kelly's direction, pretending to be surprised by this information. "How could you not want Brett to marry Arch? Arch is bae goals!" *Ugh*—bae goals? Tell your twenty-two-year-old assistant to update your cheat sheet of hip young-people sayings, because no one under the age of thirty is saying "bae" anymore, you dumb pterodactyl.

Kelly uses her napkin to dab at a bead of sweat above her lip. "I think the world of Arch. Arch and I have a special connection," she adds, defensively, in the manner of a raving racist telling you about her many black friends. "I just think that Brett is still young, and that there is no harm in taking a step back and making sure she's ready for a commitment like marriage."

I sneak a glance at Vince. His Adam's apple is moving like a Boomerang video. He knows Kelly's reservation has nothing to do with Brett being *too young*. She is twenty-seven years old. Can we stop talking about her like she's some sort of child bride? "Vince?" I say. "You and Brett had *a special connection*. And I always love to hear a guy's take on the silly matters of the heart. What say you? Should Brett marry Arch?" I smile at him, goadingly, showing as many of my movie star teeth as I can.

Vince turns to me in slow motion, seeming, finally, to catch on to what is happening. This is a setup. I came here to shred him. "I like Brett," he says, woodenly. "But I really don't know her well enough to say, babe."

"We should text her," I suggest, fairly. "Give her a chance to weigh in. We're sitting around, talking smack about her relationship—are people still saying 'smack,' Jesse? I know you're super jiggy with it." I reach into my pocket and remove my phone, tapping the green messages icon with my thumb and sending a text to someone, though that someone is not Brett.

Almost immediately, Jesse sits up straighter. The zapped posture of a person whose phone has just mildly electrocuted her left ass cheek.

"You should really get that," I tell her, in an undertone. I've always wanted to say that! *You should really get that,* like a murderer at the end of a genre novel, right before he confesses to his crimes in Scooby-Doo detail. *He.* Gosh, how sexist of me to assume that only men can be murderers.

Jesse keeps her eyes on me as she removes her phone from her back pocket and opens the text message. "It's from you," she says, unsmiling, but I can tell by the way her finger moves on the screen that she's opened the file I've shared with her, and that she is now watching the GoPro footage I clipped last fall, right before I asked Brett to move out for good.

I thought I had a rat. I would walk into my pantry to find that bags of flour and brown sugar and hot chocolate packets had been tampered with, walk out leaving a trail of powdery footsteps. I had a GoPro that I had forgotten to return to prod last season, and so I set it on the low-light feature and positioned it on a top shelf, turned toward the pantry door, to see for myself. No sense vacating my apartment to have it fumigated if I didn't have to.

The camera captured a little over three hours of footage before it ran out of space, and so the next day, I dragged my thumb along the slider at the bottom of the screen, keeping an eye out for any small moving shadows hurtling along the foot of the frame.

At the two hour and thirteen minute mark I removed my thumb. There was something, but it wasn't a filthy, disease-ridden rodent. (Well . . .) It was Brett, slinking into the pantry, poking around, sticking her fingers into the bags of flour and sugar, *licking* them clean and crudely shoving them right back in. *What is she doing?* I wondered at first. But then I remembered something I learned at a live taping for a self-care podcast that Brett loved and dragged me to back when we were friends. Self-care—what will well-to-do white women come up with next?

At this taping, I learned that binge eating is a natural reaction to deprivation, and that children whose parents put them on diets and banned sweets from the house sometimes resorted to assembling strange pastes made of raw sugar and flour just to get their fix. It's a coping mechanism that can follow them into adulthood. Vince and I never really kept sweets in the house. They left a burning sensation on my tongue because of my medication, and Vince was always more of a savory guy (is! I'm getting ahead of myself). *That must be what Brett is doing,* I realized, watching her scavenge, feeling a blooming sense of compassion remembering what Brett told me about her childhood. How everyone in the family ate a normal-sized dinner off a dinner-sized plate except Brett, who was given a weighed and calorie-totaled portion on a tea saucer. How her mother kept the cookies in a padlocked cabinet and only Kelly was given the code, because she could stop herself at just one or two. And then a second shadow appeared in the doorway and my compassion went up in a combust of flame and fury. I didn't have a rat. I had two.

"Who else has seen this?" Kelly asks me, quietly, with a single pulse of the green vein in her temple. She's just watched the clip in question over Jesse's shoulder.

"What is it?" Lauren asks, weakly, from the far end of the table, like she actually doesn't want to know.

"Why would you humiliate yourself like this, Steph?" Vince whispers next to me.

"People, people!" I admonish, cheerfully. "One at a time with the questions. Let's start with you first, love of my life and light of my loins." I turn to Vince. "I am doing this for equity's sake. Either we are all punished for aggrandizing our backstories or none of us are. No exceptions. Brett does not get to be spared by virtue of the effect she has on Jesse's granny panties."

I face Kelly. "Next! Who else has seen this? I am happy to report, Kelly Courtney, that you are the first. It's an exclusive! A scoop! A breaking-news bulletin interrupting our regularly scheduled programming!"

I lean around Vince to address Lauren's question last: *What is it?* "It's a homemade movie of Brett getting—"

"I don't want to hear another word about this," Jesse says, severely.

It is quiet. Not silent. Not with the rowdy ocean so close below, exchanging shorelines with Nantucket, ninety-eight nautical miles away. It's so much more than a view. It's the sound of power, always in your ears. That's why Jesse spends all her time at this place.

Jesse. The garden-fresh betrayal that first appeared on her face as she watched the video of Brett getting drilled by my husband from behind is already receding, creating an illusion of composure. For a moment there, I actually felt bad for her, this middle-aged woman fleeced by her proudest protégée, like some blue-haired grandma in a nursing home wiring the entirety of her life savings to help a "relative in distress" in Guam. Jesse Barnes has been elder abused.

"*Brett,*" Vince sneers, defying Jesse's mandate. "Brett is a fucking bitch and a fucking fat liar." Cleverness tends to deteriorate the closer you get to the truth—not that Vince ever knew how to turn a phrase.

"Not in my house," Jesse says, because she can't permit a man to call a woman fat in her presence, even if she is a fucking bitch and a fucking fat liar.

Vince grips my thigh under the table. "She wanted you to leave me," he tells me desperately. "She hated that you had somebody and she didn't. She was always threatened by me."

I laugh. A cold, annihilating laugh that sends Vince's hand slithering back between his thighs to check to make sure it's still there. "Take a look around this table, Vince. You are not a threat. You are a *drain on our resources*. Your day has dawned. We should preserve your body and mount you in the Museum of Natural History. Unimpeachable Men: The Dinosaurs Among Us."

Vince's breath shortens and quickens, audible only on the exhale, like being ceremoniously emasculated in front of a group of millionairesses is a cardiac event. Fun fact: Spell check red-flags the word "millionairesses," but not "millionaires." There is no entry for "millionairesses" in the dictionary, which beautifully illustrates my point—the world will only permit one of us to make it. Is it any surprise then that women continue to be so horrible to each other? Supporting your kind is supporting your own fucking mediocrity. It's *unnatural.*

Jesse slaps the table to get my attention, with a gentle but commanding thump. "Stephanie," she says. My full name—*uh-oh,* Mom is mad. "You have been through a lot over the last few weeks and I am not unsympathetic to that. But I won't sit here and listen to you drag Brett through the mud with lies and defamation when she isn't around to defend herself and offer her side of the story."

"When she isn't around . . ." I trail off in befuddled helplessness. A story ceases to have "sides" when there is empirical proof of my husband screwing my best friend in my pantry, on my Scalamandre Le Tigre sofa, on my beloved, creaky stairs. You better believe I moved that camera around for the next couple of nights so that I did not have to hear that it was "just a one-time thing" should I ever confront Brett or Vince with what I saw. I don't know when it started, but I know how. They must have met one of the nights Brett snuck downstairs to stuff her face. How did it start? Did Brett find Vince aglow by the light of a *Narcos* episode, halfway through an auction-house bottle of Brunello? Did he offer her a glass? Did he sigh sadly and say a distance had grown between us? Did he tell her he wished I could see the good in him, that way she could? Did he laugh and joke, *If only you played for my team, Courtney?* Did *Brett* kiss *him*? Did she think it wouldn't hurt me, did she think I didn't love him, did she even think? Did she tell Vince she wasn't gay, or did she let him believe she was straight only for him? That there was something different about him, something special. Brett always did know how to make ordinary people feel special.

I couldn't bring myself to confront either one of them. Going into the fourth season, I was still determined to hold my marriage together. But once Brett found out I had waged a cold war against her, she must have put two and two together and gotten *Steph knows I rode Vince like a SPOKE bike around the first floor of her house and she's trying to destroy me.* And still, she didn't apologize. Still, she chose to save her own skin over showing an ounce of humiliation or remorse. I do not blame her, but I do hate her.

"We are done here." Jesse speaks directly to the lens, in effect speaking directly to Marc. "Shut the cameras off." Marc removes the F55 from his shoulder, slowly, as though setting down a weapon. The assistant cameraman follows suit.

I want to laugh. I want to cry. Why didn't I control for this? That Jesse wouldn't do a thing about this? I thought the commander in chief of the queer world would tear into Brett for appropriating her community. I thought the same punitive action that has been taken against me would be taken against her. In all my reveries, I never considered that it would behoove Jesse to protect Brett, not for Brett's sake, but for her own. If it comes out that Brett conned Jesse so close on the heels of me conning her, Jesse is just another example of why men make better bosses.

The relief that relaxes Kelly's face would be enough to send me over the edge if I hadn't already taken the plunge. She gets what Jesse is doing. She knows Brett's secret will stay a secret. With cloying sympathy, she adds, "I know you have been under an inordinate amount of pressure since we got back from Morocco. With what happened"—she clears her throat cryptically—"there. But it was not your fault. We don't blame you and we just want to see you get the help you need."

The help I need? Oh, honey-bunny. Just like your leaky, weak-walled post-baby vagina, only surgical repair could restore me now.

"There should be an age requirement to ride those things," I say to Kelly.

"But," Jesse looks around the table, to confirm that everyone has heard what she has heard and that it doesn't make any sense, "Kweller wasn't riding."

"No, I mean like for adults. *Seniors.* Spatial awareness declines sharply after age thirty-four, or so I've heard."

"I'm sorry," Jesse sighs, "but you've lost me."

"There has never been a woman past the age of thirty-four on the show," I say.

"Whoa," Lauren breathes, her brow furrowed, taking inventory of our fallen soldiers, realizing I'm right. Jen raises a glass of water to her lips, taking a trembling sip. She has not said a word or even made a facial expression since we sat down, just sat there like a pasty statue. I had almost forgotten she was here.

Jesse fans her face. "Everyone is overheated and exhausted, Stephanie. Jen is clearly not feeling well and we should get her into the air-conditioning. We came out here and we did this for nothing.

Just let it go. Go home. Get some rest. There will be a new chapter for you, but not until you take the time to step away and reflect."

I am not going home, getting some rest, and *reflecting*. I am never going home again. I lean across the table, serving myself some salad from the large ceramic mixing bowl. These hypocrites have worked up my appetite. "Why has there never been a woman past the age of thirty-four on the show?" I persist.

Jesse turns her hands palms side up, as though I must be kidding her. "I guess not then. Sorry, ladies—and, well, I was going to say gentleman, but I'll just say Vince instead—that Stephanie is dead set on making your Sunday so unpleasant." Jesse focuses in on me, her tone that of a reasonable person tasked with subduing a madwoman. "The reason," she continues, "that there has never been a woman on the show past the age of thirty-four is because it's a show about female millennials who have accomplished amazing things without the financial support of a man."

"Thirty-four-year-olds *are* millennials." I smack her down. "In another year, thirty-five-year-olds will be millennials, and a year after that, thirty-six-year-olds will be and on and on and on. A generation's ages are fluid, not stagnant." I dazzle her with a smile. "Try again."

Jesse decides to antagonize me further by matching my smile. "Forgive me. I misspoke. It's a show about young women who have accomplished amazing things without the financial support of a man. Is that more to your liking?"

"It is extremely to my liking." I spear my bed of lettuce with my fork. The leaves are fluffy in texture, young green in shade. Rich-people-who-mistreat-their-staff lettuce. "Closer to what I'm getting at. So after thirty-four, you're no longer young?"

Jesse tilts her head at me, pityingly. "No, you're not. I'm sorry if that's a reality that scares you, but that says more about you than it does about me. I'm forty-six years old and I'm proud of my age." *Oh yeah, you celebrate it now that the cameras are off.* "I'm proud to provide young women with a platform so that they too can find themselves where I find myself today. You should move into the next bracket with grace and pride. You should pass the torch *generously*."

"I'm not passing anyone anything from where I stand today. I'm a fucking leper. No one would take anything that's been touched by me."

"I'm sorry," Jesse says, and it only sounds like she means it. "But those are the consequences of your actions. Woman-up and deal with it."

Oh, she wants me to *woman-up* and deal with it, does she? I spear a shrimp and jam the whole thing into my mouth, tail and all, feeling like Daryl Hannah in *Splash*. My fly friend does not scare off, only does a two-footed hop onto a lower tier of shrimp and rubs his fly-paws faster. I take this for anticipatory support: He can't wait for me to *woman-up*. "And what about the consequences of *your* actions?" I snarl, spewing a pink shard of shrimp shell onto the table. Jen covers her mouth with a silent gag. "You sold us on a show about sisterhood, and then you flipped the script, but *only on us*. Everywhere else, you continue to pat yourself on the back for lifting women up. I cannot read one more breathless fucking profile about you and your commitment to empowering women in the *New York Times*. I cannot listen to one more viral fucking Ivy League commencement speech where you implore twenty-two-year-olds to negotiate their salary like a man, to wear the label *Difficult* with pride. *To get that money, girl.*" I snap my fingers in the way we've come to expect sassy black women to do. "Everyone sitting at this table knows the truth. You are manning the fucking Zamboni so that we can body slam one another on clean ice. Girl fight! Reconcile. Girl fight! Reconcile. Those are our marching orders, and you get richer and more self-righteous while we get bloodier and older. And then, when we have the *audacity* to follow your own Pollyanna advice and ask to be paid more than forty-one dollars and sixty-six cents a day, you cut us loose and blacklist us from the Cool Feminists Club. This show is not a platform. It's a mass gravesite for thirty-four-year-old *difficult* women."

I get up and head for Jen's car with gamey underarms and clear eyes. I wish the cameras had captured my speech—I've been working on it for weeks—but I did the best I could do with what I had to work with, and for once, my best will have to be good enough.

I practiced this next part in my head, hundreds of times since I hatched my exit plan. Only I didn't control for another factor, which was the jughead I married. I didn't control for him being there, chasing after me, probably thinking I am about to drive straight to the *New York Times* offices and shove the video under Gary the Photographer's nose myself. He grabs my arm, spinning me around, pinning me to his chest and trying to shove his hands into my pockets, grabbing for my phone. People are shouting behind us, screaming at Vince to *let me go*. Stupid gashes. They should be begging Vince to restrain me. I sink my teeth into his wrist and keep sinking until I feel the skin give way with a satisfying snap. Vince yowls like a cat with his tail caught in the door, his grip on me loosening enough that I am able to worm out of his grasp.

I throw myself behind the wheel of Jen's Tesla. Did it lock? I didn't hear it lock. In the second and a half it takes for me to wonder this, Vince has the passenger-side door open. Goddamn you, Elon Musk. I try to accelerate before Vince can dive inside, but he manages to throw his body lengthwise across the front seats, his elbows in my lap, his head between my chest and the steering wheel. The passenger-side door flaps like one good wing as I gun it for the picnic table, for the whole vomitous, infected girl squad, though it's Jesse Barnes, patient zero, I'd most like to leave a pink smear on her eroding lawn.

"You're fucking crazy!" Vince shrieks, and he seizes the wheel, his hands over mine, forcing me to turn, turn, turn—fuck, fuck, fuck—away from my squealing, scattering targets. He can control our direction but not our speed, so time for Plan D, E, F . . . ? I've lost count at this point. I pulverize the gas pedal, Vince unwittingly aiming us for the edge, for the peacocking sea. It wasn't how I wanted it—I wanted an unholy slaughter—but as the wheels run out of ground I remind myself *done is better than perfect. Done is better than perfect. Done is better than . . .*

PART IV

Post • August–November 2017

CHAPTER 21

Kelly
Present Day

The officer is my age, but he occasionally calls me *ma'am*. His wedding band is black silicone, the kind you wear to the gym or the beach, to protect your real ring from sweat and sand. He's in good shape and he smells a little. I decide I have interrupted his Sunday afternoon run on the beach. Well. Stephanie did.

"What did Stephanie and Vince argue about at the table?"

"Um," I say, slipping my hands under my thighs. I've mentioned that I have a daughter, and I don't want him to see my unadorned finger and know I'm not married. I need to be regarded as an upstanding and dependable member of the community, and people have their notions about unwed mothers. Not that I've had much free time over the years to worry about how it looks that I have a child but not a husband. It was what it was, until the show came along and made single motherhood this very deliberate and punk-rock choice. The show. Will it survive this? Do I want it to survive this? *Yes, desperately,* I realize, the thought producing an echo of shame.

"Everyone knew that Vince wasn't faithful to Steph," I say, my posture attentive and ladylike, the posture of a woman you would be inclined to believe. "And I think Steph always knew but looked the other way until recently, when she just decided she had had enough."

"Had something happened recently to set her off?"

Yes, Officer, but you can't prove it given the fact that Jesse's phone conveniently ended up at the bottom of the pool in the mad dash to get out of Stephanie's path. *We are the only ones who watched it,* Jesse said to me, quietly, while the rest of the crew and cast huddled together in mini support groups, comforting each other and waiting for the ambulances and the Coast Guard to arrive. *A man attacked a woman and she drove into the ocean trying to escape him!* Jesse told the emergency dispatcher, after dialing 911 from my phone. It was one way of looking at it, but it seemed rash to write history with one person's clearly biased interpretation. I was still bouncing all the possible scenarios around in my head, trying to decide what *I* thought had happened. Was Stephanie just trying to get away from all of us and she became disoriented in the struggle? Was she intending to kill herself in a blaze of glory and Vince just happened to get in the way? Or, I considered with a shudder, had she come here with the intent to take all of us with her?

I couldn't look. I stayed back, with Jesse. Lauren and Jen had wandered over to the edge of the property, along with a few members of the crew. Lauren had dropped to her knees with a wail when she saw the wreckage. Jen had actually *shushed* her. Marc was the one to go and comfort Lauren, moaning in agony himself, which, shell-shocked as I was, seemed strange. He hadn't been particularly close to Stephanie or Vince, who I had no doubt were dead, shark food along with Stephanie's phone, with the GoPro app that contained evidence of Brett's affair with Vince. *Do you want people to know that Brett isn't gay?* Jesse asked, privately on her lawn, and I shook my head, speechless, in shock. I knew Stephanie was unraveling, I didn't realize she had come so perilously undone. *So just say it was a tape of the two of them having an affair if it comes up,* Jesse said. I looked at her sharply. *A tape of Brett and Stephanie having an affair,* she clarified, though I had understood. *I cut Stephanie off before she could say what was on the tape. It's not on camera. Don't you think Brett would rather have people think she had an affair with Stephanie than with Vince? She would have been single when it happened. Technically, she did nothing wrong. No! Don't text her!* Jesse snatched my phone out of my hand. *Nothing in writing. They might subpoena your phone.* So I called Brett instead. Going on thirty times now and she still hasn't picked up. She's pissed at me. This is payback for the way I toyed with her during the Mrs. game.

I do not know if I will be able to tell a bald-faced lie to a police officer, and I'm praying he does not specifically ask if Brett was having an affair with anyone. "Stephanie was definitely reeling from what had happened with her book," I say vaguely, in answer to his question.

The officer screws up his face. "Her book? She wrote a book?"

"She's Stephanie Simmons," I say, but he shows no sense of recognition. "She's a very successful author." I sit up straighter, taking umbrage on Stephanie's behalf. *She's dead. She was maybe trying to kill you. She maybe tried to kill Layla in Morocco!*

"She wrote a memoir about her childhood," I continue. "Recently. It was a bestseller. People loved it. But then it came out just a few weeks ago that she lied about a lot of her life. She lost everything—her publisher, her fans, Vince."

"Vince left her?"

Again, the ludicrous urge to defend Stephanie's honor. "*She* left *him*. She kicked him out. She was serving him divorce papers, last I heard."

The officer writes something down. He hasn't written anything down since he brought me in here, just relied on the recorder. "Did your sister come up in the argument at all?"

My throat constricts. *We can pull this off,* Jesse had said, as the sirens neared and I started to waver. *I know the police chief. I will make sure you and Brett are protected.* "My sister did come up," I say, delicately. "Vince made the comment that Brett was threatened by him. That she was jealous Stephanie had someone in her life, and that she wanted Stephanie to be alone just like her."

"Wasn't your sister engaged, though?"

"She's engaged now. But he was talking about before, when she was—" I stop, abruptly. *Wasn't your sister engaged, though?* Why is he speaking about my sister in the past tense?

"Do you think you could check again?" I ask him. "On Brett? I've been trying to get through to her, but I'm wondering if maybe I just have bad service in here. I really want her to hear about this from us, not the news. Do you know if it's made the news?" I swipe left to check my Apple-curated Top Stories for the umpteenth time but it's exclusively headlines about Hurricane Harvey. I make a mental note to talk to Brett about doing a ride to raise money for Houston when we get home.

The officer clears his throat with a fist at his lips. "As soon as we are finished here I will check." His thumb twiddles his silicone wedding band. "Tell me how Stephanie and Vince ended up in Jennifer Greenberg's vehicle."

I nod, cooperatively. Of course. Of course he has to ask this question. "Stephanie was sort of disgusted by the conversation and the way he was speaking about my sister. He called her fat too, which, you just don't do that—*ever*—but particularly in front of a table full of women. She just wanted to get away from him. I don't think she was thinking clearly. She got up from the table and he followed her. He put his hands on her."

"So it got physical?"

I nod, emphatically, relieved I don't have to lie about this.

"Did anyone try to stop it?"

"Of course we tried to stop him!" *Him*, not *it*. Why are men so obtuse when it comes to the violence they inflict against women? "We yelled at him to let her go, and we all started to get up, and so he did. Let go, that is. And when he did that, she ran for the car, and he ran after her and he, like, threw himself into the passenger seat." I demonstrate with flying Superman arms. "Like that. Stomach down, stretched out across both seats. And Stephanie started driving. His door was still open, and I think she thought she could maybe, like, throw him out of the car. But he had his hands on the wheel." I demonstrate again. "And they were driving right at us. It looked like they were fighting for control of the wheel."

"She could have braked," the officer says.

She could have braked. She could have not worn such a short skirt. She could have not gone up to his room. She could have not laughed at him and made him feel small. There is a blitheness to the statement, a maleness to it that sets me straight. My voice is different when I speak again. It is resolved. "She was terrified. You don't think or act rationally when you're in fear for your life. I think she thought he was trying to kill her." *Did she think that? Does it matter?* "I think she was trying to turn the wheel away from us, to spare us." There is such a gap between how much I want this to be true and how untrue it is that my voice catches. A memory of Layla surfaces then. Three or four. We were waiting to be seen by a Genius at the Apple store. I had booked an appointment but they were running behind, and we were going to be late for a checkup at the doctor's and then a playdate after that. I was grumbling and huffing, griping with the other customers whose reservations hadn't been honored either, my stress palpable. I had given my purse to Layla to occupy her—one of her favorite pastimes was sorting through its contents—and from her perch on the floor, my wallet and keys and loose change and lip gloss and sunglasses and dry-cleaning tickets scattered around her, she said something so quietly I had to ask her to repeat it.

"Layla, speak up," I'd snapped.

"I'm happy," she said, only a little bit louder. The girl next to me, older than me but still young, gasped and squeezed her boyfriend's hand.

"It's the little things in life," he laughed.

Would the little things in life ever bring Layla joy again had Stephanie not turned the wheel?

The door opens and another officer asks for a word. My guy stands, his chair rolling back. "Can I get you anything? More water?"

"Please," I manage, remembering how small Layla's voice was that day. *I'm happy.* "And you're going to ask if anyone's heard from my sister?"

"Hang tight," he says, closing the door.

While I wait, I check to see if Brett has responded to my anthology of abusive texts. *Nothing in writing,* Jesse had said, but when phone call after phone call went unanswered I resorted to a verbal thrashing. Even if they do subpoena my phone, there is nothing implicative in a sisterly spat. *You are a stubborn fucking brat,* I have texted. *I know you are mad at me but SOMETHING MAJOR HAPPENED and you need to swallow your pride and call me the fuck back.* To continue to punish me with silence, because I merely hinted at the real reason she shouldn't marry Arch? Grow the fuck up. I text her that now. *Grow the fuck up. Until you do, I don't want Layla anywhere near you.* My anger is only displaced fear. I'm restless to speak to Brett, to tell her what really happened, to ask her if it is a dangerous and stupid idea to lie about it. To ask her if she is even willing to lie about it. What if I say that it was Brett and Stephanie on that tape, but she tells the truth? Can they arrest me for that? I think they can. Could I lose custody of Layla if I am arrested?

I drop my head into my hands with a low groan. How do I explain what happened to a twelve-year-old? Layla is on her way up here now (*Out here,* comes Brett's voice). Our local police department in New Jersey is giving her a ride, and the officers have confiscated her phone to be sure she hears what happened from me, and not from Facebook.

The door opens. The officer is back with Jesse, of all people, and a bottle of water. The plastic is foggy from the refrigerator, still sporting a price tag, which tells me the bottle did not come from a bulk pack. An officer bought this bottle, for himself (*Because only men can be police officers,* comes Brett's voice again), and he put it in the fridge to drink later, and now it's being given to me. I need it more than he does. To have a train of thought like this, I must suspect what is going on.

"How are you?" Jesse crouches down on her heels and twists the cap off for me.

"Oh, let me . . ." The officer starts out of the room again, presumably searching for a chair for Jesse.

"He's going to tell you they can't say for sure who is responsible, but it's obviously Vince." Jesse is speaking at a fast, whispered clip. I don't understand what she is saying, and I don't really care. I'm only hoping for an answer to one question.

"Have you gotten ahold of Brett?"

"Babe," Jesse says, resting her hand on my forearm, "we have really bad news about Brett." Tears prick her eyes. "I'm so sorry."

"What about Brett?" I'm saying as the officer returns with a chair for Jesse.

"She's asking about Brett," Jesse says, in a sort of tattling way. *She's asking, not me.*

The officer sighs, putting his weight on the back of the new chair, leaning on it like it's a walker in a nursing home. "We wanted you to know before your daughter arrived that we've located your sister."

"Well . . . where is she?" I look from him to Jesse. "Is she here? Have you seen her?"

Jesse is looking at me with big *this is going to hurt me more than it hurts you* eyes, stroking the back of my head. This is the most we've ever touched.

"Ma'am," the officer says, and I feel this word far sooner than what he says next, because I am still in shock, "there is no easy way to tell you this, but your sister is deceased."

My immediate thought is that it was a car accident. That Brett implored her driver to go faster, to get her out of here, and he blew a red light, flipped taking a turn too fast on one of the back country roads. I don't think to connect what happened to Stephanie and Vince with what happened to Brett.

I am surprised that I am able to ask, "What happened?" quite normally. Jesse has taken my hand now. She's still crouched next to me on the floor.

"I need you to understand," the officer says, "that we don't have that answer ourselves, just yet. But as her next of kin, I want to provide you with all the information we have at this point in the investigation. But know that is subject to change as we gain a better understanding of what happened today."

I don't really hear him, but I nod. My head feels heavy on my neck. How did I never notice how heavy my head was before?

"Your sister was in the car that Stephanie was driving. When they went over the edge, her body was expelled onto the roof."

Lauren's wail. Marc's moan. *They saw my sister.* I wish I could be sick. I wish I could purge this feeling, flush it down the toilet, but already I know, this is not a feeling. This is a growth. Inoperable, benign but painfully pressing on a vital organ. It will be with me, hurting me and not killing me, all my life.

Still, I am trying to understand how my sister got into the car. Did she sneak into the car while we were filming at the picnic table? How did we not see her? I must look very confused, because the officer asks me if I understand.

I shake my head: *No, I don't.* "How did she get into the car without any of us noticing?"

Jesse and the officer exchange a worried look. *They haven't told me the worst of it yet,* I realize.

"I'm sorry," the officer says, "I should have phrased that more clearly. Your sister wasn't in the car. She was in the trunk."

"The *trunk*?" I'm at a loss. "When did she get in the trunk?"

"Sometime between when she came home from Talkhouse with Stephanie and when you woke up in the morning."

"Why didn't we hear her? Wouldn't she have been kicking and screaming?" As I ask the question, I work it out for myself. "Oh," I say, my voice low, the sharp threat of vomit high in my throat. "Oh. She was . . . she was not alive? In the trunk?"

The officer shakes his head, wincing on my behalf. "We believe she was deceased before she was placed in the trunk, yes, but that is one of the things we have yet to conclusively determine."

"You're saying she was murdered. Is that what you're saying?" My mouth is sticky and dry. I must look like I'm having difficulty swallowing, because Jesse brings the water bottle to my lips.

"Drink," she commands, lifting the bottle. Water leaks from the corners of my mouth, splashing my bare thighs. I rubbed my legs with bronzing lotion this morning, and the real color of my skin is exposed in jagged rivulets. *I rode in a car listening to the new Taylor Swift song while my sister's dead body was in the trunk.* Like patting my head and rubbing my stomach, it is a cognitive challenge to have this thought and swallow water at the same time.

"How did this happen?" *In the library with the candlestick* my mind answers with a giggle that tells me I am not well.

"We'll know more when the autopsy report is in, but your sister sustained a sizable wound to the back of her head. It's possible she slipped and fell, but if it were an accident, there wouldn't have been a need to conceal the body. And also. Because your sister was not, um. Well. It would have taken some strength to move her. A woman couldn't have done that on her own."

Because your sister was not thin, is what he was almost about to say.

"Vince did it," Jesse says, and the officer shoots her a reproachful look. "I don't know why she can't know that is what everyone is thinking. He found out about Brett's affair with Stephanie and he fucking lost it."

I am standing. Why am I standing? I have my hand on the wall. I am doubled over, as if I am in labor, again. Maybe I am, a little bit. This is a realization so awful it must be born.

Someone killed my sister and that someone may or may not have been Vince, but we are going to say that Vince did it. We are going to say that he did it just like we are going to say that Brett and Stephanie had an affair when they didn't. We are going to rig reality.

Jesse and the officer are telling me to sit down. I try but I immediately get back up. To sit on the truth. That's something people say, and I understand it now. There is a strain of the truth that is a cement-backed chair, a pea in your mattress, and a pebble in your shoe. Bearable, but just barely.

So I pace until Layla arrives. By that time Jesse has worked out what we should tell her.

CHAPTER 22

Kelly

I remember almost nothing of her funeral, except the parts of Yvette's eulogy already trending on Twitter.

And Arch.

Arch came with her mother, but not her father. I felt dirty about that. Like he refused to pay his respects because he knew something in the water wasn't clean.

We all rode together in the limo after the burial—my father; his wife, Susan; Layla; Arch; and Arch's mother. At the curb, right outside of Patsy's Pizzeria on Sixtieth, Brett's favorite pizza in the city and now the site of her wake, Arch asks me to hang back a moment.

"I've got her," my father says, his hand in the middle of Layla's upper back. Layla seems sleepy, cried out, numb. She has barely let me out of her sight since Brett died, and truthfully, I'm afraid to stray too far from her. Layla is a welcome distraction. So long as she is around, I can focus on comforting her. *I can suspend everything I am afraid to feel.*

"We won't stay long," I promise her as my father and Susan escort her onto the curb. My father shuts the door. My father. I don't think he believes my story any more than I do, but I also know he will never challenge it for Layla's sake. Layla may be devastated, but she is proud to be Brett Courtney's niece—the Brett Courtney the public thought they knew.

"The rain held off," Arch remarks to the gloomy window.

I nod, feeling like a spring-loaded trap moments from triggering. I have avoided being alone with Arch as much as possible this week. It was one thing to lie to her by omission when Brett was alive, quite another to insist that Brett and Stephanie had an affair ten months ago and that Vince found out about it and killed them both, which is the East Hampton Town Police Department's working theory. I have my own working theory, but it's nothing I can advance.

"Not that it would have mattered. Right?" Arch turns to me with a limp laugh, bunching a wet tissue beneath her chapped nose. She means because most of the women who attended the funeral wore sneakers, in Brett's honor. They wouldn't have had to worry about their heels sticking in the mud at the cemetery.

"It would have been okay either—"

"Was she still seeing her?" Arch demands. She cuts me off as soon as I open my mouth to respond, "Tell me the truth, Kel. Please. *Please* don't lie to me. Don't let me be the dumb girlfriend who didn't know."

Oh, the cut of that. I don't speak quickly enough to be believed. I can't speak quickly enough to be believed. I feel gagged by my grief. "She wasn't seeing her. She loved you, Arch."

Arch shakes her head disgustedly, skinning her nostrils with that wet, dirty tissue. I reach into my purse, trying to find her a fresh one so that she doesn't give herself an infection.

"She didn't love me," Arch says. "I didn't want to admit it, because I loved her. But I could tell. She was never all there. I'm not *crazy*. I won't let you make me feel crazy. I know something was going on."

I abandon the hunt for clean tissues and cover my chest with my hand. My heart feels old. It feels weak from hurting so many people. "Arch," I gasp. "Please. I need you to believe she loved you. I love you and so does Layla. We will always be family."

"Is it true?" she says to me, sounding stronger, like her anger has taken the lead now. Grief is just a partner dance between sorrow and fury. "Is it true you're going to let them show what happened? That you're getting your own show with Layla?"

I recommit myself to the clean tissue hunt so that I do not have to face her rightful disapproval. "The cameras were turned off when it happened. It doesn't really show anything."

"But you and Layla? You're doing your own show?"

"It's all focused on SPOKE. It will help so many Imazighen women and children, Arch."

Arch starts to cry again. No. Wait. Is she . . . ? She is. She's laughing. A bitter, silent, wet, and red-faced laugh. "You do it all for those women and children, don't you, Kel?" she says once she catches her breath. Then she climbs out of the car and closes the door so gently it doesn't even click. I don't imagine I'll hear from her again.

CHAPTER 23

Kelly: The Interview

Present day

I have been reinstated at SPOKE, promoted to vice president. The board immediately revoked the decision to remove me after Brett died. It would have been too much upheaval for the company to survive, and in the aftermath of Brett's death, women flocked to SPOKE and FLOW, specifically asking for me. For Layla. The demand has been so great that we are going nationwide in 2018, opening studios in Miami, DC, and L.A. Rihanna's number is in my phone. The Oscar-Nominated Female Director sent me flowers. I wonder if this is how Donatella Versace felt.

Lisa steps into the shot, conferring with Jesse for a moment, their heads tilted together. Layla and I both watch on the monitor from Jesse's guest bedroom. For "confessional" type interviews, only the DP, the EP, an audio mixer, and the talent are in the room. Everyone else is sequestered away, to minimize distraction and ambient sound.

Layla has stuffed her feet into Brett's furry Gucci slides, which are a size too small for her, but she insisted on wearing something of Brett's for her interview. "Layls," I whisper. There isn't much privacy in Jesse's cramped, expensive apartment, especially not with eight members of the crew milling about, plus hair and makeup and Jesse's two personal assistants. "Just checking in that you still want to do this. You're allowed to change your mind at any time. Even in the middle of the interview, if that's when you decide you don't want to do this."

"I know, Mom," Layla groans. She is furious with me that Brett is dead. *Only temporary*, the grief counselor has assured me.

Even though we are filming my interview with Jesse and Layla's interview with Jesse on the same day, they will air months apart. My interview will run after the season premiere of the show—soon, in three weeks—and Layla's after the finale in a few months. It can't look like we packed it into the same day, so Jesse has changed into a cashmere hoodie and has moved from her living room, where we conducted our more formal sit-down, to her kitchen, to cook and have a "casual" conversation with Layla about what she's been up to since the unthinkable happened.

"Little Big C," Jesse says into the monitor, her nickname for Layla. She's the littlest Courtney, as in the youngest, but she's also the tallest. You're not a real member of her tribe until you have your nickname. I realize with a greedy thump of my heart that I don't have one and probably never will. "We're ready for you."

"Just stop," Layla mutters to me as she hops off the bed, heading for the kitchen, even though I haven't *said* anything. Layla turned thirteen three weeks ago. Is it crazy that I'm already counting down the days until the next barbaric year of her teens? Her disposition is too wizened for that of a three-week-old teenager, but at least I can officially blame her precociousness on her teenageness. I'm wary of viewer criticism that I'm forcing her to grow up too fast. Or is it that I *am* forcing her to grow up too fast? I can't tell anymore.

I watch Layla join Jesse on the monitor. Lisa and a PA lay out the tools and ingredients needed to make *chebakia:* the food processor and the already toasted sesame seeds and the orange water and the baking sheets. Finally, at the marble island set, everyone takes their places and Lisa cues them to start the scene. "Hi, Layla," Jesse says. "It's so good to see you."

Layla's smile is embarrassed and cute. "Thank you."

"What are we making here today?"

"*Chebakia,*" Layla says. "It's a Moroccan cookie that's shaped into a flower and fried and coated in honey. It was Brett's favorite." She stares at the ingredients on the counter, unmoving.

"Tell me what I can start on," Jesse prods.

"You can crack the egg," Layla says, and Jesse grins.

"I think I can manage that."

"So this was Aunt Brett's favorite?" Jesse asks, as she splits an egg on the stainless steel edge of a mixing bowl.

"Brett's favorite. I didn't call her my aunt. She was my best friend."

Jesse picks up a whisk. "You two had an unbreakable bond."

Layla nods, adding the sesame seeds and other dry ingredients to the food processor.

"What do you miss most about her?"

"She bought me the best clothes and bags, even before she could afford to buy herself that stuff. Brett worked really hard to be successful but it wasn't for her, it was so she could help other people."

"She was truly one of a kind," Jesse says, graciously. "I know it must be difficult to talk about her, but it means a lot that you are willing to share your memories of your aunt with her fans." Jesse blankets her heart, as if to say *count me among them*. But if Jesse is a fan of anyone's it is Layla. It's like how single men joke about "borrowing" their married friend's baby to pick up women, knowing women are attracted to hard men with soft babies. Likewise, Jesse is hoping the viewer takes to her, with her tattoos and collection of fierce leather jackets, baking cookies with a sad thirteen-year-old.

Layla's hands are coated in flour, and she scratches an itch on her cheek by lifting her shoulder. "It's not difficult for me to talk about her. I don't want to ever stop talking about Brett."

The network sprung for Layla and I to meet with a media consultant before this interview, and she was the one who supplied that line—*I don't want to ever stop talking about Brett.* It positions the interview as a cathartic exercise for Layla, rather than an exploitative one. In truth, it is both. So many things are both.

There are two versions of what happened the day Stephanie drove Jen's Tesla off Jesse's cliff. The real version and the TV version. Already, in my mind, the TV version is threatening to replace the one that happened. That's how it goes with the show too, you say something enough times and it buries the real. It doesn't erase it entirely, but it makes it very, very faint, like in the movies when the bad guy takes down a message on a pad of paper, and the good guy comes and shades the page with a pencil to reveal the time and location that the bomb will detonate. An impression of the truth. That's what you're left with.

This is the story that has dried in the closed police file: Vince showed up at Jen's house in the early morning hours of August 27, after seeing the video of Stephanie disparaging him on *TMZ*. Brett is the first person Vince encountered when he entered the house, the person who absorbed the full weight of his rage. She had been making a pizza after coming in for the night—it was found overcooked in the oven. There was a struggle; Brett ended up on the floor of the kitchen. The coroner flagged a series of bloody bald patches on the top of Brett's head, evidence that Vince had her by the hair when he slammed her head into the ground. He *scalped* her, a feminist gasped on Twitter, linking to the coroner's report. Vince's handprints were also found on the trunk of Jen's car. (I can see him in my mind's eye, leaning against the Tesla's back bumper while we debated how to get to Jesse's house. *You look like you could use some AC*, he told Lauren with that signature Vince smirk.)

The autopsy, performed nineteen hours after Brett expired, determined that her blood alcohol content was .088, which means it was even higher at the time of her death. *She was at a disadvantage to defend herself*, the detective told me, *but that also means she probably didn't feel much pain or realize what was going on.* He was trying to make me feel better, but I cried harder that day than any day since Brett died. It was all so base. My sister made some mistakes in her life, but she did a lot of good in this world, and she would have walked across fire for Layla. And yet she died drunk, in a sloppy barroom fight over a man. It was about so much more than that, of course—about power, about survival—but the public would have reduced it to its Jerry Springer bones. Her death was beneath her, and maybe that's why I'd prefer her TV one.

The next morning, the police and the public believe, Vince insisted on coming with us to Jesse's house, perhaps because he panicked when he realized we were driving the car that contained Brett's body. Perhaps he wanted to monitor the situation, be sure that Stephanie didn't trash his name on camera now that they were getting a divorce. It is impossible to tell exactly what he was thinking, if he was planning on doing what he was doing, or if it just happened in a moment of passion. The police asked for footage of the day, which Jesse turned over only after the producers cobbled together enough Frankenbites to fit her account. Jesse made a large donation to the Montauk Playhouse and offered the police chief's niece an internship at Saluté, and no one ever specified that it was the unedited film they needed.

"Talk to me about how you plan to honor your aunt's legacy," Jesse says, tapping the whisk against the side of the mixing bowl before dropping it in the sink.

"I will," Layla says, "but I want to say something else first. About Stephanie." She turns the food processor off.

"Stephanie?" Jesse says, eyebrows in the middle of her forehead, although Layla told her in advance she wanted to say this. Layla feels an impassioned obligation to take up for Stephanie, the woman she doesn't know tried to hurt her in Morocco, the woman she doesn't know succeeded in killing her aunt. My stomach burbles. This is the part of the day that I have been dreading most, and there was already so much to dread. Why, *why* does Layla always have to do the right thing?

"I know Stephanie messed up by lying in her book," Layla says. "But I think that was her way of reaching out for help. We know now that Vince was hurting her, but she was too afraid or embarrassed to say that, so she made up this other abusive relationship in her book. And I don't want people to forget her, and all she's done for women."

This is indefensible, what I can't stop my daughter from doing: unwittingly pardoning my sister's murderer.

But Layla was insistent. If she was doing this interview, then she was defending Stephanie, especially once it came out that Stephanie had changed her will right before she died, leaving all her worldly possessions to End It!, the national organization devoted to providing women of color with the financial means to leave their abusers. To me, this just read like an ironic punctuation point at the end of her original plan, which was to kill as many of us as possible before she killed herself. Violence against women by a woman who left the entirety of her estate to an organization dedicated to fighting violence against women. The depravity is enough to make your head spin.

A renowned intimate violence expert that Jesse interviewed on Facebook Live said it was possible that Stephanie anticipated the worst when she ended the relationship with Vince. And so, as though signing the divorce papers were akin to signing her own death warrant, Stephanie changed her will just in case Vince came after her. If she was going to become another statistic, at least some good would come out of it. Other women in her same position could be helped.

And it made sense, the expert added, that Vince would go after Brett too. Perpetrators of intimate partner suicide-murder tend to be overwhelmingly white and male, and tend to blame others for their feelings of powerlessness in a romantic relationship. It is never the man's fault that his partner has abandoned him, it is always the doing of somebody else. He likely laid the entirety of the responsibility for the dissolution of his marriage at Brett's feet, the expert neatly concluded.

Then there were all the cell phone videos of Brett and Stephanie, dancing at Talkhouse the night before they died, having the time of their lives celebrating Stephanie's emancipation from Vince. *Only a man would see this pure and unadulterated adoration these two women had for each other as a threat*, Yvette had said in Brett's homily. *Only a man would feel compelled to snuff out these two beautiful lights. Naysayers have long disparaged what I do and what I stand for. Women have all the same rights as men—what am I shrieking on about? I shriek on until women have more than equal rights. I shriek on until women's lives have equal value.* Overnight, an Etsy merchant designed T-shirts silk-screened *Shriek on* that sold out in less than forty-eight hours. I don't know where the proceeds went.

There were others who came forward, who told stories that cast suspicion on Stephanie, like the cabbie who drove the two home from Talkhouse and the high school senior, just eighteen(!), who Stephanie deflowered in the back alley of the bar. The detectives assigned to Brett's case kept me apprised of each development, but they didn't wander too far down any roads that didn't have large yellow *Vince as hater and killer of strong beautiful women* theories staked at every turn.

There was also the question—that if it had been Stephanie who killed Brett, how did she manage to get my sister's body into the trunk all by herself? Vince would have been the only one with the strength to do that, the detectives assured me. I had a simple workaround to that conjecture—adrenaline—but I didn't bother to float it, the same way I didn't tell them the other way Vince's handprints could have ended up on the trunk of Jen's car. What would be the point when I would then have to explain that I thought Stephanie did it, and what her motive was? I needed my sister to be remembered as a martyr for the resistance, not as her best friend's husband's mistress. Tribalism trumped truth, in the end.

I sometimes wonder what Jesse has offered Jen and Lauren to keep their silence. Surely they suspect Stephanie too. Their contracts have been renewed for a fifth season, as has mine, but that would seem to be the bare minimum. Even if it had gone down the way we said it had, it would be in poor taste for the show to come back without its surviving members.

"Stephanie was as much a victim as Brett was," Jesse says, spelling it out clearly for everyone at home in case Layla hasn't stated it plainly enough. "And the network plans to honor her legacy by matching Stephanie's estate and donating that amount to End It!"

Jesse meets Camera A's glass eye. "And if you're sitting at home and wondering how you can help, you can donate to End It! by visiting the link at the corner of your screen." She addresses Layla again. "I know you have plans to help too. Tell me about those, Layla."

"My mom and me"—the awkward phrasing plays a string in my heart. She's still just a kid in so many ways—"are going to Morocco next month with more e-bikes. And we're opening a store in Union Square that sells rugs and blankets made by the women we've met through SPOKE."

"And we will be there to document your latest endeavors. Stay tuned after the hour for a special preview of *Still SPOKE*, which will follow Layla and Kelly as they work to keep Brett's mission alive." I didn't understand the name of our spinoff. Jesse's assistant had to explain to me that it was a play on the word "woke," and then she had to explain to me what that meant. *It means, like, being aware,* she told me, rolling her eyes. *But being aware of what?* I asked. *Social stuff,* she answered after a hefty pause.

Jesse smiles at Layla with unreserved adulation. "Layla, Little Big C, I can't thank you enough for being here. I think I speak for every woman watching when I say thank you for all you do." She points her finger at the ceiling. It's coated in flour. "We miss you, sister."

Layla holds stock still, smiling a stiff smile, until the sound producer declares, "Got it!"

"Phew," Jesse says, fanning her face with her hand. "That was tough, huh?" She holds up her phone. "Why don't we take a selfie?"

A gaffer opens the door to the guest bedroom. It will take a while to pack up the equipment and clear out, and it's been a long day. I let everyone go in front of me so they can get to it. As I'm walking out last, I run into Marc in the doorway, walking into the guest bedroom.

"Oops," I say, stepping aside to let him through. "Sorry."

But Marc just stands there. He glances over his shoulder, and when he's sure no one is watching, he presses something small and plastic into my hand. "Take this," he says.

I look down. I'm holding a black USB flash drive.

"I'll do whatever you want to do with it. You know I loved her." He wipes his eyes. "Ah, shit. I don't want to cry in front of you. It must be so much worse for you."

I close my fingers around the flash drive weakly, dreading its contents. I am so tired of having to make difficult decisions. "What's on here?" I ask him.

"That weekend in the Hamptons, when Lauren went upstairs after the game? She passed out with her mic still on. I'm the only one who's heard this." Marc motions for me to pocket the device, which I do, reluctantly. "It's something you should have. I can't . . . it can't be up to me what to do." He plugs a runny nostril with a knuckle. "You're her sister." He means it wholeheartedly, but with his finger in his nose like that, the statement comes out nasally, girlishly aping. A PA approaches, and Marc clears his throat and finds a manlier voice. "Listen to it alone," he tells me before doing an abrupt about-face.

CHAPTER 24

Kelly

Her scream is cut short. It isn't until I listen to the recording a third time—alone; Layla is in school—that I start to visualize some of what I am hearing. Lauren must have been startled awake by Brett, and Brett must have slapped a hand over her mouth when she cried out.

It's me. Shhhhh. It's Brett.

Bedsheets rustle. When Lauren speaks, her voice is rough and disoriented.

What . . . She clears her throat . . . *why are you . . . ? Is it time for dinner?* Fumbling. More rustling. *You have my phone.*

Just give me a sec.

Why do you have my phone?

Because Stephanie jacked mine up and I can't get the button for J to work. Brett groans, quietly. *You don't have Jesse's number?*

Lauren is awake enough now to speak with some embarrassment in her voice: *It's a new phone. I have Lisa's number.*

I don't want to talk to Lisa.

What do you need to talk to Jesse about at . . . a pause while Lauren strains to read the bedside clock, probably . . . *three twenty-nine in the morning? I knew you guys were boning.*

Lauren Elizabeth Fun, Brett reprimands, *that word ages you.*

People still say "boning"!

Old people. Like Stephanie. Who is out of her FUCKING mind right now. Do you know what she did tonight? She got up onstage at Talkhouse—

You guys went to Talkhouse?

After dinner.

Why didn't you invite me?

Um. Because your hair caught fire and you came up here to fix it but, I don't know, I guess you passed out instead?

I didn't pass out.

You're still wearing all your clothes. And your boob is hanging out of your T-shirt.

A pause while Lauren checks to be sure this is true. *You love it, you little lezzie. What happened at Talkhouse?*

So. The band let us come up onstage and sing with them—

What song?

"Bitch."

Fuck you.

Brett finds this misunderstanding uproariously funny, laughing while she sings, *I'm a bitch, I'm a mother, I'm a child, I'm a lover.*

Ohhhh. Good one for us. Very on brand.

Why do you think I requested it? Even in her final hours, Brett couldn't help but pat herself on the back. *Anyway. So after the song was over I got off the stage and I thought Steph was behind me. But she stayed up there and, like, hijacked the mic and started saying all kinds of crazy shit. About us.*

Did she say anything about me?

About all of us! How everything is made up. How we made up our fight and you and Jen went along with it. Stephanie didn't actually mention Jen or Lauren by name, but this was Brett, recruiting allies. *Just really bad stuff. It makes us look so thirsty. Oh. And then. She fucked a teenager behind the side of the bar. I'm not kidding when I say teenager. I would be SHOCKED if he was legal.*

She was trying to make you jealous.

Why would she— Brett stops. She forgot her own impending storyline. *The point is. Jesse needs to know before tomorrow. She can't be allowed to go to the brunch. She's totally unhinged and I don't want her spouting off lies about me on camera.*

Just tell Lisa.

Lisa won't give a fuck. She would one hundred percent support anything bad Steph says about me. Talk about jealousy. You know Lisa is jealous of me.

Lauren's pause is incredulous.

Don't roll your eyes. You know it's true.

I'm hungry.

Your boob is still out.

It sounds like Lauren throws off the covers. *Come on. If I'm hungry I know you're hungry.*

I saw frozen pizza in the garage, Brett says. *And seriously, put it away. I'm so sick of boobs.*

I hear a pucker, the noise a fridge makes when it suctions away from the frame. Then my sister's sarcasm, *More wine is what you need.*

My hair looks like Kate Gosselin's.

Four million people used to watch Jon & Kate Plus Eight. *Show some goddamn respect.*

Make the pepperoni one.

I thought you weren't eating bread right now.

Pizza isn't bread.

Cabinets open: searching for a plate on which to nuke the pizza, maybe. *Wait. Holy shit,* Brett says. *Does she not have a microwave?*

Infrared light and cancer cells. Blah blah.

I can't.

I know.

The silence stretches. Initially I thought that maybe Brett was trying to figure out how to turn on the oven, but on subsequent listens, I think she was debating whether or not to say what she said next. *You know it's not real. Her whole vegan shtick. She eats meat.*

Lauren snorts. *And I'm the one who sent the* Post *that video of me blowing the baguette at Balthazar.*

I'm being serious.

Glugging. Lauren already on to glass two, maybe? *I am too.*

Lauren. Brett is astounded. *Jesus.*

Whatever. It worked, right? I got another season. I got to pretend to accuse each of you of doing it and have a reason to fight with you.

But you had to step down as CEO.

It was going to happen anyway.

Brett says, *Damn, girl,* which is rich, given her own duplicity. *What are you doing?*

I think there's Tito's in the freezer.

You definitely need vodka.

Like a hole in the head. That Lauren said that, given the way my sister died not even an hour later, feels like grazing the third rail.

They putter around the kitchen for a while. Looking for snacks. Making fun of the vegan items in Jen's pantry that she doesn't even eat anymore. Lauren's voice grows increasingly garbled, and she's having trouble keeping track of the conversation. A few times, she asks how long until the cabs get here. Brett corrects her in the beginning but eventually starts playing along. Twenty minutes. An hour. *An hour?* Lauren mumbles, with attitude. *Get your shit together.*

A loud crash marks the recording at fifty-seven minutes and thirty-two seconds. My best guess is that someone slammed the freezer door too hard, because they were just discussing how nut milk ice cream isn't the most disgusting thing in Jen's freezer. I think some of the platters that were stacked on top of the unit clattered to the ground. One dog barks, and then all three. I cannot believe I slept through this. And now, on my third listen, knowing what happens next, I wonder, *Did Jen give me that Xanax on purpose to knock me out? Did she plan to confront Brett when she got home later that night?*

Oops. Lauren giggles. After a few beats, there is a noise like rubbing somebody's back over their shirt. Lauren climbing onto the sofa, just in view of the kitchen.

Don't get up, Brett says. *Really. Just lie there and spoon your Tito's. I'm fine to clean up your—oh, God. What do you want?*

You is Jen.

Go to bed, Jen pleads. *For the love of God. You've been banging around down here for an hour.*

Because we've had to, like, rub sticks together to make this pizza, Brett retorts, belligerent and rude. The two of them were never a good match, but that night, they were aluminum and bromine in a gas jar. *I mean,* Brett says, *that shitty meat you're eating from FreshDirect is more likely to give you cancer than a microwave.*

Bretttt, Lauren croaks from the couch, in some half-hearted attempt to defend Jen, lapsing into a convoluted rendition—*You're a bitch, you're a child, you're a sinner and a mother . . .*

Brett continues to open cupboard doors and drawers. The tape here is cluttered with the sound of utensils rattling, plates clinking into one another. I think, even as drunk as she was, that she was pretending to stay busy to avoid meeting Jen's eye. I think she knew she had gone too far by saying that in front of Lauren. Not like either of them had to worry about Lauren remembering in the morning. She barely seems to remember what happened next.

I thought you'd like to know that I've crafted a statement with my PR team about my decision to step away from veganism, Jen tells Brett, eloquently. At this point in the tape, I have become so inured to Brett and Lauren's slurring that Jen, speaking clearly and reasonably, is the one who makes me sit up and take note. *Green Theory has and always will be about promoting what works best for your individual body, and shedding labels is truly a healthy step forward for all women. I have a good feeling about this. I've built a strong community and I have confidence they will support me, and by disassociating from veganism, my team believes I will attract a whole new customer base.*

I know you're talking, Brett says, *but all I hear is this.* She's misquoting Emily Blunt in *The Devil Wears Prada,* making a closed beak gesture with her hand, I have no doubt.

I am talking, Jen snaps. She's mad now. Brett embarrassed her. I know what it's like to share something with Brett that you've put a lot of thought and effort into, and for the Big Chill to make you feel like a complete nerd for trying so hard. *I'm telling you this for two reasons. One, because I'm no longer going to allow you to lord it over me, and two, I thought you might want to take a cue from me. Prepare your own statement. Get ready for the ensuing shitstorm when everyone finds out that you slept with Vince.*

Thudding silence. Whatever Brett was doing in the kitchen, she's stopped.

Vince is foineeeee, Lauren says through a yawn.

Your sister told me, Jen says, probably in response to the stunned look on Brett's face. *That's bad, Brett. Not just what you did and what you've lied about, but that your own sister is so done with you that she sold you down the river. You're going to have no one, after this is over. You think Jesse will stand by your side after this? I know Yvette won't. See, she might not always like me, but she will always love me. The same cannot be true of some girl she met three years ago.*

Yvette. *Ugh.* Why did Jen have to bring up Yvette? Yvette was Brett's do-over. She made Brett feel worthy of a mother's love. Of all that Brett stood to lose if the truth came out, I believe she would have felt Yvette the hardest.

Brett makes a dismissive noise that just barely masks her full-blown panic. *Tell me, did you work with your PR team to craft a statement about the year you spent fucking Vince?*

Jen and Vince?! I scream-thought on the first listen.

Jen and Vince? On the second.

Jen and Vince. On the third, I remembered Brett trying to talk to me before we set out for the mountains in Morocco. Something about Jen. I had brushed her off. No. I hadn't just brushed her off. I had screamed at her that I never wanted to hear another bad word about Jen again. I was just so sick of feeling like she didn't have my back and also that she was set on sabotaging my relationship with the one person who did. Would things have been different if I knew?

Would I want them to be?

Vince is not my best friend's husband, Jen says, cool as a cucumber, almost as if she was prepared for Brett to bring up the dalliance. *That was your* best friend. *She was good to you. She* loved *you. And you shit all over her. Think about it, Brett. Women are going to hate you when they find out.*

Brett does seem to think about it. Then she laughs defiantly. *Was he your first or something, Greenberg? You are TOTALLY still writing Mrs. Jen DeMarco in your diary, aren't you? You know I broke it off with him, right? You know he kept pursuing me, even after I got engaged? He is capital O Obbbbbb-sessed with me. That must kilIllll you. You got yourself a little makeover with your new boobies and your long hair and you thought you were gonna sweep in and win yo man back.* Brett gasps, theatrically. *Oh my God, look at your face! You did think that. You did. You thought you were going to show Vince what he was missing and instead, he only had eyes for my fat ass. See. This is what you have never understood. Actually, I think you do understand it, and that's why you hate me. Nobody likes you, Greenberg. You are boring. Being thin is your full-time job and your hobby. Being thin is all you have to offer anyone, because you have* no *charisma*, no *sex appeal*, no *guts. Of course Vince would rather fuck me over a lonely bag of bones in an Ulla Johnson dress and your mother would still rather I was her daughter. Aw, are you going to cry? You know, I've never actually seen you cry. Do you cry, like, green kale smoothie tears?*

I held my breath here, on the first listen, because I was so sure this was when it would happen. I would have understood, on some level, if Jen had snapped after an evisceration like that. It was so mean. It was so cruel. It was so true. But somehow, it manages to get worse.

Because Jen, from what I can gather, turned away. She didn't engage. She didn't give Brett the reaction she was looking for.

Jen, Brett hisses, trying to call her back. *Jen. Stop. Jen!* And then, I hear Brett's fast feet on the limestone flooring, that unyielding flooring, and Jen's grunt. Brett went after Jen. *Brett* started it.

Lauren snores lightly as Brett and Jen tangle on the floor, groaning, breathing hard, trading curses. They kept their voices down for a reason: they didn't want to be stopped.

The crack reminds me of the coconuts Brett and I used to raise above our heads and slam into our driveway when we were kids. It is not the *crack!* of something breaking. It is the *crack!* of someone breaking something. The intention is deafening. Brett moans, almost in recognition. *Ohhhh,* this is it for me. Brett's cause of death was acute subdural hematoma, a blood clot below the inner layer of the dura. The pathologist identified two contusions to the back of her head, caused by two separate blows, only one of which was fatal. But because they came in such quick succession, she could not determine their order. Listening to the tape, I am certain it was the first.

Still, Jen might have been able to spin this as self-defense, or even an accident, up until this point. She could have called for help, and maybe Brett could have been saved. But then, a second crack. What she believed to be the *coup de grâce*. There was no calling anyone after that.

For a while, Jen's distraught breathing is the unstressed beat to Lauren's snoring. Brett is silent. Brett died fast.

She tried to drag her on her own first. I heard it. But there was no way the show's elfin flower child was going to be able to dispose of my sister's sizely body without some assistance. *A woman wouldn't have been able to do that on her own,* the officer had said, but two women could.

Lauren. Jen's voice is a close hiss. *Lauren. Wake up.*

This continues for a good minute or so.

Stop, Lauren finally groans.

No, Lauren. Wake up.

No. Hey! Stop! What are you doing? I can imagine Jen dragging Lauren off the couch.

Help me! Jen snarls at her.

Is that Brett?

Get her feet.

Lauren laughs. *Brett is DRUNK. Wake up, Brett!*

Get her—that's it. You got it. Keep moving.

Is this Brett?

Keep moving.

A door creaks open. A light clicks on.

Ow, Lauren complains, and there is a sickening plop, then another. Brett's feet, being dropped to the concrete garage floor.

Get her feet again!

Is this Brett?

A light clicks off.

Just wait here, Jen tells Lauren. *I'm grabbing my keys. Don't move.*

Lauren is actually able to wait quietly until Jen returns and opens the trunk of her car. It makes sense now, why both of them were so determined to take my car. It makes sense why Lauren didn't seem to understand her own trepidation. She must have retained only spotty memories of stuffing my sister's dead body in the trunk of Jen's car, if any at all. What would Jen have done with Brett if Stephanie hadn't done what she did, if not for that gruesome stroke of luck? She must have had a rough idea. She must have been the one to send a text to me from Brett's phone—*Called a car to take me back to the city. Over this shit.* The police pinned that on Vince too.

Okay. Lift her up. That's it. Let go. You can let go now, Lauren.

The hatch beeps once. I hear it latch shut. Jen waited to be sure it closed.

Help me, Jen says again, when they are back in the kitchen.

What is this?

Just help me clean it up.

But what is it?

It's tomato soup.

Soup?! Lauren cries.

Shhh!

Why is there soup on the floor?

You spilled it.

I'm sorry, Jen.

It's fine. Just help me clean it up. No! Don't eat it. Gross. Lauren. No! Jen retches, or maybe that is me.

I'm hungry.

I'll make you pizza after this.

Do I look like the Long Island Medium?

You're fine. Just keep doing what you're doing.

The two work without speaking for the next half an hour, cleaning up my sister's blood.

Okay, Lauren? No, Lauren. Not on the white couch. Let me just get those off you first.

Don't touch me, Lauren slurs.

Just let me get—

Don't touch—

Your jeans off—

Wanna have sex with me?

Before you get on the couch, you fucking alcoholic fucking bitch! Jen comes undone, weeping from someplace deep and irrevocably broken.

I can imagine Lauren, regarding her friend contritely, before asking, *Did I pee?*

Jen sobs *Yes!* with relief, realizing this is the only way to convince Lauren to cooperate.

Don't cry, Jen. I'll take them off.

I hear the button of Lauren's jeans cling to the zipper, the sound of denim, sanding skin.

Here, Lauren says, with so much sweetness that Jen sobs again. Her footsteps plod away, those of a woman heavier than she was an hour ago. Lauren starts to snore not long after that. From what I can gather, she never made it to the couch. It's possible that she slept in the very same spot where my sister died.

There is always a choice. There is not always a good choice. I can go to the police. I can go to Jesse. I can do nothing. I can go to Jen. Jen, my *friend*. But I knew what I would do the first time I heard my sister moan, sounding nothing like I want to remember her. Why listen to the recording again and again? The same reason I made two appointments to terminate my pregnancy. I knew the day I missed my period that I would keep the baby. But I let my father and Brett drive me to the clinic twice anyway, to watch the angry men with their angry signs, to know with *conviction* that walking through the doors marked "Reproductive Services" felt like the wrong choice for me.

I hide the MP3 player in the leg of a skinny jean and shove it in a storage bin beneath the bed for now. Luckily, Layla rarely steals my clothes. "Too tight." It is almost time to pick her up from school. I don't need to look at a clock or my phone to know this, I hear *Ellen* greeting her audience through the thin wall I share with my neighbor. I am so sick of sharing. I share the bed with Layla and my drawers with Brett's clothes. Arch folded them very neatly into garbage bags and left them with our doorman a few weeks ago, and this apartment has but one shallow closet by the front door, already stuffed to the gills. I used to hear the words *doorman* and *luxury high-rise*—which is how StreetEasy classifies my building—and picture Charlotte York's apartment, but the reality is much less glamorous. This was Brett's old apartment, the lease I took over when she moved in with Arch. It made for a suitable bachelorette pad, but it is not practical for a mother and a teenage daughter long term. I looked at a two-bedroom out of my budget last weekend. Fifty-five hundred a month in a failing school zone. No windows in the bedroom. No stove in the kitchen. That was not the first time I heard Stephanie's voice in my head: *Forty-one dollars and sixty-six cents a day.*

I did some research after that. Not on the rental market in Manhattan.

I want to stay in this neighborhood. I want Layla to continue at the school where she is enrolled, the one with the "splendid" views of the Hudson, the one that scored an A+ on teachers and an A- on diversity from Niche. I want to retain my title at the company that is my joy and passion and finally, slowly, starting to turn a small profit. I want to receive letters from Imazighen women telling me they are the first women in their villages to go to college thanks to SPOKE. I want everyone to remember my sister fondly and I want to be properly compensated for appearing on a TV show that has increased viewership at Saluté by 39 percent. I do not want to be paid per season, or even per episode. I want residuals.

I find my phone. I have just enough time to call her before I have to meet Layla. The conversation doesn't need to be long, and better to do it now while I'm fired up about it. I don't want to ever listen to that recording again.

Jesse contacts me often, and I am expected to be available, whenever, wherever. But my call goes straight to her voicemail. I take a deep breath while I listen for the beep. "Hey, it's Kelly. I need to talk to you about something." My heart beats slowly and loudly. "It's important, and I'd like to set a meeting to discuss it. Mornings after eight are best for me. Please call me when you can. Thanks. Bye." I lose my grip on the phone before I can hang up, tacking on a muttered curse to the end of the message. Through the wall, *Ellen*'s audience cheers as she introduces her second guest. Time to go.

Outside, I am annoyed to find that it is sunny. It was overcast when I walked Layla to school earlier this morning, and I didn't bother to grab my sunglasses before I left, thinking the day was still gray. Our apartment doesn't receive a lot of natural light.

I decide to just squint and bear it, figuring that it will add another five or ten minutes to go back inside and grab my sunglasses. The elevators are in high demand at this hour, and I always try to beat the dismissal bell. Watching Layla exit the doors of her school tells me more about her day and her life than she will ever offer up to me.

I make the ten-minute walk in eight, lingering on the northeast corner of the block, knowing Layla exits the south-facing door, and that I will not be in her line of sight when she does.

I don't recognize the two girls flanking Layla as she bounds down the stairs and onto the sidewalk. Then again, I don't recognize Layla. I used to arrive early to her school in New Jersey too. She walked out alone most days, or with her friend, Liz, though less and less once Liz made the junior soccer team. Brett insisted that Layla was beloved everywhere she went, but she never saw her at pickup, at a school where so few students looked like her. She never saw what I saw, which was that no one had a problem with Layla, but no one went out of their way to befriend her, either.

The city has been good for Layla; her confidence has blossomed. She picks at her face less; she is rarely with the same group of girls, a sign of not just her popularity but of her generous spirit. She is invited to so many sleepovers and birthday parties that I have to say no to some of them, which of course only makes everyone want both of us more. If anyone were to ever find out the truth about my sister, we would be loathed with the same intensity we are loved now. We would not survive it. Going to the police was an option, but it was never one I was going to take.

Layla says something that gets a big laugh. She looks almost unbelievably happy, like a kid in an old Sunny Delight commercial. No teen is that excited to discover orange juice in the refrigerator. And yet, this likeness is real. Seeing my daughter's earnest smile, her surefootedness with her new friends, I can say with conviction that I didn't make the right choice.

I made the best one available.

ACKNOWLEDGMENTS

I want to thank my husband, first and foremost, for his unflinching good mood and his willingness to run out and get me the good coffee anytime I asked. I love you so much and I'm so proud of the chance we took and the life we're building in our new city.

I also want to thank the readers of *Luckiest Girl Alive,* who have reached out to me over the last three years to share experiences so sadly similar to mine. I kept a secret for so long—out of fear, out of shame, out of conditioning—that I never knew the power of the shared experience. I am stronger because of you, so thank you. I hope you are stronger because of me too.

Thank you to my literary agent, Alyssa Reuben, for fielding countless panicked calls from me over the course of the last year and for always remaining calm, encouraging, and compassionate. You had a vision for my career before I had it for myself, and for that I will be eternally grateful.

Thank you to my editor, Marysue Rucci, for never hesitating to tell me when something is not working so that I can believe you when you tell me something *is* working, for your patience, your enthusiasm, and the well-timed martinis.

Thank you to the team at Simon & Schuster: Amanda Lang, Richard Rhorer, and Elizabeth Breeden, for your dedication to getting this book out there and into the world. To Jon Karp for throwing your support behind both my babies the way you have, and to

Zack Knoll, who I don't think I'm related to but ya never know, who is on top of things at all times like some kind of warrior-ninja.

Thank you to Michelle Weiner and Joe Mann at CAA for showing me the ropes in L.A. and for working tirelessly to give my books a second life and my writing career another dimension. And thank you, Kate Childs, rock-star addition to the team at CAA.

Thank you, Alice Gammill, world's best assistant, who is also a talented writer and will probably be in a position to give me a job one day.

Cait Hoyt, just thank you.

Mom and Dad, thank you for seeing the creative spark in me from day one, for raising me with a strong work ethic, and teaching me to value my ambition, without which I never would have been able to bridge the gap between talent and career.

Thank you to Katy Burgess and Brady Cunningham at Wall for Apricots, interior designers extraordinaire, for creating a boss office space for me in my new L.A. home.

This was a hard year. But it would have been a lot harder had I not been under the care of my wonderful therapist, Dr. Debbie Magids, and renegade dietician, Elyse Resch. Debbie first: I was in a lot of pain before I found you, and I know the healing process is a long one, but thank you for helping me find the start of the path. Elyse, thank you for helping me to heal my relationship with food and for teaching me that I am worth more than my weight—a radical notion for a woman.

Lastly, thank you to the volunteers behind the Southern California Bulldog Rescue. Without you, I wouldn't have my beloved Beatrice, who snored by my side while I slaved away at my laptop. Her sweet, mushy face and oinking sounds made me laugh on days I didn't think it possible. My heart is bigger and my days are brighter for all the work you do.